I0819053

PRAISE FOR *IT HAPPENED ONE MURDER*

"I am so glad Liz Lawson is bringing her talent to adult mystery, because *It Happened One Murder* has it all! Incredible chemistry between the two leads—Nic and Harriet, who are the perfect foils for each other and who have a history that kept me rooting for them. A twist-a-minute mystery that kept me on my toes. And that trademark Liz Lawson humor that kept a smile on my face the whole time. If you're in the mood for a satisfying romance *and* a whodunit that'll keep you guessing, look no further!"

—Alicia Thompson, *USA Today* bestselling author of *Love in the Time of Serial Killers*

"Murder is a dish best served hot in Lawson's deliciously charming, darkly comic small-town mystery-meets-rom-com. Deftly plotted and delightfully fresh, *It Happened One Murder* kept us guessing with every clue and savoring Harriet and Nic's simmering romance with every page."

—Emily Wibberley and Austin Siegemund-Broka, authors of *The Roughest Draft*

"Fast-paced, funny, and impossible to put down. *It Happened One Murder* is easily my new favorite enemies-to-lovers romance. Liz Lawson's adult mystery debut delivers irresistible chemistry and a twisty murder mystery all wrapped into one unforgettable novel."

—Alissa DeRogatis, author of *Call It What You Want*

"Liz Lawson delivers the perfect blend of second-chance romance and cozy murder mystery in this highly addictive story. If you love lighthearted but twist-heavy mysteries with a heaping side of humor, the kind of book that would sit comfortably next to Elle Cosimano and Jesse Q. Sutanto, you'll adore *It Happened One Murder*. Such a fun read that you're guaranteed to tear through!"

—Ashley Winstead, *USA Today* bestselling author of *This Book Will Bury Me*

"*It Happened One Murder* is a fast-paced, enemies-to-lovers whodunit perfect for fans of Elise Bryant and Ally Carter. I love Liz Lawson's young adult books, and I'm thrilled she's writing adult now. Don't miss this delightful blend of romance and mystery!"

—Gloria Chao, *USA Today* bestselling author of *The Ex-Girlfriend Murder Club*

"*It Happened One Murder* is the rom-com-mystery I've been waiting for. Small-town intrigue, a cast of vivid characters (and suspects!), and a juicy second-chance romance? Yes, please. Lawson's adult debut infuses humor and heart into a tightly paced murder mystery that kept me on my toes until the very end. Fun, twisty, and heartwarming, *It Happened One Murder* is a must-read."

—Amelia Diane Coombs, author of *Drop Dead Sisters*

"A deliciously twisty rom-com mystery that absolutely delivers. Enemies-to-lovers chemistry, a cleverly layered murder mystery, and an escapist beachfront backdrop. Five stars!"

—Allison Brennan, *New York Times* bestselling author of *Beach Reads and Deadly Deeds*

"*It Happened One Murder* is the perfect formula: A twisty murder mystery + a messy second-chance romance = an unputdownable read. I laughed, I gasped, I swooned, and I can't wait to see what Lawson writes next!"

—Mia P. Manansala, author of the bestselling Tita Rosie's Kitchen Mystery series

"If you like mysteries spiced up with a witty, slow-burn romance or love stories that unfold during a twisty murder investigation, you'll love *It Happened One Murder*. Liz Lawson writes with wit, heart, and suspense—all the elements of a great read."

—Karen Dukess, *USA Today* bestselling author of *Welcome to Murder Week*

"*It Happened One Murder* made my heart race for two reasons: the twisty murder mystery and the hot romance at its core. A delicious blend of thrills."

—Bellamy Rose, author of *Pomona Afton Can So Solve a Murder*

"Lawson delivers the recipe for a perfect rom-com-mystery mash-up: a dash of corruption, a sprinkle of small-town gossip, and a heaping scoop of swoon, baked at high heat. Fans *of Only Murders in the Building* will adore this devilishly delicious escapist read!"

—KJ Micciche, author of *One Week Later*

"Murder, romance, and juicy small-town drama—Liz Lawson explodes onto the scene with her page-turning adult debut. This pacey whodunit will satisfy mystery and romance readers alike with its twists, vacation-town vibes, and the heartwarming second-chance romance at its core."

—Sienna Sharpe, author of *A Killer Getaway*

"Take one plucky heroine, add a heartthrob of a hero, throw in a dead body or two, and you have the fast-paced ride that is Liz Lawson's *It Happened One Murder*. Fun, flirty, and with just the right amount of mystery to keep you reading late into the night, this book straddles a perfect line between intrigue and romance. I can't wait to see where Lawson's talent takes us next!"

—Tamara Berry, author of *Murder Runs in the Family*

"Lawson's signature excellence with murder books continues into *It Happened One Murder,* with the perfect mash-up of rom-com and mystery. With a vivid and oftentimes hilarious cast of small-town characters, a breathless mystery, and a perfectly swoony romance, this book is the ultimate escape. Readers will be racing through this book for both our killer and for enemies-to-lovers Harriet and Nic to just finally admit they love each other. An utterly charming delight."

—Carlyn Greenwald, author of *Sizzle Reel* and *Murder Land*

IT HAPPENED ONE MURDER

IT HAPPENED ONE MURDER

A Novel

LIZ LAWSON

Cover design by Emma Rogers
Cover images © riroriro/Getty Images, pink.mousy/Shutterstock,
Lana Brow/Shutterstock, MOSQUITO_vector/Shutterstock
Internal design by Tara Jaggers/Sourcebooks

Published by Sourcebooks Landmark, an imprint of Sourcebooks
1935 Brookdale RD, Naperville, IL 60563-2773
(630) 961-3900
sourcebooks.com

Cataloging-in-Publication Data is on file with the Library of Congress.

Printed and bound in the United States of America.
PAH 10 9 8 7 6 5 4 3 2 1

To anyone who's ever wondered what it would be like to fall in love while solving a crime…please see pages 1–384.

CHAPTER ONE

HARRIET

August 29
6:19 p.m.

It's always amazed me how much can change in a year.

This time last August, I was living in New York City, working as a journalist in a career I loved, absolutely thriving. Everything was great. Perfect even.

But now? A mere 365 days later? I'm unemployed, broke, back in my hometown living with my mother and her fourth husband, celebrating my twenty-sixth birthday at a party I didn't even want.

Of course, my mother isn't exactly known for taking what I want into consideration.

"Oh, *George*," she says, laughing extravagantly as she throws her head back. The Cartier bracelets ringing her wrist clink together. She's dressed like she's accepting an Academy Award in a long, green (off-the-rack, but she'd never admit it) Alexander McQueen dress with a plunging neckline, and heels high enough to slice your chest right open. And she's not alone. The invitations she sent out (for a party allegedly for me) said formal.

Formal!

Everyone is standing around her living room wearing ball gowns. It's beyond weird.

The only people I actually want to see today, my best friends Steven and Maggie, vanished twenty minutes ago under the guise of getting some air but *really* so they could smoke the joint I spotted sticking out from Steven's jacket pocket. I tried to slip away after them, but my mother intercepted me, catching my sleeve between her manicured fingers and leading me around the room like a show pony.

"You're so bad," she says to George, squeezing his arm. She lets out a gross little giggle, and my stomach turns.

"Bad?" my grandmother asks from my other side. She looks at me, and I shrug.

In my opinion, George *is* bad, though not in the way my mom means. More in the sense that he's the second coming of the Antichrist. A property developer who's just under six feet tall (but will tell you he's six two) with a full head of graying-blond hair (thanks to hair plugs), he's single-handedly responsible for gentrifying NYC's Meatpacking District and killing tons of small businesses and restaurants. Not to mention his full name—and I swear I'm not making this up—is George *George*, like he's the villain in a bad Pixar film.

He and my mom dated back when they both went to Pleasantville High School but broke up after graduation. They went their separate ways—George to college up in Boston and then to NYC, my mom to Rutgers and then back to Logan Island. Three years later, she ran into George's best friend, Jack, and started dating him. Nine months into their relationship, they got a little surprise in the form of a wailing infant. Me.

Really romantic, right? An unplanned pregnancy, a marriage forced on them by my mom's parents.

Needless to say, they divorced before my second birthday.

Now, twenty-six years later, my mom is back with George. The devil in human form, who happily destroyed innocent lives to make a quick buck. He's pretentious, snobby, and condescending. Oh, and he also happens to own the massive beachfront house where we're standing, the one my mom happily moved into ten months ago. Nothing like a little (okay, a *lot* of) money to make up for a hideous personality, right?

"George said—" my mother starts.

"*I* said," George cuts in, looking down his long nose at me, "that it's *interesting* your father thought it was appropriate to bring his new teenage girlfriend to this party."

We all turn in unison to look at my father, who's across the room, leaning against the arm of a chaise lounge. He's chatting with his sister Vicky while his aforementioned girlfriend looks on.

To be fair, she's not a teenager anymore, but she certainly was when they first met. She used to babysit me back in the day, pimples and all.

Did it creep me out when I found out they were dating? Yeah. Of course it did.

Would I ever admit that to George or my mother, thereby validating their gossipy sniping? Absolutely not.

"George, please. That's my son you're talking about," my grandmother says. She's wearing a bright purple caftan and a ruby-red necklace she once promised to me. Legally known as Gloria Baker, to me she's simply Gogo. My favorite person in my family, though the competition for that title isn't exactly fierce. "Cindy isn't a teenager."

"Her name is Cynthia," I whisper.

George smirks. "He's really hitting his midlife crisis hard, isn't he?"

"What is she *wearing*?" my mother says, doing a remarkably bad job of hiding the fact that she's staring at poor Cynthia. "Is she headed straight from here to work a corner in Atlantic City?"

I take a large sip of champagne instead of replying and almost choke on the bubbles.

"And look at Vicky!" she continues, ignoring my spluttering. Gogo pats me softly on the back. "She's not even wearing a dress!"

In my opinion, Vicky is wearing what we should all be wearing: high-waisted, wide-legged jeans, a simple white T-shirt, and wedges. It's the rest of us that are the issue.

I can't help myself. "Vicky looks cool, Mom."

My mom scowls. "She should have moved back to New York City when her mother begged her to. She's lived overseas too long. Lost her sense of decoru—"

"Cucumber sandwich?" a caterer interrupts, shoving his tray at us.

"I'm good, thanks," I say. My eye catches on his face. Something about him is so familiar. "Did you go to Pleasantville High?" I ask. How awful if he did and is now serving all his former classmates.

"I'm not from here," he says quickly, then turns to George. "Would you like one, sir?"

George, busy typing something into his phone, doesn't reply, and the caterer's face falls. His tray droops precariously to one side, sandwiches sliding toward its edge.

"Not that you asked, but *I'll* have one." My mother picks up a tiny sandwich and takes the tiniest of nibbles off its corner as the waiter shuffles away.

"I just hope," George says, pocketing his phone now that the help is gone, "that you're enjoying the party, Harriet. I spent a lot of money on it."

"I have to go to the bathroom," I say, apropos of nothing, and walk away. I'm reluctant to abandon Gogo with the two of them, but I can't handle another second of the insipid sniping they think passes for polite conversation.

I plaster on a smile as I weave through a (not so) venerable who's who of Logan Island: George's business partner, Luke Dalio, wearing a suit and a scowl, talking with Logan Island mayor Courtney DiPetrio, who graduated from Pleasantville High four years before me. Police Chief Mick Sharkey, out of his uniform for possibly the first time ever, sips his drink next to Fire Chief Dutton. And Mrs. Barbara Patterson, head librarian and member of the Logan Island Town Council, is standing alone by the fireplace.

The sight of her makes me pause. What the hell is she doing here? From what I understand, she'd rather rip out her own toenails than have a voluntary conversation with George, and the feeling is very, very mutual.

I steer around a tight circle of large, burly men I don't recognize and stop by the glass doors leading out to the back deck.

Somewhere out there in the falling night are Maggie and Steven, but in order to reach them, I'll need to pass several clumps of old classmates, all of whom will inevitably ask me the same question: *What brought you back to the island, Harriet?*

It's not that I'm *ashamed* I was fired from my journalism job in the city and forced to move back to the island because I couldn't afford rent. It's more…

Okay, fine, yeah, that's a lie. I'm embarrassed as hell about it.

Instead, I slump against the wall and open LinkedIn for the umpteenth time today, doomscrolling down my feed.

It's a knife to the stomach: a slew of articles my old coworkers recently published, jobs my classmates from NYU managed to land, and the taunt of a still-empty inbox. No new responses to the many (*many*) messages I sent out to my contacts; nothing from the positions I applied to.

And then, because I am nothing if not a masochist, I open Safari and type an *h* into the search bar.

HumansMag.com fills automatically, a testament to just how often I've trolled the site since they fired me. I skim a listicle about celebrity babies named after fruit, then angrily shove my phone back inside my clutch. I snap it shut, glaring out into the crowd.

I find Vicky's eyes across the room. Her mouth quirks up into a bemused half smile, like she knows just what I'm thinking. Like she gets it: my frustrations, my doubts, my feeling of being lost at sea. Unfortunately, I haven't had a chance to have more than a five-second-long conversation with her since she got into town, not with my mother monopolizing all my time planning this stupid party.

With that depressing thought, I push myself upright and walk through the doors to the veranda.

I promptly crash face-first into a brick wall.

"What the hell?" I jerk back, rubbing at my smarting nose.

Through my haze of pain, it takes me a moment to register what I hit. The chest of a man. A very tall man. With a very hard, wide chest.

I look up. And up. And up some more, until I finally find his eyes.

They're green, tinged by gray around their edges. The color of a stormy ocean. Deep. Beautiful. I could swim laps in them.

He's Glen Powell's better-looking twin, something I would not have thought possible until this very moment. Both of his arms are covered in intricate tattoos.

It takes me a moment to realize I'm staring. Possibly drooling. Heat flushes my cheeks, and I drop my eyes to the ground. *What's gotten into me?* Sure, it's been a while since I had intimate relations with another person, but...*drooling?* I surreptitiously swipe at my lips.

"Harriet, I am so sorry," the hot man says. He's clutching my shoulder like he thinks I'm going to topple over if he lets go. "Are you okay?"

He knows my name. How the hell does he know my name?

I say as much.

The softness around his eyes collapses. "Are you serious?"

I frown. "Serious about what?"

He barks an unamused laugh. "Amazing. Just amazing. You *are* serious. You really don't remember me, do you?"

I study his face. "Am I supposed to?"

His upper lip lifts into a sneer, and his hand falls from my shoulder. "Are you *supposed to*— Jesus Christ. *Yes*, Harriet. You're *supposed* to remember me. Seeing as I lost my fucking virginity to you."

CHAPTER TWO

NIC

August 29
6:30 p.m.

The empty expression in Harriet Baker's eyes is a kick to my fucking balls.

I'm an idiot. The minute Mom told me that we'd been offered this job, I *knew* this might happen, but I still pushed her to take it like a putz, even though our schedule was already packed tight. I hadn't seen Harriet in person in eight years. I thought maybe…

It doesn't even matter what I thought.

I spent the afternoon avoiding her as we set up in the kitchen, just in case. I didn't want my day ruined from the jump, and I figured I could catch her later, somewhere quiet. Out of the public eye.

Not that it was hard. She barely noticed we were there, service workers dressed in black and white, blending in with the background.

And look. I get it—sort of. My growth spurt didn't happen 'til the age of nineteen, when I sprouted up six inches and gained a solid seventy-five pounds. I know I look different than I did back then.

But still.

We *slept* together. Not just once but many, *many* times over the course of two weeks. Weeks that I only learned once they were over meant absolutely nothing to her.

Harriet, of course, looks exactly the same—long, glossy brown hair, wide-set blue eyes, and a cute little button nose. I was already well aware of all this because of late-night social media rabbit holes. Given her shock, it seems pretty clear she never returned the favor.

"*Excuse* me?" Harriet says. "We did not sleep together."

"Yes." I struggle to keep my expression neutral. No way will I let her see that I'm dying inside. "We did."

Her forehead crinkles. "I'd remember you."

"Well, I think you're making it pretty clear that you wouldn't, actually," I say. I smile tightly, and Harriet's expression shifts.

"Wait..." She presses her eyes shut. When they pop open a second later, her lips have parted, eyebrows soared to her hairline.

"Holy shit. We *did* sleep together!"

"I'm aware," I say dryly.

"Wow." She studies my face. "You look so..."

"Different?" I supply, lest she's about to fill in the blank with something less flattering.

"Yeah," she says after a long moment. "Different."

I press my lips together and try not to scream. This is a waking nightmare.

She rubs her forehead. "Your name was, um..."

"My name," I say tersely, "is Nic."

"Of course! I knew that," she says, lying through her straight, pearly white teeth. She takes in my uniform, the tray shoved under my arm. "Let me guess: You work for the catering company? As a cater waiter? I take it you still live on the island?"

Why did she have to say it like that, all condescending—*a cater waiter*, like that's all I am, like it's what defines me. At least I *have* a job. If the rumors are true, she's currently unemployed.

Though, of course, being unemployed means something different in Harriet's world than it does in mine. She gets to move into a giant six-bedroom beachfront house and watch the ocean from the back porch.

Me?

I'd be back sleeping on the ratty pull-out in my parents' tiny, half-finished basement, surrounded by piles of old records and stacks of used cookbooks. Developing back problems because the mattress down there is about as old as I am.

"Yeah. And I guess you live...here, huh?" I point up at the house. "With your *parents*? Aren't you a little old to be living at home?"

Her eyes narrow. I've hit a nerve.

Good.

"First of all," she says, "George is not my *parent*. Do not connect me biologically to that...that...*creature*. And second—yeah, I live here. But it's temporary. It's only been a month since I got back from New York, where I lived for almost eight years, thankyouverymuch. I'm just figuring out my next move. And third, so I didn't recognize you.

So what? You look different. You said so yourself. You don't have to be such a...a *dick*!"

I grit my teeth.

"*I*," I say in a low growl, "am not the one being a dick."

Her mouth wobbles, but she crosses her arms against her chest defiantly. "Screw—and I mean this with every fiber of my being—you."

Jesus, this woman. Anyone else would apologize, but not Harriet Baker. It's exactly how I remember her. She never backed down without a fight. It's one of the things I found so annoyingly attractive about her.

I scowl. "Yeah. Well. Screw you too. You know, as much fun as this is, *I* have stuff to do."

An expression darts across her face—disappointment? Why the hell would she be disappointed for this horrific conversation to end?

"Right. You're at work. Bye, um..."

She must be kidding. "Nic," I say.

"Of course. Nic," she says. "I know."

Without another word, I walk away.

I walk back into the kitchen and find my sister, Sara, yelling about cake.

"*Mother*," she screeches. "Where the *hell* is that ugly crystal brooch? I still need to figure out how I'm going to fix it onto the cake! As you might remember, I'm not a *pastry* chef."

She says this with all the disdain of a savory chef who thinks bakers are lower beings. She's such a snob.

Also, she needs to chill before Mom loses her patience with her. Again. Sara's been fired from this job numerous times but keeps wiggling her way back in, helped by nepotism and the fact that she's the best chef on this tiny island.

You'd think at this point, she would have gotten it through her head that our little family-run operation is not the same as the Michelin-starred restaurants she used to work for up in the city. The way she talks might have flown up there, where they're all *yes chef*, but we work for our mom's catering company, for fuck's sake.

"Could you kindly lower your voice?" I drop my tray down on the island with a clatter. "I ran out of tea sandwiches halfway through my rotation. I think we should consider upping the number on each tray."

Unable to take even the smallest amount of constructive criticism, Sara retorts, "Oh, *should* we, Nic? Maybe you should be the one holding down the kitchen, since you're such an expert."

I flinch. Low blow. She's well aware that I too had plans to attend culinary school. While she was always interested in fine dining, I was interested in learning to incorporate environmental sustainability into a restaurant. I thought maybe someday I could open my own place. One that sourced local organic products and focused on energy-efficient cooking techniques and a net-zero carbon footprint.

But then life happened. My plans got waylaid by family stuff. While my sister was up in New York City having the time of her life, I was here, helping our parents not lose their home.

Speaking of—Mom hurries toward us, waving her hands.

"Children! Please!" she says, like we're two toddlers rather than her twenty-seven and twenty-five-year-old offspring. "Nic, Matthew has only been with us for a month, and he's all alone out on the floor. That's unacceptable. I need you to refill your tray and get back out there—now. And, Sara." She strides over to the far counter and grabs the elaborate strand of Swarovski crystals that Harriet's mom informed us is supposed to go on the birthday cake. She waves it in the air at my sister. "It's right here. I am not your sous-chef. Use your eyes. If we need to discuss you going to an optometrist, we can do that...*after* this party."

She departs, leaving Sara and I locked in a standoff. Finally, I break eye contact and turn away. I learned a long time ago that going up against my sister is pointless. She is the most stubborn, strong-willed person on earth.

I fill my tray and hustle back down the hallway, past the stairs down to the basement, pivoting around a woman who almost barrels into me—clearly not watching where she's going—and enter the living room.

Five minutes later, the sandwiches are gone, and I've realized Matthew is in fact not on the floor. He's completely disappeared.

Where the hell is he? There's no excuse for going missing in the middle of a job.

I'm heading back toward the kitchen to restock and complain when an old man with a bad comb-over appears in front of me.

Harriet's stepfather, George George. With a name like that, he was probably bullied as a child. Maybe that's why he's such a prick.

"Excuse me," he says, lips pinched white, outstretched hand clasped tight in a fist. "I need to speak with someone about the food."

He unfurls his fingers. In his palm are the remains of an English tea sandwich.

"There is something in this that is"—he leans close to my ear and hisses—"*disgusting.*"

Then he grabs my hand and plops the whole sorry, half-eaten mess into it.

He has got to be kidding. "I'm sorry to hear that, sir," I say, depositing the heap of half-chewed food onto my empty tray. I don't get paid enough for this shit. "I'll let our chef know."

"*No*," he snaps. "*I* am spending my hard-earned money on your tremendously shoddy services, so *I* will let your chef know."

"Sir, I'm happy to—"

He pushes past me.

"Sir, please. Wait—"

I have to catch this idiot before he tangles with my sister. Ever since Sara got back from NYC last year, she's been a bit of a… How can I say this nicely? A total live fucking wire. A cannon so loose that it pops its lid at even the slightest provocation? I'm mixing my metaphors probably, but you get the drift. I cannot even imagine how she'd react to someone insulting her food.

Behind us, a woman's voice. "George, I've been looking all over for you! Where have you—George? Where are you going?"

Up ahead of me, George disappears around a corner into the kitchen.

A second later, Sara's voice booms. "What do you think you're *doing* back here?"

I enter the room and see her standing beside the kitchen island, brandishing her red spatula at George like a weapon.

"Excuse me, young lady," he says in that nasally voice, like nails scraping down a chalkboard. "I'm looking for the chef. I need to register a complaint—"

I try one last time to stop him. "Sir—"

They ignore me.

"I *am* the chef," Sara says haughtily.

"Well then," George says. "You should be made aware that there was something off about the sandwich I just ate." He sniffs. "The texture was strange and—"

Sara's nostrils flare. "The texture was *strange*?"

"Yes. It was off-putting," he says with a nod. "Disgusting, really."

People start trickling into the kitchen, but I keep my eyes on my sister. If I know Sara, what's about to happen is going to be bad. Very bad.

"I'm curious. What culinary school did you graduate from?" she asks.

"Erm, well, I didn't—" George starts to respond, like he thinks this is a real question and not the start of Sara systematically destroying him.

"What chefs have you shadowed? What magazines have featured *your* cooking? What's that?" She cups a hand to her ear. "None? Is that right? And yet *you* think it's okay to come in here and insult *my* cooking? Who do you think you are? A food critic? You look like someone who wouldn't know good food if it crawled its way up your ass!"

"*Excuse* me!" George says, pulling his chin into his chest. "*I* am the person paying for your services!"

My mom pushes past me, stepping between them. "Sara, that is enough!" Then she turns to George. "Sir, I'm so sorry. What seems to be the issue?"

George recognizes an ally when he sees one. "I came in here to tell your chef that her food tastes strange and was met with outrageously rude behavior. I certainly hope this isn't how you normally run your business, Mrs. Allbright."

"I cannot apologize enough, Mr. George," my mom says. "Sara—err, well. She can be a bit...precious with her cooking. How can we make this up to you. Can I get you something? A fresh glass of champagne? Something else to eat? I'm sure Chef Sara would be happy to prepare whatever you'd like."

"What I'd really like is for this...this *girl* to apologize," George says.

My mom winces, probably thinking the same thing I am.

Sara does not apologize.

"Of course. Sara...please?" She's trying her best to hold a polite smile.

This is ridiculous. Our poor mom is pushing sixty; she shouldn't be spending her time refereeing an argument about a tea sandwich between her bullheaded daughter and a rich POS in an overpriced suit.

"Absolutely not." Sara crosses her arms. "I did nothing wrong."

"Sara..."

"No."

"If she won't apologize, she needs to go," George says, looking down his nose at my family members. God, he's an asshole.

"Sara! *Please.* Say you're sorry." My mom is practically begging. Earlier this summer, she fired Sara off a job for a very similar reason, and we can't afford another scene like that. Our reputation is on the line.

"No!" Sara spits the word out. "You *never* take my side."

My mom's face darkens. She's kind when she needs to be, but

Angela Allbright is not afraid of conflict. There's no question where Sara inherited her temper.

"Then," she says, "you need to go."

Someone in the crowd behind me lets out a little giggle, and I bristle. This isn't a fucking joke; it's my life.

Sara unties her apron and throws it on the countertop. "You know what? Fine. I'll go. Happy to. Keep kissing the ass of every rich dude who thinks he's entitled to an opinion," she snarls at our mom, "and I'll see *you* in hell," she tells George George. She storms out of the room.

CHAPTER THREE

HARRIET

August 29
6:46 p.m.

"Are you okay?" My best friend Maggie nudges me. "I was literally in the middle of telling you about the couple who got caught having sex in the law library, and you just disappeared."

I shake myself. I gotta get out of my head. "Sorry. Yeah, I'm good. Keep going."

Except the thing is I'm really not. I'm actually sort of freaking out. I mean, I fully didn't recognize an entire person who was *inside* me.

But now I can see it so clearly, those weeks, *those* nights, with Nic.

It was good, by the way. The sex. Very, very good. It's why I never suspected he was a virgin. He had moves. Like this one time, when I was on top and he scooped me up like I weighed nothing and twisted me around and—

I press the cool side of my plastic wineglass against the side of my neck. It's only sixty-five degrees outside, but I feel like I'm on fire.

If he'd given me a couple more seconds, I would have placed him. I'm sure of it.

"Okay..." Maggie sounds unconvinced but launches back into her tale of horny law students.

I didn't really know Nic at all during our four years together at Pleasantville High. I was too wrapped up in my own scene—one that included my very serious boyfriend Adam Kozel, who I'd been dating since freshman year. Who I thought I was going to marry. Who disappeared on me the day after graduation and smashed my heart into a million little pieces.

A few days later, I ran into Nic, and one thing led to another. Suffice it to say he was a great distraction from my pain. Back then, he had a bad haircut and skinny arms, but he was kind. Gentle. Just what I needed to get me through that weird, awful moment of time.

When my mom told me that they'd hired All Bright Catering Company for my birthday party, I didn't put two and two together. Not until earlier today, when I caught sight of Nic's older sister, Sara, in the kitchen wearing a chef's hat and apron.

The connection hit me like a brick, heavy and hard. I turned around and ran straight back into my room, only venturing out again when guests began to arrive. I didn't see Nic anywhere, so I thought I was in the clear.

Except, obviously, I was wrong.

"Oh my god. I've been looking for you guys everywhere." Steven walks up wearing a huge grin, a fresh glass of champagne in each hand.

He shoves them at us. "Didn't you hear?" he says. "There's a fight in the kitchen!"

My right eye starts to twitch. I knew it. I *knew* this party was a terrible idea. It's probably my parents, at each other's throats like they always are.

"Jesus Christ," I mutter, then take off for the sliding door.

I hear the yelling as soon as I step inside. Surprisingly, it doesn't sound like my mother.

The hallway from the living room into the kitchen is tight with party guests, all presumably trying to get a glimpse of the drama.

I'm pushing my way through the congestion when a woman appears from it, her face tight with fury. People part in waves to let her pass.

It's Sara Allbright, her chef's hat askew, blue apron speckled with sauce.

"Hey!" I try to catch her attention. "What's going on—" But she vanishes around the corner.

I finally make it into the kitchen and find George sprawled on the floor clutching his chest. My mother's hovering over him, nervous hands fluttering through the air.

Is he having a heart attack?

I look between them. "Is George okay?"

George shoots upright. "I was just assaulted!" he shrieks. "By a *chef*!"

Right. Not a heart attack. I should have known better than to think this was actually something real.

"Oh my god. You were not," Nic mutters. He's pressed against the center island, his arms crossed tight against his chest. Next to him, an older woman dressed in a catering uniform elbows him hard in the bicep, and he winces.

Whispers grow around me, and I spot several people recording this mess. Fantastic. I'm sure it's going to be all over social media before the night's end.

I turn back to my mother and her husband. "What happened?" I ask them. I sound like I'm talking to a couple of children, which, honestly, is not that far off from the truth.

George makes a show of struggling to his feet and carefully dusting off his gray slacks before answering. "*Well*, Harriet. I came in here to tell the chef that her tuna canapés tasted odd. You'd think she'd *thank* me for the feedback, but instead..." He sniffs. "She *cursed* at me. In my own home! I've never experienced such terrible behavior in my entire life."

"Okay. But why the hell were you lying on the floor?"

"Harriet!" my mother gasps, like hearing me say *hell* took ten years off her life.

I really need to move out. I make a mental note to follow up with every job I've ever applied to on LinkedIn first thing tomorrow.

"Because she *shoved* me!" George cries. "Toppled me straight to the ground!"

The older woman steps forward, voice strained by stress. "Again, I cannot express how deeply sorry I am about all this, Mr. George. I'll personally see to it that Sara is formally reprimanded for her behavior—"

"Fired," George interrupts.

The woman looks flustered by this, but after a second, she nods. "Fired. Right. Of course."

"Who's fired?" my dad says, striding in with Cynthia, Gogo, and Vicky trailing behind them. George stiffens. He hates my dad.

"We have it under control, *Jack*," my mom says, spitting out my dad's name. She *also* hates him.

"Are you sure?" my dad asks with a smirk. "Because it certainly doesn't seem that way, *Lisa*. I could hear you from the other room."

"Well, excuse me for breathing," my very mature mother snaps.

"We don't need your help with this," George cuts in. "Or with anything at all, for that matter. I have it handled."

The three of them start loudly arguing, much to the amusement of the crowd.

What a family I have. Vicky's brow is furrowed; she probably wishes she was back in London. I don't blame her at all. Maybe I should ask her about the job market over there.

"Please. Stop." I step between them, forcing my voice to stay calm through sheer willpower and a burning desire not to hash out our stupid family drama in front of half my high school graduating class. "I'm sure whatever happened was a mistake." George starts to argue, but I talk over him. "And it sounds like this nice woman has apologized. Can we please move on?"

My dad grins. "You're right, honey. It's your birthday! We should be celebrating. George, old boy," he says with a twinkle in his eye. George scowls. "I'm sure whatever happened can be remedied with a stiff drink. Let's go grab one in the other room."

And with that, he wraps a beefy hand around George's arm and drags him out of the kitchen.

Drama over, the crowd finally disperses, on their way, I'm sure, to post all this on Instagram. The woman in the catering uniform lets out a tired sigh.

"You okay?" Nic asks her.

She blows out a slow breath. "Your sister—" Her eyes land on me, and she cuts off and shakes her head. "Never mind. Let's get back to work. We'll chat later."

She hurries away, leaving me alone with Nic.

An uncomfortable silence settles between us.

"Your mom?" I ask for lack of anything better.

He rubs his forehead. "Yup. My sister's the feisty, fired chef. It's a fun family operation." He leans back against the wall and closes his eyes.

Guilt nips at me. It's possible that maybe, just maybe, I should apologize for our earlier interaction. What if he thinks I'm as big of an asshole as George and my mom?

"About what I said on the porch—"

"No, thanks. I'm good," he interrupts, rubbing a hand against his jaw. "I get it. I mean, why would you remember me? It was just sex, right? Totally unimportant to someone like you."

Ew. *Someone like me?* What's that supposed to mean? What a dick. Of *course* I remembered him; I just didn't *recognize* him. Not that I'm in the mood to explain the difference right now.

I glare at him. "Well. This is all *so* very pleasant, but I have to go. Somewhere else. Literally anywhere else but here."

"Fine," he says, an echo of earlier.

"Fine."

I spin around on my heel and stomp out of the kitchen.

CHAPTER FOUR

NIC

August 29

8:00 p.m.

The party's winding down earlier than anticipated. It started pouring about an hour ago, which scared off half the guests.

Fine by me. I've had about enough of this job for one night.

I'm out on the back porch cleaning up stray glassware. It's chilly and humid, but even so, it's better than being in that house. I'm trying to avoid Harriet, and there are only so many rooms where I can hide.

For the first time tonight, I stop to take in the view off the porch, beautiful even through the gloom. The twinkling lights of the Yacht Club to my right, the houses peppering the coast to the left. The waves kicked up by the rain crashing against the beach. I wonder what it would be like to wake up to this every day, the privacy, the ocean yours for the taking, like you're in control of it instead of the other way around.

My eyes land on a few scattered objects down on the beach.

Trash.

There's nothing that pisses me off more than littering, especially near the ocean. It messes with wildlife, seeps into the water supply, destroys reefs.

I stomp down the stairs and swipe up the crumpled cocktail napkins and wineglass left at the bottom. I shove it all into the trash bag in my hand to sort out later and turn to head back inside.

As I do, my eyes catch on something about fifty yards down the beach by the edge of the water—short and bulky, like a chunky piece of furniture.

I squint through the dim light trying to make out details, but it's too far away, the night too dark. My best guess is that it's a party guest, passed out on the sand.

Great. It's probably someone I went to high school with, one of Harriet's many friends who ignored me back then, who I served canapés to tonight. This should be fun.

I'm tempted to ignore them, but Harriet's stepfather was such a dick about the tea sandwich, I can only imagine what he'd do if someone drowned after drinking the alcohol we served. He'd probably sue us before the body was even cold.

I didn't spend the last eight years of my life helping my mom build her business to lose it because some asshole drank too much champagne and died on our watch.

I set down my garbage bag and start trudging across the beach.

As I get closer, the shape I thought was one person splits into two. One lying prone on the sand, the other crouched above them, staring down.

In the dark, it feels wrong. Menacing. My chest tightens.

"Hey!" I yell, but the wind tosses the word out to sea. I start to jog through the wet sand toward them. "Hey!" I yell again, and this time, the croucher hears me. Their head whips up, and they leap to their feet, taking off down the beach.

In my surprise, I stumble, but I manage to catch myself before face-planting into sand.

Once I'm stable, I push into a full-on sprint, gaining on them. Closer...closer... I dive forward, crashing against their back, and we hit the ground hard.

"Ow! *Fuck!*" they shout from under me. "Get off me, you dick!"

I roll off them sideways in shock. I'd recognize that voice anywhere.

"Jesus, Nic. What the hell?" My sister is sprawled next to me on the sand, chest heaving.

My *sister*. Out here on the beach, hours after getting fired.

Out here on the beach, standing over a motionless figure. Running away from me.

Dread twists in my gut.

"What are you doing here?" I ask her.

She sniffs, pulling herself up to a seat. Her arms wrap around her legs, and she tucks her body into a tight ball. She's crying.

Sara never, *ever* cries.

"Sara. What's going on?" I ask, even though I'm not sure I want to hear the answer.

"It's... I..." She sniffs.

"What?"

She lifts a trembling finger and points toward the ocean's edge. "That."

The other person is still lying where she left them, waves gently lapping against their side. They haven't moved.

The hairs on the back of my neck rise.

I turn back to my sister. Her eyes are wide. Haunted.

"Sara." The word scrapes its way up my throat, painful. "What did you do?"

CHAPTER FIVE

NIC

August 29

8:08 p.m.

Nothing!" Sara cries. The moon slips free of the clouds, showering us with light. Her hair curls wildly around her face, her eyes scared. "I was coming back… I wanted to talk to Mom, clear the air, *apologize,* but—"

I interrupt. "Since when do you apologize?"

She doesn't answer. Just drops her forehead to her knees.

"Sara!" I bark. She doesn't move.

I scramble to my feet, heart in my throat as I approach the figure. They're face down, limbs splayed like a rag doll. The sand around them soaked red. A sickly sweet smell climbs into my nose.

Dead.

The word crashes into my mind.

No. They can't be dead. I can save them.

I can save Sara from whatever this is.

I wrap my hands around their shoulders, pulling with all my strength, trying to get their face out of the sand. They need to breathe.

I pull and pull. Their limbs are floppy, heavy, but I finally get them on their side. An eye, open and unblinking, greets me. My stomach roils, and I let out a scream.

Someone appears on the porch of Harriet's house. Then another and another. People run down the beach toward us.

It takes three people to finally roll the body all the way over.

It only registers then. Who it is, lying there, immobile.

George George. Harriet's stepdad.

And he is dead. Absolutely, definitely dead.

I puke a stomach full of tea sandwiches into the cold Atlantic Ocean.

I'm shivering.

Chief Starkey is at work on George George's lifeless form.

I think about getting up, asking him for an update, but I stay rooted to the sand.

Behind me, up on the porch, someone is screaming.

Something cool brushes against my arm, and I jump. Mom, pale beneath her olive skin. "What happened?"

My brain is mush. I push my palm against my forehead. "I don't know. I don't know."

Mom studies my face. Then her eyes land on something over my shoulder, and her brow furrows. "Is that..." she asks.

I turn. Sara, still curled in a ball on the sand.

I haven't said anything to anyone about what I saw.

"Sara?" Mom calls, walking to her.

Sara stands, waving her arms wildly as she talks. She's drawing attention to herself. She needs to stop.

Mom waves me over. "I'm going to see what's going on. You stay with your sister," she says once I join them.

When she's out of earshot, I grab Sara's arm. "What did you *do*?"

She yanks away. "*Ow*, Nic—stop! I didn't do anything! I swear to god. After I left, I wandered the sidewalks for a while. It started pouring, so I waited it out in a little alcove. While I was in there, I started thinking maybe I should come back. Apologize to Mom. And to the guy I argued with too."

I frown.

She throws up her hands. "You don't believe me, fine, but I'm not an idiot. I know I need this job. So once the rain let up, I walked back. Came in through the back gate since they gave us the code for load-in. I was hoping I could sneak inside without anyone seeing, but then I saw something down here. Something big. I thought it was an animal! A beached whale. But I... It wasn't...it was...it was... *him*. Is he..."

"It didn't look good. The blood..." I swallow. "But I'm not a doctor," I add weakly.

"*Shit*," Sara whispers. "I shouldn't have—"

She's cut off by a commotion near Harriet's house. EMTs spill through the gate, equipment in hand. One of them is my best friend, Martin Patel.

"Make some room!" he calls, and the crowd parts. Chief Sharkey gives them a rundown of the situation before stepping back.

"No breathing, no pulse," the EMT at George's head says a moment later.

Silence falls. Martin drops to his knees, a pair of shears in hand. With one swift motion, he cuts open George's shirt and peels it back, revealing a jagged stab wound in the center of his chest.

Gasps ripple through the crowd, but Martin doesn't blink. One EMT bags George while another carefully sticks cardiac monitor pads around the wound.

Martin starts compressions as the monitor powers on.

A minute drags by as we hold our collective breaths. Then the EMT says, "Flatline."

"Fuck," Martin mutters. "We need to call—"

He's interrupted by a piercing voice. Mrs. George bursts from the crowd, eyes wild.

"What do you mean? What do you *mean*?" she screeches, clutching Martin's shirt.

"Mom!" Harriet appears behind her. "Mother! Stop it!"

"There's *blood*." Mrs. George's voice pitches so high that a dog howls somewhere in the distance. "Why is there so much blood? Why is he just *lying* there? Why aren't you *doing* something?"

Martin flinches back from her assault. "Ma'am, please. I can't do my job when—"

"Mrs. George, can I help?" Chief Sharkey is back, gently taking Mrs. George's arm and steering her away.

"I don't... He isn't..." Harriet's mom stammers.

"Ma'am, Mrs. George," Sharkey says. "I'm so sorry. You have my word—we will figure out who did this to your husband."

Next to me, Sara lets out a whimper. "It wasn't me," she mumbles, face stark white. "I swear to god, Nic. I didn't do it."

"Sara—"

"They're going to blame me for this. I know it. I need to go."

"No, Sara. Wait—" If she runs off now, she'll look even more suspicious.

But she's already heading for the gate.

Mrs. George clocks her immediately. "You!" she cries, jerking away from the cop. "You're that chef! The one who was so rude to George! What are you doing here? You were supposed to leave and—*ohmygod*." Her mouth falls open. "You did this, didn't you? You killed my George!"

The officers start moving toward my sister. "Excuse me?" one of them calls. "Miss? We'd like to ask you a few questions."

Sara's pace quickens, and my heart sinks. She's going to make this so much worse for herself.

"Somebody stop her! She's getting away!" Mrs. George screams.

The officers close in, and Sara makes a decision. A bad one, like so many of hers are.

She runs.

"We have a runner!" Sharkey calls, pointing. A cop races by me, hand on his holster, heading after her. The crowd freezes, watching as the chase unfolds.

Sara's still fit from years of sports, and for a moment, I think she's going to make it. She's almost to the gate—

Then her foot snags on something in the sand and she goes flying. She lands hard a few feet away, face-first. The cops are on her immediately, one driving a knee into her back, pinning her arms behind her.

"Arrest her!" Mrs. George shouts as she rushes toward them.

The officer hauls Sara to her feet.

"I didn't do anything!" she shrieks, twisting as the officer grips her arms. Sand flies.

With some difficulty, the officer unhooks cuffs from her belt and snaps them onto my sister's wrists.

"What are you doing? Are you arresting her?" Mom runs up, Sharkey on her heels.

He steps in front of her. "Ma'am, you're going to need to back up."

My mom jabs a finger into his face. "Tell your people to back off."

My heart sinks. If she keeps this up, she's going to wind up in cuffs too.

I jog over. "Mom! Stop."

She whips around, eyes blazing. "Stop? You want me to *stop*, Nico? Don't you see what they're doing to your sister?" She starts muttering under her breath in Italian, and I catch the words "stupido ragazzo." Stupid boy. Right. *I'm* the stupid one here. "You can't do this!" she says again.

"Actually, we can." Chief Sharkey adjusts his belt. "Your daughter tried to evade police questioning, which is both illegal and suspicious. She's coming down to the station, and I can *guarantee* you she'll be spending the night. It's in her—and *your*—best interest to cooperate from here on out."

My mom's lips press into an angry line, but she stays quiet as they lead Sara away.

Sara, on the other hand, does not.

"This is bullshit," she screams, going limp in their arms like she's some sort of political prisoner.

"Jesus," Sharkey mutters. He hustles over to help his officers haul Sara off the ground.

"Sara, cooperate," I call, though I'm sure it's a waste of breath. She's always dramatic, but this is over the top, even for her.

Why the hell did she come back tonight? To apologize? Or for something else?

"Chief Sharkey?" Martin calls up the beach. His voice has an edge to it that makes my blood run cold. Martin's been a paramedic for six years. He's pretty much unflappable.

For his voice to sound like that...something must be very wrong.

I turn slowly.

He's pointing at the sand. A glint of silver catches my eye as he nudges it with his boot.

"You're gonna want to see this."

Sharkey jogs over, and I follow without thinking. When Martin sees me coming, horror flickers across his face.

Sharkey crouches next to him and lets out a low whistle.

"Good lookin'," he says, clapping Martin on the back. "This is huge."

I lean in, peering over their shoulders. I need to see it. No matter how bad it is.

"Nic—" Martin looks up at me, voice tight. "Don't—"

But it's too late. The sight hits me like a punch to the gut.

Sara's biggest job in New York was under a James Beard–nominated chef at a French restaurant named Pêne Dormant. On the one-year anniversary, he gifted her a set of knives, which she brings everywhere. A reminder of her former life, of what could have been.

They're very expensive. Very unique.

And the pearly white handle of one is sticking out of the sand, right next to George's dead body.

CHAPTER SIX

HARRIET

August 29

8:42 p.m.

George George, my mother's fourth husband, is dead—*murdered*—and I feel...nothing.

Is something wrong with me? Am I a sociopath?

Sure, George was never my favorite person, but still. I know him. *Knew* him. And he was stabbed to death right out there on the beach.

Possibly by someone I know.

Maybe even someone sitting on this porch.

The thought hits me hard. I hunch into myself, scanning the crowd. Could it be one of the caterers huddled around Nic's mom? Or a town council member—Barbara Patterson maybe, who's whispering by the back stairs.

After the cops dragged Sara away, they gathered the rest of us here and asked us not to leave. Now we're stuck, sizing each other up with suspicion.

It's freezing out here; the rain blew the humidity of the day out to sea, and I'm shivering in my stupid dress. Across the porch, I see Gogo and Vicky huddled together wearing jackets and scarves, my mother beside them, a mink fur draped over her dress.

I eye her. I'm currently giving her a wide berth; when I tried talking to her a few minutes ago, she screamed this was all my fault.

Someone pokes my shoulder. Steven, holding two bottles of champagne and a coat.

"Thank god. Give me that." I reach for a bottle.

He drapes the coat over my shoulders and sits. "Have you talked to your mom?"

I take a small sip from the bottle. "I tried. You know how she is."

"Yeah. I know." He tucks a leg under himself, settling back against his seat. "This is crazy. Someone *killed* your stepfather. It's unbelievable." He thinks for a second. "Okay, maybe not totally unbelievable, given who George was and all but...still. Murder? Like, who does that? Are we in a soap opera?"

I almost smile. Steven continues talking a mile a minute, shifting into a monologue about Martin Patel: how hot he is in his uniform, how he looks even better in person than on Instagram, how Steven always had such a big crush on him back in the day. It's fine by me. I don't have the energy to keep up my end of a conversation right now.

"Oh my god, this is bananas." Maggie staggers up, interrupting Steven's monologue. She falls into an empty chair and slips off her heels, rubbing her stockinged feet. "I've read about criminal cases in school, but I never thought *I'd* see something like this close-up." She leans forward, squeezing my hand. "How are you doing?"

I shrug. "I'm weirdly...okay? I think maybe it hasn't sunk in yet."

"Yeah. That's normal. After my mom died, it didn't really register for months. I kept expecting her to walk through the front door—" Her voice breaks, and she falls quiet. Her mom was diagnosed with an aggressive form of cancer our freshman year of high school and died two short months later.

Now it's my turn to squeeze Maggie's hand. One thing I've learned in my twenty-six years on this planet is that there is family you're born into and family you choose, and sometimes the latter is far more important.

Before I can respond, we're interrupted by a ding from Steven's phone. He sucks a sharp breath through his teeth as he reads the screen. "Shit," he says. "The local news got hold of the story."

He holds out his phone. The screen reads BREAKING: LOCAL REAL ESTATE SCION GEORGE GEORGE FOUND DEAD IN SUSPECTED HOMICIDE.

My stomach sinks. "How did they already find out?"

Steven gestures with his chin to the thirty or so people around us. "People love to insert themselves into drama. I mean, it's what you did when you were writing for *Humans*, right?"

I'm sure he didn't mean anything by it, but his words sting nonetheless.

I stand. I need some air, some space to breathe. "I'm going for a walk."

"Har," Steven says. "I didn't mean—"

The missing tears are pricking at my eyes. "It's fine," I say with a tight smile, then hurry across the porch and down to the beach.

I realize my mistake the moment I hit the sand: It's packed down here. Cops, EMTs, town government folk all mill around the beach. It's still very much an active crime scene, with the police tape to prove it.

If anyone spots me, they're going to be seriously pissed. I consider retreating back up to the house, but I really do need some space. I slip into the shadow beneath the porch and press myself against the back side of a wooden support beam.

I lean against it and close my eyes, enjoying the momentary peace. Maybe when I open them, I'll find all this was nothing more than a stress-induced nightmare.

I wonder how Nic and his mom are doing. It's not like the cops really think Sara did it, do they? They only arrested her because she took off running.

But then again…why *did* she run?

"…create a mess." A familiar voice shakes me from my thoughts. Chief Sharkey, his voice clipped.

I peel one eye open. He's nearby—back out on the beach.

"Well," a woman replies.

I hold my breath, straining to hear.

"It's going to get a lot worse if—" Her words are lost under the roar of the waves. "…we need to protect the project. His death could knock things sideways, and we can't let that happen. Even if it means compromising a little, pinning this on someone who's an easy—"

Pinning this on someone? What does that mean? I strain to hear more, but she cuts off as a phone rings.

"Hello?" Sharkey says. "Hi. Yes, of course. I'll look into it right now."

"Was that—" the woman asks.

"Yeah. Gotta go deal with it. You'll contact the DA's office?"

"Tomorrow, first thing."

Then silence as their words spin through my mind.

CHAPTER SEVEN

NIC

August 30

7:32 a.m.

The sky blazes red and orange as I pull onto my parents' street on the south end of the island, a quick five-minute drive from my apartment downtown.

Even though sometimes all I want is to move off this tiny island, I have to admit that right now, there's comfort in its familiarity. The vegetable garden out front of the Alfonzos' house, where Mrs. Alfonzo has grown pumpkins in the fall, asparagus in the spring, and tomatoes and cucumbers all summer long since I was a kid. The Parkers' house across the street still decked out in red, whites, and blues from the Fourth of July, committed as always to their over-the-top holiday celebrations.

The north side is where the rich people live—where the party last night was. Developers like Harriet's stepfather got their greedy hands on it years ago, razing all the small beachfront cottages and replacing them with gated mansions and spots like the Yacht Club.

Now they've set their sights on my side of the island, but instead of giant single-family homes, they want to build high-rise hotels and luxury apartment buildings. People are up in arms about it, which I totally get. A lot of the families here have lived on the island for generations. No one wants to see small businesses vanish or neighborhoods bulldozed.

Not to mention no one wants to lose their home.

George George was notorious around here for his development schemes, including a proposal to build a giant hotel complex just a few blocks away from here, where the Windswept Motel used to stand. Thankfully, the island's zoning board has pushed back against him time and time again, and it seems like, for the moment at least, we're safe.

I stop in front of my parents' row home and turn off the ignition.

I yawn, big and deep, and drop my head to the steering wheel. I got a grand total of three hours of sleep last night, and that only after a hefty shot of whiskey. I was up late making a huge list of lawyers to call if—or maybe more accurately *when*—things go south with Sara. The cops here are notorious for treating people on the island's two sides very differently. *Very* differently.

A few years back, a jewelry store downtown was robbed, and they immediately arrested a couple kids who live two streets over from here on the grounds that they'd been seen in the area shortly before it occurred. It wasn't until their parents scraped together enough money to hire a decent lawyer that anyone bothered to look at footage from the red-light camera down the street. It turned out it wasn't them at all—it was a group of rich teens here on vacation.

A sudden, sharp rap on the car window startles me out of those depressing thoughts. My head jerks up, and I find Martin peering in at me with a grin on his face.

I roll down the window and swipe at him. "What the hell, man? You almost gave me a heart attack."

He jumps back, laughing. He's certainly in fine spirits for someone who had another person's blood on their hands yesterday, though I suppose that's par for the course with his job.

"Sorry. Didn't mean to scare you," he says, although his smirk says otherwise.

"Whatever." I climb out of the car and join him on the sidewalk. "You here visiting your ma?"

Martin and I both grew up on this block and have known each other since we were in diapers. My mom has the embarrassing pictures to prove it.

"Yeah. Dropping some stuff off." His mom was diagnosed with stomach cancer a few months ago, and he comes by to administer her meds when his dad is at work.

I peel my shirt off my moist back and give it a shake. It's humid as hell out here, and dawn has barely broken. The Jersey Shore at its finest.

"How's she?"

He shrugs. "Okay. Sort of. The chemo is helping, but she feels like shit pretty much all the time. Worst thing is my dad found this new clinical trial up in Detroit, but we can't afford the cost of travel. They're already in a ton of debt because their insurance doesn't cover a lot of the stuff it should..."

His lips pinch white, and anger surges in me. It's such bullshit that his mom—one of the sweetest people I know—is drowning in medical debt while the people on the other end of this island have more money than they'll ever need.

"Anyway," he says. "It is what it is. You here because of Sara?"

I nod.

Martin grimaces. "I thought, day after the party, we'd be talking about you seeing Harriet for the first time in years. Not your sister behind bars. I'm sorry about..."

He trails off like he doesn't quite know how to finish the sentence. A gull shrieks overhead.

Finding the knife? Totally screwing Sara by telling Sharkey about it instead of surreptitiously digging a hole and burying it so far down that no one would ever find it?

"You know," he finally says.

"Yeah. It's not your fault." I was pissed at him for a split second last night, but I'd be kidding myself to think no one else would have spotted it. "I get it. You were doing your job."

"Yeah, well. Sometimes, my job is bullshit." We lapse into momentarily silence and then: "How do you think it ended up there?"

A headache tugs behind my eyes. "I don't know. I don't know, man. Maybe somebody stole it when we weren't looking? It has to be that, right? It's the only explanation."

I may have had a moment last night when I thought—well, what anyone would think after finding someone standing over a dead body. That maybe my sister had killed him.

But I've thought about it pretty much nonstop since, and now I'm convinced she didn't do it. Sara's a hothead, sure—the number of times she's been fired by Mom speaks to that—but she also calms down, fast. If she was going to kill George for insulting her cooking, she would have done it right there in that kitchen, crowd or no crowd.

Martin, loyal friend that he is, immediately agrees. "Right. Of course. Have you heard if she's coming home today?"

"Yeah. She should be back soon, and she hasn't been formally charged or anything. Though my mom sent her cousin Barry down to the station to 'help,' so we'll see how long that lasts."

Martin grimaces. "Barry...like her cousin who failed the bar eight times Barry?"

"The very one."

"Shit, man." Martin kicks a pebble off the sidewalk with the tip of his boot. "Well. I shouldn't be telling you this, but if your mom is planning to rely on Barry for help..."

He's wearing an expression on his face I recognize. It's the same one he was wearing our senior year of high school when he told me he'd overheard Michael Dalton in the locker room telling everyone that I had a tiny dick.

I *hate* that expression.

Also, for the record, I don't have a tiny dick—Michael Dalton is a fucking liar and is currently serving ten years in minimum security prison for mail fraud.

"What?" I prompt impatiently.

"I was talking to some of the cops last night, and—" He hesitates. "I don't know how to say this any other way, so. Sara's their lead suspect right now. In fact, she's their *only* suspect."

I squint down the block at a gull, squawking as it splashes in a puddle. What I wouldn't give to trade places with it right now.

"Shit."

"Yeah," Martin agrees. "Shit is right."

CHAPTER EIGHT

HARRIET

August 30

9:18 a.m.

I grab a bag of dark roast with shaking hands and busy myself making coffee. My mom's asleep still, knocked out by the pills I gave her late last night, and the house is quiet. Too quiet. My imagination's playing tricks on me, every creak and groan making me jump.

The beach greets me through the window over the kitchen sink. The waves, lapping up against the shore, George, brutally stabbed to death—

No.

I rip my eyes away.

Once I get the coffee brewing, I pick up my phone, open TikTok, and am immediately greeted by yet another video of Sara flying across the beach. There are thousands of comments, hundreds of reposts. It's gone very, very viral. Whoever posted the original is such a dick.

I saw it for the first time late last night on the *Humans* landing page, which I was masochistically scrolling after consuming an entire bottle of champagne.

And then I…

A memory hits. *Oh shit.*

I fling TikTok closed and open my email. Please, please, *please* tell me I didn't do what I think I—Oh. Oh no.

There it is, sitting in my sent folder.

An email to Frankie. My old boss at *Humans*. The person who fired me in cold blood after I outed a celebrity's secret pregnancy. Which was a god's honest mistake.

The last time I spoke to her was six months ago, when she was screaming at me for getting the magazine into a shit ton of trouble and telling me that I was under no uncertain terms *fired as fuck*. After that, I spiraled for a while. Sank into a deep depression for about a month or so, spent another three months desperately applying to other jobs while living off my grandmother's generous donation of rent money. Month five, I finally conceded defeat and slunk back here with my tail between my legs.

What the hell was I thinking, emailing that witch?

I wasn't is the obvious answer.

The coffee machine lets out a loud beep to tell me it's finished brewing, but I ignore it. Suddenly, caffeine is the last thing on my mind.

I remember it clearly now: sitting on the living room couch, chugging straight from the bottle. Hunting down Martin's Instagram since I couldn't find Nic's and zooming in on every photo with him in it. The memory of our two weeks together wriggling into the back of my mind as I scrolled until it got too sharp, too painful, and I had to stop. I opened HumansMag.com, and my worlds collided—not in a good way. They'd posted the viral video of Sara along with an article riddled with errors. I didn't recognize the byline—probably the person they hired to replace me.

I saw red.

And then I emailed Frankie.

Two paragraphs, half the words misspelled, the general gist of it being *you guys don't know what you're talking about, you should never have hired me* (a lovely typo—I meant *fired* me), *the local police are corrupt, maybe someone should investigate THEM instead of the other way around.*

Right. If she didn't already have my email blocked, she will now.

Which sucks, because buried beneath my drunken spewing is an actual, important truth: I overheard a very shady conversation out on that beach, and I'm pretty sure Sara is in serious trouble.

The sound of the doorbell cuts into my thoughts. I send a longing look at the untouched coffee carafe and rush into the front hall before they can ring again and wake my mother.

Through the front windows of the house, I catch sight of an unmarked black Crown Vic parked in the driveway.

The cops.

"Dammit," I mutter. A quick glance down confirms I'm still wearing my pajamas. Just the outfit I would have chosen for a chat with the authorities.

I swing open the front door. "Can I—"

My eyes land on the male detective, and my brain goes blank.

No.

This cannot be happening.

I'm going to throw up. Just when I thought things couldn't possibly get more fucked up.

Standing on the porch is my ex-boyfriend, Adam Kozel, staring at me like he's seen a ghost.

I almost slam the door in his face but manage to stop myself just in time. He is, after all, an authority figure, even though I once saw him do a sixty-second keg stand.

"Everything okay?" Kozel's partner, an older Black woman, looks between the two of us with a curious expression. "Adam?"

He looks almost exactly the same. White, almost translucent skin, short brown hair, a sharp jawline, lashes annoyingly long and thick. I was always jealous of those lashes.

I note with pleasure the two deep lines etched into his forehead. Although as a man, people probably think they give him *character*.

Steven mentioned he'd heard Kozel was a detective, but I thought he worked at the county sheriff's office over on the mainland, which is a solid forty-minute drive away. He should not be here, on my doorstep.

"*Adam?*" his partner asks more sharply.

Kozel slaps on a smile like the sociopath he is. I shouldn't be surprised he's working with the LIPD; he's probably just as corrupt as they are.

"Yup. All is well. Thanks, Sandy. This is, um, Harriet Baker." He clears his throat. "We... Well, we know each other from high school. I hadn't realized—I didn't know she was back in town."

Sandy's eyebrows lift. "Another one from high school, huh? Guess I should stop being surprised by that."

"Anyway," Kozel continues smoothly. He's always been smooth, even in the most awkward situations (see: sociopath). "Hello, Harriet. It's so nice to see you—"

He's lying, obviously. There's no way he's happy to see me, not after how he ghosted me back in high school.

"I just wasn't..." He clears his throat. "Well. I was expecting your mother to answer the door. We're very sorry about—your stepfather, was it?"

I nod.

"Your stepfather's, his, um, his passing..."

Again, Sandy's eyebrows jump as Kozel stumbles over his words. She cuts in. "Ms. Baker, hello. Detective Sandy Jones, Atlantic County Sheriff's Office. We were brought onto the case late last night to assist the local PD. They're less experienced with this sort of matter. May we come in? We'd like to speak with you and your mother about what happened."

I glance behind me, trying to think of a legitimate reason to send them away. "My mom's still asleep—"

"You could wake her?" Detective Jones says. She frames it as a question, but I can tell it's really not.

"Yeah. I guess. She's sort of a monster when she gets woken up. But..." I trail off, hoping she'll get the hint, but she just stares at me. My shoulders slump. "Fine. All right. Come in."

I lead them into the living room, and they settle on the couch.

"I'll be right back," I say. My top priority is to get Adam Kozel the hell out of here as fast as possible. If that means rousing my mother and dealing with her wrath, fine.

I head up the stairs and take a sharp right toward her room.

The door is cracked, and I peek inside. It's dark, the curtains pulled tight against the morning sun.

"Mom?"

No answer.

I try again, louder this time. "*Mother!*"

Still nothing.

I flick on the overhead lights. Admittedly rude, but desperate times.

The comforter emits a loud groan.

"Mom?" I say more gently. "The cops are here."

Another groan.

"They want to talk to you! About...you know. George. And—"

"Harriet?" My mother's head emerges. She blinks at me, black mascara ringing both eyes like a sad raccoon. "Why are you in here? What did you say? *Who's* here?"

I swallow, loath to remind her of everything. She's still half asleep.

"The cops."

"The—" Her eyes widen. "The police? Are here?" She takes in the empty space next to her in the bed and lets out a choked sob. "To talk about my George?"

I nod.

"Have they arrested that horrible woman yet?"

"I don't know."

Her mouth sets in a determined line, and she sits up, fluffing her blond bob.

"Tell them I'll be down in five."

I back out of the room slowly, reluctant to face Kozel again.

Five minutes later, my mom appears wearing a full face of makeup and a floral housedress. She's smiling, but her eyes are red-rimmed, the buttons on her dress crooked.

A twinge of pity hits me. A very small twinge, which disappears as soon as she walks into the room, sees Kozel, and exclaims, "Adam *Kozel*? Oh my *goodness*. It is so lovely to see you!" She flutters a hand over her heart. "I heard you're a *detective* now. I always knew you'd do big things with your life."

She shoots me a look that clearly says *Harriet, how could you let this A+ specimen of a man get away?*

This is my own personal version of hell.

My mother always adored Kozel. When we broke up, she was convinced it was my fault, and nothing would change her mind. It was so typical of her, I wasn't even surprised.

I wish I was back in New York.

She settles into the armchair next to me, then leans forward and grasps Kozel's hand between her own. "How *are* you, Adam? I'm sorry. *Detective* Kozel." She bats her lashes, and Detective Jones frowns. "Are you *married*?"

Kozel gently extracts his hand while I take deep, slow breaths to keep from screaming.

The woman just lost her husband. She is devastated.

"Because Harriet isn't," she continues. "She moved in with me recently because she lost her job and—"

I'm going to kill her.

"Ms. George," Jones interrupts.

"*Mrs.* George," my feminist mother says.

Jones's frown deepens. "Right. *Mrs.* George. I'm Detective Jones. We're here to—"

My mother interrupts her now. "I *assume* you're here to tell me that you've arrested the woman who murdered my George. That *cook*."

"Ma'am, we're still in the process of gathering evidence—"

My mother gasps. "Excuse me? Gathering *evidence*? You already know who did it! You have her in custody! Her knife was found in the sand next to George, for god's sake! What more do you need?"

Before Jones can respond, Kozel jumps in. "Now...Mrs. George—"

"Please, Adam. Call me Lisa. We were practically family at one point."

Kozel's eyes cut to my reddening face, then back to her. "Lisa. Right. As my partner was saying, we're very sorry for your loss. We're told Mr. George was a good friend to the Logan Island police force. His death is a great loss to the community as a whole. As I'm sure you realize, we believe George's death was not from natural causes."

"Of course it wasn't!" my mother cries. "Which leads me back to my original question: Why hasn't that awful woman been charged?"

"We're working on it," Kozel says vaguely. "In fact, we're here because we want to hear your account of what happened last night. Not just the argument between Mr. George and the—" He coughs. "The cook but the rest of it too. I remember you were always so observant when I was younger, and as I told my partner on the way here, I'm sure you noticed things *no* one else did."

Kozel is many things (sociopath, liar, the list goes on), but a dummy he is not.

My mother titters. "Oh, Adam. You *do* flatter me," she says, then launches into it. "Well. As you know, last night we hosted a party here in celebration of my daughter's twenty-sixth birthday. I would have invited you, Adam, but you know how stubborn Harriet is—"

"*Mother!*" I snap.

"What?" she says with a frown, like she can't imagine why I'm annoyed.

"Nothing," I mutter.

"Well then." She turns back to the detectives. "As I was saying before I was so *rudely* interrupted: We invited some old classmates from PHS, George's business associates, VIPs in the town government—"

Detective Jones flips the page of her steno pad. "Can you confirm the names of the attendees for us, please?"

"Actually, I can do one better. I'll get you a full list." Rising from her chair, my mom heads over to her desk. A moment later, she returns with her iPad in hand. On the screen is an Excel spreadsheet, which she proudly shows the cops. "Would you like me to print it for you? There's a printer back in George's office."

"That would be very helpful," Kozel says with a smile.

My mom hurries out of the room, and an awkward silence descends. I study the ceiling, trying to avoid Kozel's eyes, which I can feel running laps around my face.

"The beach," Jones says, disrupting the silence. She's flipping through her notebook. "We understand it's private, but it's also geographically inaccessible, correct? One side blocked by a rocky hill, the other by a thicket of trees?"

"Correct. The only paths in and out are through the gates, and they all have codes."

She scribbles this down. "Great. Can you tell us who has the codes? Anyone other than residents? Workers? Friends?"

I shake my head. "Not really. At least not ours. George changed the code weekly."

Her eyes flick up. "And was that new behavior?"

I shrug. "I don't know. I was living up in the city until a couple months ago. My mom would be the one to ask."

"I'm so sorry to hear about your job, Harriet," Kozel says, pretending like he has an empathetic bone in his body. "All you ever wanted was to work in journalism."

I ignore him.

My mom returns, a piece of paper clutched in her hand.

"Here you are," she says, holding it out to Kozel. "You'll recognize *many* of the names as local VIPs."

Kozel scans it, then looks back to her. "Are you aware of anyone on this list who wanted to hurt George?"

"Your daughter mentioned he changed the gate code frequently," Jones adds. "Was that something new? Was he concerned about his safety?"

"Absolutely not! George was beloved on this island. He was a member of the town council. A figurehead. A leader! Everyone respected him."

Her eyes fill with tears. I extend a box of tissues, and she pulls out a handful, carefully blotting her cheeks so as not to mess up her blush.

"You can't think of *anyone* who wanted to hurt your husband?" Jones asks.

"Well, of course I can," my mom huffs. "That cook! But outside of that, no. George was an angel."

"Are you serious?" The words are out of my mouth before I can stop them.

Three sets of eyes land on me. "Harriet? Is there something you'd like to add?" Kozel asks.

"I'm sorry, but—" How do I say this without getting myself kicked out of the house? My mother's glare is burning a hole in my cheek. "George wasn't... Mom, you *know* he could be very...difficult."

"How dare you!" she snaps. "I knew you disliked him, but to *say* such a thing! Really, Harriet. He hasn't even been gone for a full day. You have absolutely no respect for the people who—"

Kozel stands. "Lisa, I'd really like to get your perspective on the fight between Sara—err, the chef and George. As I said before, I remember you being so observant. Would you be willing to step into the other room with me so we can chat? Just the two of us."

Her eyes light up. "Absolutely."

He leads her out of the room. Once they're gone, Jones leans forward. "So George had a lot of enemies?" she asks softly.

A part of me wishes I'd just kept my mouth shut—less risk of fallout with my mom later—but it's too late now.

I plunge ahead. I need to get it on record that lots of people hated George.

"I don't know how much you know about my stepfather, but he was not an easy man. Especially if he didn't get his own way."

Jones flips to a new page in her notebook. "Can you be more specific?"

"Well." I pick at a loose thread on the pillow next to me. "Take, for example, the fight over development of the island. When George moved back here after decades up in Manhattan, he arrived with all these ideas. Ideas a lot of locals really hated. He wanted to build apartment buildings, luxury hotels, high-end shopping—things that were strictly forbidden under the zoning laws here. But did that stop him? Of course not. Instead, he managed to get himself elected to the town council and was working to change those laws from the inside. And let me tell you, people were *pissed*." I glance toward the doorway my mom and Kozel disappeared through, but it's quiet. "If I were you, I'd look at everyone he interacted with at the party, especially the people who've spoken out against his development plans. Take Barbara Patterson, the head librarian—she was vehemently opposed to everything George stood for and really hated him. Honestly, I thought it was weird she was there."

"Got it, thanks." Jones snaps her notebook shut without asking anything further.

I'm caught off guard. I thought she'd have follow-up questions, ask me more about Patterson and George's relationship, about who else I think could have done it.

"I'm just saying, you guys should investigate other people. Outside of Sara Allbright, I mean. Just because my mom says she's guilty doesn't mean she is."

"Of course, Ms. Baker," Jones says smoothly. "We're exploring all possible angles."

She'd make a good politician; I can't tell if she's telling the truth or lying to my face. I'm tempted to ask her about the conversation I overheard on the beach—what she thinks Sharkey meant by *pin it on someone*. Is anyone actually investigating this, or has Sara's fate already been decided?

But would she answer me honestly?

Is she after the truth, or is she just another cop looking for an easy conviction?

She stands, smooths her slacks, and calls, "Detective Kozel!"

A beat, then Kozel appears.

"Ready to go?" she asks him.

His eyes cut to my face, and my cheeks warm. I look away.

"Yup. All set," he says.

"Great." She turns to me. "Thank you for your time. We'll be in touch."

CHAPTER NINE

NIC

September 3

3:23 p.m.

Sara's at the other end of the long metal prep table from me, chopping onions. Normally, she makes a show of it, but today her knifework is sluggish.

She's sniffing as she slices, and I'm pretty sure it's not because of the onions.

The last time I saw Sara cry was… Honestly, I don't even know.

"Are you okay?" I ask. I'm worried. I've been worried since she stepped foot through the door of my parents' house on Sunday morning, and it's only gotten worse as the days have passed. Martin's sources inside the PD tell him that things do not look good for her; the cops have all but given up looking for other suspects.

If they even tried at all.

Which means she's in trouble. Massive amounts of trouble. And if things get as bad as I fear they will, my mom's cousin Barry isn't going to cut it as her lawyer.

The issue is we can't afford someone better. The public defenders here are all fresh out of law school, living at home, working for the government until they can land a gig in the private sector. They wouldn't handle my sister's case any better than Barry. I spent the last two days hustling my ass off, calling every lawyer's office in a fifty-mile radius. The prices I was quoted were astronomical—or at least sounded that way to me. And no one is willing to cut us a break.

The system on this island—in this *country*—wasn't built for people like us. It was built for the people on the other side, who buy sailboats for fun, who belong to the Yacht Club. The rich people.

Sara looks up, glaring at me through glassy eyes. "I'm *fine*," she snaps.

The door to the warehouse bangs open, and Esme Peters appears, trailed by Matthew Prado.

Esme's worked for All Bright Caterers for eight years, ever since we opened our doors. She and my mom grew up together, have known each other for decades, and she's been an invaluable asset. Matthew, on the other hand, only started a month ago. He's from somewhere around NYC, and why he moved here of all places is still a mystery to me. He just showed up one day, résumé in hand, asking for a job. He's lucky we even had an opening; we don't usually hire new people toward the end of the season, but one of our regular caterers moved down to Philly for grad school.

"Sara." Esme wraps her in a hug. "Are those silly police officers still bugging you?"

Sara pulls back, blinking fast. "I didn't do it! You know that, right?"

"Of course, honey," Esme says. She digs into her shoulder bag. "Here, I brought you something." She presses a small pile of rocks into Sara's hand. "Black tourmaline. Put a piece in every corner of your home for protection, okay?"

"Yeah. Thanks," Sara murmurs, distracted by the sounds of the front door opening behind me.

I turn as Adam Kozel appears through it, flanked by an older woman. I'm caught off guard for a moment—Kozel is the last person I expected to walk through that door—but then I remember: he's a cop now. I remember when Martin told me that, I thought it seemed fitting. Kozel *was* always the type to follow the rules without question.

To be clear, I don't mean that as a compliment.

I never had any real reason to hate Kozel back in high school—we didn't really interact, me being a total loser with one friend and he being the most popular guy in our grade—but I still managed to resent the hell out of him. And after everything went down with Harriet and me like it did, I decided that was mostly his fault too.

They stop in front of my sister, official in their matching gray, ill-fitting suits.

"Sara Allbright?" the woman says.

"Y-yes?" Sara looks at me like she's hoping I can protect her from what's coming next.

"I'm Detective Jones from the Atlantic County Sheriff's Office. And this is my partner, Detective Kozel..."

"Adam," Sara finishes. "Yeah. I know Adam."

"Of course. I should have guessed," Jones says. "We're here with regard to the murder of George George—"

Sara interrupts. "I didn't kill him." Her voice is steady, but the knife clutched in her fist trembles.

The detectives exchange a look.

"Did you work at Pêne Dormant in New York City?" Kozel asks. I note with satisfaction that he butchers the French.

"Yes?" Sara says. "What does that have to do with anything?"

"You were a cook there—"

"I was *sous-chef*," Sara snaps. I wince. She needs to pull back on the attitude. These people do not care about fine dining titles.

Kozel pauses. "Right. Sous-chef. You worked there until it closed down, correct?"

"Yes," Sara says, lips disappearing into a thin white line. "But we didn't *close*. We were forced out of business."

Pêne Dormant. The place where she got those damn knives that killed George, gifted to her by the head chef, Jules. When she landed that job, I really thought she'd found her place in the world. But a year later, the building sold and the new owner tripled their rent overnight. The restaurant shut down, and Jules, whose real name was John, moved back to Iowa and married his high school sweetheart.

Sara lost her fucking mind. I'm pretty sure she and Jules/John were sleeping together, so with the sale of that building, she lost her job, her relationship—all in one fell swoop.

After that, she bounced around. Landed a few gigs working for mid-tier restaurants but was fired from them all. Eventually, the opportunities ran out and she moved back, started working for us.

She hasn't been the same since.

But I have no idea what any of it has to do with the murder.

"Porcha puttana." My mom hurries out from her office. "What is going on out here?" She surveys the two plainclothes detectives. "You are the police, correct?"

"Yes, ma'am. We are," Kozel says.

My mom frowns. "Sara, che diavolo sta succedendo?"

"I don't know!" my sister replies.

"Mrs. Allbright, I can answer that," Kozel says.

"You speak Italian?" she says, eyebrow jumping.

He smiles smugly, and I roll my eyes. "Solo un po'. We're here because we have a few more questions for your daughter—"

"She already spoke to the police!"

"Yes, ma'am. But that was before my partner and I were brought over from the mainland. Since then, new information about Sara's relationship with the deceased has come to light, and we need to ask her about it."

"Ms. Allbright," Jones directs to my sister, "you moved back to Logan Island in..." She consults the notebook in her hand, though I'd bet she knows the information by heart. "2024. Is that correct?"

Sara crosses her arms. "Yes. So?"

"Curious timing," Jones says. "Don't you think, Detective Kozel?"

"It does seem quite coincidental," he says with a little shrug.

I'm not usually a fighter, but I seriously want to knock him in the mouth right now.

Sara looks at them. "What's coincidental?"

Jones sidesteps her question. "Before that, you were living in New York City?"

"Yeah, so?"

"Well, Mr. George moved back to Logan Island from New York in 2023 after selling his commercial real estate busin—"

Sara interrupts again. "You're kidding. You're here questioning me because that guy and I lived in the biggest city in the country at the same time and then both moved to the island? I grew up here! I had a legitimate reason to come back. I'd never even talked to him before that night!"

"We think you did," Jones says. "In fact, according to several posts on LinkedIn from early 2022, you had *quite* the vendetta against GG Capital Group. We dug up several heated—borderline threatening—comments left by someone with your name."

"So what?" Sara's chin juts like she's ready for a fight. "Those assholes shut my restaurant down!"

"Exactly," Jones says.

I tense, waiting for the other shoe to drop. "*Those assholes.* At GG Capital Group. The real estate investment company George George founded. While living in New York City. At the same time as you."

And there it is.

"George George founded..." Realization dawns across Sara's face. "I didn't know that! You think I *knew* that? And what, you think I waited three fucking years to get revenge? That's insane!"

"Murder often is," Jones says, nodding.

Sara holds up the knife still grasped in her hand, brandishing it in the air. "Jesus Christ!" she shouts. "This has to be a joke. I didn't *kill* him! I didn't kill anyone!"

"Sara!" I hiss. What the hell is she doing? Is she trying to get herself arrested?

"Whoa there," Jones says, hands raised. "Ms. Allbright, I suggest you put that down *immediately*."

"Sara," Kozel says. "That is not a good idea."

Sara blinks at the knife like she's not sure how it ended up in her hand. She drops it to the floor with a clatter, and Kozel darts forward, snatching it.

"I wasn't going to hurt anyone—I just—"

"You need to come with us," Jones says. "*Now.* We can do this the easy way or the hard way. It's up to you."

"She wasn't going to hurt you!" Mom cries. She reaches out to Sara, but Jones blocks her with a straight-arm.

"Mrs. Allbright, please don't make this any more difficult," Kozel says softly. "We're just taking Sara in for a chat. Nothing more, nothing less."

I'm not sure I believe that. The way Jones straight-armed my mom, her tone with Sara—this doesn't feel like "just a chat."

It feels like they've already made up their minds about charging her.

Sara's face is pale; she's cowed in a way I've never seen. "I think I need a lawyer, Mom. A real one. Not Barry."

"Ms. Allbright." Jones gestures to her. "Shall we?"

Sara gives a tiny nod, and the detectives lead her away.

CHAPTER TEN

NIC

September 3
8:52 p.m.

Martin's already at the bar as I push through Hendricks' front door, a glass of whiskey resting in front of him. He's still in his EMT uniform, fresh off a shift saving lives.

I, on the other hand, smell like an onion.

"I need a drink," I say by way of greeting.

Hendricks is downtown, close to our catering space and walkable to my apartment. In the height of the summer, it's a total tourist trap, filled with college kids from Philly and NYC who stuff eight, ten, twelve people into the houses they rent, and I avoid it at all costs.

Right now, though, it's not too bad. The college kids are back at school, thank god, so even though the town is packed with tourists, it's mostly families who don't venture out to bars late at night.

It's quiet. The way I like it.

Martin tips his glass toward me. "Whiskey?"

"Please."

He signals to the bartender, and I settle onto the stool next to him.

"Any word?" he asks.

Sara is still down at the station. My mom and Barry headed there two hours ago, and I spent the time between frantically googling law firms again to no avail.

I shake my head. "Nothing yet. I still can't fucking believe this. They've got to realize they have the wrong person."

"I hate to ask but...did you know about Sara's connection to George?" Off my questioning look, Martin adds, "My source down at the station told me about it. I'm sorry to hear it, man."

"Yeah. It's messed up. And no. I didn't know. Honestly, I don't think Sara did either. She seemed shocked. I get it'd be a massive coincidence, but you know how she is. Could you really see her plotting to kill someone for *years*? She doesn't have that sort of patience."

"This is true," Martin says.

"Also," I say, studying the labels on the bottles behind the bar, "not to change the subject, but were you aware that Adam *Kozel* is the detective on this case?"

He chokes on a mouthful of his drink, spluttering into the crook of his elbow. "Yeah," he says once recovered. "I'd heard that."

"And you didn't bother to let me know?"

He winces. "I thought maybe it wasn't the right time to bring it up?"

The right time. Sure. What a chickenshit.

"So instead, you let me be blindsided."

He winces. “I’m sorry. I should have given you a heads-up.”

I roll my eyes. “Yeah, you should have. He’s still such a tool.”

The bartender sets a glass in front of me, and I slug a huge sip of whiskey. It hits the back of my throat, burning.

“From what I hear, Kozel is actually a pretty decent guy these days,” the traitor next to me says. “It might not be the worst thing, having him on Sara’s case. Personal issues aside.”

“No one asked you.”

“I’m just saying. I doubt he thinks your sister is a murderer. He knew her.”

“I wouldn’t be so sure,” I say gloomily. “You weren’t there.”

“How’d he look anyway? Still hot?”

I roll my eyes. “He looked fine.”

I don’t add how fit he looked—way fitter than me. I wonder if Harriet’s seen him. Not that I care, especially given our interaction at the party.

“Harriet,” Martin says, like he’s reading my mind.

My heart skips. “What?”

“Harriet,” he says, tilting his chin. “Just walked into the bar.”

It’s like the start of a very bad joke.

“The devil herself,” I mutter.

“She’s with two people,” Martin says, taking a sip of his drink. “Oh! Steven Martinez and Maggie Sutherland. I heard Steven was living down in Philly with some guy for a while, but they broke up a few months ago so he moved back. According to my sources, he’s single.”

I eye him. He’s certainly well-versed on Steven’s relationship status.

“Do you want to ask them to join us?” I say warily.

His eyes light up.

"If you do," he says.

"Sounds fantastic," I say with clear sarcasm. Yes, what I want to do right now is hang out with Harriet fucking Baker, who didn't remember sleeping with me and whose mother accused my sister of murder.

Martin ignores my tone. "Great," he says with a smile. He hops off his stool and walks to them. He and Steven exchange a few words, Steven nodding keenly.

Then Martin points at me. Harriet's eyes find mine, and her face darkens. I swallow, forcing myself to hold her gaze until she looks away.

When Martin and Steven head my way, she trails after them.

Great. I'm tempted to start banging my head against the bar top but instead take a long sip of whiskey.

Martin slides back onto his stool, pulling out another for Steven.

"Hey, Nic," Steven says as he sits. "Fancy seeing you two here. I'd say it's been a while, but it really hasn't, has it? You know, you were amazing that day, Martin."

Martin grins modestly. "Thanks. Just doing my job."

Maggie and Harriet have stopped in the middle of the room and are clearly arguing about something. Me, no doubt.

I drain my drink and push the glass away. Normally, I'm more than happy to be Martin's wingman, but I'm too tired and too worried about Sara.

I lean over to whisper in Martin's ear. "I'm gonna take off."

Before he can respond, Maggie and Harriet arrive to us. Or, to be precise, Maggie arrives and Harriet sort of...hides. Behind her. Like a giant baby.

God, that woman.

We catch eyes, and she narrows hers.

I roll my own.

Maggie's caught in the crossfire. After a second, she sighs loudly.

"Hi. I'm Maggie Sutherland," she says, holding out her hand.

Yeah, no shit. Jesus, what is *up* with Harriet and her friends? I've seen Maggie around the island over the years—we've never really talked, but she should still recognize me.

"You're Nic, right?" she continues.

I blink with surprise. "Yeah. Nic Allbright."

"It's been a while, but I think we were in the same geometry class sophomore year."

I nod, heart warming to her.

"Mr. Patterson," she adds. "With the bow ties?"

I let out a laugh, my first in days. "I forgot about those bow ties."

She grins. "And you remember—" She turns as Harriet ducks behind her back. "Harriet. Hi, Harriet. What the hell are you doing?"

"I'd say she's hiding," I say a little nastily. I can't help it. She's acting like I'm diseased.

Harriet draws herself upright and plonks her fists onto her hips.

"I'm not *hiding*. I thought I recognized someone. Over there. Across the bar." She makes a vague gesture toward the opposite end of the room.

"Right," I say, making clear I very much do not believe her. "Sure."

She glowers at me.

Maggie raises a brow. "Okay. On that note, I need a drink. Har, you want anything?"

"Whiskey. Neat."

I'm impressed, even though I'd never say it.

"You and your whiskey," Maggie says with a teasing grin. "I remember when you started drinking it because you thought people would take you more seriously as a journalist."

Harriet's face blooms red.

"You?"

It takes me a second to realize Maggie's talking to me.

"I..." I drag my eyes from Harriet's face to my empty glass.

Do I really want to go home and sit in silence, panicking about Sara's legal representation? Waiting on news that could very well be bad?

Not particularly.

"Yeah, okay," I say. "Thanks. Glenlivet on the rocks."

With Maggie busy, Harriet is finally forced to speak directly to me. "You're not going to ask if one of us wants your chair? Wouldn't that be the gentlemanly thing to do?"

I look over my shoulder, pretending like I don't know who she's addressing. When I turn back, a scowl has settled on her face.

"Oh. I'm sorry." I press a hand on my chest. "Were you talking to *me*? I didn't realize you were acknowledging my existence."

She steps closer, and suddenly the air between us is crackling with old, familiar tension. "God, you're annoying. Obviously, I was talking to you."

"Wouldn't asking if you want my chair be considered, I don't know—misogynistic?"

She gives me a withering look. "No. It would be considered polite."

I stand. "Do you want to sit?"

"No, I'm good," she says with a smile.

Right. Of course she is. She's so annoying. So combative.

Which, to be fair, is sort of a turn-on.

Maggie leans back against the bar as she waits on our drinks. "Okay, so Kozel," she says to Harriet. "I've barely had a chance to ask about your run-in with him. Did he look the same?"

I guess that answers the question of whether she's seen him.

"No," Harriet says quickly, eyes darting to my face. I flex my biceps.

Maggie's ruddy complexion grows even redder, and she claps a hand over her mouth. "Oh shit. Nic. Sara Allbright. The one the cops brought in in connection to the...the..."

"The murder?" I finish when it becomes clear she's not going to.

"Right. That. She's your sister, isn't she? I knew that, but my brain is mush after spending the week buried in law books. I'm so sorry."

Before I can respond, Martin lets out a groan. He's staring at his phone in dismay.

I lean toward him. "Everything okay?"

He meets my eyes, and my heart sinks.

"It's Sara," I say.

He winces.

"What is it?"

He hesitates.

"Just tell me."

He sets the phone down and turns to face me. "The fingerprints came back. From the knife. And there was only one pair on it."

"Sara's," I say.

"Sara's," he confirms.

I knew her fingerprints would be all over the knife—of course they would be. But I'd been holding out hope that someone else's would be too. It would force the cops to consider other suspects, and this whole mess would start to untangle.

"Yeah. And that, coupled with everything else..." He's wearing the same expression he was that morning outside my parents' house. The one I hate. "The DA is planning to formally charge her. With first-degree murder."

The words hit me like a stab to the gut. Harriet, Steven, and Maggie are quiet.

My stool scrapes loud against the linoleum floor as I push back from the bar. "Already? They can't be serious. That's fucking ridiculous!"

Martin sets down his phone. "It is, but do you remember the last election cycle? A district attorney was elected for Atlantic County, and according to my sources, she was—"

"Good friends with George," Harriet interrupts. At least she has the decency to look ashamed. "So's Sharkey, actually. And Mayor DiPetrio. George was a big donor to all their campaigns."

"Yup," Martin says. "And this new DA's trying to make a name for herself. A murder trial could be huge for her, particularly since the victim was a well-known Manhattan property developer."

"So, what: Sara's a pawn? Someone she can use to further her career?"

"I wish I could say no," Martin says. "But it sure sounds like that."

"We covered stories like this in my journalism courses," Harriet murmurs to Maggie. "It's insane how willing politicians are to play with people's lives."

Does she think that's helpful? I'm about to rip her a new one when something clicks.

Harriet. Harriet wrote for a national outlet up in the city. Sure, their main focus is celebrity fluff pieces, but it still has a huge readership.

"You," I say, pointing.

She looks confused. "Me?"

"This is your fault."

"It's not—"

"*Your* father got himself killed—"

"Stepfather," she mutters.

"And now my sister could spend the rest of her life in prison. Why did he insist on starting that fight with her? Why couldn't he leave well enough alone? What is it with you rich people? Why do you think you own the fucking world?"

Her mouth drops open. "I don't," she says, her voice small.

"Nic—" Martin's hand finds my arm. "Hey. This isn't her fault."

He's right. I'm letting my anger get the best of me. I need Harriet's help, and this isn't how to get it.

I down the rest of my drink and take a deep breath before speaking again. "Okay, listen. My family can't afford a decent attorney. My mom's cousin Barry's representing Sara, and he once told me he's pretty sure the earth is flat. So you can see what sort of predicament we're in here."

Harriet nods.

"Sara is innocent. You might not be aware of this because of where and how you grew up, but the cops on our lovely little island have a long history of scapegoating people like me and her."

"I know," Harriet says. "And I'm sorry, but—"

"Let me finish. And if she's charged—*once* she's charged—she's screwed. That's the end of the hunt for other suspects, if the cops even looked for any to begin with. Barry won't do shit to help her. That's where you come in. You used to work at a big, fancy publication up in New York, didn't you?"

Harriet shakes her head. "Yeah. But not anymore."

"Right, not anymore, but you *know* people. You need to use your connections and write about all this. Tell the world what's happening to my sister. Maybe someone will read it who can help her."

"Nic," Harriet says quietly. "I *did* email my editor."

I blink. "You did?"

"Yeah. But she hasn't responded, and I don't think she will. You don't understand. I got *fired*. I haven't been able to find another job and it isn't—"

She keeps going, one reason after another about why she can't help.

I stop listening. Of course she won't. It was stupid of me to think she would.

I finally interrupt. "I need to go."

"Do you want company?" Martin asks.

"*No*," I snap, then soften. None of this is Martin's fault. "I have to find my mom. But tell me if you hear anything else, okay?"

"Will do."

I'm almost to the door when a hand grabs my elbow. I turn.

Harriet.

"What?" I bark. Her face falls. For a moment, my heart stutters, and I remember the Harriet Baker that was mine for two weeks. But this woman in front of me isn't her.

"I—" She falters. "I'm sorry. About all this. I really wish I could do something, but—"

I'm not in the mood to hear any more of her excuses.

"Right." I shake her hand off me. "I'm sure you fucking do."

And with that, I stalk out of the bar.

CHAPTER ELEVEN

HARRIET

September 3
10:48 p.m.

I'm drunk when I get home. Drunk enough that it takes me three tries to get the front door unlocked, the key heavy in my hand. Inside, the house is dark, my mom probably passed out upstairs from her sleeping pills.

I head to the kitchen, pour myself a glass of water, and chug it straight down. I let out a loud, very elegant belch, then wipe my mouth with the back of my hand and set the glass into the sink. A bleary glance at the clock on the stove informs me that it's 11:00 p.m.

Back in the city, I'd still be at work. Here, it's so quiet I can hear the hum of the fridge.

Work.

Frankie.

What if she wrote back?

I dig my phone out of my bag and click my mail, holding my breath as I watch new emails load. But apart from a few marketing emails, there's nothing new.

When I first saw that email I'd sent to Frankie, I was appalled. But maybe I was onto something. Nic's right: Publishing an article in *Humans* really could help Sara.

Maybe I should email Frankie again. Call her even. Harass her until she agrees to give me a platform to tell this story. There's so much I could say. I overheard Sharkey plotting something. I was *there* when George was murdered! It happened at *my* birthday party, for fuck's sake!

Screw Frankie and her silence.

I open a new message and start typing furiously, mostly using my pointer fingers.

As I write, Steven's voice loops through my head. He reminds me how horrible Frankie was to me, how she completely screwed me over, how depressed I was in the aftermath. I shove those thoughts away again and again.

Sara needs this. Nic needs this.

I need this.

I can't live under the same roof as my mother for much longer without losing my mind.

By the time I sign the message, I'm sweating and a little nauseous.

I straighten from my hunch, close my eyes, and press Send.

My phone buzzes with an incoming call approximately thirty seconds later. A number with a New York area code. I don't have it saved anymore, but I'm pretty sure it's Frankie's direct line at the office.

Holy shit! She's actually calling me.

It's nearly midnight, but I guess some things never change. She always was a workaholic.

I swipe to answer and press the phone to my ear. "Hello?"

"Surprise!" Frankie purrs, like the last time we spoke was ten minutes ago, not almost six months. "I bet you never thought you'd hear from *me* again, did you, Baker?"

The sound of her voice makes the muscles in my throat contract. She's the person who hired me fresh out of NYU. Who taught me the ropes, introduced me to the right people...

And who unceremoniously fired me four years later like a shot through the heart.

"Hello, Frankie," I reply, unwilling to match her familiarity. "I hope you're well. I assume you received my emails about the situation in my hometown?"

She laughs. "*The situation in my hometown*," she mimics. "No, Baker. I'm calling you to have a nice little catch-up."

God, she's an asshole. I struggle against my instinct to hang up. "Right."

"So," she continues. "That video of the person flying across the beach was recorded at *your* birthday party, huh? What a small world. It's hilarious stuff and matched to the perfect song. Wish my social media team was that savvy. After watching it, I told the head of that department they better step it the fuck up. Do you know the person who posted it?"

This has absolutely nothing to do with my email. I answer through gritted teeth. "I don't."

"Wait. Seriously? How? Weren't they at your party?"

"Yeah. But there were people there I didn't really know."

"Are you...are you actually saying that you didn't know all the guests at your own party? Wow." She lets out a mean little laugh.

I hate her. I think again about hanging up even if that would mean blowing my one chance to help Nic and Sara. It's important, but is it worth dealing with this bullshit?

Then my eyes land on my mom's oversize purse splayed on the counter, the plastic prescription pills bottles that belonged to George. Their crap is everywhere in this too-quiet kitchen. Even my bedroom is crammed with boxes of their old clothes, discarded electronics, random junk they never use but won't throw away.

Nothing here is mine.

And I want something that is. Even if it means dealing with the likes of Frankie.

Plus, Nic will shit himself when I tell him I made it happen.

"About my emails," I say, trying to steer her back on track.

"Right," she says. "Your emails. Lucky that I unblocked your address a few weeks ago so I got them. When I read your first one, I have to admit: I was skeptical. You were ranting about corruption, using a lot of misspelled words. I thought maybe you'd gone off the deep end since you got yourself fired. But the one tonight? Now that piqued my interest. You overheard the police chief talking about shady stuff on the beach? Tell me more. Pitch it to me, Baker. But do it well this time."

My eye twitches. "Right, that conversation," I say. "Well. It was between the chief of police, Sharkey, and..."

And who? I have no real idea who he was talking to, but I can't say that to Frankie. She'd eviscerate me.

"...and the mayor," I say, lying a little. Sometimes lying is necessary though, for the greater good. I warm to the idea taking shape in my head. "They said they were going to pin it on someone."

"*Pin what on* someone?"

"The murder, I assume."

"You *assume*?" Frankie says. "What did you hear exactly, Baker? Are you wasting my time here?"

I rub the bridge of my nose, but it does nothing to ease the headache roaring into my skull.

It doesn't seem much of a leap to assume their conversation was about pinning George's murder on Sara. Sure, I didn't actually hear them say her name, but that's what's happening, isn't it?

If another teeny tiny lie gets this article green-lit, so be it. That way, I'll have time to investigate and *prove* it. Frankie will never be the wiser.

I clear my throat. "Sorry, I probably should have added—they explicitly mentioned Sara Allbright by name. That's the woman from the viral video, the one they arrested. The police chief said to the mayor that they needed to pin the murder on her so they could close the case. They're worried about...about an open murder investigation tanking next summer's tourism."

Frankie lets out a low whistle. "Jesus, Baker. I really do not understand how your brain works. Talk about burying the lede. You should have put that in your first fucking email!"

Finally, I have her on the hook. "Well. Yeah. Probably. And listen to this—I actually know Sara from high school. I bet I could get some face time with her in jail and include her perspective in the article. That would be a big draw for readers, right?"

"Really?" Frankie sounds skeptical. "Why would she talk to you? You're the stepdaughter of the guy she's accused of murdering."

She makes a decent point, but I bet Nic could help on that front. He doesn't exactly, you know, *like* me much, but he wants me to write this article. The least he could do is get me in front of his sister.

"I know her brother. Well, actually"—I cringe—"we, um, we dated. Back in the day."

Dated is stretching the truth (again), but it sounds better than *banged for two weeks at which point I stopped calling him back.*

"Did you now?" Frankie says.

"Yeah. He'd make sure I get in front of Sara. Also, I could dig into whether the cops even bothered looking at other suspects. If they ignored leads, that'd help prove my theory. And!" I add, because knowing Frankie, she'll need even more convincing. "What if I figure out who actually did it? Remember that case in Maine? The Instagram wellness influencer accused of killing her boyfriend? How her best friend set out to prove her innocence and documented the whole thing on social media? People ate that shit *up*! She was on the *Today* show, even got a book deal! If I solve this, think of the traffic *Humans* would get."

She's quiet for a long moment, and the future flashes before my eyes. Me, stuck in this godforsaken house for the rest of my life. Nic, glowering whenever I run into him at the grocery store. My mom wearing the same white nightgown for months on end. Me, taking up crochet and adopting five to seven stray cats. A modern-day *Grey Gardens*.

"Hmm. All right, I'll bite," Frankie finally says, bursting the picture growing in my mind of my mom and I dressed in oversize fur coats and headscarves. "Go for it, Baker. Write the story. Figure out if that little island of yours has a corrupt underbelly. Do it well, and this could be enough to make us forget about the Belinda incident. I'm thinking a lead time of a month."

A month? Shit. "Of course," I say, swallowing my anxiety.

"I also want to make sure you to understand a few things. Should your investigation cross into less than legal territory—or even less than *ethical* territory—and you find yourself in trouble, *Humans* will not indemnify you for any legal costs incurred. In other words: You'll have to handle that shit on your own dime."

I squint at my reflection in the darkened computer screen. It's not a huge surprise they're willing to throw me under the bus, but did she have to put it *quite* so bluntly?

"Also," she continues, "you won't be paid until I approve the article for publication. And on the very, very off chance it ends up going viral, *Humans* owns the rights. Any book deals, movie deals, whatever—they go through us. Got it? It'll all be outlined in the paperwork I send over."

I had not in fact understood *any* of that. "Right. Yeah. Of course," I say.

"Good," Frankie says. "I'm curious to see what you come up with. And Baker—don't make me regret giving you another opportunity."

Oh my god. Is this actually happening?

This is *actually happening*.

I'll need to avoid defaming anyone, which means spending time verifying sources and fact-checking on my own—I know better than to think *Humans* will do it on their end. With the trial still pending, I won't even be able to access police records—unless I can convince Kozel to leak them to me, which is unlikely given our past.

Every doubt I've been shoving down springs to the surface: I'm not a detective. I'm not even an investigative journalist—I wrote articles about celebrity gossip, for fuck's sake. Do I really think I can single-handedly uncover the dark underbelly of our quaint little vacation town? I don't know how to solve a *murder*.

Someone killed George in cold blood. If they find out what I'm doing...I'll be next.

CHAPTER TWELVE

NIC

September 4

8:34 a.m.

Friday morning, I wake bleary-eyed, the pounding in my head threatening to split my skull in two. I didn't drink that much at the bar, but once I got home...

I catch sight of the half-empty bottle of whiskey across the room on the coffee table as I stumble to the bathroom. My stomach heaves.

Right.

Once I got home, shit got real.

I spent three hours painstakingly writing down everything I could remember about the party while drinking down that bottle: the timeline of events, the people in attendance, the details about the body I hadn't already blocked from my mind. The deep slice across his chest, leaking red onto the sand.

As far as I could tell, none of it would help Sara.

In the bathroom, my reflection greets me: bloodshot eyes, hair sticking out every which way from my head.

I look like the walking dead.

This week has been a nightmare, and last night was the poisoned cherry on the top of a shit sundae. My sister going down for the murder of some rich asshole. Harriet not able—or not *willing*—to help.

The injustice of it all makes me want to puke.

So I do.

Once that's over and done with, I spend several long moments horizontal on the bathroom floor and then punch out a text to Martin, reassuring him I didn't drown a puddle of self-pity.

He responds that Sara's arraignment has been set for Tuesday—she's going to be stuck sitting in that fucking jail cell an extra day because of the Monday holiday.

After I read this, I lie back down on the cool tile for a while, staring at the ceiling, contemplating how all this is really Harriet Baker's fault.

My reasoning is this: If she hadn't been born, the party never would have happened. George wouldn't have been killed, and therefore, Sara would be free.

I finally manage to heave myself off the ground and head into the kitchen, where I'm greeted by an empty bag of coffee beans. I let out a groan. Of all the mornings. The universe is clearly conspiring against me. I was all ready to brew a pot and whip up breakfast using the random assortment of foods in my fridge, an activity that eases my mind. Helps settle me. But instead, I'm being forced out of my apartment to hunt for caffeine.

Back in my bedroom, I pull on a pair of sweats and a T-shirt and head out the front door. There's a coffee place two blocks over. I usually try to avoid it; each cup is five dollars, and I don't have that kind of money. But it seems I have no choice.

Damp, cool early morning air slaps me in the face as I walk out the front door. By the time I make it to the shop, I can't wait to get inside.

Its warm interior is a relief, but the feeling is cut short as my gaze lands on the last person I want to see: Harriet Baker, holding a paper cup, looking offensively fresh given the early hour. Whereas I resemble a hungover toad.

What the hell is she doing drinking coffee on this side of town?

She spots me, and a smile stretches across her face. Like she thinks we're friends.

"No," I say as she approaches.

She stops in front of me, face falling. "What do you mean *no*?"

"I mean, *no*. I can't deal with this—with *you*—right now. I need coffee. My head hurts. My sister's in jail. She's going to be charged with something she didn't do. You won't help. And you're *smiling* at me like you think it's—"

She punches her fist into her hip. "*Excuse* me? Is it illegal to smile now? Maybe you should rethink being such a dick to me, because I'm actually here to—"

"Uh, excuse me?" a shaky voice interrupts. I turn to find a pimply teenage boy, wearing an apron that says *Java the Hut*.

"What?" Harriet snaps.

He flinches back. "I...uh...I..."

"You don't have to be so mean," I tell Harriet, even though I was going to do the exact same thing if she hadn't beaten me to it. "Can we—can *I*—help you?" I ask the kid, extra polite.

"Yeah, um, well," he stammers. "It's just...you're sort of standing in a puddle of coffee?" He indicates the ground, where there is indeed a very large puddle of coffee beneath my white sneakers.

Harriet smirks. "Whoopsie. Hope your shoes are okay."

I edge out of the puddle. "You know," I tell the kid, "you should put up a sign to warn people."

"Uh, yeah. There actually is a sign?" He points behind me, where—sure enough—a yellow caution sign sits.

"Oh."

"Yeah. Um, also, before you walk away, would you mind wiping off your shoes? So, you know, you don't track coffee all over the floor?" He hands me a filthy dish rag.

"Fine." I swipe at the soles of my sneakers, shove the towel at him, then stride to the counter to finally, at long last, order my coffee.

"Hey," a voice says by my elbow.

Harriet. She's following me. Once upon a time, finding her next to me would have made my day, but right now, it just pisses me off even more.

"*What?*" I snap. She's staring at me with those big doe eyes, like a puppy begging for food. It's annoying.

"Did you know Steven and Martin left the bar together?"

I stare at her. If she expects that piece of news to soften me up, she has another thing coming.

She chews on her lower lip. "Well, actually."

I flare my nostrils. "Actually?"

She scoots around someone trying to grab their order. "I'm actually here because I need to talk to you."

"About Steven and Martin? I could have told you that was coming."

"No. About something else."

I give my head a sharp shake. "We have nothing to say to each other."

"I have things to say to you!" she says like she can't believe I just said that. "Lots of things in fact."

"Fine, let me rephrase: *I* have nothing to say to *you*. Understand?"

Another teenager behind the counter—don't these kids have to go to school?—clears her throat. "Can I help you, sir?"

"Yeah. One large, black coffee. To go."

"Should we leave space for—"

"No!" I'm the one snapping this time. I need to chill. "Sorry. I mean, no, thank you. Black is fine."

"Okayyy, sure. Whatever." She grabs a to-go cup and heads to the machine.

"So," Harriet says. "The thing is—"

"You're still here?"

She rolls her eyes. "You're being rude."

"Oh, I'm *sorry*," I say, not sounding a bit sorry. "My sister is being charged with a murder she didn't commit, and they're arraigning her on Tuesday. How dare I be in a bad mood?"

"Your sister is *what*?" The barista is holding out my coffee with her mouth hanging open.

"*Nothing!*" I grab the cup, throw some dollars in her direction—possibly too many, but who cares; I just want to get the hell out of here—and hightail it out of the shop.

Once I hit the sidewalk, I pause to take a sip of my drink, and someone crashes into my back. Coffee spills out through the black plastic lid, scorching my hand.

I spin around. "Are you serious? *Why* are you following me?"

"I told you! We need to talk!" Harriet says.

"And I already told you *no*. Please leave me alone."

She grabs my sleeve. "Nic. I'm serious."

There's a spark where her fingers touch my shirt, but I ignore it. "Kindly take your hands off me."

"I will if you give me a minute to say what I need to say. If you don't, I guess I'll be holding your shirt for a long, long time."

"Are you *threatening* me?"

She bats her lashes, which, annoyingly, makes my stomach lurch with longing, a long-buried memory invading: the feel of those lashes on my cheek, my neck, my inner thigh as she—

"Of course not." She interrupts my little fantasy. "Think about it like this: The faster we talk, the faster I leave you alone. So you might as well get it over with."

"You're annoying."

"Thank you," she says, smiling with all her teeth. My stomach jumps again.

Since it's clear I won't be rid of her until I acquiesce to her demands, I point to a nearby table. "There."

"There what?" Her full lips quirk up to one side.

I give her a withering look. “Don’t make me change my mind.”

“Fine, fine.” She bounces to the table with far more energy than is socially acceptable for nine a.m. “So,” she says once we’re seated.

“So, what?” I say flatly.

“I want to...” She hesitates. “First, I guess, apologize? For what happened at the party. And before that too. Back in high school. I... Look. I was in a really bad place that summer after Kozel left and...it wasn’t personal.”

My jaw muscles clench. Not *personal*? Is that supposed to excuse her behavior? It certainly seemed personal at the time.

She reads my mind. “No, wait. I don’t mean... My boyfriend who I thought I was going to marry had just left town without telling me. I was a mess. And I didn’t realize it was your first time, and I’m sorry I stopped answering your calls. I’m also sorry I didn’t recognize you when we ran into each other. But you do understand not *recognizing* someone is not the same as not *remembering* them, right?”

That does have a ring of truth to it.

“I suppose,” I grumble.

She studies me. “You are aware that *you* owe *me* an apology too. Right?”

It *is* possible I was maybe a wee bit of a jerk to her too. I let my anger get the better of me, which I don’t normally do. Not that it excuses anything, but I’ve been carrying around the hurt of that summer for eight long years. Even when I dated other people—people who meant something to me, people who I thought I loved—I never felt as connected to them as I did to Harriet during those two weeks.

“You’re right. I’m sure all your sexual partners are very important to you." At least I'm pretty sure. "I shouldn't have said that. I'm sorry, okay?"

"Okay. Thank you. Now, let's start over. It's good to see you again, Nic. How have you been?"

I'm really too tired for this shit. "Yeah. You too. Can we skip to the reason you're here?" I set my paper cup down on the table and take its lid off to let it cool.

"Oh! Right." She perks up. "I talked to my old editor last night!"

"Your editor?" It takes a second to land in my brain. "Wait, *what*? You did?"

"I did."

"Why the hell didn't you say that when you first attacked me in the shop?"

"I didn't atta—" She shakes her head. "Never mind. I tried to, but you kept running away."

"Oh." I listen as she tells me how she emailed her old editor again after the bar. How they ended up talking on the phone, Harriet pitching the idea, putting her reputation on the line for me—for Sara. It's just starting to really sink in, how hard she went to bat for us, when she mentions a conversation she overheard—

"Wait, you overheard *what*? Again, Harriet—why didn't you tell me this before?"

She has the decency to look ashamed. "You were mad at me!"

"I'm *still* mad at you." Though, I have to admit, less so than before.

"Well, I'm telling you now, okay? Anyway, she was excited about the concept. Though I did have to sort of fudge a couple details. But it's okay. She gave me the green light, and now I can—"

I interrupt. "We."

She pauses. "We?"

"Sara's my sister. Her arraignment is in four days. If you think I'm not doing this with you, you've lost your damn mind, sweetheart." The word slips out of my mouth before I can stop it. *Sweetheart*. I haven't called her that in eight years.

Her cheeks redden, and our eyes lock for a long moment—too long—my mouth going dry.

"You really want to help?" Harriet asks after a long moment.

I tear my eyes away from hers and grab my cup. I take a sip of coffee, stalling to gather myself before I answer. What the hell was that? Have I lost my mind? Clearly, I'm still attracted to her; I'm a big enough man to admit it. But I'm no longer a seventeen-year-old virgin. I need to control myself, keep in mind that empty fucking look in her eyes when she said we never slept together.

Right.

"I do," I say. "Your article will give Sara's case some much-needed exposure. And once people read about it, they'll have to see something shady is going on. So what's the plan?"

"Well." Harriet tugs in her chair and leans across the table. "First, we need to prove that the police didn't do their due diligence. Did they look at anyone else or just immediately focus on Sara? From what I understand from Maggie, most of the evidence against her is circumstantial. Like, any defense attorney worth their salt could get the fingerprints from the knife tossed."

"Even more reason to do this then. Maybe we can get the attention of a decent lawyer who'd be willing to take the case for cheap."

"Oh, good point." She takes a sip of her drink. "From everything I heard on that beach and how things have shaken out over the last week, it's clear the police are hurrying to pin this on Sara—but why? Is it because of the project Sharkey mentioned? If so, what is it?"

I can't believe I'm about to suggest this: "Doesn't your ex-boyfriend work for the LIPD?"

She cringes. "Technically, he works at the sheriff's office on the mainland, but yeah. They brought him in for this."

"Maybe you should talk to him. He might let something slip about the case."

Harriet's eye twitches. "I thought about that, but what if he's involved with whatever Sharkey's tied up in?"

"Still worth trying," I say, hating every word.

"I guess."

I smile like I'm not dying a little inside, sending Harriet back into the arms of her ex. Maybe they can thank me in their wedding vows.

"Also." She lowers her voice. "I've been thinking about the timeline."

I set my cup down in front of me. "Same. I actually wrote it all out last night, but I don't see how it helps."

"Well, it made me realize something. George was outside during a torrential downpour, but he *hated* the outdoors. In fact, he hated discomfort of any kind. So, ipso facto, what—or *who*—managed to lure him out there?" Her cheeks are flushed, her brown hair loose and wild around her head. "I'm thinking George knew that what was going to be discussed was sensitive enough that he didn't want to risk being overheard."

That makes sense. "Then it couldn't have been Sara! They didn't even know each other."

"Except the cops will say they did. Martin told me about those LinkedIn posts—"

Martin has such a big mouth when he drinks. I interrupt. "That was just a shitty coincidence."

She holds up a hand. "Okay, I can believe that, but it's what the *cops* would say. That she got him alone on the beach and *WHAM*!"

She slams her hands down flat against the tabletop, and my coffee jumps, a splash of dark liquid spraying across the center of my T-shirt.

"Shit!" I grab a napkin but only manage to smear it.

Harriet winces. "Sorry. If you dab, it'll come out more easily—no, like this." She grabs a napkin and climbs halfway across the table, wiping up my T-shirt. Her hair swings down, and a handful of strands whisper against my forearm, soft and gentle. She smells so good, like lavender and citrus.

I wonder what would happen if I twisted them around my hand, pulled her close and—

She abruptly pulls back, clearing her throat. Her cheeks are red. "So yeah. That's what I was thinking about the timeline."

The air in front of me suddenly seems very cold. I cough, trying to steady myself. "Right. But I still don't see how it helps. It doesn't even narrow down our list of suspects. Didn't a ton of people have issues with him he wouldn't have wanted to discuss in public?"

I push my fingers into my temples. My head's throbbing again. Am I being an idiot by insisting on doing this with her? What if we end up crosswise with the cops and get thrown behind bars too? Harriet would probably hire some big-shot attorney from the city to defend her, and I'd be stuck with Barry.

My parents would drop dead from the stress.

But I encouraged my mom to take the job for Harriet's party, and now Sara's in jail. Logically, I know those things aren't connected, but it sure feels like they are. It feels like by wanting to see Harriet one more time, I unwittingly pushed over the first domino and the rest came crashing down.

"Okay," I say. "So you need to get in front of your ex-boyfriend"—she rolls her eyes—"but what should I do? I gotta go help my mom with a couple things at the office, but then I'm free. Unfortunately, most of our upcoming jobs have canceled since Sara's arrest."

"Good question." Harriet taps her finger against her chin. "Let's brainstorm. First—our suspects. The gate to the beach had a code, and George changed it daily. The only people with it the day of the party were my mom, George, me, and..."

"Us," I say. "The caterers."

She grimaces. "Yeah. So if it wasn't any of you—"

"It *wasn't*!" I snap.

"Of course it wasn't," she says quickly. "Which means George must have been killed by a guest who went out to the beach through the house."

"Hang on," I say. "If they went through the house, how did they get outside and then back inside without anyone noticing? The only way to the beach is through the living room, right?"

Harriet shakes her head. "There's a door in the basement."

I straighten. "Well, there couldn't have been many people who knew about that door, right? That can help us narrow things down."

"Unfortunately, George insisted on giving tours of the entire house to pretty much everyone who ever entered. Lots of people had seen it."

My shoulders slump. "Shit."

"Yeah. So back to the guests. What was their relationship like with George? Take my mom. She worshipped him. Relied on him for far too many things, in my opinion. I would be absolutely *shocked* if she's our killer, so I think she can go way down on the bottom of our list. No motive. Then there's Luke Dalio, his business partner. You've heard about the high-rise hotel George was trying to build on the old Windswept Motel property?"

"Yeah, of course. Mom's talked my ear off about it. I don't know if your side of the island is aware, but everyone over here *hates* that idea."

The Windswept Motel sat on that land for the better part of eighty years, across an inlet from Atlantic City. Tourists loved it—it offered both small-town charm and easy access to AC's nightlife—but a couple years ago, it burned down in a massive fire caused by faulty wiring. It was pretty horrific—several people were severely injured, and a kid almost died.

A few months later, the owners ended up selling off the land to George and moving down to Florida.

George's plan for it only came out later: a giant high-rise hotel complex, which he claimed would finally make Logan Island relevant. Except when he put the proposal in front of the zoning board and town council, he was immediately denied. He lost his shit and has been fighting with them ever since.

"Yeah, I know," Harriet says, a little haughtily for someone who lived off island for almost a decade. "My point is that George had more experience than Luke figuring out how to slice through red tape. Luke will be lost without him. Plus, Luke isn't the kind of guy who'd get his hands dirty. Not the murdering type."

I'm getting impatient. "Okay, so who do you think *is* our killer?"

Harriet chews on her lip. "As I mentioned to Detective Jones, Barbara Patterson is definitely someone to consider. She *despised* George. She's heading up an antidevelopment group and was always calling the cops on his construction sites, digging through records to try and prove that he was dirty. I could see her getting angry enough to do it."

"Harriet, Patterson is, like, *eighty*," I say.

"Don't be ageist. Old people can be brutal. Plus..." She snatches up her phone, types something, then spins it so I can see the screen. "According to Google, it doesn't take much strength to stab someone. Especially with a very sharp knife."

"Well, shit. Sara sharpened those things daily. Actually." An idea is sprouting in my mind. I have doubts about Patterson being our murderer, but Harriet could be onto something in a broader sense. "My mom and Mrs. Patterson go way back. I could ask Mom what she's heard from Patterson about it. See if she knows who else is in that group—and if any of them were at the party."

Harriet's eyes light up. "Great idea."

Those wide blue eyes. Full pink lips. She looks so innocent, so sweet. I could fall under her spell so easily.

I need to be careful, in more ways than one.

"Thanks," I say.

She nods. "All right, so you talk to your mom. And I'll… I guess I'll see if I can get Kozel to tell me anything about their investigation. We can reconvene tomorrow. Sound good?"

I drop my eyes to the black liquid inside my paper cup, the tiny bubbles rippling to its surface. Remind myself again that the only way I'll get out of this unscathed is if I keep my distance.

"Sounds good," I say, watching as the bubbles burst, one by one.

CHAPTER THIRTEEN

HARRIET

September 5
8:02 a.m.

You okay?"

A familiar voice startles me out of my trance.

I'm sitting at the same table where Nic and I talked yesterday, nursing my second lukewarm cup of coffee. I haven't seen him since our little run-in, and he hasn't responded to the text I sent him earlier this morning. So here I am—again.

I'd been hoping he would be too, but he's nowhere to be found.

Instead, *this*.

I turn and there he is. Adam Kozel, a small grin playing on his lips. His hands are shoved deep into the pockets of his shorts.

"You look a million miles away."

"I'm fine." I'm about to blow him off when I realize this is the perfect opportunity to fulfill my promise. I can talk to him right here on this sidewalk and then never have to deal with him again. I plaster on a smile. "It's good to see you, Adam."

He tilts his head. "Are you *sure*, Harriet? Because when I saw you the other day, things were a little awkward."

God, he's annoying. "No, they weren't," I lie.

"I do admit," he continues like he didn't even hear me. Typical. "I was caught off guard when you opened the door."

"Uh-huh," I say, digging my fingernails into the back of my thumb. *Be nice, Harriet.*

He gestures to the empty paper cups in my hands. "Do you need help with those?"

"No, thank you." Being polite to him is giving me an ulcer. It better be worth it.

I walk to the trash can and toss the cups at it. One bounces off the rim and hits the sidewalk below.

Heat flushes my face.

I bend to pick it up and stuff it into the can, hoping maybe Kozel didn't notice.

"Are you *sure* you don't need help?" He smirks, and my pledge to behave evaporates.

"I'm a perfectly capable adult, *Adam*," I snap, the scowl I've been holding in crawling onto my face. "I managed to get through all four years of college without you. I lived in the big, scary city of New York without you. Imagine! How ever did I survive?"

His smile flattens. "I was trying to be nice."

"Aren't you always?"

"What's that supposed to mean?"

"It means *I'm fine*!"

"Is this about high school?" he says, and my spine stiffens. How dare he bring that up?

An older woman exits the coffee shop, and we both fall silent. Kozel tips his head in greeting as she walks by.

As soon as she's gone, I turn on him. "Is *what* about high school?"

"How you're acting. Is it because of—you know. How we left things?"

Oh, that's rich. "How we *left* things? That implies we had a conversation. Not that you straight-up ghosted me and the next time I heard from you was when you knocked on my mother's door the morning after my stepfather was murdered!"

He winces. "Like I said, I didn't know you'd be there."

He's got to be kidding. "Are you—*That's* your response? You didn't know I would *be* there? Right. Cool. I gotta go."

I whirl around on my heel and start down the sidewalk toward my car. Kozel hurries to keep pace with me. "You're misunderstanding," he says. "I was *glad* when you opened the door, Harriet. I've thought a lot about you over the years. I would love to explain if you—"

"Goodbye," I say.

"Harriet—"

"Goodbye, Adam." I pick up my speed.

A text from Gogo arrives as I'm climbing into the car.

Hello, Harriet. Your aunt Vicky and I are on our way to your dad's house and would love it if you would join us. We should be there in twelve minutes. We can chat over tea. Love. Your grandmother (Gogo)

I consider ignoring it and heading home. The morning hasn't exactly gone well thus far, and a part of me wants to go into hiding for the rest of the day.

Except I have an article to write, an investigation to pursue, and I just blew what might have been my best chance to talk to Kozel. I can't go home and watch Netflix. If I can't make this article happen… I shake my head. I don't even want to consider what that would mean. For my life. My future. I can't help but feel like this is my last shot to prove to the world that I'm not a total failure.

Gogo and Vicky—and even my dad—were there the night of the party. They could have some insights to share about everything.

I drive southwest across the island with my window down, the warm late-summer breeze in my hair. I haven't been to my dad's since I got back from the city. Back in high school, we were tight—in fact, I lived with him my senior year because I couldn't stand to be in the same room as my mother.

But then George came back into the picture, and it all went downhill. I got the feeling my dad was…maybe jealous isn't quite the right word—more like *irritated* that George and my mom had reconnected. There's a lot of history between the three of them, most of it not very good. Either way, my dad began dying his hair an unnatural shade of brown, bought a Corvette, began to date people half his age, and forgot all about me. Our relationship never recovered.

I steer my car onto his street. Either side is lined with two-story bungalows and the occasional transplanted palm tree. Halfway down the block, I spot Gogo's bright-blue Lincoln Continental and pull into the space in front of it. I hope my aunt drove that thing here; Gogo failed her last driver's test.

"Harriet!" Gogo's in the foyer, arranging flowers in a vase. She looks at me with surprise. "What are you doing here?"

I'm on my way down to kiss her cheek, but I pull back. "You asked me to come?"

She blinks, then gives her head a little shake. "Oh, right. Of course! My little peanut."

She takes my hand and kisses the tips of my fingers. Her skin is crepey, wrinkled, pale. I try not to focus on it—or her memory slip.

"I'm glad to see you. *Cynthia* is here. It's only been fifteen minutes, and she's already tried to get me involved in three separate MLM schemes. Here. Come. Sit."

Gogo leads me into the empty living room and settles on the couch. She has on an oversize wool coat even though it's seventy degrees outside, and the fabric overwhelms her small frame. She looks like a child playing dress-up.

"Where is everyone?" I ask.

"Hmm, well. Vicky's fixing me a cup of tea, and your father and Cynthia are upstairs. They're packing."

"Packing?" I frown. "For what?"

She raises her eyebrows. "They're going to Europe tomorrow. I assumed you knew."

"Europe?" I in fact did not know that. An awful thought occurs to me. What if my *dad* killed George, and that's why he's skipping town?

I shake myself. I can't start accusing every person I find vaguely suspicious of murder. This trip was probably planned months ago. It's not like he keeps me abreast of his comings and goings. Plus, it's my *dad*. We might not be best friends, but he's not a killer.

"When did they plan this?" I ask Gogo, trying to keep my tone neutral.

"I don't remember, to be honest," Gogo says. "You'd have to ask your father. Regardless, off they go! Fingers crossed Cynthia doesn't come back pregnant!"

I balk. That's almost as horrifying a thought as him murdering someone. "Oh my god, Gogo. No."

"I'm just saying," she says with an impish smile that pulls at my heart. "She's still young and fertile. Stranger things have happened."

"Gross, Gogo. I'm gonna to go find Vicky." I bolt out of the room before she can say anything more.

I find Vicky on the kitchen floor, half buried in a cabinet.

"Hey! What are you doing in there?"

She startles, smacking her head on the frame as she pulls free. "Ow! Shit!"

"Oh crap. Are you okay?" I should have given her some warning before barging in here and basically yelling. "Do you want some ice?"

She rubs at the spot. "No, no. It's fine."

"I'm so sorry," I say, extending a hand to help her up.

"Not your fault. Gogo mentioned you were coming. I should have known it was you."

She smells of jasmine. Her hair is slicked back in one of those severe buns that only people with extremely symmetrical faces can pull off, and she has on a cute black turtleneck and a pair of dark blue jeans. It's hard to believe she's in her mid-fifties; she could pass for my older sister with the right lighting.

"I'm actually on the hunt for a teapot," she says. "Any idea where it could be?"

"I don't think my dad owns one, actually."

Her eyes widen. "He doesn't? How does he make tea?"

I tap the device next to her head. "In this."

"Are you—In the *microwave*? Good Lord. Absolutely not." She starts rummaging through a different cabinet. "I refuse to make tea in that...that *thing*. There must be a pot somewhere I can use ..."

I try to think of a casual way to steer the conversation away from tea and toward the question of whether my father is a murderous psychopath. "Hey, speaking of my dad. Gogo mentioned he's going on a trip. Was that planned?"

She looks up at me, brow furrowed. "What do you mean?"

My stomach drops. Did Gogo imagine an entire *trip*?

"Gogo said he and Cynthia are going to Europe tomorrow?"

Vicky sits back on her haunches. "Oh, right! Sorry, I thought you knew? Their trip is the whole reason I'm here. Your father is attending a medical conference in Greece and bringing Cynthia along. They're staying for a few weeks, so I agreed to come help Mom. We've been planning this for...gosh. Three months now?"

"Right. I knew. I'd just…forgotten." I'm lying of course. I try to brush it off, but it stings.

Vicky rises with a grunt, a small silver pot clutched in her hand. "This should do." She sets it on the stovetop, then stretches high, groaning as she leans to each side.

"Are you okay?"

"Yeah. Just sore. Long-haul flights and jet lag—the older I get, the worse it is."

"Right, jet lag," I say, like I have any idea what I'm talking about. I pick up the pot and fill it with water, then set it back on the stove and snap on the burner. "The worst."

I haven't been out of the continental U.S. since my junior year of college, when Maggie, Steven, and I met up in Cancun, and Steven and I almost got arrested for indecent exposure. Thank god Maggie was there to persuade the policía to let us go—it was actually the moment we all realized she'd make a fantastic lawyer.

I spent the next few years promising myself I'd travel more as soon as work slowed down. But—spoiler alert—it never slowed down. Not until the day it stopped completely.

Speaking of work.

I clear my throat. "Hey, I was wondering. About the other night…"

"The other night?" Vicky asks as she pulls open the fridge. "Gogo likes milk in her tea, but I don't know if your dad—ah, here we go." She reappears, carton in hand. "Of course. George. I tried calling your mother, but she hasn't gotten back to me. I meant to reach out to you too, but, well—things have been so busy with your grandmother. How are you holding up?"

I swallow. "My mom's mostly been holed up in her room. I don't think she's really talked to anyone, so I wouldn't take it personally."

"Don't worry." She sets the milk on the counter and checks the pot. "I know better than to take anything your mother does personally. I hope she's holding up. Please tell her to reach out if she needs anything, okay?"

I nod. "I will."

I should ask her now. This is the perfect chance; we're already talking about it... Why am I having so much trouble getting the words out of my mouth?

"Can I ask you something?" The words clunk from my mouth, heavy and awkward, but I need to ask my questions before I lose another chance to get some answers.

She picks up a tea bag from the counter and rips the package open. "Of course. What's up?"

I wrap my palms around my upper arms. "I've been thinking about what happened to George and...I don't know. I have some questions?"

Her eyebrows arch, and she sets the steaming cup back on the island. "What do you mean? Don't they have a suspect in custody?"

"They do." I consider whether to tell Vicky about my article and what Nic and I have planned, but I'm not totally sure if she'd be on board with it. "I'm trying to understand how something like that could have happened. You know? Out on the beach, behind my mom's house. During my *birthday* party! It's insane."

Much to my surprise, tears spring into corners of my eyes.

"Hey." Vicky sets the mug down. She walks over and wraps her arms around my shoulders, which only serves to expand the lump in my throat. "Are you okay?"

I nod into her hair. "Yes. Sorry. The past few days have just been a lot. I'm tired."

She pulls back, studying my face. "Understandable. I wish I could help answer your questions, but I must admit—the night is a bit of a blur."

I sniff, giving her a little smile. "They were pouring heavy."

"They were," Vicky agrees. "I—" Her phone begins to buzz on the counter, and she cuts off. She picks it up, frowning at the screen. "Shoot. Work. Do you mind making Gogo's tea and taking it in to her? I have to grab this."

"Sure. Of course."

"Thanks, Harriet," she says and picks up the call.

I find Gogo's still sitting on the couch where I left her, fiddling with her jacket. My heart twists. She looks so fragile, so much smaller than she used to.

She takes the mug from me carefully. "Where's Vic?"

"Phone. Work."

Gogo's lips press together. "Of course she is. That woman works too much! I always imagined she'd come back stateside eventually, but it seems more and more like it'll never happen. At least not while I'm still here to see it."

"Gogo. Stop." I hate when she talks like that.

She's quiet for a beat, then: "It's so nice to see you, peanut. I've been worried about you. Your ex stopped by my house a few days ago, as handsome as ever—"

I stiffen. *Et tu, Gogo?*

"—and an even bigger ego. Which is really saying something, isn't it?" She grins and pats me on the hand. "Don't worry, dear. I remember how he behaved after graduation. I can't believe he's the detective on this case. Have you had to see him?"

"Yeah. Unfortunately. He came by my mom's to ask us some questions. Actually." I lean toward her, seizing the opening. "I have some questions of my own about it. Did you notice anything strange that night?"

"Anything strange?" Her brow furrows. "What do you mean?"

"Anyone who seemed—"

She interrupts. "I thought I saw a newspaper article that said an arrest was made. Am I mistaken?"

"You are not," I admit.

She studies me over her tea. "Are you doing the thing you do?"

"The thing?" I say, pretending like I have no idea what she means.

"Your *nosiness*. It's why you were so good at your job at that tabloid—"

"Online magazine," I interject.

"—but also why you were almost expelled your junior year of high school. Remember? You thought something fishy was going on with the swim team, so you snuck into the locker room while the boys were changing—"

I clear my throat. One of the issues with family: They know everything about your past misdeeds. "Oh, right. That. This isn't that! I'm just curious."

"Curious? Didn't curiosity kill the cat, Harriet?"

I roll my eyes. "Well, good thing I'm not a cat. I'm asking for my own sanity. It happened right outside my mom's house, and I'm staying there. What if...I don't know. What if the cops got it wrong? What if whoever killed George comes back? Just help me put my mind at ease. Please."

She takes a small sip of tea. "All right. I'm happy to indulge you. Let's see. I saw you talking to an attractive man at one point."

Nic. It has to be Nic. He was by far the hottest man at the party. Even though it's annoying to admit.

"I know I've been single for a while, but seeing me talk to a man was strange?"

"Not strange so much as...surprising. I distinctly remember you saying one of the reasons you didn't want to move back to the island was because of the—how did you put it? The 'inbred dating pool'?"

That does sound like me.

"Yeah, and?"

"I'm just answering your question."

"As you well know, I meant anything strange with *other people*."

She winks. "Oh, silly me. Well, let me think. Well, there *was* an odd situation between George and a caterer—"

"The fight?"

She shakes her head and settles her teacup on its coaster. "No, no. Not the chef. A boy. He kept following George around. Did you notice that?"

"I didn't. Who was it?"

"Hmm, not the handsome one you were flirting with—"

"I was not flirting!" More like sticking my foot so far down my throat it choked me.

"Whatever you say, dear. Either way, the one who I'm talking about was younger. He seemed on edge. Every time he came out of the kitchen, he went straight to George. George kept waving him off, and each time, the boy's face...well! It just crumpled. But you know how your stepfather was. It wasn't unusual for him to get into tiffs with the waitstaff."

"That is true." I file this piece of information away to ask Nic about. There's a part of me that wonders if I can rely on Gogo's memory, but the way she was teasing me about Nic, the details she mentioned—she seems steady. Certain. "Did you notice anything else?"

Gogo rubs her chin. "I'm not sure."

She gazes down into her teacup, and I wait.

Finally, she looks back up, and I can tell immediately that something has changed. The light behind her eyes has dimmed. "Where's Vicky?" she asks.

"Probably still on her work call. But did you—"

"I wish she'd move back, but it doesn't seem like that's going to happen, does it? At least not while I'm still around."

My heart cracks in two. She's so sharp one minute and so lost the next. I should say something to Vicky or even my dad, but it feels like a betrayal.

I wonder if they know. I wonder if we all know, and we're all pretending it's not happening. Hoping it will go away.

I chew my bottom lip, a heaviness settling in my chest. "I love you, you know." My voice is tight, choked by withheld tears.

Gogo pats my hand. "I love you too, peanut."

CHAPTER FOURTEEN

NIC

September 5

11:14 a.m.

Mom?" I call as I step inside the warehouse. "I'm here!"

The only response is opera music drifting from the back office. She must be buried in admin again. The worst part of the job, in my opinion. I walk by our cooking stations, dark and quiet, the burners snapped off, the silver counter empty. It's eerie, the exact opposite of a normal Saturday in the late summer when we're in here, all hands on deck, prepping for whatever party we have that night.

What I wouldn't give for it to be a normal Saturday. I miss it. I miss the smells, the sounds, even Sara's shouts.

I head back to the office and find my mom at her desk, half hidden behind a teetering stack of paperwork as predicted. "Hey, what's up?"

"Nico, hello." She sets down the paper in her hand and takes off her glasses, rubbing her fingers against the bridge of her nose. Bags sag under her eyes, so dark they could be mistaken for bruises. "Thanks for coming. This shouldn't take long. I don't want to hold up your afternoon."

"It's fine. I don't have much else going on," I say.

Her face falls. "I'm sorry," she says. "I've been scrambling to book us new jobs, but there's nothing, and we're hemorrhaging the ones we had. All those Labor Day parties, down the drain. Esme and Matthew are coming by for their checks in a bit, and I fear they're going to be very disappointed by their size."

"It's not your fault." My voice cracks. Of course it's not her fault, but it's still worrisome. People we've known for decades, canceling on us because of my sister's arrest.

"Have you been down to see Sara recently?"

"Yesterday. I'm hoping to get there later today too, but we'll see how things go here."

She sounds exhausted, not a surprise all things considered. Her daughter behind bars, her business floundering—it's a mess all around.

"Mom, you're friends with Barbara Patterson, right?"

She leans back in her chair with a frown. "Barbara? I suppose so, yes. Why do you ask?"

I drop into the closest chair. "Well, I drove by the old Windswept property on my way here and—have you heard anything else about the development they were trying to build there? Has Barbara mentioned it recently?"

"The development? Where is this coming from, Nico? Cosa stai combinando?"

"Just wondering."

She narrows her eyes at me like a bloodhound catching a scent. She's always been able to tell when I'm telling half-truths.

I groan. "Fine. Harriet and I—" The name slips out before I can stop myself.

Mom's mouth drops open. "*Harriet?* Harriet Baker? Quella piccola strega in erba? Are you joking? You and Harriet—*what?*"

"Um." I know better than to mention the article or our investigation. She'd never believe Harriet's intentions are pure. "Nothing. I ran into her earlier, and we had an *argument* about the land. Whether George actually would have been able to develop it."

Her lips press together in disapproval. "Una maleducata, proprio come sua madre. Except, unfortunately in this circumstance, she is right."

"What do you mean?"

"I mean that Barbara pulled me aside during that party, all riled up because the permits George and his partner needed had been approved."

"They *were*? How? I thought they'd been denied, like, ten times."

"They had. Unsurprisingly, Barbara had some theories about how it finally happened. She thinks it had something to do with Joel Benone's resignation."

"Joel Benone?" I ask.

"The zoning board chair, Nico. You need to be more aware of the leadership in this town, mio caro. He resigned because he was 'ill,' but I promise you, the man's never been sick a day in his life. And the new chair? Just so happens to be Mayor DiPetrio's cousin."

DiPetrio's *cousin*? That family isn't even trying to hide their nepotism. "That sounds incredibly shady."

"Barbara would agree with you. She's been convinced for years that George and his business partner are in bed with the town government, and with this new appointee, I have to say I'm starting to agree. Personally, I hope with his death the project goes away, but I guess we'll see."

"Do you happen to know," I say, trying to keep my tone casual, "if Barbara is working this weekend? At the library? I have a few questions for her."

She raises an eyebrow. "What's this sudden interest in town politics, Nico?"

My face grows red. "Nothing! Just trying to prove a point to Harriet is all."

"Well. Unfortunately for your little debate with the daughter of the devil, Barbara is out of town on her annual vacation until early next week." She rises from her chair with a groan, clutching her lower back. "Shall we get started on the boxes?"

"I guess," I say, suddenly itching to head to the van, mind racing with everything I need to tell Harriet. "Hey, I can handle the boxes solo if your sciatica is acting up."

"Are you sure?" she asks, already halfway back into her chair.

"Yeah, absolutely. I got it. You rest," I tell her, glad for the opportunity to be alone.

"Hello?" Harriet answers.

"I talked to my mom." I pop my earbuds in so I can talk while I work.

"Who is this?"

Apparently, she doesn't have my number saved in her phone anymore. "It's Nic," I say, trying not to let it bother me. "Nic Allbright."

A laugh. "I'm kidding. I know it's you."

I tug the first big box through the double doors of the van as I try not to smile.

"I was actually going to text you," Harriet continues. "I'm on the way home from my dad's, and I saw my grandma there. She mentioned something we should probably look into. Apparently, someone on the catering staff—a young guy but not you—was paying George a lot of attention during the party. Did your mom tell you guys to give George special treatment because he was paying?"

As she speaks, I lug the box to the front door and set it on the stoop. I don't want to carry it all the way inside just yet in case Mom asks who I'm talking to.

I clap my hands together to get the dust off them and head back for the next one. "Huh. No. That had to have been Matthew Prado. He's the only other guy on our staff right now. What was he doing?"

"From what she said, it sounds like whenever he came out with a new tray, he'd go straight to George and try to chat him up. George blew him off every time—not a surprise, given George's *charming* personality. Gogo said the kid seemed upset by it."

"Okay, well, that's weird." I swing both van doors open this time, and a giant mountain of boxes greets me.

Shit. This is going to take hours.

Instead of grabbing the next one, I settle in the open doorway, my knees groaning with pleasure. "I wonder what that was all about. I don't think Matthew knew George, but I'll see what I can find out. Did your grandma say anything else?"

"She says *lots* of things, Nic."

"That's not what I meant."

"I know. Sorry, just being a dick. Nothing else on my end. What about you?"

I wipe the back of my arm across my forehead. "Well," I say. "According to my mom, the permits George needed to build on the motel property had finally come through, and Patterson was extremely pissed."

"Patterson! I knew it!" Harriet says. "She was there that night. She probably stole the knife from the kitchen, lured him outside and—"

As much as I want Sara out of jail, I can't help but pump the brakes. "Hang on. You sound like you're in an episode of *Forensic Files,* Harriet. I think you're jumping to conclusions. Being mad at someone doesn't equal murdering them. Plus, even if Patterson could have stabbed him—which I still don't totally believe—George was at least a decade younger and much, much stronger than her."

"Yeah, but maybe she surprised him. Caught him off guard. You found him. Were his hands cut up?"

My mind drifts to the beach. George's body splayed on the sand. The blood.

So much blood.

Bile rises in my throat. Nope. Can't do that right now. "I don't remember. I'll ask Martin if he's heard. He's friends with a few of the medical examiners."

"Great," says Harriet. "Well, at the very least, Patterson should be on our suspect list, right? Along with that caterer?"

"I suppose." I'm not fully behind the idea of Patterson, but I'm also not sure about Matthew. Two maybes is better than nothing though.

"Great. When can we talk to her? Maybe we can get her to incriminate herself."

I ignore the second part, which, again, makes her sound like she's a character in a bad crime novel, and say, "Unfortunately, my mom said she's out of town until sometime next week."

"What?" Harriet gasps. "She left town? That's *incredibly* suspicious. Not to mention annoying. How the hell can we grill her if she isn't even here?"

A thought occurs to me. I'm a little reluctant to suggest it for personal reasons, but Sara needs my help, and if Patterson's our best suspect right now, I'll do what I gotta do.

I clear my throat, watching as a car pulls into the lot, does a three-point turn, and then drives back out. "We could talk to Mindy Washington. She works at the library. She and Patterson are close."

"Who?" Harriet says.

She's got to be kidding. "Mindy Washington? She was in our class in high school? We only had two hundred people in our grade, Harriet."

"Nope. Don't remember her. Which, might I add, is different from not *recognizing* someone."

A bead of perspiration trickles down my cheek. I flick it away, deciding to ignore her little dig. "Well, she could probably help."

"You think she'd give us information on her boss?" She sounds skeptical. "Why?"

I hesitate. The real answer is because Mindy sort of has a thing for me. We went on a few dates earlier this year, but I quickly realized she was more into it than me. I've kept my distance recently—we've been friends since middle school, and I don't want to risk ruining that for a short-term fling.

"I think she'd answer some questions," I confirm without explaining further. Why am I reluctant to tell Harriet about my dating life? A question for a later time. "Also..." I hate to bring it up, but it seems necessary. "Adam Kozel. You mentioned earlier that you'd get in touch with him. Have you?"

"Um," she says. "Well. No. Not yet."

"Maybe you can invite him to dinner or something? Get a few drinks in him, loosen his tongue..."

"Perv." She breathes a laugh, and a shiver runs down my spine. I mentally kick myself for having that sort of reaction to her. I barely know her. I never really did.

"That's not what I meant," I say for the second time this conversation. I'm irritable all of a sudden, which I decide to blame on all the boxes I still have to lug inside.

"I know, I know. Sorry. Mouth ahead of brain, as usual."

"But really," I say. Could she just get on board with this? If I can go see Mindy, she can have one fucking conversation with her stupid ex-boyfriend. "Us questioning people is helpful, sure, but Kozel has access to official casework. He actually knows what's going on inside the LIPD."

She groans.

"You agreed to do it," I say sharply.

"I'm going to, okay? *God*," she says with obvious annoyance. "Why are you being so pushy?"

This of course makes me want to push her even more. I hop up to my feet and start pacing next to the van. "And what about your neighbors? There are other houses on the beach, right? Have you even thought about seeing if those people saw anything?"

"The middle house is empty..."

"What about the third house?"

"An old lady lives there. I doubt she could have seen anything."

"Didn't you tell *me* not to be ageist?"

"Fine," she grumbles. It's clear she's not thrilled by the idea, but right now, I don't really care. "I'll go talk to Mrs. Carter. You see when your friend Mindy is around. And don't forget about Matthew either."

"Fine."

"Good."

I roll my eyes. "Goodbye, Harriet," I say.

She sniffs. "Goodbye," she says, and with that, she's gone.

CHAPTER FIFTEEN

HARRIET

September 5

12:53 p.m.

Nic and I hang up as I pull into the driveway of my mom's house.

Through the windshield, I watch as the breeze picks up the loose ends of the police tape still wrapped around the gate, tangling them together in the air. Nic's right—not that I'd ever admit that to him. I should probably go talk to Mrs. Carter, as much as the idea pains me.

I climb out of the car, pulling my sweater tight as the wind winds around my bones. This side of the island faces the Atlantic and runs a full ten degrees cooler than over by my dad's.

I could grab a jacket from the house, but if I go inside, I might chicken out again.

I march to the gate, punch in the code, and duck under the tape, stepping onto the sand.

There are only three houses on this small stretch of private beach. George was killed at edge of the water between our house and the middle one—owned by some billionaire NYC hedge fund manager who never even uses it. The third house, farthest from my mom's, is the one I mentioned to Nic. It's occupied by Mrs. Ruth Carter, an eighty-six-year-old widow who, it's safe to say, is not my biggest fan.

August of last year, my mom and George went out of town, and I decided to take advantage of the empty house and come down to visit Maggie and Gogo. The weather was beautiful, so Maggie and I decided to do some topless sunbathing—*as one does* on a private beach. Well, if we're being precise, *I* decided and dragged Maggie along for the ride.

Little did I know that Mrs. Ruth Carter is one of those little old ladies who love to snoop.

From her reaction to our boobs, you'd have thought we were out there murdering whales. She literally called the cops and tried to have us written up for indecent exposure. Maggie managed to argue our way out of it, but suffice it to say, I am not eager to interact with her again.

That said, given Mrs. Carter's propensity for prying into other people's business, she definitely could have seen something the night George died, and I would be an idiot not to talk to her. It's possible the cops didn't even think to interview her—she's old, and we all know what little value our society places on older women.

I trudge toward her house, hands shoved into the pockets of my shorts, chin tucked to my chest, keeping my gaze on the sand. The sun is bright, but still it's creepy being out here alone. I hurry past the place where George was found, but at the top of the porch stairs, I force myself to turn back. I find it easily.

Which means Mrs. Carter could have seen something.

"What are you doing?"

I whirl around. Mrs. Carter stands in the open doorway glaring at me, a teacup clenched tight in her fist.

I take a breath, trying to relax. What did I expect? George's ghost?

"What are you doing on my property?" she asks, annoyance pinching her lips white. A gust of wind lashes us with its cool tendrils, and she flinches. For a second, I almost feel bad for her—she looks so brittle and birdlike in that thin sweater. But then she says, "Do I need to call the cops on you again, young lady?" and I remember that while she may be eighty-six, her tongue is as sharp as the knife that murdered George.

She doesn't need my worry; in fact, she'd probably yell at me if she knew it had even crossed my mind.

"I'm here because I'm wondering *about* the cops, actually," I say.

"What's that supposed to mean?"

"Did you see all those people out on the beach the other day? I'm curious if you—"

Another gust hits us, and Mrs. Carter sighs like she thinks the weather is somehow my fault. "It's freezing out here. If you insist on badgering me with questions, you need to come inside."

She turns on her heel and disappears into the house.

I hesitate, feeling like I'm about to enter the dragon's lair. But if I want to talk, it's clear I have no choice.

I walk through the door into a high-ceilinged room. Every corner is filled with large, green houseplants, teetering stacks of hardcover books, and art. Lots and lots of colorful art, mostly featuring boats. Ocean landscapes with boats, abstract oils of boats, watercolors of boats. I don't know what I was expecting after my encounter with her last summer (cages filled with flying monkeys?), but it certainly wasn't this.

"My late husband," Mrs. Carter says, watching me take it all in, "was a boat enthusiast. I never liked them much myself. Too much water."

I stop myself from asking why exactly she decided to live on the edge of the ocean if she's not a fan of water.

She sets her cup down on the coffee table. "Now, what's this about?"

I shift between my feet. The way she's staring at me, unblinking, makes me feel about two feet tall.

"Well, you know," I start.

"I don't, actually." She settles on a deep blue crushed-velvet couch. A curious choice for a beach house. I walk toward it, and she points to an armchair across the way. "There."

"Right." I scoot around the table and drop onto it. I clear my throat. "My stepfather George died. Did you hear that?"

"Yes, of course," she snaps. "I'm old, not dead. You think I didn't hear that mess the other day? And before it, the party. So loud, all of it. Some of us prefer our quiet."

"Well. I was wondering if you saw anything that night. Something that could point to who killed George?"

"From what I heard, they already have someone in custody. The cops showed her photo when they came to my door."

Ah, so they were here. "Sara Allbright?"

"That's the one. Pretty girl, not sure how she got herself tangled up in this mess—"

I interrupt. “Plenty of murderers are good-looking. Take Ted Bundy.”

“Who?” She waves a hand. “Never heard of him. My point is, seemed like those officers had their minds made up. So why are you here, bothering me with your questions?”

I weigh how much to tell her. On the one hand, Kozel will be livid if it gets back to him that I’m asking questions about this case. But on the other, do I give a shit? It’s not illegal to ask questions; in fact, the world would be a better place if more people did. Plus, Mrs. Carter is nosy as hell; she might be more willing to open up to me if I loop her in on a secret.

I scoot forward and lower my voice, even though we’re obviously alone. “Please don’t repeat this, but…I think they have the wrong person.”

Her eyebrows jerk up, like a bunny catching a curious scent. “Do you now?”

I nod. “Yes. And I’m here because I’m writing an article about it. For *Humans*.”

Her brow scrunches. “For humans?”

“It’s a digital magazine. Fully online—”

She looks at me like I have three heads.

“Never mind. In short, I want to figure out who else could have done it. I don’t think the cops are doing their job. I think they decided Sara would be an easy person to blame. It was her knife, she’s from the south side of the island, and she can’t afford a good lawyer. From what I understand, it’s their typical MO.”

She sniffs and picks up her teacup. “Don’t have to tell me twice.

The cops here are idiots. Especially that Mick Sharkey. How he became police chief is beyond me. His minions asked me several perfunctory questions, but I could tell they thought I was just a batty old woman with bad eyesight." A sour expression crosses her face. "They acted like I was already dead. I might be old, but I'm not useless."

"*I* don't think you are. And I'd love to include your thoughts in my article, which will appear in a *national* publication, if you're on board."

"I'm listening."

I slip my phone out my pocket. "Would you be okay with me recording this?"

She eyes it. "All right. I suppose."

"Great. Thank you." I open the voice memos app, hit Record, and set the phone between us on the coffee table. "To start—you said Sharkey's an idiot. Why's that?"

She snorts. "Have you *met* Mick Sharkey? Man wouldn't be able to find his way through an open door. The only reason he got that position is because DiPetrio knew he'd do whatever she told him to. Wouldn't be surprised if she rigged his police exam so he'd score high enough to be considered. And now he's filled the department with a bunch of yes-men. You should have heard their questions. Absolutely ridiculous."

"What did they ask?"

"If I saw anything out on the beach. Particularly, if I saw that girl."

"Had you?"

"Yes." She pauses as she takes a sip of tea.

My stomach plunges into my shoes. She *saw Sara*? Am I going to have to tell Frankie that I was wrong? Tell Nic that his sister is guilty? Am I going to—

Then she adds: "She was out on the beach earlier that afternoon."

Once I've recovered, I continue, "What about later?"

"Nope. But I couldn't see much of anything later. It was too dark. Too rainy."

"Oh," I say. I just wasted twenty minutes of my life coming over here. I reach out to turn off the recording. "Okay. Well, thank you for your time."

I pick up my phone and stand, but she stops me with a sharp shake of her head. "I have to say, I'm disappointed. When you showed up on my porch, I thought maybe you'd be smarter than those moronic cops."

"So you *did* see something?"

"No!" She sets down her cup with a clatter. "You're asking the wrong questions, just like they did. They kept asking *Did you see anything? Are you* sure *you didn't* see *anything*? Like they thought I didn't understand the question. But it was dark and rainy. I'm eighty-six years old. Of *course* I didn't see anything."

I slowly sink back down to the chair. "I'm sorry. I'm confused."

"I didn't *see* anything, but..." She gestures toward her ear, and it clicks.

"You *heard* something," I say. Why the hell couldn't she just say that? She's acting like this is some sort of logic puzzle I'm failing.

"There you go. Now you're thinking with your whole brain."

Right. My *brain* is the issue. I turn back on the recording.

"Did you tell the cops?"

She pulls her chin to her chest. "I certainly did not! They only asked me that one question. Left right after. Heard them talking as they walked away about how they knew coming to my house would be a waste of time because I'm 'so old.' Idiots," she adds darkly.

"They should have been more respectful," I say. Never hurts to butter up a source—a lesson the cops could stand to learn.

The edges of her mouth pull up—not a smile exactly, but something that less resembles an upside-down U. "That's right, young lady. They should have! Maybe then I would have told them that as I was moving my potted hoya out to the porch that night—her soil had dried out, so it was the perfect time for her to drink—I heard a man's voice, clear as day, from the direction of your house."

I freeze. This could be it. I might have saved Sara. Nic will be so happy. Kozel will be so mad. My article will be huge. Drive so much traffic to the website that Frankie will shit herself. She'll *have* to hire me back full-time. I'll get my old life back.

It'll be proof that I *am* good at this after all. Not just a tabloid writer—a real journalist. Talented. Smart. All the things that I stopped believing when Frankie fired me that day.

I push the phone forward, heart thumping in anticipation. "What did you hear?"

Mrs. Carter's brow furrows. "Loud voices. Sounded like an argument. I walked to the railing to see if I could figure out what was going on. We have to keep vigilant, you know. Never know who's out and about."

"Uh-huh. And the voices? What did you hear?"

"I didn't catch most of it," Ruth says, squinting at me. "But I did hear one thing. A man's voice. George. I'd know it anywhere. So nasally and clipped. He said, plain as day, *This is getting pathetic. Let it go.*"

That's far more cryptic than I'd hoped. I frown. "Did you hear anything else?"

"Nope. That's it. I stood there for a bit longer, but the rain started coming down in sheets, and I had to get inside. My hip acts up in bad weather."

I sit back, trying to quell my rising disappointment, my vision of the future vanishing as quickly as it came. "You didn't hear who he was talking to?"

Her glare returns. "I already said. I did not."

Right, okay. It's not as clear as I'd hoped, but maybe it can still be useful. "What time was this?"

"Just had my evening tea, so 7:35. I have my tea at 7:25, and I always drink it in ten minutes."

7:35 p.m. Shortly before Nic found the body. Which means whoever she heard him talking to was likely the killer.

This is getting pathetic. Let it go.

I turn the phrase over in my mind, picking at its strands. The wording suggests it wasn't the first time they'd argued, which confirms my theory—George knew them.

I consider whether I should call Kozel and tell him what I learned. The thing is I can easily see him blowing it off. Saying George was talking to Sara. Telling her to let go of the argument they had in the kitchen.

No. There's no need to tell him. I'm going to keep this little piece of information to myself.

Myself and Nic.

Our first real clue.

CHAPTER SIXTEEN

NIC

September 5

2:02 p.m.

I finally finish unloading the boxes, which took twice as long as Mom said it would, mostly because I did it alone. Not that I'm complaining. Her back's been a mess lately; lifting one of those things would have thrown it out completely.

Back in her office, I suggest she call the jail, see if she can go visit Sara before it's too late in the day. She protests at first, telling me there's too much to get done here, but it doesn't take much to convince her, and because the Logan Island Jail isn't exactly highly trafficked, she's able to get an appointment at three. While she's on the phone, she books me an appointment for tomorrow morning.

It's about time I ask my sister what happened that night.

She leaves with a reminder to wait for Matthew and Esme, and I sink down into her chair, propping my feet up onto the edge of the desk. I slip my phone out of my pocket and find a string of text messages from Harriet, updating me on the conversation she had with her elderly next-door neighbor.

My heart leaps as I read the final one.

And—GET THIS—she heard George out on the beach talking to someone!!!

What did they say?

She responds immediately.

Where have you been??

Performing manual labor. Not sure if you know what that is?

Yes, Nic. I do. Thanks so much for asking

Whatever. Anyway, what did she hear?

Right. She heard George say This is getting pathetic. Let it go.

I frown down at the words on the screen.

I finally respond.

My phone starts buzzing in my hand.

"Hello?"

"Sorry," Harriet says, "I don't usually call people, but—I don't know what it means exactly. It's the only thing she heard so there's no context."

"Did she see who he was talking to?"

"Well...she didn't exactly *see* anything. It was dark and rainy. Plus, she's pretty old. Her eyes are bad."

My shoulders slump. "If her eyes are bad, are you sure we can trust what she told you?"

Harriet pauses. "I think so. She says her hearing is in perfect condition. Plus, she'd known George for years. She would have recognized his voice. I don't know if you remember, but it was...distinct."

If by *distinct* she means annoying as hell, then yeah. "Okay. So George was out there. But...we already knew that. What would have been useful is the identity of the other person."

I can almost hear Harriet's eyes roll through the phone. "Yeah, obviously, thanks, Nic. But think about the phrasing. *Getting* pathetic. *Let* it go. It all implies that this wasn't the first time they'd had this argument, which means he knew his killer. It fits Patterson, but what about the caterer? You weren't sure if they knew each other, right?"

"Matthew? I don't think so, but I don't know him that well. He only moved to town about a few weeks ago."

"In August?" Harriet says with surprise. "*Why?*"

I hadn't really thought about it before, but she's right. It's weird.

Most people don't move to the island at the end of the summer season. "I don't know. But he's on his way to the office, so I'll see what I can find out."

"You're still at work?"

I roll my eyes. "Yes, Harriet. Some of us work to pay our rent."

"Oh my god, I *know* that, okay?" She makes an exasperated noise. "Could you please stop implying that I'm some sort of trust fund baby? Do you think I'm living with my mom for my health? I had a job. I got *fired*. I moved back here because I couldn't afford rent. Just because George was rich doesn't mean I am."

I fall quiet, suddenly ashamed. I'm being an asshole. I need to cool it.

"Sorry," I mumble.

"It's fine," she says, but it's clear she's annoyed, and I guess I can't blame her.

I'm about to apologize when there's a noise from the front room and a voice calls, "Hello? Angela? Are you here?"

"Shit, I gotta run," I tell Harriet as Esme's puff of blue-gray hair appears in the doorway.

"Nico! It's good to see you. How is everything? Your sister? Any news? Where's your mother?"

"Okay, go deal with that," Harriet says. "Talk later."

We hang up and I stand. "Hey, Esme. Nothing new to report about Sara. My mom went to see her, actually."

Esme walks over, wrapping her arms around my chest, enveloping me in the scent of burnt sage. "I'm glad," she says as she pulls away. "Sara needs all the support we can give her right now."

I nod.

"Has she been using the crystals I gave her? Black tourmaline. They should help her stay calm and centered so she can support Sara in a loving, openhearted way."

I clear my throat. I've known Esme my entire life—she and my mom have been friends for the better part of forty years—and she's always been the same. Warm, weird, and full of slightly bizarre wellness advice. "I'm not sure. You'd have to ask her."

"I assume she hasn't." She shakes her head. "I've told her time and again how helpful they are! Your mother is so bullheaded sometimes. I guess that's where Sara gets it—" She stops, her cheeks growing red. "Oh, Nico, I'm sorry. I didn't mean—"

Hearing her stumble over my sister's name deepens my exhaustion. But I can't be mad at her for it. Esme doesn't have an unkind bone in her body.

"It's fine. You're not wrong," I say, ready for a change in subject. I pick up an envelope from a stack of papers. "Listen, here's your check. I'm sorry if it's less than you'd hoped."

Esme rips open the envelope, wincing as she sees the number printed on the paper inside. She also works part time at the Logan Island General Store, a small grocer and deli next to the police station, but it's slow in the offseason. Very slow. She relies on these gigs to supplement her income, and the fact that her check is three-quarters what it would have been without all the cancellations has to hurt.

I know it hurts me.

"Well, thanks." She folds it in half and sticks it into the pocket of her overalls. "Are we still on for next Thursday?"

"For the moment, yeah." Given everything, I don't have high hopes the job will stick around. Still, I keep that to myself as I follow Esme into the other room. "I'll let you know if anything changes. Or if we get anything new on the books."

She pats me on the arm. "Thanks, Nico. You're a good boy."

The front door bangs open, and Matthew enters, his hands stuffed deep into the pockets of his gray shorts.

"Hey," I greet him. "What's up, man?"

"Hey," he says gruffly, joining us.

Esme frowns. "Your chakras are out of balance." She reaches out to cup his face, and he cringes away. "Are you eating?"

Matthew cuts his eyes to me, and I shrug. "Yeah. Why?"

Esme's lips press together tight. "You seem—"

"I'm just tired."

Her drawn-on eyebrows jump. "Well, all right. If you're sure. I'll check in about the Thursday job later, Nico." She hikes her bag onto her shoulder and heads out the door.

"She's weird," Matthew mutters once we're alone.

Esme might be a little odd, but she's not wrong. Something is definitely off with Matthew. Dark purple hollows hang under his eyes, and his shirt is wrinkled like he slept in it. He's never the most put-together guy, but this is something else.

"You sure you're okay?" I ask.

He sniffs, running a fingertip under one eye. "Yeah. Like I said. Just tired. Worked last night bartending at the Yacht Club, and I didn't get home till after two."

I'm about to go grab his check but pause as what he said registers. *The Yacht Club.*

I'd forgotten he works there. He mentioned it during his initial interview but hasn't said a word about it since. Of course, he hasn't really talked about much of anything with me—he's been pretty quiet whenever we're around each other.

If he bartends at the Yacht Club, chances are he *did* know George. I'll have to confirm with Harriet, but I'd bet money George belonged there—every person in his tax bracket is a member.

I slowly turn back. "Two a.m.? Shit. Late one."

"No kidding," he mutters. "Gonna try to get some extra sleep this afternoon, so if you don't mind grabbing me the check?"

"Right, right, of course. It's in the back office." As we walk back, I continue, "I'm sorry I haven't asked—how *is* that job going? At the club? I know the members there can be a little brutal to waitstaff."

His eyes flick to my face. "It's good."

Not the most descriptive answer I've ever received.

"Have you met anyone?" I ask as we turn the corner to the office.

"What?"

"Like...have you made new friends?" I cringe. I sound like his mother.

"Uh. Sure. I guess?" he says, shooting me a skeptical look.

Right. Too much. Except if I back off, I might never get answers out of him.

I grab his check and hold it out. "Here it is."

"Thanks," Matthew says, reaching for it. As he does, I pull it away, and his hand is left dangling empty in midair.

"Did you ever run into the guy who died at the club?" I ask. It's clear I'm starting to weird him out, but I need answers. In three days, Sara's set to be arraigned. "George George?"

"What? No. Never met him." He snatches his check from my fingers. "If you don't mind, I gotta run."

I trail after him into the other room, still peppering him with questions. If he didn't have anything to do with George's murder, he's going to think I've completely lost my mind.

"Never? No conversations? No interactions at all? Even at that party at his house?"

"No," Matthew says, stopping short next to the row of burners. "Okay? I never talked to the guy in my life. Can I go now?"

"Yeah, of course," I say. He just directly contradicted what Harriet's grandma told her about what she saw at the party. Was she mistaken?

Or is Matthew lying?

I rack my brain for something—anything—that would get him to open up. But it's too late. He's at the door, pulling it open, and then he's gone.

CHAPTER SEVENTEEN

HARRIET

September 5
4:23 p.m.

When I get back from Mrs. Carter's, I shut myself in my room and spend an hour staring at a Word doc. What I need to do is *write* this article instead of just talking about it, but my brain is as blank as the page on my screen.

Eventually, a stream of texts from Steven rescues me from my misery. They inform Maggie and me that he is in *love,* and we are officially required to be bridesmaids in his spring wedding to Martin.

I really hope Martin is as good a guy as I remember. Steven comes across as cavalier, but his heart's as fragile as they come.

I turn back to my computer and get a few more words down before I'm interrupted again. This time, it's Nic, updating me on his conversation with Matthew. He asks if George was a member of the Yacht

Club (of course he was) and whether Gogo could have been mistaken about Matthew's behavior.

I'm hesitant to say yes—it feels like a betrayal—but I have to admit it's possible. As much as it breaks my heart, there is something going on with Gogo. Something bad.

Nic and I go back and forth, discussing whether Matthew's a real suspect or just a really private introvert. Then he has the nerve to ask if I've talked to Kozel.

I drop the phone onto my bedspread.

Even though I know it's ridiculous, there's this tiny voice in my head asking if Nic keeps insisting I talk to Kozel because he's hoping we'll get back together. (I know I sound insane. To be fair, Kozel's mere existence is incredibly triggering to me.)

When I pick the phone back up, there's yet another text:

Sara's arraignment is in THREE DAYS, Harriet.

Right. Good reminder that Nic does not in fact want me to run back into the arms of my awful ex. He simply wants to save his sister from going to prison for the rest of her life.

Dammit.

I swipe out of his text, into a new one, and type a number I—unfortunately—still have memorized from way back when.

Then I write:

Hello. This is Harriet. Harriet Baker. I'm writing against my will to see if you're free for dinner soon you JERK?

No, probably not.

I hit Delete and try again.

> **Hello, Adam. This is Harriet. It was nice to run into you earlier. Are you free for dinner soon? I would love to catch up.**

Better, even though my eye is twitching and I'm vaguely nauseous.

I press Send and wait, but no blue bubbles appear. My anxiety grows as the seconds tick by; I can't just sit here staring at the screen, waiting for his reply. It's giving me major flashbacks to high school.

Tucking my phone into the pocket of my jeans, I shove off the bed and head into the hallway. The room George and my mom stuck me in is just down the hall from George's home office. I've tried its doorknob a couple times since the cops went through it—if George had anything to hide, that's where it would be in the house—but it's been locked up tight. My mom's got the only key, and I can't exactly ask her to let me in without getting into a conversation I don't want to have, so I've been checking it every time I walk by.

I twist it, and it turns in my hand.

I'm two steps away before my brain catches up.

It *turned*! Holy shit!

I backpedal and stop, staring at the round silver handle, suddenly gun-shy.

If I go in there, could it be considered breaking and entering? I'm technically a resident of this house, and it's unlocked, but...still. What if I find important information? Could I use it in my article?

Maggie should be able to answer that.

Do you have a second?

sure. what's up?

How can I ask this without arousing her suspicions?

is it illegal to go into an unlocked room in your house and look around?

Huh? no of course not

Okay, that phrasing was a little *too* mild. I try again.

Well what if it's like...an office that's not yours? And it's normally locked? And you go through someone else's private stuff?

There's a pause.

Harriet.

What?

what are you up to?

Nothing!!!

Seriously. It's for—

I scramble. Maggie is always on my back about doing more creative writing.

A short story I'm writing

Riiight. A story. I'm sure.

MAGGIE!

Fine. The answer is—it depends. It's probably not outright illegal but whoever you're "writing" about should probably consider that they might be toeing some ethical lines

Hmm. Ethical lines.

Frankie's never cared about a little thing like ethics, but what if my article gets picked up by the wires? What if some Hollywood producer comes a-knocking, asking to buy film rights—

Don't do anything dumb. Can't afford to bail you out of jail rn

Sorry, Maggie. Before I can make millions from selling the rights to my article, I actually need to *write* the damn thing. And in order to do that, I need information.

I twist the knob again, but before I can push it open, my phone buzzes.

Hello, Harriet. I'm surprised to hear from you, but yes, I'm around tomorrow. Dinner sounds good. Piccolo–7pm?

Ugh. I guess it's really happening. Dinner with my asshole ex. Just what I've always dreamed of. He better have something useful to tell me about Sara's case.

I shove the phone back into my pocket to deal with later. Like when I'm not in the middle of breaking into—ahem, I mean *exploring*—my dead stepfather's office.

One more glance around to make sure my mother hasn't suddenly appeared, and I step inside.

The falling evening sun filters through the blinds behind his desk, casting shadows across its surface, against the coffee mug perched on its edge. The musky scent of George's cologne winds into my nose, sending a shiver up my spine. Being in here is spookier than I expected. Like he just stepped out and will be back at any moment. Best to get this over with as fast as possible. My mother could be lurking out in the living room, and I don't want to deal with the consequences if she catches me in here.

I slip over to the desk and start my search.

First, the desk drawers. The first is filled with manila folders—property tax bills, insurance EOBs, checks with scrawled deposit dates. None of it seems helpful, but I take a few pictures and shove them back inside.

The next drawer is locked tight. Now we're talking. Why lock something unless you have something to hide? Except, of course, I need a key.

I rifle through the other drawers, searching, but find nothing.

There has to be another way.

It hits me.

I pick up my phone and google *how to pick a lock*. Page after page of search results appear on the screen. I love the internet. All the information I'll ever need in the palm of my hand.

A minute later, the drawer pops open.

I'm greeted by a small stack of miscellaneous items: a few newspaper clippings about George's old company acquiring a large piece of land in Manhattan back in 2001. Several engraved invitations to charity galas (lol at the thought of George being charitable). An obituary for a handsome guy named Adrian Pruner who gives strong JFK Jr. vibes—square jawed, thick brown hair swept neatly to the side. According to the dates under his picture, he died at twenty-four.

Damn. What a waste. I wonder how George knew him. I wonder if his death is what turned George into such a prick. It's possible: Grief does weird things to people. Like my mom after her third husband died. I swear a piece of her soul burned out there on that boat with him.

I snap photos and keep digging.

Nothing...nothing...I'm hungry... Maybe I should just put everything back and go make myself some frozen pizza—

Then I reach the bottom of the drawer and forget all about food. A single sheet of notebook paper with handwriting scrawled across it.

Dear George,

You are a selfish monster with no respect for other people, no regard for history, and a blatant indifference to the damage you've inflicted on our fragile environment. If you were to disappear from this earth, we'd be all the better for it. But you already know that, I'm sure. What I'm writing to tell you is something else. Something I hope will keep you up at night and haunt your dreams.

I know what you did.

And I'm going to prove it, if it's the last thing I do.

Barbara Patterson

I read it again, then again, forgetting how to breathe. A piece of evidence—*real fucking evidence*—where one of our suspects is threatening George.

And it was just sitting in George's desk. Did the cops see the letter when they searched the room? Sure, it was in a locked drawer, but wouldn't they have asked my mom to open it?

Just as I'm about to snap a photo of the letter, my mother appears in the doorway. Her eyes narrow as she spots me. "Harriet! What the hell are you doing in here?"

Crap.

I shove the letter into my pocket and slam the drawer shut—directly onto my fingertips.

"Fuck!" I yank my hand free and flap it in the air.

"Language!" my mother snaps.

"Shit!" I say, mostly just to annoy her.

She purses her lips. "Might I ask what you think you're doing? Are you going through George's desk?"

"Um. No?"

Her eyes narrow. "You just shut that drawer on your fingers. That wouldn't have happened had it been closed."

A fair point.

"Yeah, fine. I was looking for…a pen? I couldn't find one in the kitchen, so I came in here and thought maybe he would have one and…um." Jesus Christ; what am I even *saying*? I force a laugh, trying to play it off.

"I want you out of this office, Harriet. Now."

I come out from behind the desk with my hands up. "I wasn't in his office."

She's not amused. "You are *still* in his office."

I roll my eyes. "Fine. If you want me out so badly, can you please move so I can leave?"

She steps aside, and I scurry past her into the hallway. She joins me, pulling a key out of her pocket.

"What's that?" I ask, even though I know exactly what it is.

The key to George's office. Which she's locking behind us.

Fuck.

She stalks off without another word.

I linger behind, slipping Patterson's note out of my pocket and reading it again. She didn't directly threaten him, but the tone of the note is still ominous. I picture George receiving it, fury boiling up inside him. Confronting Patterson outside the library late one night...

And then he wound up dead.

Nic and I are set to meet in the morning to question his friend Mindy about Patterson, but this new evidence has lit a fire under my ass.

I click a quick picture of the letter, text it to Nic, then call him as I walk back to my room.

"Hey," Nic says, sounding breathless. "I can't really talk—"

"Did you see what I texted you?" I ask as I settle back on the bed.

"Let me look." A pause, then, "*Damn!* Where'd you find this?"

"I finally got into George's office. Found it one of his desk drawers, but my mom caught me a second later and kicked me out before I could do much else."

"Well, this is great," he breathes. "Seems like our plan to talk to Mindy tomorrow was a good one."

Pride bubbles up in my chest. "Thanks. But I was thinking—with this new evidence, why wait?"

He clears his throat. "Yeah, okay. I'm at my parents' house. Barry's here updating us on the case, but I think he's wrapping up. Let me text her and see if she's around."

I hear clicking as Nic types. Voices rise in the background of the call, arguing in Italian. Guilt nips at me; I should let him be. I'm not used to being around people so close with their families. Ever since Maggie's mom died back in high school, she and her dad have been like two ships passing in the night, and Steven's parents are great, just independent. His dad once had hip surgery without even telling him it was happening.

"No dice." Nic's back. "She just sat down to see a movie over in Pleasantville. That said, she'll be at the library tomorrow morning."

Not ideal, but there's not much I can do about it. "Okay. We'll meet there like we planned. Nine a.m.?"

"Sounds good." He goes quiet. For a moment, the only sound is his breathing, soft and steady in my ear. Goose bumps prick along my arms. "We have two decent suspects now, don't we, Baker? And it's only been a few days. This is good. We make a good team."

A grin spreads across my face. Is he warming up to me? Maybe even on his way to forgiving me?

"It is. It's very good." I pause, not ready for the conversation to end. "Oh! I almost forgot to tell you—I'm having dinner with Kozel tomorrow night."

He pauses. "Oh. Great."

He doesn't sound like he thinks it's great. In fact, he sounds like he's mad.

Finally, I break the silence. "So that's good, right?"

"Right. That's...great. Hey—sorry, Harriet, but Barry's at it again. I gotta go. I'll see you tomorrow, okay?"

The line goes dead, and I'm left staring at the dark screen, wondering what just happened.

CHAPTER EIGHTEEN

HARRIET

September 6

9:10 a.m.

I'm late. Ten minutes, to be exact.

I was on the way out the door when my mother stopped me to talk about planning a memorial for George. His funeral can't happen until his body's released by the authorities, so she's decided we need to do something in the meantime to remember him by. I agreed to help organize a gathering next week at the Yacht Club; she looked so sad standing there in the foyer, I didn't have the heart to say no.

Nic's standing by the front of the library with his arms folded, foot tapping against the sidewalk. As I watch, he checks the watch on his wrist. A perfect picture of impatience.

I'm out of breath as I jog up to him.

"Sorry, sorry," I pant, doubling over to slow my breathing. "I'm here."

"I see that," he says.

I gulp another breath, then straighten.

"You okay?" he asks, eyes softening.

Something inside me stirs. Something warm and deep and extremely inconvenient. I tell myself it's nothing. It's just because I haven't had sex in… Well. Let's just call it *a while*. Nic is a very attractive human being. He looks like Glen Powell, for fuck's sake! I mean, have you *seen* the wet T-shirt scene in *Twisters*? C'mon. I'm a red-blooded woman. Of course I'm going to find him attractive.

It has nothing to do with remembering how sweet and gentle he was back in high school. Absolutely nothing at all.

"I'm fine. My mom," I add, desperate to break the tension crackling between us. "She caught me on my way out and harassed me until I offered to help organize a memorial for George. Then I almost drove through a stop sign and got pulled over and—anyway. I'm only ten minutes late. The library can't be crowded already, right? Have you seen Mindy? Is she here?"

Nic's eyes have grown wide. "Did you have too much caffeine this morning, Harriet?"

"Um, yes?" I say, lying out my ass. If *only* it was caffeine that's got me this twisted. "Also, I'm excited. We're making progress and…"

I'm distracted as a woman appears behind him, framed in the library window.

A woman about our age. Silky blond, curly hair. Glowing, smooth skin. Bright-blue eyes.

She's gorgeous. She could pass for Kate Hudson's younger sister. There's no way that's…

Nic turns. "What are you—oh!" A warm smile spreads across his face—a smile, might I add, that did not appear when *I* showed up.

Not that I care.

He waves.

"Is that...?" I'm not sure I want the answer. When Nic first mentioned Mindy, did he say how well they know each other? Are they... together?

"Yeah. That's Mindy." He shrugs.

Did everyone turn into a supermodel since high school except for me?

I grab his sleeve, yanking his face down close to my own. He smells good. Better than I remember.

I blink the thought away. "That cannot be Mindy Washington. I don't remember her being so...so...you know..."

"That's Mindy," he confirms, gently extracting my hand from his arm. "And I didn't realize you remembered her at all."

Before I can respond, she knocks on the window and motions for us to join her inside.

"She seems very excited. To see you."

"You ready?" he asks and then walks away without waiting for a reply.

I trail after him.

Nic never said anything about being in a relationship, but we only reconnected a week ago, and most of that time has been filled with conversations about murder. Again, it's not that I care. But if he has a girlfriend, it feels like something I should know. Because we're going to be spending time together and all.

Mindy envelops him in a hug. "Nic!" she says breathlessly. "I talked to Martin, and he filled me in on everything. I've been *so* worried. How are you? How's Angela? Your dad? Can I do anything to help? Maybe start a meal train?"

"Thanks," Nic says. "I appreciate that, but we're okay."

"Well, just let me know. I'm here to support you, however I can."

I'm watching the exchange like a tennis match. Her hand hasn't left his bicep, and something's bubbling up inside me. Something that feels a lot like...

"Do you two spend a lot of time together?" I blurt, stepping out from behind Nic.

Mindy's hand finally falls away from his arm. "Oh my gosh! I'm so sorry, Harriet. I would have said hello sooner, but I've just been so worried about Nic and his family. It's great to see you. I heard you were back in town! How long has it been? Years? Since graduation, I think?"

"Probably," I say. "What have you been up to since? I guess you and Nic still hang out?"

And *bam*—there goes her hand, back to his arm. "Yeah. We hang out sometimes. Right, Nic?"

She smiles up at him, and my heart skips a beat.

Sometimes. What the hell does *that* mean?

Nic's silent.

"Nic?" Mindy says, her smile faltering.

He blinks. "Yeah. Yes! We do."

Another, even bigger smile breaks golden across her face. God, why is she so *pretty*? I look away.

"So, Nic—I know why you're here," she says. "But, Harriet, what can I help you with—" Her mouth drops open. "Wait. I'm such a jerk! George George was your stepdad! It's so terrible, what happened to him. Awful, awful stuff. I cannot believe someone in our beautiful little town *killed* him. I do hope you know it couldn't have been Nic's sister, Sara! She's a wonderful human being and absolutely not a murderer."

"Actually." I leap at the chance to get us—*me*, really—back on track. This visit is about Patterson, not Mindy and Nic's totally sweet and not at all jealousy-inducing romantic relationship. "That's why we're here."

Her brow furrows. "*We?*" she repeats softly.

"We're trying to help Sara," Nic says, "and were wondering if we could ask you a couple questions. If possible, somewhere a little more private?"

Mindy hesitates. "I'm supposed to be manning the front desk, but hang on. Lemme see if Fred will cover for me."

She walks over to an older gentleman who's shelving books. They confer, and he nods.

When she gets back to us, Mindy says, "Okay, we're good. I have ten minutes. Let's head back to one of the study rooms."

We wind through the stacks, through the children's section where a couple toddlers are sprawled on the floor, past the chapter books, and finally into a small room with floor-to-ceiling windows.

"How can I help?" Mindy asks once the door is closed. She leans against the table and folds her arms against her chest. "I don't want to disappoint, but I didn't really know Mr. George other than by reputation, and, well—he wasn't exactly well-liked around these parts. Particularly since he convinced the city council to gut the library's budget. So sorry, Harriet."

"It's fine," I say.

"When did that happen?" Nic asks.

"Earlier this year. Barbara had been speaking out against the island's development, and Mr. George didn't like it. It was his way of retaliating. It was brutal. If it weren't for private donors supplementing what we lost, we wouldn't have been able to buy new books this year. It's hurting the town, the people who live here—the *children*. But I guess some people don't give a quack who they hurt if money's involved."

"That's awful," Nic says. He looks about thirty seconds away from wrapping his arms around her.

She gives him a sad smile. "Thanks. It's been rough."

I clear my throat. "Look, I should level with you here, Mindy. I'm a journalist."

She manages to rip her eyes away from Nic. "Oh right! I'd heard that," she says brightly.

"Oh." She sounds like she means it, but I can't help but wonder what else she's heard. That I was forced back home with my tail between my legs? "Well. I'm currently doing some freelance work, and *Humans* hired me to write an article about what's going on here. George's death, Sara's arrest, all of it. The LIPD is barreling forward to charge Sara, but why? Did they do their due diligence before arresting her? Did they properly investigate other suspects—any at all?"

"And Nic is…helping?"

I glance at him. "He is. I mean, I'm writing the piece, but the investigation is a joint effort."

"Oh," she says, mouth tilting into a frown. "Okay. Unfortunately,

I'm not sure I'll be much help. Like I said, I didn't really know Mr. George."

"Of course," Nic says, like he's forgotten we're not actually here to get Mindy's opinion on my stepfather. They're looking at each other like I'm not even here.

"But," I say before they can start making out in front of me, "your boss did."

Mindy raises her brows, barely taking her eyes off Nic. "Barbara? Sure. She did, but so what?"

Something tightens in my center. I will not let this...this *Tinker Bell*–looking supermodel blow me off so easily.

"So. So she *hated* George. Everyone knew it. And yet she came to my party. I wasn't close with her, so it leads me to wonder—why? Why was she there? Was it because she had...plans?"

Nic's mouth drops open. "Harriet!" he snaps. "Mindy, I'm so sorry—"

Mindy interrupts, glaring at me. "What exactly are you asking me, Harriet Baker? Because it sounds a *lot* like you're accusing Barbara of murder, which is absolutely outrageous!" She steps closer to me, waving her finger in the air between us. "If you must know, Barbara went to your party because Mayor DiPetrio would be there. She wanted to catch her in a social setting. Talk about library funding. We're desperate. We can only afford a few new releases a month. Our patrons are suffering!"

"What makes you so sure Barbara couldn't have done it?" I reply. "She hated George—you said so yourself! George wrecking your funding? That's a little thing we call motive. Plus, I found a very incriminating letter she wrote to George in his desk drawer. She *threatened* him."

Somewhere in the back of my brain, I recognize I'm being a total asshole. A woman who hates on other women. The worst kind.

But the way she's defending Patterson, like her shit's made of gold, is pissing me off. Must be nice to have a boss who doesn't treat you like crap. Must be nice to have a boyfriend who's hot and kind. And have a steady job. And a beautiful little upturned nose straight out of a Disney cartoon.

"Okay, that is *enough*!" Mindy says, voice sharp. "Nic, I know you want to help Sara, but this is outrageous! Barbara is the best person I know. Did she have problems with George? Sure she did, but she was far from the only one. She did not *kill* him, and I won't stand here and listen to this crap!"

"Mindy, that's not what she's saying—" Nic tries, but she talks over him.

"What is *wrong* with you, Harriet Baker? You think you can waltz back into town and start accusing good people of murder? You had better not write about Barbara in your little article. And if you do we'll...we'll *sue*! For defamation. And you better bet we'll win."

Silence falls and a whisper floats through my mind, cruel and familiar. It sounds a lot like Frankie. *You're a crap journalist, Baker. Always have been, always will be.*

I break eye contact with Mindy, cheeks heating.

Nic steps between us, his jaw tight like he's struggling to stay calm.

"Mindy. I am so, so sorry for..." He glances at me and then away just as quick. "We don't actually think Barbara did it. We're just exploring every angle, you know? The cops are charging Sara on Tuesday, and the only lawyer my family can afford is my mom's cousin Barry, who took the bar eight times before passing. I'm desperate. Sara's screwed if we don't figure this out."

Mindy softens. "I understand. But Barbara is one of the most upstanding women...no, one of the most upstanding *people* I know. She could never, ever kill someone. Okay?" She pets Nic's arm. "I have to get back to work. But I'm serious—you better not go spreading this malicious gossip around town, or you'll be very sorry." She directs this bit at me.

"We won't," Nic says. "I promise."

"Thanks. I know I can count on you." She leaves the room without another glance in my direction.

As soon as she's gone, Nic turns, anger flashing on his face. "What the hell was that? Is that how you usually conduct your interviews? Jesus, Harriet."

"What?" I ask, like I don't already know.

"Are you seriously asking me that? You jumped down Mindy's throat as soon as we walked into this room! Did you really think she was going to answer anything after that?"

No, of course I didn't, but I still couldn't make myself stop for some reason.

I really blew it. I let my stupid mixed-up feelings get in the way of being professional. Now Nic probably thinks I'm a screwup. Probably thinks, *Oh, now I understand why she got fired.*

I should say something. Apologize even.

"I'm sorry. But don't you think it's at least *possible* that Mindy's view of her boss is a wee bit distorted? Last time I checked, upstanding citizens do not send letters telling people the world would be better off if they disappeared."

He shakes his head. "That might be, but she's Mindy's hero. You should have let me take the lead and not ignored me when I tried to stop you. If we're going to be partners, you need to respect what I have to say. Got it?"

"Fine! But since she isn't going to help us with Patterson, we need to do it on our own. We should try to get into her office and take a look around."

"*Get into her office?* That's—"

"A good idea? Maybe tomorrow? I'd suggest sooner, but I'm going out with Kozel tonight, and he'll probably be more reluctant to spill the dirt if I was just arrested for breaking and entering."

"—illegal?" Nic finishes.

"And? Sometimes you have to go the extra mile in order to get what you need!" I'm well aware of how ridiculous I sound, but I can't seem to stop.

He looks less than pleased. "I doubt your editor will be happy if you start committing felonies, Harriet. Can't include *that* in your article, can you? Instead of trying to get us both arrested, why don't you just ask Kozel if he's heard anything?"

I hate that he's right. "*Fine,*" I say, sounding like a petulant child. This morning has not gone according to plan.

Nic sighs. "Look, I have to get going. Are you ready to head out?"

I nod and trail after him through the library, my eyes trained on the worn heels of his shoes as we twist through the stacks.

Once we're back outside, he stops. "I'll see you later, Harriet," he says, squinting off down the street.

My heart sinks. Did I fuck up so royally that I've scared him off for good? "Wait. Where are you going? I thought we could chat. Come up with our next step."

"I have an appointment."

"An appointment? Like...a dentist appointment?"

He shakes his head.

"Doctor?"

"No."

If he thinks I'm going to let this go, he has another thing coming. "What then?"

He scowls at a nearby tree. "Look, if you must know, I'm going to see my sister. But you can't just show up at the jail. You have to make an appointment. I made one yesterday. I need to talk to her, alone."

"Excuse me? You made an appointment without even *telling* me?"

"Yes."

"I need to come!"

"No. You don't. This is exactly why I didn't tell you." He's infuriatingly calm.

"What the hell, Nic? You just said inside that we're supposed to be working as a team. How am I supposed to write this article if I don't talk to Sara? I know what questions we need to ask her. Interviewing people is literally my job!"

"Your job—" He rocks back on his heels. "Harriet. I made the appointment because I want to make sure Sara's okay. I thought about inviting you along, but I thought she'd be more likely to talk if it was just me. I gotta say, now I'm pretty glad I *didn't* ask you, after seeing how you treated Mindy in there. If you did that to Sara, she'd flip her shit. And if you two ended up in a fight, things for her would go from bad to worse."

He starts to walk away.

"Nic!" I scramble to come up with something that will change his mind.

He pauses. "What?" He sounds weary. Of me.

"I'm sorry," I finally offer.

The look he gives me makes me melt into a puddle of shame.

"That's great, Harriet, but I am going to see my sister. Alone."

CHAPTER NINETEEN

NIC

September 6

9:42 a.m.

Harriet is following me.

She's been tailing me since I left the library, not even bothering to hide it. She really has some nerve.

I pretend like I don't see her until I reach the station and come to a sudden halt outside its double doors.

Harriet runs straight into my back. "Are we going in?" she asks into the fabric of my shirt.

I turn to find her wearing an eager expression. She's like a really cute, really annoying puppy. If she had a tail, I swear to god it would be wagging.

"I am going in. You are staying here. Or better yet, going home."

"Wait." She presses her palm flat against my chest. Through my

T-shirt, her hand is warm. A second later, she blinks at it like she's not quite sure how it got there, and her cheeks burn red. "Oh. Oh *god*. Sorry." She pulls it back and stuffs it into her pocket before speaking again. "Look. You're right. I… I came on too strong with Mindy. I'm sorry." She cringes, like it pains her to say it. "I'm usually better at all this, I swear, but if you let me come see Sara, I'll let you do the all the talking. Promise. I won't say a single word. I just—I want to help. Write this article. But part of that is talking to the person wrongly accused. We're running out of time, Nic. Her arraignment is in two days."

Her eyes are locked on mine, deep and blue like the sky, full of pleading. Her tongue darts out, licking her full bottom lip, and for a second, I almost forget myself. I think about cupping her cheek, pulling her close. Kissing her until all this—all the pain and anxiety of the last week—fades away.

"So?" Harriet ventures, more timid than I've ever heard her. "What do you think?"

I feel myself caving. She's right—she needs to write the article. And in order to do that, she probably does need some face time with my sister.

If we can't figure out who really killed George by the time Sara's arraigned, she'll be charged with murder, and then shit's going to get real—real in a way that Barry absolutely can't handle. She'll need a real lawyer, and if we're lucky, Harriet's article will help get us one.

"We agreed to do this together, right?" Harriet says. "Give me a chance to show you I can be gentle."

I suck in a deep breath through my nose. "Fine. I doubt they'll even let you in, but if they do, it's your funeral."

I should have known that Harriet would manage to persuade the cop at the front desk to let her join me even though she isn't on the pre-approved list. This place isn't exactly Alcatraz. Now we're sitting in a small interview room, waiting for my sister to join us.

Unfortunately, Sara's incarceration in our hometown jail is only temporary. From what I understand, if she's officially charged and we can't make bail, she'll be transferred to the Atlantic County Jail—a much bigger, much scarier facility on the mainland. I worry she won't survive it, given her inability to shut the fuck up.

We're sitting shoulder to shoulder on plastic folding chairs in front of a scratched-up metal table. The walls are bare, their gray paint peeling in spots.

"Can you please stop doing that?" Harriet whispers.

"Doing what?"

She slaps her hand over mine, pinning it down to the table. "That! You keep tapping your fingers, and it's driving me crazy." I'm about to snap that *everything* she does drives me crazy, but her voice softens. "Sorry. I should have—You're probably freaking out right now, huh?"

Her hand is still resting on mine. I stare down at them. Does she even realize what her touch is doing to me? It's been eight years since we slept together, but right now, it almost feels like no time has gone by at all.

She smells the same, of cinnamon and apples.

Her fingers tighten on the back of my hand, her pupils darkening, and I flash back to that very first time, that very first kiss we had in the front seat of her car.

She was crying about Kozel. I wanted to find the guy and kick his ass for upsetting her so much, but instead I finally worked up the nerve to reach out. Tuck a wayward hair behind her ear, my fingertips caressing her smooth cheek.

"Nic, I—" she whispers now.

The door to the room swings opens with a bang, and we spring apart.

Sara appears, clothed in an orange jumpsuit, her hands cuffed in front of her body, and for a moment, I hate myself for what I was just thinking about Harriet. This isn't the time or the place.

I need to stop. Concentrate on what's important. Not the girl who abandoned me that summer but the sister who I grew up with, who used to make shadow puppets on the walls of my bedroom to make me laugh.

The cop settles Sara into the chair across from us, then retreats into the shadowy corner of the room. It's only been a couple days, but her hair is already greasy and limp, her nails bitten down to the quick. She looks like a prisoner.

A pang of pity hits me, so hard and sharp that I lose my breath. I have to get her out of here.

Then she opens her mouth. "Are you fucking serious, Nic? You brought *her*?"

Shit. "Wait, hold on. Let me explain, okay? She's here to help. She—"

Sara doesn't let me finish. "*Help?* Her mom accused me of murder!"

I lean forward onto the table. "Can I please explain?" The cop in the corner is watching our exchange with a frown.

Sara shakes her head. "Absolutely not. I have nothing to say to her. Her family thinks I'm guilty."

This is going pretty much how I expected. Which is why I wanted to talk to Sara alone.

"Sara, c'mon. Please. Harriet is—"

Harriet, doing the very thing she promised not to, interrupts. "Listen, Sara. I get it. If I were you, I wouldn't be thrilled to see me either. But I'm not here on behalf of my family. I'm a journalist. And I'm writing about what's happening to you for *Humans*. It's a national outlet that I worked for up in the city."

She sounds confident, controlled—totally different from the chaotic steamrolling back in the library.

"Thrilling," Sara says with an eye roll. I think about interrupting, but she's actually letting Harriet complete whole sentences, so I decide to see what happens.

Harriet continues, lowering her voice. "I want to show how you're being persecuted by the—" She tilts her head toward the cop in the corner, who's now intently focused on his phone. "I mean, we all know that if you were from George's side of the island, this wouldn't be happening to you."

"That's for damn sure," Sara says.

"But in order to write it well, I need your help." Harriet leans forward, her full attention on my sister. "Please," she adds.

There's a long silence.

"Okay," Sara says finally.

"Okay?" I say with surprise. Incredible. A surge of admiration rises in me. That was impressive. Harriet Baker just won over my sister. Not an easy undertaking.

"Okay!" Harriet claps her hands together, which is annoyingly adorable.

"What do you want to know?" Sara leans back in her chair, scowling. She's trying so hard to seem tough, but I saw how her mouth wobbled at the corner when she first sat down. The way her hands shook. The pitch of her voice—a whole register lower than normal, like she's trying to signal she's still in control.

Harriet glances over like she's finally asking my permission to keep going. I'm not about to stop her now. I nod.

"Let's start at the beginning," she says. "You left the party early, correct?"

Sara nods.

"Right. And what did you do after you left?"

Sara rubs her forehead. "I don't know? Umm...well, I didn't have a ride, so I headed out to the main road, but it started pouring after I'd only made it a couple blocks. I waited it out in an alcove, thinking about..." She shakes her head. "Stuff. I decided I should probably apologize for what had happened, so once the rain let up, I walked back. Your parents had given us the gate code, so I decided to go around back and in through the basement door. I didn't want to risk running into anyone. But as soon as I got to the beach...I saw..." She swallows. "Him. The body."

"Did anyone see you while you were out walking?"

"I don't think so. Some people passed me in cars, but I have no idea how you'd track them down, and I doubt they'd remember me. The weather was horrible."

"Okay, well, did *you* see anything suspicious?"

"Like what?" Sara asks with a frown.

Harriet leans forward. "A car speeding away? Someone hurrying from the house?"

"Nope."

"How about on the beach? Anything weird there?"

"No. Outside of a fucking dead body, of course. I *wish* I had. I wish I'd gotten there ten minutes before, when that fucker was getting stabbed. I wish I'd—"

"*Sara!*" I cut her off, afraid she's about to say *I wish I'd been the one to stab him.*

"What, Nic?" Sara snaps. "Jesus, will you let me talk? I was going to say: I wish I'd seen who did it. Then I wouldn't be in this mess, would I?"

"No," Harriet says. "You would not."

"Right. You get it," Sara says to her.

Harriet nods sagely, and I roll my eyes.

Sara continues, "I mean, this whole thing is ridiculous. The cops think it's some big clue that one of my knives killed him, which is so stupid. I'm sorry, but it's not like the kitchen was locked down. Any number of people could have swiped it! And of course my fingerprints were on it. It was *my* knife!" She takes a deep breath. "And let's not even talk about the stupid LinkedIn comments they found, which I posted about a million years ago. It's the most absurd, horrible coincidence.

I didn't know the guy! All I knew was that those assholes forced our restaurant to shut down! And now they're saying that someone overheard us arguing in the basement shortly before the kitchen fight—"

The last bit pulls me upright. I don't remember hearing anything about that.

I interrupt. "An argument?"

"Yup." She rubs at her eyebrow, another of her tells. "Apparently, someone heard George shouting at someone down there, and of course, they're trying to say it was me. Which is impossible! I was in the kitchen the whole fucking time."

My mouth drops open. "*What?* Either Mom and I were in there with you pretty much the entire afternoon. Why hasn't anyone asked us about that?"

"I don't know, Nic!" she says.

The guard's head jerks up at the volume of her voice.

Sara holds up a hand. "Sorry. I'm calm. I'm calm." Once he's focused back on his phone, she whispers, "I don't know, and there's nothing I can do about it. Do you really think this article could help me?"

"I do," Harriet says with a determined nod. "What you just said, Sara...that's exactly what I'm talking about—why *haven't* the cops asked about your whereabouts during that argument? They should have asked around, confirmed whether it was you. Because if it wasn't—"

"It wasn't!" Sara barks, and the cop looks up again.

Harriet backtracks. "No, no. I know. I'm sorry. I misspoke. Let me rephrase—*since* it wasn't, figuring out who it *was* seems important to me. Doesn't it to you? If we can, their case against you will fall apart."

"We're going to do everything in our power to get you out of here," I add.

The corner of Sara's mouth wobbles again. I want to take her hand, but I can't, so I say something I hope might help.

"I love you, Sara. Everything is going to be okay."

As soon as it's out of my mouth, I realize how weak it sounds, and from her expression, it's clear she believes it as much as I do.

CHAPTER TWENTY

HARRIET

September 6

7:32 p.m.

Kozel's waiting in the foyer of Piccolo when I walk in the door. He's wearing jeans and a light gray sweater I swear he had back in high school.

"Harriet, good to see you," he says, going in for a hug before awkwardly switching to a handshake when I don't move. "I think our table is ready if you are?"

"Sure."

We follow the hostess to a table tucked into the far back corner. I've been dreading this dinner, but seeing Sara in jail today reminded me what really matters. This isn't about what happened back in high school. If Kozel will tell me anything that could help her, I need it.

Plus, it hasn't even been seventy-two hours, and Frankie's already on my back asking for a progress report. I spent a large part of the afternoon working on the piece but only managed to eke out a rough opening paragraph:

Murder in Paradise

Logan Island, NJ, a tight-knit community of 1,500 full-time residents, was rocked last week when one of its prominent residents, George George—a former Manhattan real estate mogul—was found stabbed to death on the private beach outside his home. The police were quick to arrest local chef Sara Allbright, claiming the murder was an act of revenge.

It's not great. Dry. Boring. Regurgitating facts that have already been reported numerous times. Which is all the more reason I have to get through this meal without punching my ex-boyfriend in the face—which will take every ounce of my self-restraint.

I slide into the chair across from him.

"I have to admit, Harriet. After the other day, I was surprised to hear from you," Kozel says as he picks up his menu.

"What?" I say, feigning shock. "Why?"

He gives me a skeptical look. "You didn't exactly seem thrilled when we ran into each other. But regardless, I'm glad you texted me. I would love to explain why I did what I did after high school—"

"What are you having?" I interrupt. What a self-centered prick, thinking I even *care* about that. It's been eight years! I'm over it.

I mean, have I wondered late at night when I can't sleep why my first real boyfriend turned out to be such a dickhead? Sure.

But do I want to talk about it? With *him*? Nope. No, I do not. I want to pump him for information and get the hell out of here.

Kozel tries again. "Harriet, could I—"

I glare at him over the top of my menu. "No."

He rubs a hand over his scruff. "You're exactly the same, you know that?"

He is *such* an ass. I am absolutely not the same. I'm much more bitter and broken.

"I lived in New York for almost eight years, Kozel. You think that didn't change me?"

He shrugs and snaps his menu shut. "What brought you back here anyway?"

"Life" is all I'm willing to say.

He pauses, water glass halfway to his lips. "Wow, Harriet. So illuminating."

"What brought *you* back?" I shoot back, even though I promised myself I wouldn't ask him any personal questions. "After you left like you did, I didn't think you'd *ever* come back, but I guess I was wrong. About a lot of things."

"As I said, I would like to explain that if you'll let me."

"No, thank you," I reply.

"But you just asked—"

"Yeah, sorry." I wave a hand. "I forgot—I don't care why you're back. It was a hundred years ago."

He shifts in his seat. "All right. Fair enough. I suppose I deserve that. But I'd still like to—"

I interrupt again. "What *I'd* like is to hear about your work as a police detective."

"My work as—" He frowns. "Harriet, if this is about your stepfather, we're working hard to get his killer behind bars. Permanently. Her arraignment is in a couple days. It's a start. You have to be patient."

"Did you guys look at anyone else before filing charges against her?"

"Anyone else?" He sounds confused.

"Well, as you probably know, someone overheard George having an argument in the basement shortly before he was killed, but Sara says she never left the kitchen."

He narrows his eyes. "When did you—Are you *writing* something about this?"

I'm stunned into silence. How did he guess that? I was going to tell him—*obviously* I was going to tell him, or our conversation wouldn't be on the record—but I had planned to ease him into the idea of it. Maybe slip it into conversation after getting him nice and drunk.

"Possibly?" I hedge.

A bread basket arrives, and we both fall silent. Distraction by carbs. Thank god.

As soon as we're alone, Kozel starts interrogating me. "Harriet. Is this why you asked me to dinner? Because of an article? I believe in the free press, of *course* I do, but...aren't you a little too close to it? Either way," he continues, "as I am sure you're aware, I'm not at liberty to talk about the case. Not even with you," he adds as I open my mouth to argue. "Plus, what are you even planning to write about that hasn't already been covered thoroughly by local media?"

"I'm…I'm just writing about what happened," I say feebly.

He raises a single skeptical brow. I used to be so jealous that he could do that. Right now, though, I want to shave it off his face.

"George used to live up in the city," I tell him. "He's a known entity. Plus, my editor *likes* the personal connection. And also…"

Do I go there? Do I dare say *Also, I don't think Sara's guilty? Also, did you even look at other suspects? Also, are you a corrupt cop?*

Maybe not that last one.

The waiter arrives to take our drink order and saves me from having to finish my sentence.

"A glass of pinot noir, thanks," Kozel says. "Harriet?"

If he won't ask my questions sober…

I pick up the wine list.

"Why don't we get a bottle?"

He shrugs. "Sure, why not? It's a special occasion of sorts. A bottle of the pinot okay?"

I nod. A bottle of grain alcohol would be fine by me so long as it got him talking.

He puts in the order.

An hour later, his cheeks are flushed, and he's started to slur his words. He's had far more than half the bottle. I've been topping up his drink whenever he's distracted—a frequent occurrence. An extraordinary number of people have stopped by our table to talk to him, and we've barely had a moment alone. He's been asked about everything from a broken stoplight off Main Street to whether George's murder was actually a mob hit.

"Sorry for all the interruptions," Kozel says after his old high school football coach walks away. He just spent five minutes asking for advice about a speeding ticket. "Now you know why I don't spend much time on the island. Once I started working at the sheriff's department, people started hitting me up for favors." He throws back the rest of his wine and sets his glass down. "On that note, I gotta get going. Early morning tomorrow."

Shit. Dinner's over, and I haven't even had a chance to bring up Sara's case again. If he leaves now, this will have been a huge waste of time.

I smile. "Or we could get another drink?"

"I'd love to another time, but I really do need to get going."

I brace myself for what I'm about to say. The very thing I've been trying to avoid. "I'll let you explain. Why you, you know, left. Back then." My stomach churns at the thought.

He pauses. "Really? Without interrupting or making snide asides?"

I swallow. "Yes."

"Promise?"

I struggle to keep my eyes from rolling backward into my head. "Yes."

He grins. "Okay. One more drink."

CHAPTER TWENTY-ONE

HARRIET

September 6

9:39 p.m.

Kozel is stumbling as we leave the restaurant, so I steer him away from his car and into an Uber.

"I really am sorry, Har," he says. He stops by the open door of the car and turns back with his lips puckered.

Is he trying to *kiss* me? Jesus. "Time to get to bed."

"But Harriet—"

I push him away. "I'll see you later, Adam."

He blinks blearily, then climbs into the waiting car. As the Uber pulls away from the curb, his window lowers. "I'll call you," he shouts.

I give him a thumbs-up, thankful that he probably won't remember saying that in the morning. In fact, my hope is that he won't remember most of what he said once we paid our bill and moved to a quiet corner at the bar.

For someone so desperate to explain himself, his reason for ghosting me was extremely mediocre: all *if I'd told you I was leaving, it would have made it impossible to actually go*. Blah blah fucking blah. Basically, he was too big of a wimp to tell me he didn't think we had a future together.

But once that was finally over, I got some good stuff. Some *very* good stuff. Unfortunately, Kozel was still sober enough to say it was all off the record, but even so, it confirmed what Nic and I suspected: There are other people who might have killed George, and the cops ignored it.

Apparently, he and his partner wanted to keep digging rather than press charges against Sara, but they were overruled by Sharkey and some other higher-up. The next thing he and his partner knew, the case was pushed through to the prosecutor, and Sara was formally charged.

Kozel told me their decision was political, that they wanted the case shut as quickly as possible, but he wouldn't—or couldn't—tell me why. Which begs the question: What the hell is the LIPD trying to hide?

I asked who he and Jones had on their list of suspects, but he wouldn't give me any names, even after I plied him with yet another glass of wine. Said he'd get fired. Which I suppose is true.

Once I'm in an Uber, I text Nic to fill him in, but he still hasn't replied by the time I get home. The house is dark, my mother either out (unlikely) or drugged up in her bedroom (far more likely).

I make my way to my room, drop my bag onto the bed, and head into the bathroom. I'm halfway through my skincare routine when the sound of glass shattering breaks the silence of the night.

I freeze, cotton pad halfway to my face.

What the hell was that? I grab my phone off the counter and shoot off a text to my mom.

Was that you?

I wait and wait, but she doesn't respond. I call her, but it rings out to voicemail.

My face is white in the mirror: a bunny caught in the headlights of a car. I should call 911. But what if it's nothing? Or should I text Maggie? She always knows what to do. But what if she insists on coming over and there's someone out there? She could end up hurt. Or dead.

I'm staring at the phone, weighing my options, when a text from Nic appears.

How was dinner?

I hit the Call button.

"For someone who claims to hate talking on the phone," he says by way of greeting, "you sure love calling people."

"I think there's someone in the house," I say in one breath.

"You know—wait. *What?*" he says, voice shifting from teasing to concerned.

"I'm in the bathroom, and I just heard a big crash down the hall—" I choke on the word.

"What kind of crash? Did you call the cops?"

"No. What if it's nothing? It could just be my mother, stumbling around. Or, I don't know. Something that fell off a wall. I could be overreacting."

"I'm coming over."

"No, no. It's fine!" I say, even though I'd give anything for him to be here right now. But—again—what if I'm wrong?

Or worse. What if I'm *right*?

"I'm already out the door. I'll be there in seven minutes. Stay on the phone."

I hurry into my bedroom and press my ear against the door. It's quiet. I put my hand on the knob. If I go out there, there's probably less chance of something happening to me than to someone coming in cold, right? I can be quiet, whereas Nic's going to drive up in a car, headlights and all. Which means I should go out there.

"Don't leave your room," he barks, like he knows exactly what I'm thinking.

His tone irks me. "Stop being so bossy."

"You need to call the police, Harriet."

"Fine. But first I'm going to take a quick look. Just check out the situation."

"*Harriet!* Stay in your room!"

I've never been good at following orders. I drop the phone by my side and crack the door, edging my way into the dark hall.

"Mom?" I hiss.

The sound of the ocean is my only reply.

The sound of the ocean... Why can I hear the ocean so clearly from here?

It takes me a moment to realize it's coming from the direction of George's office. My throat goes dry. What if the sound I heard was his window breaking?

Nic's voice screams from the phone. "Harriet? What the *hell* are you doing?"

I put it up to my ear. "I'm in the hall."

"Christ, Harriet. Go back to your bedroom! I'll be there in four—"

I drop the phone again. Take a step forward. Another. Then I hear it: papers rustling, a cough through the door.

My heart stops. There's someone inside George's office.

What if they find me out here? I should go back to my room. But what if they're in there, stealing valuable evidence?

I bring my phone back up. "Someone's in George's office."

"*Go back to your room!*" Nic shouts in my ear. "I'm calling 911."

"Absolutely not! What if they're stealing something that would clear Sara?"

"Harriet. Do not—I repeat—*do not* do whatever you're thinking about doing. I'll be there in two minutes. Could you please—Jesus! I just blew through a red light. You're being an idiot!"

"I gotta go." I hang up and take a step toward the office. "Hello?" I call.

The shuffling inside stops, and silence hangs in the air, thick, suffocating, winding down my throat. Then a loud scrape, the roar of the ocean, a thud, a grunt of pain.

And footsteps. Coming straight toward me.

All the fear I've been pushing down rises, and I take off back to my room, slamming the door. I lock it behind me and lean against it, the pounding of my heart in my ears all I can hear.

Nic's right. I'm an idiot.

Once my breathing slows, I press myself back against the door.

Silence.

Then my phone buzzes, and I jump about twelve feet into the air.

I'm here. Front door locked—how do I get inside??

I direct him to the spare key, typing fast, misspelling words.

Found it. I'm in. Where are you?

My bedroom. Back hallway, last door on the right. Be careful

I brought a weapon

I'm typing a response when there's a soft knock against the door.

"It's me."

I twist the lock, crack the door, and there he is. Nic, his green eyes tight with worry. He came all this way to help me. No one's ever done something like that for me before.

"Are you okay?" he asks in a low voice.

"Yeah. Did you hear anything?"

He raises a judgmental eyebrow. "No. Your little hallway stunt must have scared them off."

"I didn't want them stealing evidence!"

"You could have gotten yourself killed, Harriet." He sounds decidedly unhappy at that prospect.

"You'd miss me, huh?" I say as I join him out in the hallway.

He rolls his eyes. "Don't flatter yourself." A silver metal object resembling a hammer dangles from his hand.

I point to it. "Is that a cooking mallet?"

"Yeah. I told you I brought a weapon."

"Uh-huh."

"Harriet?" My mother stands a dozen feet away wearing a long nightgown, ghostly in the shadowy hall. Of course. *Now* she wakes up. Classic. She rubs her eyes. "What's going on? Who is that?"

She's going to flip if she realizes it's Nic Allbright.

As if reading my mind, he ducks behind me.

"My friend...Sam. From high school. You remember him." I'm banking on the fact that she barely noticed my friends back then.

"Of course," she says, brushing a hand through her hair. "Hello, Sam."

Nic raises a hand in greeting. "Uh, yeah. Hey."

She flicks the hall lights on, the sudden brightness blinding.

"I thought I heard shouting," she says. "Was that you?"

"There were noises. From George's office."

"Noises? But it's locked."

"There was this big crash... I tried to call you, but you didn't pick up, so Ni—I mean, Sam came over. We think someone broke in."

"*What?*"

"I called the cops," Nic offers.

"Where's the key?" I ask her. "We need to get in there."

"Absolutely not!" she cries. "I'm not letting you get yourself killed!"

"Mom—" I'm interrupted by the wail of a siren out on the driveway.

She twists. "That must be the police!" She disappears around the bend of the hallway.

"Are you okay?" Nic asks softly. His eyes are worried. Soft.

All of a sudden, I feel like crying.

I run my tongue along my teeth a few times before I respond. "All good. Let's go make sure that woman doesn't scare off the cops."

CHAPTER TWENTY-TWO

HARRIET

September 6
10:18 p.m.

After greeting the police in hysterics, my mom finally calms down enough to locate the key and unlock the office door.

"Stay here." Officer Delgado disappears into the room with his partner, Officer Raskin, at his heels.

"Window's shattered," Raskin calls. "Looks like somebody kicked it in. My guess? They entered that way, but they're long gone now."

Delgado reappears around the corner, motioning to my mother. "Mrs. George, if you could come in here and take a look around? We need to know if anything's missing."

My mother hesitates. "Are you sure they're gone?" she asks with a tremble in her voice.

"Yes, ma'am," Delgado says. "No one here but the two of us."

She walks in, and Nic and I follow.

My breath catches. Behind George's desk is a gaping hole where the window used to be. Shards of broken glass are strewn across the carpet like shrapnel.

Someone did this. Someone was in here while I was washing my face on the other side of the wall.

My mother heads to the desk, opening drawers, rifling through his papers. I hold my breath; did she know about that letter from Patterson? What if she realizes it's gone?

"Anything missing?" Raskin asks after a moment.

My mom straightens, shaking her head. "I don't think so, but I can't say for sure. I don't know exactly what was in there."

I guess George's shadiness is working in my favor. I turn back to the cops, ready for them to start their forensic examination of the room.

But Raskin just nods. "Great. In that case, my partner and I will draw up a report, and then you can get back to your night."

He can't be serious. "A *report*? What about fingerprinting the room?"

"Ma'am, long time ago, the department decided processing standard B and Es for latent prints wasn't worth the time or resources. Most burglars these days are smart enough to wear gloves."

I glare at him. Did he really just *ma'am* me? I'm only twenty-six years old. "You're kidding, right? My stepfather was just murdered right outside this house! Whoever broke in is probably the person who killed him!"

My mom looks at me like I'm Benedict Arnold. "The person who *killed* him? What are you saying, Harriet?"

Officer Delgado scratches his balding head. "Ma'am, you are aware the person who killed Mr. George is behind bars?"

"First of all," I say, my voice shaking with frustration, "she is just a suspect. She hasn't been charged with anything. And second, don't you think this break-in means you have the *wrong person*?"

"Harriet!" my mother cries. "That girl threatened George! She ran from the police! You seriously think—"

Delgado puts a hand on my shoulder, and it's all I can do not to shake it right back off. "Look, Ms...."

"Baker," I say through gritted teeth, stepping away from him.

"Right. Ms. Baker." He stuffs his errant hand into the pocket of his pants. "As much as we appreciate your *theories,* Sara Allbright is set to be arraigned in two days. At which point, she *will* be charged. The fact that she hasn't been yet is simply a formality. What happened here tonight has all the signs of a straightforward break-in. Mr. George was a successful businessman with a high net worth, and the case has been all over the internet. Somebody saw an easy target—a house with no man around—"

My eye starts twitching yet again. At this rate, I'm going to develop a permanent tremor.

"—and decided to see what they could grab." He hacks a cough into his fist. "Or it could have been one of those true-crime weirdos who like to play detective. Think they're smarter than the police. It's stupid and dangerous, but there you have it."

"Are you really not going to do anything?" Nic speaks for the first time. His voice is so soft I can hardly hear him even though he's right next to me.

Delgado turns. "What's that, son?"

For the first time, Nic steps into the light of the room. "Someone broke in—smashed the window, scared the shit out of Harriet. And all you're going to do is fill out a report? That's fucking ridiculous!"

"Son, let me remind you, you're speaking to an officer of the law," Delgado says. "Watch your tone."

My mom lets out a screech, pointing at Nic. "I knew I recognized you! Out in the hall, I thought I was mistaken. That Harriet wouldn't go that far..." She turns on me, eyes ablaze. "You let him into my *house*? After what his sister did? Is this how much you hate me?"

Hate her? I'm used to her histrionics, but this is over the line, even for her.

"He came over to help me!"

"He's the one who broke in!" my mother screeches.

Nic takes a step backward, shock blooming across his face.

"Someone breaks into George's office, and right after, he appears out of thin air?" my mother continues. "That's no coincidence. He probably did it to throw suspicion off his sister!"

"Mother!"

My mother ignores me. "Arrest him!" she shouts.

I can't take any more of this. "Stop it. *I* called him! Okay? I got home, heard some noises, and called him—"

She recoils. "You *called* him?" she says, like that's the most offensive thing she's ever heard.

"—and he offered to come over."

"For all you know, he was already here! I want him arrested immediately!"

"I was in my apartment when she called," Nic says in a flat voice.

"Not to mention," I add, "do you really think he would have answered if he was lurking around outside?"

Officer Delgado clears his throat. "While the timing is certainly coincidental, what we need to do right now is get our paperwork in order so we can leave you to your night."

"But—" my mother says.

"We understand your concerns, Mrs. George. We really do. But we can't arrest him—"

My mom starts to argue, and he holds up a hand.

"*Although* we can't arrest him, we're happy to escort him off the premises if you'd like that."

"Are you serious?" I say. "I *invited* him here!"

Nic's jaw is tight, his expression stormy. "It's fine, Harriet. I'll see myself out."

"Nic, I'm so sorry—"

But before I can finish the sentence, he's gone.

CHAPTER TWENTY-THREE

HARRIET

September 11

9:08 a.m.

Our investigation has stalled. I haven't really talked to Nic since he stormed out of my mom's house, not for lack of trying. He texted after Sara's arraignment to say she'd been officially charged and denied bail, but when I called him, he didn't pick up.

I'm trying to give him space, but it's been five days, and the deadline Frankie gave me is looming, keeping me up at night. She's sent me several emails asking for pages, but I've ignored them—not the right move if I ever want to get my job back. At this point, I'm starting to worry I'll never get the damn thing written. My *Grey Gardens* nightmare is coming closer and closer to fruition with every passing day.

I've tried to plow forward solo, but it's felt like hitting my head against a concrete block. Kozel has clammed up, pissed that he ran his mouth while drunk. Patterson's back from her vacation (at least she didn't go on the lam), but every time I stop by the library to talk to her, Mindy intercepts me like her personal bodyguard.

I even stopped by the Yacht Club a couple times to see if I could find that caterer, but he wasn't working.

This morning, I woke up frustrated as hell and sent Nic a message begging him to come to George's memorial at the club today. Actually *begging*, which I *never* normally do.

He has to come. Patterson will be there and, according to a bartender I talked to the other night, so will Matthew.

Two birds, one Nic and Harriet–size stone.

He finally responds as I'm walking into the ballroom with my mother.

I cannot show up at your stepfather's memorial.

Your mom will try to have me arrested.

Again.

He has a point, but also…

Matthew and Patterson will be here. You have to

No

PLEASE. I cannot do this alone.

There's no reply, so I add:

Sara needs you.

The three bubbles appear.

Not cool to invoke my sister's name, Harriet

Well she does

There's a pause, which my mother fills by ordering me to make sure the staff is folding the bar napkins in the way George always liked. "In thirds, not in quarters," she says, as if anyone gives two shits about it but her.

I keep the thought to myself. "Sure, okay."

I'm about to walk away when I hear a loud sniff. She's gazing out at the terrace overlooking the ocean.

"George asked me to marry him out there." Her voice wobbles. "On the veranda."

Suddenly, I feel like a real asshole. Sure, my mom drives me crazy, and yes, George wasn't my favorite person, but still. She *loved* him. I've been so caught up with the case that I'm not even sure I've said how sorry I am that she lost him.

"Mom…are you okay? If you need to talk—"

She blinks like she just remembered where she is. Her lips tighten. "No, Harriet. I do not need to *talk*. What I *need* is for you to check on the napkins. For the love of god, can you just do what you're asked for once in your life?"

My throat tightens. "Yeah." I hurry away before she can spot the dumb tears that have popped into my eyes.

Nic responds as I'm walking up to the bar.

Fine I'll be there around eleven. Friend will let me in the back. See you then

Suddenly, the day seems brighter.

I will see you then!!!

I shove my phone back into my pocket and turn to the bar. The bartender is crouched behind it, organizing bottles.

"Hey," I say, peering down at him. "Do you mind—"

He looks up, and I lose my train of thought. I'm 99 percent sure this is Matthew.

"Can I help you?" He stands, wiping his hands with a soggy towel. The same strange feeling I had at my party passes over me, like I know him somehow.

"My mom's hosting this event? And she had a very specific request. About napkins."

He throws the towel down on the bar top, looking vaguely annoyed to be interrupted by something so silly. "Okay?"

Screw the napkins. I change course. "Listen, you work with Nic Allbright, right?"

"Yeah. Why?"

"You guys were catering my birthday party when that guy"—I

point to the giant photo of George my mom propped against the far wall—"died."

His cheeks redden. "Oh. Right. Hey."

"Hey. Thanks for working yet another party thrown by my mother. Hope no one dies at this one."

My poor attempt at humor falls flat; he doesn't even crack a smile. "Yeah. No problem. I have to finish setting up, so if you want to explain about the napkins?"

"I—okay." I show him what she wants done.

"She wants me to refold *all* of them in thirds?" He shakes his head, like he's used to fielding bizarre requests of club members. "All right. Sure. I can do that."

"Cool, thanks," I say, glancing over my shoulder as my mom screeches something across the room.

"So about George—" I say, turning back to Matthew, but he's gone. I catch sight of the back of his shirt disappearing through the doors to the kitchen.

I think about chasing after him, but before I can, my mom grabs me, ordering me to handle yet another menial task like I'm her assistant, not her daughter.

The party starts uneventfully, the room filling with George's friends and enemies.

Steven and Maggie show up a half hour in, rescuing me from a painful conversation with my mother and Mayor DiPetrio.

Steven kisses me on the cheek by way of greeting. "Har, are you aware there is a very attractive man staring at you?"

I pull back. "Who?"

He flicks his eyes in the direction of the bar. "You really didn't notice? The bartender can't take his eyes off of you."

I glance over. Sure enough, Matthew is staring at me. When he sees me looking, he quickly turns away.

Steven and I don't always have the same taste, but I can usually at least understand where he's coming from. "You think *that* guy is hot?"

"Yeah? I mean, he's objectively attractive. Like, Maggie, right? I'm not crazy?"

"He's hot, yeah," she confirms.

"Okay, to each their own I guess?" I say as I wonder if the two of them need glasses. "That's Matthew. He was at my birthday party."

"Oh!" Maggie's eyes widen. "The hot cater waiter. What's he doing here?"

"He works here part-time. According to Nic—"

"*Excuse* me?" Steven interrupts. "Did you just say 'according to Nic'? As in *Martin's* Nic? Since when do you two speak?"

I haven't told Steven or Maggie anything about the article or our investigation. They'd lose their shit if they knew I was writing for Frankie again. Plus, Steven might slip up and tell Martin, who has friends inside the LIPD. Things could get all sorts of awkward.

"Um. Well. We ran into each other at the library—"

"The *library*?" Steven says, like he's never heard me say the word before.

"Yes. The *library*," I say with an eye roll. "You may have forgotten—I'm a writer? I'm literate. I read books."

He holds up a hand. "Okay, okay, I get it. Sorry."

"Right. Anyway, we got to talking."

"About some random person who works for his mom? How would that even come up?"

Oh my god, why is he grilling me about this? "I don't know, Steven! God, what are you, a detective? Am I on trial? My point is Nic mentioned it. Okay?"

Maggie grins. "Nic's cute. He has that whole nice-guy-but-also-really-hot thing going on. I totally ship you two."

"You know," Steven adds, "from what I gathered from Martin, he's also been half in love with you for about a decade."

My stomach lurches.

Maggie and Steven have no idea what happened back in high school. My brief relationship with Nic (if you can even call it that) isn't something I publicized. I was heartbroken and rebounding, and even in my state of grief, I could see that what I was doing was pretty fucked up.

I mean, could I see that Nic was falling for me in a way I couldn't reciprocate because my heart had splintered in two?

Yes.

Did I care? Unfortunately, not really. I just wanted a warm body to quiet the pain of Kozel's disappearance.

This is all to say: There's no way he still *likes* me. Not after how I treated him. Sure, he seems less overtly pissed, but he's made it clear he thinks I'm a self-centered rich girl.

Something must have gotten twisted as the story was passed down the chain. Martin misunderstood Nic. Or Steven misunderstood Martin. Nothing beyond that.

Do I wish it was true?

The question floats, annoying, through the edge of my mind.

I swallow. I need to put a stop to this line of thinking immediately. Our relationship is based on a shared goal. Nothing more, nothing less. The last thing I should do is complicate it.

"Are you okay?" Maggie asks.

"I need a drink!" I declare, mostly to change the subject.

We head across the room—filled with many of the same people in attendance at my birthday party.

Mayor DiPetrio. Mick Sharkey. George's business partner, Luke Dalio. Even the old high school football coach. But there's no sign of Barbara Patterson.

I'm starting to worry she might not show.

"Can I get you something?" Matthew asks when we're at the bar.

"Champs for me, thanks," Steven says.

"I'm good with water," Maggie says. "I have to study later."

As I'm ordering, Barbara Patterson sweeps into the ballroom wearing a purple dress with puffed sleeves and a silver bangle belt. An outfit appropriate for a birthday party or wedding—not a memorial. If I had to guess, I'd say it's one last enormous F U to George.

Mindy enters on her tail, dressed more fittingly in a short black sheath dress. They stop a few feet into the room, and Mindy whispers something in Patterson's ear.

Steven nudges me. "Harriet."

I tear my eyes away from the librarians and find Matthew staring at me.

"What do you want?" he asks.

“Oh, sorry. Just a glass of champagne.”

Matthew pours the drinks, and I watch Patterson and Mindy make their way through the room, stopping every few feet to chat with guests.

“Here you go.” Matthew slides three glasses to us. “Anything else?”

I grab my flute, fiddling with its stem. I’ll ask him my questions, then I can catch Patterson once she’s settled. “Nic mentioned you’re new to the island. You just moved here in August?”

Matthew scratches the back of his neck. “Yup.”

“What brought you? Family?”

“Just looking for something different.”

“Different?” I ask. “How so?”

He shrugs. “I don’t know. Mostly, I didn’t have a lot going on.”

“But you moved here in August.”

“Yeah? So?”

“So...*why*?” This is like trying to pump water from a brick wall.

“I just *told* you!” He’s growing visibly agitated by my questions. A sign of guilt?

“Did you and George—”

A throat clears behind me, sharp and impatient, and I realize a long line is forming behind me. Oh. Maybe that’s why Matthew looks so stressed.

I force a laugh. “Sorry. We’ll talk later.”

“Great,” he says, like he’d rather do anything but.

“What the hell was that?” Steven asks as we walk away, my face hot with embarrassment.

"Nothing. Never mind. So how are things going with Martin?" As hoped, the question distracts him.

We stop in the middle of the room, and he starts giving Maggie and me a play-by-play of his burgeoning relationship. As he talks, I try to pinpoint Patterson's whereabouts. Mindy's over by the veranda doors talking to some women I don't recognize, but Patterson's nowhere to be found.

Where did she go?

I'm about to excuse myself to go look for her when a hand lands on my arm.

"Harriet, where have you been? I have been trying to find you for *ages*."

My mother.

"Hi, Mrs. George," Maggie says. "I'm so sorry for your loss."

My mother ignores her. "Harriet, the bar has run out of seltzer." She says this like I'm personally responsible for the shortage.

I take a deep breath through my nose. "How can I help?"

She heaves a sigh. "*Obviously*, you should find the manager. Tell her that she *must* find *more*!"

She's grieving, I remind myself.

"What's her name?"

"Ella," she says, then walks away.

I drain my drink. "Sorry. Gotta take care of this."

"Do you need help?" Maggie asks gently. They're well aware how my mom can be.

"Thanks, but I got it." I work my way back through the crowd to the bar. Matthew has disappeared, replaced by a girl who can't be a day over eighteen.

"Where's Matthew?" I ask her.

"I don't know!" Her voice cracks like she's about to burst into tears. "He said he needed a break, but that was twenty minutes ago! I'm supposed to be waitressing, not bartending. I don't know how to make drinks! We're out of seltzer, and people keep yelling at me!"

"Is there more?" I ask.

"Yeah, back in the kitchen, but I can't exactly go get it. Look at all these people!"

"I'll see if I can find it, okay?"

"Ohmygod thank you so much. And if you find Matthew, *please* send him back. I didn't sign up for this shit!"

I turn toward the kitchen, but just past the edge of the bar, a hand catches me by the sleeve.

"Harriet, hello," Luke Dalio says. He's wearing a gray suit and a somber smile.

I stop with a sigh. So close and yet so far.

I've only spoken to Luke a few times, but he's always struck me as mostly decent. I've never understood what he was doing working with George.

"Hi," I say with forced politeness.

"It's crazy, what happened. To George," he adds.

"Yeah. Awful."

"How's your mom holding up?"

"She's okay. Actually, she's over there," I say, pointing to her. "I'm sure she'd love to chat about George."

He nods. "I haven't had a chance to speak with her yet. I'll go say hello. It was good to see you, Harriet."

"Sure, yeah. You too." I hurry away.

The kitchen is busy with noise: waiters filling trays with food, the crash of pots and pans, cooks barking orders. I ask one of the waiters if he knows where the seltzer would be, and he looks at me like I have two heads.

The next person barks at me to get out of their way, and that's when I decide maybe I should just find it myself.

CHAPTER TWENTY-FOUR

HARRIET

September 11

11:00 a.m.

As I'm rounding a corner in the back hallway, I smash into something hard.

"You can't help but run into things, huh?" Nic says with a shake of his head. He's wearing a bemused smile and a dark green shirt that matches his eyes with a hoodie tied around his waist.

"Only *you*." I swipe my phone from the floor, heart fluttering. I tell myself it's because of the stress of the kitchen and my brisk walk through it.

Nic raises a brow. "Only me?"

"I mean, your chest is very broad—" I force myself to shut up before anything even more incriminating can come out of my mouth. *Your chest is very broad?* What's next? *Your thighs are so thick? Your jaw is so perfectly chiseled? I want to run my fingers down it and—*

He clears his throat; I can't read his expression. Thankfully, he changes the subject. "What are you doing back here? Shouldn't you be out with the guests?"

"I was, but I'm trying to find some seltzer. But instead, I ran into you."

"Right," Nic says. "Me."

He falls quiet, and I scramble for something to say that isn't brutally awkward this time.

"Patterson just got here."

This perks him up a bit. "She's here?"

I nod.

"Well, that's good news at least. So what's our plan?"

"Our plan?" I repeat, gnawing on my bottom lip. It's been almost a week since I've seen him. What if I say the wrong thing? I don't want to scare him off.

He sighs. "Harriet, you forced me to come here, and you don't have a *plan*?"

"I mean, I've been doing stuff!" I say defensively. "I asked Matthew some questions, but his answers were really unhelpful—"

"Sounds about right," Nic mutters.

"—and Patterson just showed up. I was about to go talk to her when my mother forced me into this stupid hunt for sparkling water. I'm sorry about the other night, I really am. I hate that she did that when you just trying to help."

Tears have sprung into the corners of my eyes.

"Hey." Nic's voice softens. "That wasn't your fault. I know that."

"But you're pissed."

He rubs his forehead. "I'm not so much pissed as...I needed to regroup. Did I want to come today? No, not really. I can't go talk to Patterson with your mom out there. I looked through Matthew's file yesterday but found nothing suspicious. Same when I googled him. Our leads are weak, and Sara's going to be transferred to that other jail on Monday. I'm—"

He cuts off, blowing out a breath.

Without thinking, I step forward, closing the gap between us. Our eyes lock, and my breath hitches. God, he's beautiful.

Look away, I tell myself, but I can't. Or maybe I don't want to.

Our faces inch closer, and my body flushes with heat. I've wanted this since my party—maybe even before that. I remember how good it was back then—

There's a loud shout from the kitchen, breaking the moment in two.

Nic pulls back, clearing his throat. "Well. We're both frustrated. Let's table that and find—what did you say you're looking for?"

I swallow as disappointment fizzes through me. "The seltzer. You work in catering. Where would it be?"

He shrugs. "The walk-in fridge?"

"Do you happen to know where it is?"

"I do." We curve around a bend, and Nic stops, gesturing to a closed metal door. "This is it. I worked at the club briefly while we were building the business. And who knows?" he adds in a mutter. "I might need the job again soon."

He yanks the handle, and the door swings open. I step inside, shivering as the cold hits my skin.

Nic flicks on the overhead light and sucks in a breath. "What the—"

A giant metal shelving unit lies broken in the center of the room. Cartons of food are strewn across the floor, split open, bloodred sauces staining the gray linoleum bright.

Nic lets out a low whistle. "What a mess."

That's when I see her.

Purple dress twisted. Silver bangle belt snapped in two. Eyes wide open, staring blankly at the ceiling. Neck twisted at an impossible angle.

"Holy shit," Nic says. "Is that—"

Barbara Patterson.

CHAPTER TWENTY-FIVE

NIC

September 11
11:32 a.m.

Barbara Patterson is *dead*.

I drag my hands through my hair again and again.

Dead.

Dead, dead, dead.

Two bodies in as many weeks. So much for sleep.

"Are you okay?" Harriet asks for a third time.

We're sitting at a table in the back hallway, surrounded by club employees. The cops arrived fifteen minutes ago and shepherded us all here with instructions not to leave. The coroner's office should be here any minute.

The party guests are still in the ballroom. I assume they've gotten word about what's going on, but who knows? With the way the cops treat rich people in this town, it's possible they're drinking and eating without a care in the world.

I finally speak. "This is fucked."

"I know. I don't understand what happened," Harriet says. She pushes a hand against her eyes. "I *saw* her out there. I didn't have a chance to talk to her. And now—"

"Where is she?" a broken voice calls from the other end of the hallway. Mindy Washington appears, cheeks streaked with mascara.

She spots us.

"Nic!" She runs over, throwing her arms around my neck, burying her face in my shoulder. "I can't believe this," she sobs. "I was just talking to her, and now…now…"

A wail of grief. I pat her back, like it's any comfort at all. There's nothing I can do here. Nothing that will change this.

She pulls away. "I heard you found her. What *happened*? Did she… Did someone…"

She's dancing around the thing we're all wondering.

Did someone murder Barbara Patterson?

"I don't know," I say. "The cops haven't said."

As if summoned by my words, Adam Kozel appears, Detective Jones by his side.

Harriet jumps to her feet. "Finally! What's the word?"

Kozel puts up a hand. "I'm sorry, but I can't answer anything yet. Everything's still in progress. In the meantime, I have some questions for you and Nico. If you'll come with me?"

I climb to my feet and give Mindy an apologetic frown, then follow Kozel and Jones to a quiet spot down the hall.

"To start," Kozel says, "what were you doing in the fridge? Neither of you are employees of the club."

Harriet glances at me. "I was looking for seltzer."

He frowns. "I'm sorry. I'm a little confused here, Harriet. Why were you restocking the bar?"

"It's a long story."

"I have time."

She heaves a sigh. "My mom was on my back to find some, and the original bartender had disappeared. His replacement was about fifteen years old, totally overwhelmed, so I offered to grab it. I came back here, ran into Nic, and he said it'd be in the fridge." She shudders. "That's when we found her. Lying on the floor."

"Did you touch anything?" Detective Jones asks. "Move the body?"

Harriet shakes her head. "The only thing I touched was the door."

"Nico? Anything?" Jones asks.

"The light switch," I say.

"Well, that explains what Harriet was doing, but—Nico. What about you?" Kozel asks. "According to Mrs. George, you are not an invited guest."

An alarm goes off in my head.

"He was meeting me—" Harriet says.

I cut her off. I can fight my own battles, thank you very much. I glare at Kozel. The way he's saying *Nico,* over and over, is starting to piss me off. It's what my parents used to call me when they were angry.

"I got here about three minutes before I ran into Harriet. You can ask Alec Sanchez—he let me in the back door. You think in those three minutes, I had time to find Patterson, lure her into the fridge, and kill her?"

Kozel holds up his hands. "Whoa, buddy. Nobody's accusing you of anything here. Just trying to build a timeline."

I scowl. I'm not his fucking *buddy*.

"I would like to ask a few more questions though, Nico. If that's okay with you?"

I love that he's trying to make it sound like I have a choice. "Fine."

"On your way to the fridge, did you see anything strange? Anything that seemed out of place? Anyone acting suspicious?"

"I don't think so."

"How about you, Harriet?"

"Not that I remember."

"Hi, Detectives." A chef walks up to our little circle. "How much longer are you holding us here do you think? The people are getting restless."

Kozel looks at his partner. "We need to get everyone's info before they can leave," she says. "But we'll have someone get started on it, okay? Sit tight."

The detectives turn back to us. "Don't go anywhere, you understand?" Kozel says, a note of warning in his voice. "We'll be back shortly."

Harriet nods.

The detectives move on, leaving us with the chef.

"You're the ones who found her?" he asks. "What were you doing in the fridge?"

Harriet repeats what we told the cops.

"The bartender went missing?" the chef asks once she's done. "White guy, mid-twenties, brown hair, about yea high?" He holds a hand by his chin.

Harriet nods.

"Yup. Thought so. That's Matthew. Knew he shouldn't have been working today. I told Ella that, but did she listen? Course she didn't."

"Why?" Harriet asks.

He huffs. "Because she *never* listens."

"No, I mean, why didn't you think he should work today?"

"Oh. Because of him and Mr. George. Matthew's been pretty torn up about what happened."

Harriet glances at me. I know what she's thinking. Matthew told me he barely knew George.

"They knew each other?" I ask, straightening.

"Oh yeah. They'd chat whenever Mr. George was in here."

"Has anyone seen Matthew recently?"

"No idea. Lemme ask my manager. Hey, Ella?" the chef calls to a harried-looking woman deep in conversation with a couple employees. "Sorry to interrupt. Real quick—these people are looking for Matthew. You seen him?"

"He took off about a half hour ago."

The chef turns back with a shrug. "Guess he's gone. Knew he shouldn't have worked today."

"He left," I repeat. A jolt of adrenaline surges through me. "Right before we found Barbara."

He lied about knowing George, then took off right after Patterson died, and the cops are standing around doing jack-shit. Implying *I* did something wrong.

"Do you think—" Harriet says, but I'm already marching over to the detectives. I jam my finger into Kozel's back.

"Nico, I'm in the middle of something," Kozel says, not even bothering to turn around. "I'll be back with you in a bit."

If he thinks he can blow me off, he has another thing coming. "I need to talk to you. Right now," I growl.

Harriet's caught up, and she's watching our exchange with concern.

Kozel heaves a sigh, finally turning. Irritation is etched across his face. "All right. Can you finish up while I handle this?" he asks Detective Jones. She nods.

I lead him back to where we'd been standing with Harriet trailing after us.

"You need to find Matthew Prado," I say once we're alone.

"Matthew Prado?"

"Yeah. He bartends here. Works for my mom sometimes too. He was at Harriet's birthday party. You need to find him."

"Why's that?" Kozel says.

"He disappeared today. Right around when Barbara Patterson died."

"What do you mean *disappeared*?"

"I mean, he left in the middle of his shift."

"Okay? And why is that important?"

"Because! Because he took off! It's suspicious as hell! Two people have died now, and he was there for both of them."

Kozel scratches the back of his neck. "Well, so were you. And Harriet. And a lot of other people out in that ballroom. Did Matthew have something particular against Barbara Patterson that you're aware of? Or George?"

I shake my head. "That's not—You're not getting it. Matthew *knew* George. They talked whenever George came into the club."

"Okay?" Kozel says with impatience.

"Except Matthew works for my mom, right? And when I asked him about George after the murder, he told me he didn't know him!"

"He lied," Harriet adds. "Why would he lie unless he was hiding something?"

"I don't know." Kozel's eyes are fixed on something behind me. I glance over my shoulder and see Sharkey and a couple other cops making their way toward us. "Let me ask you again: Do you have any concrete reason to think Matthew wanted either of them dead?"

"Isn't figuring that out *your* job?" I step forward, noting with pleasure I have several inches on him.

"Nic," Harriet whispers. Her fingertips graze my arm.

"It's possible Matthew just didn't feel up to sharing his emotions with you, his employer. Or perhaps he simply didn't want to get involved." He pats me on the arm. "I have to get going but appreciate you coming to me with this. We'll keep it in mind."

Translation: They'll do jack-shit.

"You need to find him! You need to stop sitting around with your thumbs up your—"

Kozel's jaw clenches. "Nic, this is not a good idea," he says in a low voice. "Trust me. You need to back off."

"Ha! *Trust* you? What a fucking joke. I'm supposed to *trust* you after you let my sister take the fall—"

"Nic." Harriet's tugging on my arm. "Nic, don't."

I can tell I've pushed things too far, but I'm too angry to care.

"I'm going to take him home, okay?" Harriet says to Kozel. "It's been a long week. He needs a break. You know he didn't mean any of that."

Kozel waves a hand in my direction. "Fine. Get him out of here. We'll be in touch."

CHAPTER TWENTY-SIX

NIC

September 11
12:28 p.m.

Outside, Harriet smacks me on the shoulder. "What the hell was that? Are you trying to get yourself arrested?"

Before I can respond, she grabs my arm and drags me to her car. "Get in."

I'm too tired to argue.

I climb into the car and lean my head back against the headrest. I can't believe this. Another person dead. I guess it could have been a freak accident, but that type of shelf doesn't just fall over.

Matthew was at both events. And now he's gone.

Harriet gets in, watching me for a long moment before speaking. "I know things are fucked up. I know you've had a terrible week. And I'm sorry. I really am. I wish I could rewind time, make it all go away.

But what did you expect Kozel to do back there? We have no proof Matthew did anything wrong—not yet at least—and we *never* will if you end up behind bars. Sara needs you. *I* need you. If the last few days proved anything to me, it's that I can't do this alone."

The sunlight filters through the window behind her, catching on the tiny hairs on her cheek. She's gorgeous. I want to pull her close, tangle my fingers in her hair, push my tongue between her lips to distract myself from all this shit, but also because she's being so kind. She's *been* so kind.

I don't know if what I see in her eyes right now is real or just my imagination. I'm afraid of misinterpreting things, of assuming she feels what I do. What if she doesn't? What if I make a move and she pulls away?

I misread her once, all those years ago. I thought we were on the same page, then she just up and disappeared. The same thing could be happening right now.

I can't risk it. I need her to write that article.

I clear my throat. "Okay," I say.

Harriet nods and turns back to the wheel. The car roars to life as she twists the key in the ignition. "Great. Let's go find Matthew."

We pull Matthew's contact information from his file and head toward his apartment, the weight of our search settling in the car between us.

Harriet pulls to the curb outside a six-story building, its red brick facade worn down by years of salty air.

"This is it," she says. "Let's call up?"

I nod. We gather by the call box, and she presses the buzzer. Once and then again.

No one answers.

"Okay. Maybe not home," Harriet says. "Which fits if he just killed Barbara, right? I wouldn't go back home after I did something like that either. Let's call him? Try the cell number on his contact sheet."

I do, and it rings out to voicemail. "Nope."

"What about his emergency contact number? Maybe they'll know where he is. I'll make the call."

"It's there. Somebody named Ana Davis." I show her the contact sheet, and she plugs the number into her phone.

"It's ringing," she says a moment later. "Hello? Hi, yes, Ana? Hi. I work with Matthew? Matthew Prado? Yeah, about six feet tall, early twenties? I guess we're talking about the same person, but I'm not sure why..."

"What's she saying?" I whisper, and Harriet holds up a finger.

"Anyway, I'm so sorry to bother you, but we're short-staffed tonight, and I'm a little desperate. I wanted to see if Matthew could cover a shift, but I can't seem to get a hold of him. You're listed as his emergency contact—" She pauses. "No, the catering company where he works? All Bright Catering? Oh. He is? Do you know why? No, that's okay. I appreciate it. Yeah, yeah, I'm sure. Thanks." She hangs up and turns to me. "Get this. When I asked for Matthew Prado, she said she doesn't know anyone by that name, but her son's name is Matthew. Matthew Davis. And he fit my description. It has to be the same guy, right? Did he give you guys a fake last name?"

I stiffen. "*Davis?*"

I was there when he filled out his paperwork. I saw his license, his electrical bill—they all said Matthew Prado. Has he been lying since the first day I met him?

She nods. "Yeah. And get this—she said she was sorry, but he called about an hour ago. Told her he was coming home. He must have taken off right after Patterson died."

"Dammit!" I slam the sole of my shoe into the brick wall. I can't believe this. We've spent the past week chasing threads that led nowhere, focusing on the wrong shit.

And all along, he was right there.

Matthew.

CHAPTER TWENTY-SEVEN

HARRIET

September 11
1:08 p.m.

"I knew something was off!" Nic's pacing, red-faced. I've never seen him like this—losing control. "I let myself get distracted by a fucking *eighty-year-old* woman. You kept insisting she could have murdered George, but I knew—I *knew* it was an insane theory, and now she's dead and he's gone, and Sara's *fucked*!"

"Nic."

He ignores me.

"Nic!" I say more loudly.

"*What?*" he snaps.

I hold up the contact sheet. "We have his mom's address. She lives in New Rochelle, just north of the city. That's, what—a three-hour drive from here?"

"So?"

"So I think we should go find Matthew. Get the evidence we need to go to the cops. Evidence they can't ignore this time."

He stills. "Drive up there?"

"Why not? He only has a couple hours on us. What if he's on his way to say goodbye because he's planning to flee? We could be working on borrowed time."

"Borrowed time because you said an eighty-year-old was a killer," he mutters.

My eye twitches, an argument rising in my throat, but I stop myself. "Then let me make it up to you."

I shoot off a cryptic text to my mom, telling her I have to deal with a couple things, and we take off.

The drive through the bottom half of Jersey goes quickly; traffic is minimal since it's still early Friday afternoon, but as we approach the city, it starts to thicken. We slow to a near standstill, right next to the industrial smokestacks of Elizabeth, New Jersey.

"Stinks," I say. Nic's been reading something on his phone with a frown, and when I speak, he blinks at me like he forgot I was here.

"What?"

I motion to my window. "That. It smells. I've always thought it sucks that it's the first part of New Jersey a lot of people see."

He drops his phone to his lap. "What do you care? I thought you hated Jersey."

"I mean…I don't *hate* it. It's just growing up, the island always felt way too small. My parents were divorced, living a mile apart, and they... Well. It was not what anyone would call a friendly situation. My mom constantly poking my dad, my dad responding. My mom's multiple marriages, my dad's midlife crisis. Gogo was around, but she had her own life. I never really had a place I felt like was home, you know?"

He doesn't respond right away, and my throat tightens, worried I overshared. What was that? Those are things I never say, not even to Steven and Maggie. In fact, I'm not sure I've *ever* put those feelings into words.

I'm about to change the subject when Nic leans forward and grabs a bottle of water from the floor.

"Here." He hands it to me, and I take it gratefully. "Family's hard," he says quietly as I take a pull from the bottle. "As you've seen, my family isn't exactly a picture of function either. My sister's never learned to control her temper. My dad's been out of work for years. And my mom's business *was* doing well, but now... I don't think I ever told you this way back when, but I got into culinary school up in New York. I had this whole plan—concentrate in farm-to-table for my undergrad degree, then get a master's in sustainable food systems. Eventually, open my own little place that incorporated all those things under one roof."

"You did?"

He nods. "I was all set to go, but then my dad lost his job and couldn't land a new one. The rest is history. Eight years later, my mom has—or had at least—a successful catering business I helped build, my dad's, well...same old, same old. And I never moved off the island."

"Why not?"

He cuts his eyes to me. "You don't get it, Baker. My parents were barely hanging on. I couldn't abandon them. They needed me. Every time I thought maybe things were easing up, things would happen to prove otherwise. I mean, look at this. Us. Driving up to New Rochelle for my sister. I can't abandon them. I won't. That's not what you do to people you love."

His words hit me square in the chest. My entire life has been predicated on the idea that, in fact, you *do* abandon the people you love. My mom's divorces, my dad's lack of communication, Kozel.

And then I turned right around and did it to Nic.

He settles his head against his headrest and closes his eyes. His eyelashes are long, black, tangled at their edges, and it takes everything in me to tear my eyes away from him and back to the road.

CHAPTER TWENTY-EIGHT

HARRIET

September 11

4:48 p.m.

Traffic on I-95 N slows more and more the farther we get into the city, and it's almost five o'clock by the time we reach Ana Davis's house.

"This must be it." I pull up along the curb outside a two-story row home. A black mailbox is bolted beside the front door, the numbers 9538 painted in uneven white strokes across its face.

Now that we're here, it's hitting me. If we're right about Matthew Prado/Davis/whatever his real name, he killed two people in cold blood.

Is going in there and confronting him a smart idea? Should we call the cops instead? Except what would we tell them? That he left town of his own accord and we followed him? If I'm not mistaken, we'd look like the crazy people in that scenario, not him.

"I think I should go in alone," Nic says, interrupting my worrying. He unties his hoodie from around his waist and drops it on the floor. "This is my issue. If you got hurt because of it, I'd never..." He trails off, chewing on his bottom lip.

I wipe my sweaty palms across the waistband of my shorts. I'm not about to wimp out now. "Absolutely not. I'm coming."

He looks at me with a frown. "Harriet..."

"Don't bother wasting your time trying to change my mind. You know how stubborn I am."

"Okay. But if there's any sign of trouble, you need to leave. Immediately. Okay?"

I roll my eyes, trying to pretend like there isn't a lump of fear lodged in the center of my throat. "Save your machismo bullshit, please. I can handle myself."

"Harriet." His voice is low. "I'm serious. I can't go in there worried something will happen to you. I'll be too distracted."

I meet his eyes, and my heartbeat stumbles at the expression in them—worried, steady, full of care.

"Okay?" he says.

"Fine. Let's go."

Out of the car, the neighborhood is quiet, the only sign of life the shouts of kids in the distance. I trail behind him to the front stoop, and Nic rings the bell.

A few seconds later, the door swings open, revealing a woman about my mom's age with graying brown hair and a kind face. My shoulders drop away from my ears. If Matthew's mom is home, there's less chance of this ending badly.

At least I hope there is.

"Can I help you?" she says, hand still planted on the doorframe.

Nic clears his throat. "Hi there. We're looking for Matthew? Matthew Prado...err, Davis? He's been working for my mom's catering company, and we need to, um... We just had a couple questions we need to run by him."

She looks between us. "And you drove all the way down here to do it?"

"Uh, yeah. He wasn't picking up his phone, and it's important."

"I spoke with someone from his work earlier this afternoon. Why didn't they ask me to pass on your questions to him then?"

"They're sensitive," I tell her. "Money stuff."

A cloud passes over her face. "Money stuff? What kind of money stuff?"

"Just a few—"

"Now that I think about it," she continues. "They also called him Matthew Prado. Are we sure we're even talking about the same person?"

"I think so? He listed you as his emergency contact in his employee file." I nudge Nic, who holds up the photo of Matthew's information so she can see it.

She looks at it with a frown. "Huh. The rest of that fits my son Matthew, but why..." She gives her head a little shake. "This is all very confusing. Why don't you all come inside? We can try to get it sorted. What did you say your names are?"

"I'm Harriet," I say, "and this is Nic."

"Harriet and Nic." She steps back from the door, giving us space to walk inside. "At the very least, it's nice to meet some of the people he's been spending time with recently. He's been so reticent ever since he moved up to Boston—"

"Boston?" I interrupt. "He doesn't live in Boston."

Her chin tucks back. "What do you mean?"

I look at Nic. "We live in New Jersey."

"New..." A deep line appears between her brows. "Where in New Jersey?"

"Logan Island."

"*Logan* Island?"

"Mom?" someone calls. "Who is it?"

Ana's head swings in the direction of the voice, then back to us.

"Is that Matthew?" Nic asks.

"I... Well, yes. I'm still... I don't understand. I knew he was working at a catering company, but I thought—"

Matthew appears on the stairs. "Mom?"

His eyes land on Nic. On me.

His face pales.

"Hi, Matthew Prado," Nic says. "Or should I say Matthew Davis?"

"These people are here to see you," his mom says. "They say...they say you've been living on Logan Island? And why—they seem to think your last name is Prado?"

Matthew is silent.

"Matthew? What's going on?"

His face collapses.

"Matthew?" Ana says again.

"I'm so sorry," he says. "I didn't mean to do it."

CHAPTER TWENTY-NINE

NIC

September 11

4:59 p.m.

Matthew slowly drags himself down the stairs, stopping a few feet from me and Harriet.

Harriet's hand finds my bicep.

"You didn't mean to do what?" I ask.

"Why didn't you tell me you were living on Logan Island?" his mom whispers.

He's silent.

"What did you do?" I step forward, and Harriet's hand falls off my arm. I want to shake him. Hard. Force a confession out of him. Ask him why the hell he was willing to let my sister take the fall for what he did.

"Nic," Harriet says softly.

Matthew's mom is staring him in horror. "Why, Matthew?"

"*Because!*" he explodes.

Harriet lets out a quiet gasp behind me. We should have brought something with us—a knife, my kitchen mallet. I glance around the room; an umbrella leans again the wall to my left. If things go south, will it be enough to stop him?

Matthew continues, "Every time I asked you about him, you changed the subject. Said we could talk about it later. But we never did. We never do! And I needed more than that. I needed information! I don't think it was unreasonable of me to want to know about my father."

"Your father?" Harriet steps next to me. "Holy shit. I knew something about you was familiar. Something about your mouth—"

"I was trying to *protect* you!" his mom cries, paying Harriet no mind.

"I didn't need protection. I needed answers! I'm twenty years old. I could have handled it."

"But how did you find him?"

Matthew's lips tremble. "Your old journals. I dug them out of the back of your closet when you went to visit Aunt Betty last year."

"Those journals." Ana closes her eyes.

"It was on the back page, his name—all his addresses over the years. You were tracking him this whole time."

Ana tugs at her hair. "I—"

"If you'd just told me the truth, I wouldn't have gone to meet him. He was awful." Matthew slumps against the wall.

"Did he do something to you?" Ana asks, reaching toward him.

Matthew shakes her off. "No. Well, not at first. He was nice at the beginning."

The pieces are starting to slot into place. "But by the night of the party, he'd stopped being nice," I say.

Matthew turns like he just remembered they're not alone. "What the hell are you doing here, Nic?" he snaps. "Other than fucking up my life?"

I step in front of Harriet. The umbrella is within arm's reach. I can take him. I'm four inches taller. Twenty pounds heavier at least. "I'm here because my sister's in *jail,* you asshole. She was arraigned on murder charges. Are you okay with that?"

"*Murder charges?*" Ana breathes.

Harriet's hand finds my arm again, her reminder to keep control. I continue, "You said he was nice, and then he wasn't. Was that after you told him who you really were?"

Matthew's mouth pinches.

I keep going. "I bet it pissed you off that your father wanted nothing to do with you. So the night of the birthday party, you lured George out to the beach. And then you killed him. And then you let my sister take the fall."

"*What?*" Ana cries.

Matthew laughs with no humor. "Are you serious? *That's* why you're here? You think I killed that dickhead?"

"It fits," Harriet says. "You had motive. Means. Opportunity. The thing I still don't understand is what did you have against Barbara Patterson?"

Matthew throws his hands up into the air. "Who the hell is Barbara Patterson?"

"The person you killed today before skipping town," Harriet says.

"What?" he scoffs. "You both are crazy. I left today because I finally realized I had no reason to be on that island. I was only there because of George, and he was dead!"

"Then why didn't you leave right after he died?" I ask. "Why wait?"

"I don't know. I wasn't thinking clearly. I mean, someone *killed* him. One minute we're talking, and the next he's dead on the beach."

Ana puts a hand over her mouth.

"I don't buy it," I say. "We have a witness who saw you pestering George, getting upset when he didn't acknowledge you. You disappeared for a while in the middle of that shift. Was that when you killed him?"

"Nic, I didn't—Jesus! Yeah, I was acting a little weird around the guy—I was trying to work up the nerve to tell him he was my dad, for fuck's sake! When you say I *disappeared* was probably when I was in the basement talking to him. And—"

I wonder if that was the fight Sara mentioned.

"Did you guys yell?" Harriet asks, reading my mind.

"What?" Matthew looks annoyed by the interruption.

"When you guys were down there. Did you yell?"

"No. No yelling, but he was still a total asshole," Matthew says. "It caught me by surprise. He was always nice when we'd talk at the club! After a couple drinks, he'd start telling me stuff—stuff I thought meant he trusted me, liked me. Issues he was having with his company. His partner. But in the wine cellar, he was a totally different person. Said he didn't believe me, and even if it *was* true, he didn't care—he wasn't going to give me any money. Then he told me to get the fuck out of his house. He was awful, but I never touched him!"

"I'm so sorry," his mom whispers. She's crying.

"Can you prove it?" I ask. Sara's in prison; I'm not going to let him walk away without concrete evidence of his innocence.

He glares at me. "You want proof?" He pulls his phone out of his back pocket and swipes at the screen. "Here."

He hands it to me. On the screen is a long string of messages, all sent between 7:15 and 8:00 that night. Harriet peers over my shoulder as I scroll through them.

Matthew continues, "I read that George's estimated time of death was 7:35. The time stamps on these texts proves I was texting my mom at the exact time he was killed. Do you really think I was typing with one hand while I stabbed George with the other?"

His words are like a direct punch to my sternum. Another theory, blown to bits. One more nail in Sara's coffin.

"Fuck," Harriet breathes.

"I sent her those after George blew me off. Had to remind myself I have one parent who cares."

"I love you so much," Ana says. She wraps her arms around his chest and buries her head in his chest.

Matthew pets the back of her hair. "I'm so sorry, Mom."

"No, *I'm* sorry." Her voice shakes. "I should have trusted that you could handle the truth. He just… He isn't a good man, Matthew." She pulls back, wiping under her eyes.

"Did you guys date?" Matthew asks. "And if so, *why*?"

She winces. "It was…complicated."

"You said you would tell the truth."

"I—" Ana's lips press together. "All right. I worked at his company. One night, I had too much to drink, and..." She hesitates.

Harriet stills next to me, Ana's words sitting heavy in the air between all of us.

"Did he rape you?" Matthew asks, voice raw with anger.

She puts a hand on his arm. "No, no. I'm sorry, I should have been clearer. Yes, I was stupid, young, too drunk for my own good, but it was consensual. Once I told him I was pregnant, George just wanted me gone. I got a substantial payout, left the company, and never saw him again."

"Jesus." Harriet shudders. "What a creep. I still can't believe my mom married him. I don't care if they *did* date back in high school. She's an idiot."

"Oh," Ana says, her voice softening. "I wonder... Sometimes when you've known a person for a very long time, it becomes difficult to see them clearly. I worked with George every day for years and didn't realize how awful he could be until I ended up pregnant. It was impressive, really, how well he hid it." She lets out a bitter laugh. "And he wasn't just awful in his personal life. Those last weeks I was with the company, I started noticing things I had overlooked before. Things he was twisted up in that weren't exactly ethical. Or legal even. I heard he sold the business a few years back?"

"Yeah," Harriet says. "For millions."

"Millions. I shouldn't be surprised by that. It's a lot easier to make that sort of money when you don't care where it comes from or who gets hurt in the process. A couple years after I left, I ran into some old friends from work. They mentioned George was trying to broker a deal with the owner of some waterfront property in the Meatpacking District, but the guy didn't want anything to do with him." She pauses. "I don't know why, but I kept an eye on it. Habit, maybe? And wouldn't you know—two months later, the building on the land burned down. Total loss. A death. Insurance claims were through the roof. After that, George was able to buy up the land for cheap."

Hearing all this is making me even angrier about what's happening to my sister. There have to be *tons* of people who want a scumbag like that dead.

"A death?" Harriet asks, fingers pressed against her lips.

"Unfortunately, yes. The property manager—a lovely man named Adrian—was inside when the blaze started, and they didn't get him out in time. It was a real tragedy. He was supposed to get married the following weekend."

"And you think George did that?" Harriet asks. "He *killed* someone?"

Ana studies us, eyes moving slowly between Harriet and me like she's weighing just how open to be. "Like I said, after the fire, the owners were more than willing to make a deal, which always struck me as incredibly convenient for him. That said, this is all speculation, so please don't go quoting me on that."

"What happened when the NYFD investigated?" I ask. "They must have, right?" I've learned that much from Martin.

"Yes, they did." Ana pauses, then adds more quietly, "Not to sound like a conspiracy theorist, but George was very buddy-buddy with several fire inspectors. I remember them coming by the office a few times, having lunch, joking around like they were old friends. I didn't think much of it at the time, but..." She shakes her head. "Never mind. I'm sure I sound crazy. At the end of the day, they determined the cause was faulty wiring. An old building, outdated infrastructure. But I couldn't help but wonder."

Faulty wiring. The words snag in my brain.

"Harriet. The Windswept Motel," I say, grabbing her arm.

"The Windswept..." Her face pales. "*Oh*. The fire."

"The fire."

An accident caused by faulty wiring. No one ever questioned it.

"It parallels what happened in New York," I say. "Land George wanted but couldn't get. An accidental, total-loss fire. And suddenly the owners are willing to sell."

Martin worked that scene. One of the people he treated, a six-year-old kid, almost died from the severity of his burns. Normally unflappable Martin suffered insomnia for months after, couldn't sleep, couldn't get it out of his head.

"You know a kid almost died in the motel fire," I tell Harriet. "Martin saved his life."

"A kid?" she whispers.

I nod.

"I lived under the same *roof* as that man. I feel sick." The distress on her face makes me want to wrap my arms around her. Protect her. "I wonder... The note I found in George's desk from Barbara said she knew what he did. Do you think she figured out he was responsible?"

"Maybe," I say. "But it couldn't have been George who killed her. He was already dead."

"True." Harriet's eyes lock on Matthew, who's been murmuring with his mom. "You said George mentioned problems he was having with his business partner?"

Matthew nods. "That's what he told me. Said there was tension between them but didn't get into any details."

"Right." Harriet looks at me. "I think we need to figure out what exactly was going on between George and Luke. Where the tension stemmed from. Luke was involved with the Windswept Motel build, but *how* involved? Did he know about the fire? Did he know that Barbara had figured out—"

She's interrupted by a loud cough.

"Not to be a dick," says Matthew. "But as fascinating as all this is, I sort of need to talk to my mom about some stuff. Could you guys please get the hell out of my house?"

CHAPTER THIRTY

HARRIET

September 11

5:22 p.m.

We're greeted by a torrential downpour as we step onto Ana's porch. By the time we get to the car, I'm soaked to the bone, hair matted to the side of my head, goose bumps rising in waves along my arms. It's dropped at least twenty degrees in the past twenty minutes.

"I'm soaked," I say, shivering. "And cold."

"Here." Nic grabs the hoodie he discarded earlier from the floor and hands it to me. "Put this on. It's dry."

"Thanks." I start wiggling out of my wet T-shirt.

"What are you *doing*?"

I look over and find Nic staring at me with horror.

"I'm cold!" I say, my shirt halfway over my head. "Haven't you ever seen someone in a bikini? There's literally no difference."

"You could have at least given me a warning," he mutters, turning his face toward the window.

I pull on the hoodie and toss my soaked shirt into the back seat. "I'm done. You can stop being such a prude now."

He glances back over, cheeks flushed red, pupils dilated.

Oh. Warmth floods my lower belly; a throbbing starts between my thighs.

I recognize that look from our two weeks together. He wants me. And fuck if I don't want him too. If I leaned into him, I wonder what would happen. I wonder—

A loud thump against the windshield makes me jump.

"What the hell?" Another thump. "Holy shit. It's hailing golf balls. Traffic is going to be insane."

Nic's already looking at his phone. "Google Maps says it's going to take us five hours to get back."

"*Five* hours?" It's after 5:00 p.m. Dusk is settling in—my least favorite time to drive. And now it's hailing? This is going to be a disaster.

He nods. "There's a big accident where 95 meets the Parkway. People drive like shit in the rain."

"Not to sound like an old lady, but any chance you could handle driving back?"

Nic grimaces. "Normally, yes, but I didn't bring my glasses, and I need them to drive."

Rain and hail are pounding against the windshield. I watch the drops land and spread on the glass as I try to figure out what to do. "I guess we could—"

"Should we—" he says at the same time.

We both fall quiet.

"You first," he says.

"We could see if we can crash somewhere for the night? Maybe Matthew would let us?"

"Yeah. It could be a little awkward to ask him for a place to crash, given we just accused him of murder."

"Fair point. I guess a hotel then?" My heart's pounding harder than it should be. It's an innocent suggestion, one I'm making because we have no other options. It's not because I want to spend the night under the same roof as Nic.

Right. Absolutely.

Nic licks his lips. "A hotel is probably our best bet."

By the time we find a hotel with vacancy, it's after six. Night has fallen, the rain coming down in sheets. If I was driving on the highway in this, there's a solid chance we'd end up in a ditch.

Which would be much worse than finding out the hotel only has one room available.

At least that's what I tell myself.

"Are you sure you don't have *anything* else?" I ask for the third time, trying to keep the desperation out of my voice. "A room with two double beds even."

The woman behind the computer sighs. "Ma'am—"

I bristle as she *ma'ams* me.

"—as I told you before, we are almost fully sold out tonight. There's a convention in town. We have exactly one room left. A king room on the second floor. Take it or—" She gestures toward the glass windows of the building. "Roll the dice out there."

"Fine," I say, voice tight. I can't bring myself to look at Nic. "We'll take it."

"Great," she says, like she mostly thinks it's great that she won't have to deal with me for much longer. "One key card or two?"

"Two!" Nic says quickly. The woman slides two key cards across the counter to us, and we take them and head to the elevator.

The ride upstairs is quiet. I can't read Nic; I'm trying to figure out how we got here. *There's only one bed?* The universe is clearly conspiring against me.

"This is it," I say, stopping outside the room. We both stare at the door. God, this is awkward. We're acting like strangers, not two people who have spent the better part of the last week together. Two people who, once upon a time, spent weeks secretly hooking up.

"I guess we should go in?" he says. He doesn't move.

"Right." I insert my key card in the slot, and it beeps green.

The room is fine. Standard, nothing to write home about. And sure enough, it has exactly one (1) bed.

"Beats sleeping in the car." I force a laugh and toss my purse onto the small round desk in the corner.

"Yeah," Nic says, lingering awkwardly in the entryway. "I'm gonna—" He disappears into the bathroom without finishing his sentence, and the shower turns on a moment later.

The shower.

He's in there taking a shower.

Which means he's naked.

Naked.

Nic is naked.

I realize I'm standing in the center of the room not breathing.

If I'm going to survive the night, I'm going to have to pull it together. It's not like I haven't seen him naked.

Immediately, an image of Nic naked snakes into my brain.

Okay, no. That wasn't helpful. I need to back up. We're partners. *Business* partners. Not sex partners.

Sex.

Oh my god.

I grab my purse. "I'm going to go down to the bar!" I call, not waiting to see if he heard me or not.

I slide into a seat at the hotel bar. It's shabby, with strong chain-hotel vibes, but at least it's not that fucking room with one bed.

I order a drink, then open the Notes app on my phone and start jotting down everything we learned today before it slips away.

George might have been an arsonist. He might have set a fire in NYC that killed someone. *Adrian.*

The name nudges at me. Where have I heard it before?

Shit. I swipe over to my photos, and there it is: *Adrian Pruner*. The obit I found in George's desk. He must have kept it—out of guilt? Or because he was proud of the whole thing? At this point, nothing would surprise me.

The ensuing investigation into the fire claimed it was caused by faulty wiring—which, coincidentally, was also the official cause of the Windswept Motel fire. George had struggled to buy both pieces of land until the buildings burned. After that, the owners changed their minds and sold.

Side by side, the parallels are glaring.

If George really was bribing or colluding with cops or fire inspectors, it would prove our theory about police corruption. Except I have no hard facts to back it up.

If I publish without proof, could someone sue me?

I text Maggie.

Yes, someone could sue you for defamation!!! You're a journalist, Harriet. Didn't you learn that in college?

Well, yes. I *did* learn that in college, but I was hoping maybe the law had changed in the last four years.

We need proof. Cold, hard *proof* that George was twisted up in all sorts of awful things. Arson, bribery, murder.

But how?

Ten minutes and one bourbon later, I've recorded the rest of what Matthew and his mom told us and written two new lines for my article.

Murder in Paradise

Except beneath that sophisticated facade, George George was, by some accounts, a terrible man. A man who impregnated a woman, then paid her off to deal with it alone. A man who allegedly conducted his business in ways that were less than ethical—or even legal.

A familiar figure appears at the entrance to the room as I'm finishing my drink. His still-damp hair is tousled, and as I watch, he runs a hand through it, his eyes landing on me. He smiles, dimples appearing on either side of his mouth.

I am in serious trouble.

"Hey." He slips into the seat next to mine.

I'm suddenly shy. "Hey. What's up?"

"What are you doing? I didn't know where you'd taken off to when I got out of the shower."

"Yeah, sorry. I said I was leaving, but I didn't know if you'd heard me. I came down here to write."

He tilts his chin at my empty glass. "What are you drinking?"

"Bourbon."

"Nice." He signals for the bartender, ordering himself one. "Want another?"

I should not have another drink. That would be a very, very, *very* bad idea.

"Sure."

One more drink. One more drink, and I will keep my hands to myself and not have three drinks because three drinks might lead to... My eyes run down the sharp edge of his jaw, his neck, the bicep muscle peeking out from his T-shirt.

His skin was always so soft.

I should absolutely not have another drink.

I'm about to say as much when Nic clears his throat. "This weather is wild, huh? End of the summer storms are crazy."

Before I can respond, someone squeezes in on his other side, and he's forced to tug his chair toward mine.

"Sorry," he says as our legs bump. My breath catches. This is pure torture, I swear to god.

I clear my throat. "It's okay."

The bartender slides our drinks over, and I take a long sip. I need to pull it together. Be normal.

Cheers from the TV overhead distract us. "Are you a baseball fan?" Nic asks.

"Eh, not really a sports fan, actually. You?"

He shrugs. "Sort of? Not really. I mean, I like the Giants, the Yankees well enough, but I'm not spending my weekends watching it. I'd rather watch *The Great British Bake Off* or try out a new recipe in my spare time."

Well, I am officially dead. That's the cutest thing I've ever heard.

"It's my passion, I guess you could say. Like you with your writing." He hesitates. "Speaking of, how *is* the article coming? That was some crazy stuff we learned earlier."

"Yeah. I mean, I always knew George was a creep. Just not that he was *that* much of one. I can't believe my mom married that bastard. It's sickening."

I take a long sip of my drink as Nic fiddles with the edge of a paper napkin. "Are you okay?" he asks finally.

"No. Yes. I don't know. I can't believe my mom sometimes. She's been married four times, and I wonder sometimes if she has any standards at all. First it was my dad, who, let's be honest, she only married because she got pregnant with me, then this dickhead hedge fund guy—that marriage only lasted for a hot minute, thankfully—and then she married her third husband..."

Another sip of my drink.

"Maxwell. But he died. Which was too bad. He was the only one of them I actually liked. I mean, I like my dad of course, but..." I shake my head. "You get it."

I think I might be a little drunk.

Nic nods. "Oh wow, yeah. I remember that. A boating accident, right?"

I look at him with surprise. I don't think I ever talked about any of this back in the day; I was mostly focused on turning my brain off. It was only toward the end of those two weeks that we started sharing anything personal. And that's when I ran.

"Yeah. It was awful. My mom was a mess after. I think it killed her faith in love. Which, let's be honest, was minimal to begin with. A couple years later, she ran into George, and that was that. They'd dated back in high school, and he was filthy rich. An irresistible combo."

Nic runs his thumb over the condensation beading on his glass. "Or maybe, like Matthew's mom said, even though he was horrible, it seemed safe, because she'd known him for so long."

"I think you're giving her too much credit. Pretty sure the size of his bank account had more to do with it than anything." I take the remaining sip of my drink, and my stomach growls, a reminder I haven't eaten anything since breakfast. "Anyway, if we're going to continue talking about my mother, I need another bourbon. We aren't exactly what you'd call close. I'm pretty sure I've been consistently disappointing her since birth."

Nic tilts his head. "How's that possible? You went to NYU. You had a great career—"

"*Had* being the operative word," I say, motioning to the bartender. I know I said I'd stop at two, but I need to wash this conversation down with something stronger than water. "Want anything?"

He's barely touched his drink, but now he takes a long drag of it. "Actually, yeah. I'll take another."

"Great." I order two bourbons and a plate of french fries, then continue. "Currently, I am a failure because I'm twenty-six and single. At my age, she was married with a baby after all. No matter that her parents pushed that marriage on the two of them, and they broke up before I even turned two. I'm unemployed. Freeloading under her roof. Plus, she's never been shy about letting me know that I ruined her life. You know, unplanned pregnancy and all."

"That's awful, Harriet," Nic says quietly.

"It is what it is," I say with a smile, raising my drink. "Cheers."

His expression grows serious. "You don't have to do that, you know."

"What?" I ask, pulling my glass back. A flicker of embarrassment runs through me.

"Blow things off like that. Make a joke out of everything. You can tell me stuff. I want to..." He shakes his head.

"Well," I say when it's clear he's not going to finish his sentence. "At least I escaped for a while. But it's like I said in the car: The island's always felt way too small. Especially after Kozel did what he did."

"You mean after he *ghosted* you?" he says sardonically. He's not being mean exactly, but his meaning is clear. Kozel did to me exactly what I did to him.

Heat flushes my cheeks. "I guess."

"Shit," he says off my expression. "I didn't mean… Look, it's okay. Back then, was I pissed and hurt? Yeah. I was. I thought we— It doesn't matter what I thought. And then at the party when you didn't recognize me, all those latent feelings popped back up. But it's been eight years. I know I look different. I get it. We're fine. It's cool, okay?"

He sounds like he means it, but I can't let myself off the hook that easily. "Nic, no. It's not. I acted like an ass. As soon as things started getting real between us—that night at my house. You came over, cooked me dinner, like you were my boyfriend, and started asking me all those personal questions. I could tell you actually cared about my answers. I got totally freaked out. I went into the bathroom and stared at myself in the mirror, and it was like… I don't even know. Like everything that had happened over the course of that month crashed into my brain, and I just wanted to run away from it all."

"You don't have to do this—"

I nod emphatically. "Yes. I do. I should have talked to you, at the very least, instead of disappearing. I'm sorry. You deserved better. You're the guy who tried to patch up my broken heart when I was quite literally blinded with grief. You're the guy who's set aside your resentment toward me in order to help your sister. You're the guy who stayed behind on the island to help your mom instead of leaving. You're amazing."

His eyes soften at the edges. "Harriet—"

And just like that, reality slams back in at the sound of my name. What am I doing? I've said too much. I feel naked. Raw. Exposed.

"Anyway!" I down half my bourbon in one fell swoop, coughing as the burn of the alcohol smacks against my throat. "Shit!"

I lean forward, pressing my hand over my mouth, trying to get the rest of the liquid down so I don't spray it all over the bar.

"Are you okay?" Nic says. His hand lands on my back, softly patting.

I hold up a finger.

After a minute, my coughing finally subsides. "Jesus," I choke out, wiping the tears from under my eyes. "That's what I get for being so fucking sincere. Gross. I don't know what came over me."

Nic rolls his eyes. "Well, it's appreciated. I know, *gross*. But it is."

An hour later, I am properly drunk.

Exactly what I promised myself I would not be. Whoops.

I'm clinging to Nic's arm as we walk into the brightly lit lobby. He smells so good. His arm is so solid. He's so kind, reliable, steady. So different from every other person in my life.

"Are you okay?" he asks as he steers me toward the elevator bank.

"I'm fine. Why?" I slur. "You know, I'm a real dumbass for not recognizing you at my party. I should have known who you were. I should have *invited* you."

Nic presses the button for the elevator, and the doors open.

"I'm serious," I say as we walk inside. "You're awesome. You're the best." I lean into him, into his warmth. I nuzzle my nose into his armpit.

"Let's get you to bed," he says, patting my shoulder.

The word *bed* sends a jolt through me. "Are we sleeping together?"

I feel him stiffen. "What?"

Oh god. That sounded bad. "No, I mean. Not like *that*. In the same bed. There's only one. Bed, I mean." Even in my drunken state, I'm aware I should stop talking. I pop my mouth shut.

"You take the bed. I'll sleep on the floor."

The elevator stops, and I tumble out of it, Nic catching me by the back of the arm before I face-plant onto the tattered carpet.

I bat my lashes at him. "We could have another drink from the mini fridge."

"Or," he says, "you could get some sleep."

"Or!" I counter. "We could get some more whiskey."

He pats his pockets. "Where's your key? I think I left mine in the room."

"Here?" I hold it up, and he snatches it from my fingers. "Hey!"

He steps past me to unlock the door, and I lean in, rising onto my toes to lick the curve of his neck.

I *lick*. His *neck*. I'm drunk but not so drunk that I don't immediately realize that was fucking weird.

He turns, wiping at the spot. "What was that?"

"Nothing," I say.

"Did you just lick me?"

If only the floor would open up and swallow me whole. "No?" I venture.

He raises a brow. "Uh-huh."

"I..."

I look up into his eyes and lose my train of thought. He's so close his breath tickles my cheek.

"Hey," I say, leaning into him. "Hi."

Jesus Christ, I want him.

Our bodies connect, my chest pressing against his. My hands find his waist, the seam of his shirt, fingertips slipping under, dancing over ripples of muscle, across his skin. He's so warm, so alive, so close. Such a good brother, son, friend. He's...so fucking hot.

"I remember, back then," I murmur. "How it felt to kiss you. How it made everything else in the world disappear."

"Harriet," he sighs my name low. "I..."

"Shh." My fingers roam, finding the soft trail of hair that runs down off his belly button. I follow it down, down, down...

His Adam's apple bobs. He reaches up and plants his hand over mine. "Harriet." He clears his throat. "You're drunk."

"I'm not—" I start to protest.

"You are. And..." Another sigh. An exhale. "This... I can't. You're not thinking clearly."

"I'm thinking *so* clearly."

He shakes his head and gently pushes me away, turning back to the door.

My heart sinks as he pushes it open. I trail in behind him with my tail between my legs, and he tugs apart the bedsheets. "Here. Get some sleep, okay?"

I sit at the edge of the bed, slip my shoes off, and by the time I look up, he's disappeared into the bathroom. I'm still in his hoodie and my slacks from the memorial, and I slowly unzip the top, hoping he'll reappear.

He's still in there by the time it's off, and I decide to lie down for just a moment to wait.

CHAPTER THIRTY-ONE

NIC

September 12

9:02 a.m.

Harriet's sprawled out in the center of the bed, snoring, when I slip back into the room. Her hair is a mess around her head, her makeup smudged around her eyes, and I've never seen someone so beautiful. I woke up early, around six o'clock, stiff from sleeping on the floor all night, and went down to the lobby to grab coffee and work on some stuff for the case. I wanted to give her a chance to sleep it off. She was pretty hammered last night, not a huge surprise, given how quickly she was downing bourbons.

Walking away from her was hard as hell—I remember our chemistry back in the day, how good it felt... But I couldn't do it. Not like that. If anything was to ever happen between us, I'd want us both to be sober. One hundred percent sure we were both on board.

She groans, flopping to her side, one of her eyes peeling open. It lands on me. I smile. Her brow wrinkles, and she bolts upright, pulling the sheets up to her neck. Her eyes are glassy, hair sticking up off her head every which way. It's really cute as hell.

"Hey," I say.

She stares at me. I see the moment the memory of last night smacks back into her brain.

She cringes.

Not exactly the facial expression I was hoping for.

"I was so weird last night, wasn't I?" She rubs her eyes. "I told myself not to drink too much but clearly blew right by that promise. It's been a long week. Guess I needed to blow off some steam. I didn't mean to...you know. How embarrassing. Please forget it ever happened."

How embarrassing?

The words sting more than they should. We're here because of Sara, I remind myself.

"It's forgotten," I say, forcing a smile. Thank god I wasn't an idiot. Thank god I didn't hook up with her.

"Did you just wake up?" she asks.

"Actually, no." I hold up the cup in my hand. "Went down to the lobby for a while. I grabbed this for you."

"Oh my god, *thank* you."

I hand it to her and settle on the desk chair. "I was thinking about what Matthew and his mom told us. How it could connect to the Windswept Motel fire. I thought talking to the old owners of the motel could be a good next step, so I got their number from my mom and called them. Gotta say, Mr. Lewes told me a *very* interesting story. We already knew that George had been trying to buy their property for years, right? Well, according to Lewes, they didn't want to sell because business was good—and the motel had been in their family for something like eighty years. But in the months leading up to the fire, things started going south. Their Tripadvisor page was slammed with negative reviews. Guests started complaining about the phones in their rooms ringing at all hours of the night. For the first time, the motel had vacancies in the summer. Lewes reported it to the LIPD, but the cops barely gave them the time of day. It was high season. They claimed they were too busy."

Harriet balances her cup on her knee. "Shit, really? Did Lewes think the harassment could be traced back to George?"

"No. But Mr. Lewes is a really nice guy. Did you know him well?"

Harriet shakes her head.

"Yeah. He was sort of known on my side of town for taking care of people. One family on our block lost their home in the 2007 mortgage crisis, and he let them stay at the motel for free for months while they got it sorted out. This is to say, just because he didn't suspect George doesn't mean George wasn't behind it."

"And then the fire happened?" Harriet asks.

"Then the fire happened. After it, George approached the Leweses with yet another offer. By then, they were worn out. Too tired to deal with wrangling with insurance companies in order to rebuild. They accepted his offer and moved down to Florida."

"Damn. That's quite a story. Nice work."

A swell of pride rises in me.

"All that makes me even more convinced that we need to figure out what was going on between Luke and George," she says. "Did Luke know about all of it? Was he on George's side? Or Barbara's?" She takes a tiny sip of her coffee, and her nose wrinkles.

"Yeah, that sounds good. Oh, also—I asked my dad if they've released Patterson's cause of death to the public. Nothing yet, but I'm going to see if Martin knows anything. I stupidly didn't realize 'til I was talking to my dad this morning that if Patterson was murdered, it would be *huge* for Sara. The cops wouldn't be able to claim she killed Patterson from *prison*, right?"

"I'm not sure the same—" Her face goes pale, her hand smacking down over her mouth. "Oh *god*."

Her coffee cup clatters onto the side table as she scrambles out of the bed and rushes into the bathroom. The door slams behind her and a faucet blasts on, almost loud enough to cover the sound of retching.

Ten minutes later, she reemerges. Her face is clear of makeup, her hair wet, and her shirt buttoned crookedly. She gives me a sheepish smile. "Sorry. I needed to, uh, get myself together."

I get the feeling she doesn't want to talk about her adventure in the bathroom. "It's okay. You good to take off soon?"

Her eyes flick to the unmade bed and back to me. "Yes, absolutely," she says hurriedly. "I'm ready now."

We're walking through the lobby when her phone rings.

She looks at the screen with a grimace. "Do you mind holding on a sec?" She gestures with her phone, and I see the name *Frankie* on the screen. "I gotta grab this really quick."

"Oh. Sure." I want to ask why she can't just talk to this Frankie person in front of me, but I don't. Things are awkward enough after last night.

She smiles gratefully and rounds a corner into a little alcove, leaving me stewing in my thoughts. Who the hell is Frankie? Does Harriet have a boyfriend she just conveniently forgot to tell me about? Why else would she need privacy to talk to him?

I edge closer to the gap she disappeared through, telling myself it's just self-protection. Her voice is low, but I can hear it, just barely, over the hum of voices in the lobby.

"Frankie, yes, I know. Yes." I hear her sigh. She sounds frustrated. "Of course I want my job back."

I stop breathing. Her *job* back? Frankie must be her editor.

"I'm trying—yes. I'm *trying* to get it done as fast as possible. Once I get the right angle—" She cuts off. "Yeah. I'm staying close to the brother. He's—"

Her voice drops again, but I don't need to hear any more.

It's enough.

I'm quiet as Harriet steers us onto the highway. Quiet as she settles us in the middle lane, heading south.

"Are you okay?" she asks after ten minutes of silence.

I realize my leg is bouncing aggressively. I force it still. "Yeah. Fine."

Fine. What a fucking joke. I thought we were in this together, that we were in the pursuit of justice for Sara. That Harriet decided to write the article because she was appalled by what was happening to my sister. That she believes in Sara's innocence. That maybe she had the same feelings growing for me that I have—*had*—for her.

But she's getting a *job* out of it? She hadn't bothered to mention that little fact.

Convenient.

And calling me *the brother,* like I'm not even important enough to have a name, like I'm nothing more than a source, a lead, an assistant helping her to get her career back on track. What'd she tell her editor, that she knew me way back when? That she knew I'd help her with anything she asked because I'm a sucker?

She's not wrong. I *was* stupid enough to think she cared.

"Great." She flicks on the turn signal and pulls left. "So last night while I was writing, I realized what we're missing here is evidence. Cold, hard proof. We have a lot of theories, but I can't publish an article based on those alone. I'd get my ass sued. We need something concrete that shows George set those fires. That he was colluding with government officials. And like I said, we need to figure out how Luke plays into all of it. I mean, right now, we don't even know for sure whether Patterson's death was an accident or murder."

I scowl at the Welcome to New Jersey sign looming up ahead. "Seriously? You think Patterson happened to wander into that fridge as a giant shelving unit toppled over? Those racks are bolted to the wall. They don't just spontaneously fall."

"That's not what I said. I just think—"

"I think the same person killed George and Patterson."

"Why?"

"It just makes sense."

"I mean, I get that. But we need to focus on facts. And the fact is we don't know that. If Patterson *was* murdered—"

I interrupt. "Logan Island isn't exactly a haven for criminals, Harriet. If two people were murdered over the course of as many weeks, that's weird. Sometimes the simplest explanation is the best. Occam's razor. Two deaths, one killer. If I'm right, it means Sara couldn't have done it, and our goal is to get her out of jail—*right*?"

I can't help but wonder if she hopes there are two separate killers. It would give her more juice for her article. A better chance of getting her old job back and getting the hell off the island.

Harriet's frowning. "We can't force things to fit our narrative, Nic. In order for me to write this article, we need to focus on the truth, not whatever's convenient."

Easy for her to say. Her sister isn't the one behind bars. "So Sara can get justice. Right?" I ask again.

"Yeah," she says as she slams on the brakes, the car in front of us suddenly slowing. "Jesus, these fucking assholes can't drive worth a damn."

"So what do you suggest?"

"We need to think out of the box," Harriet says. "Try something new. Maybe get into the office George and Luke shared over on the mainland. See what we can dig up."

Not this again. "You mean break in? That's not something new. It's exactly what you suggested about Patterson's office last week."

"Yeah, but we never did it."

"Harriet, if you find something in that office, can you include *that* in your article? Shouldn't we start by, I don't know, looking at public records?"

"Pfff," she scoffs. "FOIA requests can take *weeks*. Even months. You want your sister sitting behind bars for that long? She's headed to that AC jail any day now."

"Not once they figure out Patterson was murdered. They'll have to let her out then."

"What—no. They won't."

I throw my foot up against the glove compartment. "Yes. They will."

"Nic, I know you want your sister out of jail. I do too—"

"Do you?" I mutter.

"What's that supposed to mean?" She shoots me a wounded glance. "I do. That's why I think getting into that office is important. And listen, we won't have to break in. George's keys are in my mom's bedroom. If I can get her out of the house for a bit, I can sneak in there and snag them. Then we can drive over to the mainland and let ourselves in. It's not breaking and entering if there's no breaking, right? If anyone catches us, I'll just say I left something inside—a sweater, maybe—and I need it back. I mean, I *was* his stepdaughter. It's not beyond the realm of possibility." She senses my hesitation. "If we want to figure out how involved Luke was, this is our best bet. His files, his computer even—it'll all be there."

I gnaw on my inner cheek. I said I'd do anything in my power to help my sister. This is my chance to prove it.

"All right," I finally say.

Harriet smiles. "Once we're back, I'll drop you off, head home, and find the key. I mean, if we've got a key, what's the worst that can happen?"

CHAPTER THIRTY-TWO

HARRIET

September 12

12:52 p.m.

I pull into the parking lot of the Yacht Club, empty outside of Nic's car. It's hard to believe that George's memorial was just yesterday.

Harder to believe it was just yesterday that Barbara Patterson died.

I drop Nic by his car, glad for the silence of an empty car. I need to process what happened last night—or rather, what didn't. Why did he reject me? Did I misread things?

Our conversation at the bar felt so intimate, I thought we were on the same page, that he'd forgiven me for what I did eight years ago. That it was finally going to happen.

There was only one bed after all.

But then he very literally pushed me away. The memory sits like a lump of coal, hard and black and ugly in my mind. It's clear I was wrong about everything. He was so testy in the car—probably annoyed I'd put him in that position. He's a nice guy after all. I'm sure he doesn't like having to reject people. I can only assume he has to with frequency. I mean, *look* at the guy.

By the time I'm pulling onto my mom's street, I've decided that the only thing to do is move on. Refocus. Remember what actually matters—why we're spending time together.

I park in the driveway, and I text my aunt Vicky.

> Hi! Is there any way you could do me a huge favor?

> Harriet—hi! What's up?

> I think my mom needs to get out of the house for a while. Can you invite her to coffee?

There's a delay in her reply. She's probably trying to figure out a way to let me down gently. She and my mom haven't been close in many, many years.

I'm about to text again when there's a response.

> Why don't you take her out to lunch?
> I'm sure she'd love that!

There's pretty much nothing my mother would like *less*, but I don't feel like explaining our tenuous relationship to Vicky over text.

Outside of the memorial, I'm really the only person she's seen since George died. Spending time with someone different would be good for her

After a minute, I send another message.

You guys used to be friends. This would be a good opportunity to catch up.

I can't leave your grandmother ☹

You can bring her.

I really think it'd be good for her mental health. I wouldn't ask otherwise

I need this to happen. I need to get to those keys.

Please??? I'll owe you big time.

Finally, Vicky responds.

All right...if you really think it would help. But I can't guarantee she'll say yes

THANK YOU!!!

I climb out of the car and head into the house. I'm digging into the fridge when my mom walks into the kitchen.

"Hey," I say, popping my head around the side of the door.

She jumps back with a hand against her heart. "Harriet! You scared me. What in the name of god are you doing?"

"I live here?" I say, a noodle dangling from my lips.

She continues. "And where have you *been*? I cannot believe you disappeared from your father's *memorial*—"

"*Step*father!" I can't help but interject.

"—and after yet another person was murdered! You didn't come to check on me. You just *took off*! What could you have possibly had to deal with that was more important? You don't even have a job, for crying out loud."

"I had to go see someone in the city," I say.

"For what? You got fired!" Thankfully, her phone buzzes in her hand before I can respond. "Hang on." She squints at the screen, then mutters, "Your aunt. What is she..." She types something and shakes her head. "Well. Vicky claims I'm the only one who—" Her phone buzzes again. "Oh, good grief."

"What is it?"

My mom sighs. "It appears I have to run out for a bit. But when I get back, we are going to finish this conversation."

As she gathers her purse from the counter, a thought occurs to me.

"Hey, Mom?"

She glances at her watch. "Yes?"

"Did Luke and George have a good relationship?"

Now she looks at me, frowning. "*Excuse* me?"

"Like, were things going well between them? With their business?"

She looks thoroughly annoyed by my questions. "Of course they were, Harriet. Luke *adored* George. George was a mentor to him. A *father* figure!"

"Right, okay." I figured that was probably the answer I'd get, but I thought I'd try my hand anyway.

"Have some respect," she snaps and then departs, leaving me alone in the house for the first time in two weeks.

CHAPTER THIRTY-THREE

NIC

September 12

1:15 p.m.

I walk over to Joe's Diner just after one to meet Martin.

The diner is a long, narrow, silver bullet of a building, which has been around longer than I've been alive. As I push through the door, I spot Martin in a booth, root beer and a plate of fries in front of him.

My shoulders relax at his familiar face. It's only been a few days since we saw each other, but they've been some of the longest of my entire life.

"Fry?" he says by way of greeting as I slip in across from him.

"Yeah, thanks." I grab a couple and stuff them in my mouth.

"How're you doing with everything?"

Before I can respond, a waitress stops at our table. "Anything to drink?"

I order an Arnold Palmer and another plate of fries, and she heads off toward the kitchen. "Things are okay," I say to Martin. "Just tired. Got back into town—"

"*Back* to town?" Martin asks. "Where were you?"

Shit. I really am tired, or I wouldn't have said that. I haven't told him about Harriet's article or the fact that we're looking into things. He works closely with both the fire department and the LIPD; he hangs out socially with them. I don't know if he'd believe his friends might be corrupt.

I trust him, of course I do, but what if he's drinking and lets something slip about what we're doing? We'd be screwed.

"Yeah. I went up to New York. It was supposed to be a quick trip, but I ended up staying overnight because of the storm—"

He interrupts. "I'm confused. You find a dead body, and then five seconds later, you take off for New York? What's going on, man?"

"I…um. I went up there with Harriet," I finally say for lack of anything better. It's the truth, but not entirely.

"*Harriet?* Somebody told me that it was you two who found Barbara, but I thought they must have been mistaken. I didn't know you guys were hanging out. Wait." His eyes narrow at me. "Why *are* you guys hanging out? The last I'd heard, you were mortal enemies."

He's so dramatic. "We weren't mortal enemies!"

"If I'm not mistaken, you referred to her as *the devil herself* when we ran into her at Hendricks."

God, why does the man have the memory of an elephant?

He's staring at me, waiting for an answer.

"Actually…um. We're the opposite of mortal enemies," I say. "We're dating."

What I just said sinks into my brain. We're *dating*? I really wish I'd gotten more sleep last night.

"Oh. My. Fucking. God." Martin slaps a hand over his mouth. "You're *dating*?"

Shit. This is bad. This is very, very bad.

"I have to admit, Steven and I talked about how you two seemed…" A grin fills his face. "Honestly, very enemies-to-lovers. Like you were either going to strangle each other or start making out on the bar."

It's too late to take it back. That would lead to even more questions I don't want to answer. "Yeah. Well."

Martin leans across the table. "Tell me everything. *How* did this happen?"

I cough. "Uh, well, we ran into each other the day after the bar and got to talking—"

"Wait." His expression darkens. "I can't believe I— This isn't exciting, it's insane! Don't you remember how she treated you back in high school? How wrecked you were? She broke your heart!"

"It wasn't *broken*."

He raises an eyebrow. "You showed up at my house crying."

"One time!"

"More than one time."

I suddenly regret the length of our friendship.

"She ditched you with no explanation. Have you guys talked that through?"

I'm silent as the waitress sets down my fries and drink.

Once she's gone, Martin continues, "I just don't want her to hurt you again. It's been eight years, and you've barely dated."

"That isn't because of *Harriet*!"

He raises an eyebrow.

"It isn't! There are limited options around, you know? And most of them are so..."

Boring.

"So *what*?"

"Never mind." I don't need a lecture from Martin on my taste in women. "And to answer your first question, yes. We *have* talked about what happened, and she apologized."

Martin sits back in his seat and picks up his phone. "Well, that's good."

"And Harriet is...is— What the hell are you doing?"

He's typing away furiously. "Texting Steven."

"Wait—" I say, but it's too late.

"Done. He's gonna die. Or—does he already know?" He shakes his head, staring at the screen. "No, if he knew, he would have told me."

I stifle a groan. I am so screwed. "Anyway, after we found Patterson, we drove up there."

"Yeah." He sets the phone onto his napkin. "Patterson. I wanted to ask how you're doing with that? Two bodies in a month is some heavy shit."

The image of George's limp body flashes through my mind, now joined by Barbara Patterson, bleeding out in the fridge.

So much death.

"I'm okay," I say. "But it was certainly surprising."

"That's one word for it. Poor Mrs. Patterson. She was a hard-ass, but still. She didn't deserve to die like that."

"Yeah. Awful." I take a sip of my drink. "Have you heard anything? About whether it was an accident?"

Martin glances around the restaurant, then leans in. "You didn't hear it from me, but they think she was killed. Word is they think she was hit on the back of the head, died, and *then* someone pushed the shelving unit over."

I frown. "Why go to all that trouble if she was already dead?"

"Current theory is that whoever killed her wanted it to look accidental. But there was a contusion on the back of her head inconsistent with the injuries she sustained from the shelf."

I knew it. "So she was murdered," I say to confirm.

"Seems like it, yeah."

I pick up my phone. "Good."

Martin looks at me like I'm crazy. "*Good?*"

"Well, *Sara* couldn't have killed Patterson, obviously. Which proves she didn't kill George."

"I hate to say it, but that's not what it proves."

He sounds just like Harriet. "Yes, it does."

Martin sighs. "Nic. You've been under a lot of stress lately. You're not thinking clearly. Just because someone else died—"

"Was *murdered*!"

"Shh!" Martin twists around to make sure no one heard my outburst. When he turns back, he's pissed. "Keep your fucking voice down! I could get fired for telling you that. Don't make me regret it. You know I don't think Sara's guilty, but think about it like a cop. There's no reason to think the same person killed both of them, and as much as I hate to say it, the evidence against your sister is strong. Strong enough that the

DA charged her. I understand this whole situation is impossibly hard, but you have to trust the American justice system—"

I snort.

"—because there's not much else you can do. Except maybe try to convince your parents that she'd be better off with a public defender than cousin Barry."

"They won't listen." I rub my forehead. I know he's right. I knew Harriet was right back there in the car. I just didn't want to let myself see it. "I'm sorry. I won't get you in trouble, I promise. I'm just exhausted. Every time I think she's caught a break..."

"I'm sorry, man," Martin says, patting my arm.

"Yeah. Thanks." I know he means it, but all the sorrys in the world aren't going to save Sara.

After we leave the diner, I drive straight to Harriet's.

She answers the front door with a frown, brandishing her phone like a weapon. She's changed into jean shorts and a button-up, her hair piled high on her head. She looks hot.

Hot and mad.

Of course she is; the thought of us dating must be appalling to her. *The brother.*

"So we're dating now, huh?" she says before I can get a word in edgewise. "Thanks so much for the heads-up, Nic. What the hell were you thinking?"

My jaw clenches at her tone. "Martin was grilling me about New York, and it just came out," I say. Does she really have to act *so* fucking annoyed about this?

"It just *came out*?" She stares me for a long moment, her expression unreadable.

"I'll call him right now and take it back. But he's going to have a lot of questions. Do you want everyone in a thirty-mile radius knowing what we're doing?"

She makes a face and steps back so I can walk into the house. "No. It's fine. But in the future, could you please keep me in the loop so I don't have to learn about shit like this from Steven?"

"If I'm ever in another situation where I have to lie about us dating, I'll be sure to give you a heads-up," I say, stopping in the foyer. I cross my arms.

"Whatever. I have news, so it's good you're here anyway. I found them." She rummages in her back pocket and pulls out a set of keys, dangling them between her fingers. "For George's office!"

"Great," I say tersely.

Her face falls. "What's the matter with you?"

"Nothing."

"You look mad. What did I do?" She swipes at her cheeks like she'll find an explanation there.

I force myself to breathe. I need to fucking relax. Martin's right. Eight years ago, I stupidly let myself fall for her, and it nearly destroyed me. I can't let myself make the same dumb mistake.

"Nothing," I say again. "It's fine. Everything's fine. I'm just tired."

"I told you that you shouldn't sleep on the floor!"

The words hang in the air between us, a reminder of last night. Of how mortified she was this morning.

"It's fine." I need a change of subject. "I saw Martin." I fill her in on what he told me about Barbara Patterson's death. Harriet listens, her eyes softening as I tell her what he said about the two murders. How it doesn't help Sara at all.

"I'm sorry, Nic," she says. "I know that isn't what you want to hear."

"Yeah. Well. We're going to George and Luke's office, right? We'll find something that *will* help her."

She blinks in surprise. "Are you saying— You want to go *now*?"

"It's Saturday. The office will be empty, right?"

"Yeah, I guess? I mean, George is, well, dead, and I sorta doubt Luke is sitting there working the week after his partner was killed." She heads into the kitchen and returns a moment later, a pair of sneakers clenched in her hand. "Ready?"

I nod. "Ready."

CHAPTER THIRTY-FOUR

HARRIET

September 12
2:38 p.m.

Nic and I drive back over the bridges connecting the island to mainland New Jersey. We haven't spoken much since we left my mom's.

He's been so grumpy all day. I know he's tired, but so am I, for fuck's sake. Plus, I drove three hours this morning, and here I am again, behind the wheel of my car. I'm sure he's disappointed that it wasn't as easy as *someone killed Patterson, therefore Sara's innocent*, but it feels a little like he's taking it out on me.

The only sound is Google Maps, leading us through Pleasantville and into the empty parking lot of an office park.

I've never been here, and I'm startled to see how small it is, how squat and decrepit. George's company in Manhattan was housed on seven floors of a giant, modern high-rise in Midtown. Working here was a real step down.

Or…maybe not. George wasn't an idiot, but he *was* a snob. He'd never have worked in a place like this unless there was a reason. Maybe he learned up in NYC that it was better to fly under the radar.

"Don't park here," Nic says as I pull into the lot. "Park back out on the street."

I stop. "What if we have to make a quick getaway?"

He heaves a sigh, and I bristle. "There are only two other cars in here, Harriet. If we park here, it'll be obvious we're inside."

I've had about enough of his attitude. "To who exactly? You think someone's going to see a parked car and immediately think, *Wow, those people must be inside the building committing crimes?*"

"I'm just saying—we need to be cautious."

"Yeah. I get that, thanks."

"Then you agree we should park on the street?"

"That's not what I said."

We glare at each other for a long moment. Too long a moment. Apparently, my body hasn't gotten the memo that we're not interested in him anymore. Heat spreads through my insides, and my eyes dart to his mouth, the way his stubborn lower lip juts out.

It's so juicy. I want to lean over and press my mouth against his. Take his lip between my teeth and gently bite it. Fuck him just one more time to get him out of my system.

Except I like him too much. I know I do. I wouldn't be satisfied with just one more. I'd want two and three and four, and it doesn't even matter because he doesn't want me at all.

"What?" Nic says.

I'm still staring at his lips. I force myself to look up into his eyes. "Nothing. I was just thinking. About where to park. Like I said, what if someone catches us inside?"

"You said this wasn't illegal because you have a key."

"Yeah, I mean, it mostly isn't, but we should still have an exit route. Just in case."

He turns toward his window. "Fine. Have it your way."

"Okay," I say, feeling strangely deflated.

I park the car.

The lobby is small, dingy. There's no front desk, no place for a receptionist to sit. Just a two-car elevator bank, gray threadbare carpeting, and a palm tree wilting in one corner.

It's so small-time. George ran a multibillion-dollar real estate empire in Midtown Manhattan, and now...this?

Again, I wonder: *Why?*

A directory hanging by the entrance informs us George's office is on the second floor. Nic strides ahead of me to the elevator call buttons, jabbing the arrow up.

The ride up is short, tense, my heart creeping up into my throat.

I have a key, sure, but I'm not an idiot. I know this isn't *really* legal. If we find something big—evidence that proves corruption or ethical violations—I can't just include it in my article without some serious legal tap dancing. But at least I'll know what direction to take it from here.

It's better than nothing.

This is our best option. There are too many loose ends, too many unanswered questions, and the clock is ticking. Sara's getting transferred to Atlantic City county jail any day now, and that place is nothing like the jail on Logan Island.

We find the office halfway down the hall. There's no sign, just the numbers 202 glued to the face of a door.

Inside, we find a small reception room with two leather chairs. A small coffee table. In the corner, another wilting palm.

"Where should we start?" Nic asks.

"Through there?" I point to another door on the far wall. "I assume that's where we'll find the offices."

We start moving at the same time, and my forearm hits Nic square in the groin.

I jerk away. "Sorry," I choke out. Of all the places to make contact. I want to sink down into the center of the earth.

An emotion flashes across his face, gone before I can place it. "It's fine." The words are tight with unleashed anger.

Is he mad? It was a *mistake*. "I didn't mean—"

He interrupts. "After you." He sweeps his hand toward the back of the room.

We find ourselves in a short, dark hallway with two doors off it.

"Their offices?" Nic asks.

"I assume so. Try the first one."

I hold my breath as he twists the knob. George was so paranoid that it's entirely possible he kept his office locked up tight.

When it turns, I let out a breath. He pushes the door open. The room is small, spare—just a couple of filing cabinets pressed up against the wall beneath a narrow window and a large L-shaped desk in its center. On it is a desktop computer.

"Jackpot." I head to it.

"How long have they had this office?" Nic asks.

I settle into the desk chair. "About four years, I think. Why?"

He shrugs. "I don't know. Where's all the personal stuff? Pictures or whatever? I've never worked in an office, but I was under the impression that people usually decorated them?"

"Well, I can't speak to Luke, but George wasn't exactly known for his sentimentality." I flick on the computer, and it whirrs to life.

"Whose computer is that?" Nic asks. "Whose office is this?"

"Actually, I'm not sure." I open a drawer and rifle through it until I find an envelope with a name printed on its front. "George's."

"Are you in?" Nic walks over and peers over my shoulder. "Shit. A password?"

"Yeah. I should have known he'd have one. Same guy who changed the gate code to the beach weekly." I study the keyboard, thinking. "I bet I can figure this out."

Nic makes a skeptical noise that rankles me. "If you get it wrong too many times, you'll get locked out."

I swivel around. "Oh, I'm sorry. Do you have a better idea? Some hacking skills I'm not aware of? If so, I'm all ears. Most people have really basic passwords, like..."

I type my mother's name and birthday and press Enter. The box on the screen shudders.

No, that makes sense. It's like I just told Nic—George wasn't the sentimental type. His password won't be something personal.

"You only have four attempts left," Nic points out unhelpfully.

"Yeah. I can read, thanks."

He huffs a sigh.

I try again. George's old company name.

No.

"Three more."

The name of his old company plus—according to Google—the year he founded it.

"Two."

I whirl toward him, glaring. "Do you think that's helpful?"

"Just saying," he mutters. He wanders over to the window, peering through its metal blinds. He's driving me bananas.

"Relax, okay? Even if we do get locked out, it's not for forever. Just an hour or two. We can do something else while we wait."

He turns, crossing his arms. "Yeah. You *would* say that."

"What does that mean?"

"Nothing," he mutters as he walks over to the door. Is he seriously leaving?

"Where are you going?" I ask.

"To the other room. We don't have all fucking day, you know." He disappears into the hallway before I can respond.

God, he's being *such* a dick. "Whatever," I mutter.

I look back at the box on the screen. It really isn't the end of the world if I get locked out for a bit. Nic is just stressed and not thinking clearly.

I try one more combination. His company name plus his birthday.

The box disappears, and the desktop unfolds on the screen. *Oh my god.* I did it. For someone allegedly so concerned with security, that was pretty fucking easy, but I guess it speaks to what an egomaniac the guy was.

I should go tell Nic we're in. But he's being so annoying; I don't really want to deal with him right now. Let him go through Luke's stuff. I'll handle this, and then we can talk.

I turn back to the computer, navigate over to the email icon, and start scrolling down George's inbox. There's lots of back-and-forth between him and the other members of the town council—lots of back-and-forth between him and Patterson without anyone else weighing in. I skim a few from Mayor DiPetrio talking about the new zoning board chair, but nothing jumps out at me as blatantly illegal. Maybe a little bit of collusion?

I grab my phone, snap a couple photos to send to Maggie, then type *Luke Dalio* into the search bar.

We need to figure out if what Matthew said was true. Were George and Luke really having issues? Or was George just venting to a stranger after a few too many cocktails? If they were, I need evidence. Evidence that's strong enough to convince the police that Luke had motive to kill him.

Hundreds of results pop up on the screen. A lot of the exchanges are short. Terse, even.

I skim through exchange after exchange about the motel property.

Approximately one million emails later, I'm starting to lose hope. Is Sara doomed? Should I get a job working at the local supermarket instead of pretending that I'll ever work in media again?

Nic hasn't reappeared. I wonder if he's having better luck.

I find him in the office next door, crouched in front of an open filing cabinet, surrounded by stacks of folders.

"What are you doing?"

His head jerks up. "Jesus. I didn't hear you come in."

"Sorry."

He rubs his fist against his temple. "It's fine. I was just reading through all this crap. Did you get into the computer?"

"Yeah. I figured out the password. GGCapitalGroup10301975. His company name plus his birthday. No thanks to you."

He pulls himself up to his feet and sets the paper he's holding down on the desk, his eyes flashing. "I just didn't want us to get locked out. That would set us back hours. Sara's getting transferred this week. Not that you care."

"*Excuse* me?" He keeps making these little digs at me, and I'm sick of it. "Of course I care. What the hell do you think I'm doing here if I don't?"

He moves out from behind the desk, striding toward me. Suddenly, there are mere inches between us. Our eyes lock together, the green of his irises deep and silken. His pupils dilate, and my breath catches.

"Honestly, Harriet, I don't know."

I swallow. The heat of him, so close, is scrambling my thoughts. "I care," I whisper.

I don't know who moves first. Me, him, it doesn't matter. His hand finds my cheek, my fingers running down his broad chest, his tangling into my hair. He yanks me closer.

"Harriet," he breathes, and the sound of it—my name—sends me over the edge. Our mouths collide.

Finally.

I run my tongue along his bottom lip, so perfect and soft, and it's everything I've ever wanted. Everything I want right now. He moans into my mouth.

My hands roam, up his muscled back into his soft, soft hair, and I pull him closer. I want to feel him. I *need* to feel him. All of him, against me.

His fingers dance against my stomach, tugging my shirt, my bra up as he finds my breast, my nipple, and then the tip of his tongue is there, soft and wet, running circles around my areola, his teeth scraping against it.

Oh god.

He scoops me up and sets me on the desk. "This needs to go away," he growls, tugging my button-up shirt off over my head, then taking his off in one deft motion. His body is wiry and strong, muscled. A colored tattoo of a bushel of herbs winds down the smooth skin of his abdomen.

Then he's back against me, his tongue on my neck, my chest, my breasts. His mouth, his lips. I'm on fire. He's hard against my leg.

A moan escapes me, and he smiles. "You like that?" he whispers in my ear.

In reply, I snake a hand around his back, pulling him between my legs, my hips bucking into his groin, and he gasps.

"Jesus, Harriet."

"You feel so good," I murmur. "You feel *so* fucking good." His mouth runs down the side of my neck. "Oh my god, Nic, I forgot how good this feels."

He freezes, then pulls away, cold settling against my warm skin. He wipes his mouth with the back of his hand and steps back.

"What is it?" My hands flutter over my chest, suddenly self-conscious.

"What are we doing?" Nic's voice is tight. He takes another step back, then another.

"What do you mean?"

"I mean," he says, "what the fuck *is* this, Harriet? You, me, this whole thing. Why are you writing that article? For Sara...or for yourself?"

I'm stunned into silence. What is he talking about? He still has his shirt off. *I* still have my shirt off.

I scoop it from the desk beside me and struggle back into it and my bra.

"I heard you, you know," he continues. "Earlier today, on the phone with *Frankie*. You don't actually care about me—us—at all, do you? All you care about is getting your job back. Leaving. You called me *the brother*."

My heart drops. He heard me? He heard me and said nothing until now. The car ride back, when I thought he was quiet because of what I'd done. It was all because of that stupid phone call to Frankie.

"Wait, hang on. It's not what you think," I say, stumbling over my words. "Yeah, okay, sure, I guess when I first came to you, I thought you could help get me in front of Sara, but—"

His nostrils flare. "Exactly. You were using me."

"Nic..." My palms are sweaty. I rub them against the front of my shirt. "Stop. Yes, okay, Frankie said if I wrote something good, there might be a chance...but I want to help Sara. I swear to god."

"Sure." He turns away, slipping into his shirt.

Anger shoots through me. He knew about this article from the jump. He was on board with it. And *now* he's giving me shit?

"What is your *problem*? You're mad because I might get something out of it too?" As soon as the words are out of my mouth, I regret them.

His jaw muscle clenches. "Yeah, exactly. Here I was, stupid enough to think you were doing this out of the goodness of your heart. Because you..." He shakes his head. "Never mind."

"Never mind *what*?"

He's backing away, pushing a hand through his hair over and over until it stands on end. "I'm not letting you do it to me again, you understand? I'm not letting you waltz back into my life because it's convenient for you and then disappear when you've gotten what you need. You're the same selfish person I knew back in high school. The same person who fucking *ghosted* me after two weeks of—" He cuts off, shaking his head. "God, I'm dumb. Fool me once, right?"

"Wow," I say slowly, his words settling into my center, heavy and painful. "Thanks. That's how little you think of me, huh? Good to know. What's next? Are you going to claim that I *kissed* you for my job too?"

His expression is unreadable.

A whisper in the back of my mind asks if he has a point. What *was* I planning to do here? Get involved with him and then...what? What was my endgame? If the article turns out well, my plan *is* to go back to the city.

Which would mean leaving him behind. Again.

Would I have told him before I left this time?

I feel sick. Like I can't breathe. Like if I don't leave this room right now, I'll start to scream.

"I need to go."

I turn to leave, but he grabs my sleeve. "Harriet, wait. I—"

I yank away. "Let me go."

"But you're my ride—"

Oh.

"You're a grown-up. Find another one."

I don't wait to hear his reply. I hurry into George's office and grab my things, my bag bumping against a stack of papers, toppling half of it to the ground. If I stop to clean it up, there's a chance I might fall apart right here on the floor, and I can't—I *won't*—do that with Nic around. I'd rather die. I scrape the papers together, shove them into my bag, and hurry out of the office.

I don't let the tears come until the elevator door shuts behind me.

CHAPTER THIRTY-FIVE

NIC

September 12

4:25 p.m.

After Harriet storms off, I shove our argument out of my mind and angrily search through Luke's papers, where I find absolutely nothing of use.

I move to George's office and log into his computer using the password Harriet told me. It takes some digging, but I finally strike gold when I recover the recently removed items from his email. An exchange between George and user10974776@gmail.com—clearly a throwaway account—all about Luke. His drinking, his erratic behavior, his tendency to run his mouth.

The final email in the thread ends in a warning: George needs to handle Luke before things spiral further.

Handle? What the hell does that mean? Was George planning on killing Luke? Did Luke catch wind and kill George first?

Or am I overreacting? Maybe *handle* meant…I don't know. Send him to rehab.

But doubt gnaws at me.

Then I uncover something even more interesting. A forwarded invoice for "consulting services" from a Gmail address belonging to someone named Ryan Krischer. It's for thirty thousand dollars, dated four days after the motel fire.

A quick search of locals with that name turns up his LinkedIn. He's a Pleasantville native and a bank teller at a local Chase. Why the hell would George pay a random bank teller so much money? The timing is suspicious as hell too. But I can't see any connection between Krischer and the LIFD. Maybe I'm conflating things, seeing links where there aren't any, because I'm so tired, so fucking pissed off about what happened between me and Harriet.

The audacity of her trying to pretend that she's not only here for her career. I know what I heard. I'm not some dumbass seventeen-year-old virgin anymore, thinking with my dick and not my head.

I push her out of my mind, turning back to the screen and snapping photos of the emails and invoice to look into later.

Doing this alone has made the process twice as long, and I still need to figure out how I'm getting back to the island. I'm reluctant to take an Uber because it'll run me fifty dollars, but I'm due at my parents' house for dinner in thirty minutes.

Then I hear the sound of a door opening in the inner office.

Did Harriet come back for me?

"You know you're—" I start but cut off when a man appears in the doorway.

Mid-forties and balding, with deep frown lines carved around his mouth. Decidedly not Harriet.

"Who the fuck are you?" he says. "And what the hell are you doing in George's office?"

CHAPTER THIRTY-SIX

HARRIET

September 12

4:49 p.m.

After a drive that's mostly a blur, I pull up in front of Steven's apartment building.

I haven't felt this way in a decade, not since Kozel ghosted me.

Stupid. Blindsided. Like my heart's been torn in two.

I can't believe I let this happen. I knew I shouldn't act on my feelings for Nic, knew I should keep it strictly professional, but I let my stupid heart take over. And for what—so he could turn around and accuse me of being *selfish*?

I'm writing an article about his sister, for god's sake! I've spent the last two weeks doing almost nothing but trying to figure out how to get her out of jail.

Because you wanted your old job back a voice whispers in my head.

"Hello?" Steven says through the intercom.

"Hey," I say. "Can I come up—"

Before I can finish the sentence, the door buzzes.

I trudge up the narrow set of stairs to the third floor, dodging around a dripping surfboard propped against the wall, and knock on his apartment door.

Much to my surprise and dismay, Martin answers. I need to talk to Steven, and I was hoping to do it alone. Or at least without Nic's best friend listening in.

Martin's smile falls as he sees my tear-streaked face. "Hey. What's going on, Harriet? Are you okay?"

At his questions, tears spring back into my eyes. I blink fast, trying to hold them at bay.

"I'm sorry to just show up like this—"

"No, please. It's totally fine."

"Harriet!" Steven appears behind him. He gasps when he sees my face. "What happened? Come in, come in."

He guides me over to the couch, settling next to me. Martin takes the chair on his other side.

"I... Nic..." My voice breaks.

I avoid looking at Martin as I fill them in everything—Sharkey's *pin it on someone* comment, the article I pitched to Frankie, Nic's involvement, what we've learned so far, and how we covered up what we were doing by pretending to date. Then I get to the worst part of all—how I managed to let real feelings get tangled up in everything.

Once I'm done, Steven lets out a low whistle. "Okay. To summarize—because I gotta admit my head is spinning—George had an illegitimate child. You suspect that not only did George burn down a building in NYC and kill someone in the process, but he might have been behind the motel fire last year. And the LIFD helped cover it up—"

Martin makes a noise that sends a shiver up my spine. Steven and I both turn to find him hunched into himself, his face pale.

"Martin? What is it?" Steven asks with concern.

"The motel fire. I was..."

"Oh, honey. Of course." Steven scoots down on the couch and rests a hand on Martin's knee. "What happened with that kid... It must have been incredibly traumatic."

"It's not just that." Martin's voice is pained. "After the fire, there were rumors. Whispers that the inspectors found signs of arson but still blamed it on the motel's old, crappy wiring. I went to my supervisor and told him what I'd heard, but he brushed me off. Said I should know better than to listen to silly rumors. When I pushed, he asked if I was accusing the fire inspectors of lying and reminded me that's a serious charge. I backed off. I'd known the guy for ten years. I thought he was one of the good ones. But a couple months later, wouldn't you know—the fire department got a major bump in their budget, pushed through by the city council. I told myself it was just a coincidence, but now..."

Steven wraps his arms around him, and Martin buries his face in his shoulder.

"I work with the LIFD all the time," Martin says, his voice muffled by the collar of Steven's polo shirt. "I drink with them. They're my friends. What if they were all in on it? What if my *boss* was?" After a minute, Martin raises his head and wipes his eyes. "Look, Harriet," he says. "If I'd known what you and Nic were up to, I would have told Nic he was being a total idiot. That he should leave it to the professionals. But." He rubs his hand against his jaw. "It sounds like Sara needs you in her corner. You guys have to keep digging until you uncover the truth."

"Speaking of that—" Steven turns to me with his brows raised. "Harriet, my dear. You're writing about Sara's case for *Humans*, of all places? Why in god's name did you think that was a good idea?"

Shit. I'd been hoping to avoid this conversation. Steven *hates* Frankie. A lot.

"She came to you, right?" Steven presses. "Frankie came to *you*?"

"Well..."

His jaw drops. "You're kidding. Harriet Baker. *You* pitched it to *them*. Why the fuck would you do that to yourself?"

He is well aware *why*. "Jesus, Steven. I need a job! I can't live with my mother for the rest of my life! I don't even know if I can live with her for another *month* without losing my shit."

He purses his lips. "Okay, I understand that. But there are other places. Other magazines. Might I remind you how Frankie screwed you over? That bitch threw you to the wolves!"

"This is different," I mutter.

"Oh really? How exactly? Are you back on their payroll? Has she given you any guarantees? Or even fucking apologized?"

My stomach knots. "I... No. But I was the one who fucked up and got fired! Frankie says this is how I can prove myself to her again."

Steven looks at me with pity. "Har, that woman has been gaslighting you for years. She always managed to convince you that you were in the wrong—including with that situation."

"What are you talking about? I screwed up!"

"Harriet. Do you really not remember what happened?"

"That *is*—"

He cuts me off. "Honey, I'm sorry, but you've forgotten the truth. Frankie knew Belinda Howard didn't want her pregnancy made public—they'd told her that when they set up the interview. But she didn't bother sharing that information with you, so you included it. Anyone would have. It was huge news." He leans in, voice tight. "And then Frankie went ahead and published it, knowing full well that Belinda's people would lose their shit. And when Belinda's publicist called freaking out, she blamed it all on you. Said you'd gone rogue. You got fired, and I bet *Humans* made double their ad revenue off the clicks."

I sink back into the couch, closing my eyes. Frankie claimed she'd told me to take it out, and when I said I didn't remember that, she doubled down. Told me I was careless. Incompetent. She made me question myself, made me wonder if I was losing my mind.

Steven continues, "Harriet, you called me when it all started going down, insisting that she hadn't told you. But as time went on, and she told you over and over again that she had, your story started to change. The thing is—I believe *you*. Frankie had fucked with you for *years*, so it's no wonder you believed her, but you were great at your job. If she'd told you not to include it, you wouldn't have. You didn't do anything wrong—she did."

Steven's words knock the wind out of me, and suddenly it's all so clear: Frankie used me to get exactly what she wanted. She wore me so far down I had started doubting myself, my memory.

"You see it now, don't you?" Steven says. He's scooted back next to me, gently stroking my hand. "Listen. None of it was your fault, Har, okay? But I can't stand idly by and watch you go through all that again."

What am I doing? Writing an article for *her*? Trying to prove my worth to a person who doesn't give two shits about me? Trying so hard to get back to my life in the city when I'm not sure I was ever really happy there. I was working seventy hours a week, surviving on next to nothing because New York City media jobs don't pay livable New York City wages. I had almost no friends. Most of the people I knew from college had moved out to the suburbs or disappeared into relationships.

Nic was right to yell at me. I'm an asshole.

Nic.

"Where is he?" Martin asks, and I realize I said his name out loud.

"I..." I swallow. "I left him at George's office." I left him because I was too stubborn to admit out loud that maybe some of what he said was valid. Too stubborn to tell him the most important reason I was doing it: because of him. Because he's important to me. Because I have fallen for him so hard it scares the shit out of me.

"Excuse me?" Martin says. "You left him at George's *office*? Where is it?"

I wince. "Um, Pleasantville?"

"You left Nic on the mainland. Does he have a car?"

I shake my head.

Steven groans. "Harriet."

"I'm sorry! Like I told you, we got into a fight about...you know. Everything. We kissed and—"

"Excuse me, you *what*?" Steven whips toward me.

"—then he accused me of being selfish. It pissed me off! I figured he could, I don't know, take an Uber or something."

"An Uber from Pleasantville costs, like, fifty dollars," Martin says. "That's a lot of money to Nic."

"I didn't think about that," I say meekly.

"Yeah, clearly," Steven mutters.

God, I'm a shit. I need to make this right. I need to prove to Nic that I care about *him*, not my stupid career or Frankie's opinion or the life I left in New York.

"I'm sure he just took one anyway," Martin says, gentler than I deserve.

I pull my phone from my bag. "I'm going to call and offer to pay for it."

Martin coughs. "Not to be prescriptive, but…I wouldn't. It would probably just piss him off more."

I pause, my phone halfway to my ear. "True. Okay, maybe just a text? To check that he's okay?"

Martin nods.

I shoot one off, and we wait, but there's no response.

"Can you try?" I ask Martin. I feel so pathetic.

He kindly doesn't make a big deal of it. "Sure. Hang on." He puts his phone to his ear. After a minute, he shakes his head. "No answer."

"Shit."

"Well," Martin says. "He's probably heading home to change. He's going to his parents' tonight for dinner so they can go over more stuff with that idiot Barry. If you leave right now, I bet you'll catch him at his apartment. You can talk it out in person."

My palms grow clammy. In *person*? That's so grown-up. Mature.

I'm more the *let me send a text and hope for the best* type, but I guess I can try it.

"Do you think he'll forgive me?" It feels like my nerves are using my stomach as a trampoline. If he doesn't forgive me, what will I do? It's only been a few short weeks, but I already can't imagine my life without him.

"I think he will, yeah," Martin says. "But either way, you guys need to work something out. Sara needs you."

CHAPTER THIRTY-SEVEN

NIC

September 12

5:35 p.m.

"What the fuck are you doing in George's office?"

I jump up from the chair and press myself against the wall next to the window as the man steps into the room. He's wearing an expression that makes my blood run cold—tense, menacing.

He looks like a man with nothing to lose.

He's between me and the door; there's no way out. I'm trapped, and my phone's still on the desk. Fuck. I was too freaked out to think about grabbing it.

"Hello? Who the fuck are you?" He moves toward me, and I shrink back like a fucking coward. Thank god Harriet isn't here to see this.

"Oh, um. I think there's been some confusion." I clear my throat, trying to steady my voice. "I'm supposed be doing an audit for a

Realtor—" I'm struggling to remember a name off the directory in the front lobby. "Cindy Nordyke? Do you know her? I could be in the wrong place—"

He snorts. "Right. An audit. On a Saturday. In September. How did you get in here?" His eyes narrow. "You know, you look familiar. Have we met?"

"Nope. Anyway, I probably should go—"

"Actually," he says, "I think you should stay. We can chat about what the fuck you're doing in my office."

This must be Luke.

I'm scrambling to put together words. "My boss is expecting my call. If he doesn't hear from me, he's going to wonder what happened and—"

"Save it." Luke strides behind the desk and crouches in front of the row of drawers. He yanks on the bottom one, but it doesn't open.

I glance at the door. I wonder if I could make it there before him.

"Fuck," he mutters, rummaging through the pocket of his pants. He pulls out a small key chain and unlocks it.

I think I could make it. I take a deep breath, psyching myself up.

Three...

He pulls it open.

Two...

Reaches inside.

One...

And stands.

Holy shit. I freeze.

He's holding a gun.

CHAPTER THIRTY-EIGHT

HARRIET

September 12

5:36 p.m.

I give myself a little pep talk on the way to Nic's apartment.

I can do this! I can handle a little face-to-face conflict. I'm twenty-six years old. When my grandfather was my age, he was fighting in Vietnam!

My grip tightens on the wheel as I pass the coffee shop where Nic and I first agreed to work together. Where this all began. I tell myself again: I can do this. I can. I can't lose him.

I can't.

I won't.

I park and walk over to the call box. I'm scrolling through the names, practicing what I'm going to say in my head, when someone says, "Harriet?"

I turn to find Mindy Washington, her eyes puffy and red. She's clutching a black binder against her chest.

"Hey," I say.

"Are you trying to find Nic?"

I glance at the call box. "Yeah. Why, are you?"

"I am. I..." She gestures with the binder. "I actually have something to show him. Is he home?"

"I actually just got here. Lemme see." I press the button.

We wait, but he doesn't answer.

"I guess he's not home," Mindy says.

"Maybe..." I buzz again.

Nothing.

Where could he be? It's been over an hour since I left him. Did he decide against getting an Uber because of the expense? Why isn't he answering his phone? What if something happened to him?

I shake myself.

I'm overreacting. There was probably a long wait for a car so he went straight to his parents' house.

"I guess he's out?" Mindy asks. She joins me on the building's stoop.

"I guess. He's having dinner with his parents, so maybe he's there?"

"I'll call him." She tucks the black binder under one arm and puts her phone to her ear. After a beat, she says, "Voicemail. Darn! I really needed to talk to him about something."

I point to the binder. "That?"

She hesitates, then nods. "I...I found it on Barbara's—" Her voice breaks, her eyes filling with tears.

"I'm so sorry about Barbara," I say. "It's horrible."

She wipes her cheeks with her shirtsleeve, sniffing quietly. "Thanks. I'm having trouble accepting it's real. When I got to work today, I expected her to be there, working in her office. But…" She sniffs again. "Never mind. I'm sorry. I should go. Can you tell Nic I stopped by if you find him? It's important. I…I think I found something that might help his sister."

She starts down the steps.

"Mindy, wait!"

She turns. "Yeah?"

"What do you mean that you found something that might help his sister?"

She eyes me with suspicion. "I don't know if I feel comfortable talking about it with you, Harriet."

I suppose I can understand that. Our last interaction wasn't particularly pleasant, what with me accusing her boss of murder and all.

"Fair enough," I say. "Look, the last time we talked—I shouldn't have implied that Barbara had any part in George's death and—"

She interrupts. "You didn't *imply* it. You flat-out said it! I'm a librarian. I believe words matter."

She's not going to let me off the hook as easily as I'd hoped, and I actually admire her for it. "You're right. I said that. I was…" The word is sticky in my throat. "Wrong. And I'm sorry."

She glances up at Nic's building. "He really isn't home?"

"I mean, I don't think so? Unless he's just ignoring us." Which, come to think of it, is a possibility. "But I'm here."

Mindy chews on her lower lip. "I don't know…"

"I'm trying to help Sara too. The issue is there's a ticking clock.

Sara's set to be transferred to the jail over on the mainland soon, and that place is *rough*. We need to figure out who really killed George before that happens. If you have something in that binder that might help, please—show me. I promise, Nic would want you to. He and I are partners."

"Oh." Red splotches bloom across her cheeks. "Right. I know you'd said you guys were working together, but I thought..." She shakes her head. "It's obvious he likes you as more than that. I mean, I *knew* he wasn't interested in me, but I still couldn't help but hope... Never mind. I've been doing what I always do, living in the fantasy I created in my head instead of accepting reality. Barbara is always telling me—*was* always telling me..."

She closes her eyes and sucks a deep breath through her nose.

"But that doesn't matter!" she says as she opens them again. "What matters is helping Sara out of this mess." She taps the binder. "I found this about an hour ago, buried in Barbara's desk drawer. I was going through her things to make sure there wasn't anything private in them, or, you know—anything embarrassing. Stuff she might not want other people to see."

I nod.

"Well. As you probably know, Barbara was the founder of the Logan Island antidevelopment movement, which she created after jerks like George George—" She cringes. "Sorry."

I wave off her apology. "It's fine. Continue, please."

"Which she created after *people* like George started trying to build up the island. Recently, she had been digging into the sale of the Windswept Motel property. I'm sure you know that your stepfather had been after it for years, but the Lewes family kept turning him down?"

I nod. "Yeah. And then it conveniently burned down, and they changed their minds."

Mindy's button nose wrinkles. "Barbara had her suspicions about that fire."

"We do too! We think George set it."

Her eyebrows jump. "That's pretty much what she thought too. Here—" She flips open the binder to a piece of notebook paper with handwriting scrawled across its face.

Talked to JZ. Said he was surprised about "faulty wiring"—when he was on site, it looked like the fire had started in two separate places.

I look at her. "Who's JZ?"

"I can't say for sure, but I dug around a bit. I think it's Jason Zimmerman. He was the junior fire inspector last year, but he left a couple months after the fire. His boss, Michael Krischer, is the one who signed off on the report."

"Shit, that's pretty damning."

"Yeah. But not damning enough. So back to the property. You know about his plans to build a huge luxury hotel there?"

I nod. "Of course, it's all he talked about."

"Well..." Mindy holds out the binder to me. "Look what else is in here."

I take it from her. Inside is a mess of papers—news articles, printouts with scribbles across them, hand-drawn maps, a blueprint.

I look up at Mindy. "What is this?"

She leans in. "Well, from what I can see, it looks like Barbara uncovered evidence proving the hotel wasn't really George's end goal. He wanted to build a casino."

"A *casino*?" I almost drop the binder in my surprise. "How was he planning to do that? Casinos are only allowed within the Atlantic City borders."

Mindy takes the binder and flips to a hand-drawn map. "Exactly. Which means to do to it, you'd either have to blatantly ignore the law, which would be obvious to any outside observer, or find a way around it. Barbara thought George had done the second." She turns the book toward me. "Look at this map she drew. There's Atlantic City." She taps the top of the page. "That's the property where the motel used to sit—on the southernmost tip of the island. They're separated by less than a half mile of water."

I realize what she's saying. "Oh my *god*. So if those borders were just expanded—"

"Building a casino would be perfectly legal," Mindy finishes. "Yup. Which would mean huge money for everyone involved."

"Changing the borders of a city can't be easy though, right? Or someone would have done it years ago."

"Yeah. It's not. It's also supposed to be put to a vote. But like I said, Barbara thought George had figured out a way around it." Mindy lowers her voice. "A little over two weeks ago, she went down to town hall and requested the plans for the site that the new zoning board chair had just approved—"

"Mayor DiPetrio's cousin?"

"Yup. Convenient, huh? And—" Mindy flips a few pages. "It seems like Barbara found features on the blueprints that didn't add up. A heavy-duty HVAC system that was well beyond what a hotel normally needs, a layout that matches casino floor plans she found online."

"Did she think DiPetrio and her cousin were involved?"

Mindy leans in, her eyes widening. "Actually, Harriet, I think—and Barbara thought—that *far* more powerful people than DiPetrio's family were involved. Annexation is an incredibly difficult process. Like you said, if it was easy, people would do it all the time. Barbara's notes included the fact that, according to New Jersey state law, annexation can only occur where land is contiguous...or if a property owner gives their written consent."

Puzzle pieces are slotting into place in my mind. The motel. Why George needed it. "Which means once the motel burned down and the Leweses sold their land—"

Mindy finishes my thought. "The process could start. But the thing is that just makes the property *eligible* for annexation—it doesn't automatically happen. Atlantic City would have to pass an ordinance agreeing to it. Same with Logan Island. And then, since it was likely to be controversial, state legislators might have gotten involved, and they could have blocked it on their end too. But if *they* were involved in George's scheme then..."

Jesus. My breath catches. "Then they wouldn't have blocked it. You guys think it goes all the way to the state senate."

Mindy nods. "That was Barbara's suspicion, yes."

I can barely breathe. We were right. George was wrapped up in something huge and corrupt and potentially very, very dangerous. And we still don't know if Luke was involved.

I left Nic all alone in that office. My hands start shaking. What if

Luke showed up? What if…what if the reason Nic isn't answering his phone is because he's in trouble?

Mindy must see something change on my face. "What?"

"I have to figure out where Nic is. Hang on."

I bring up our text thread on my phone. Martin said to talk to him in person, but since I can't find him, this will have to do for the moment.

I'm sorry. Please call me. I'm worried.

I send it and wait.

Nothing.

My heart sinks. Where is he?

Maybe Martin's heard from him.

I punch out a text to Steven.

Nic's not at his apt. Have you guys heard from him yet?

A second later, my phone rings.

"Hey," Steven says. "Martin wants to—" There's a scuffling sound, then Martin's voice comes down the line.

"Hey, Harriet. Nic's supposed to be at his parents' house right now. I just sent his mom a message. She said he hadn't arrived yet, so she called him. He didn't answer." Martin's voice is tight with worry. "His mom's been really freaked out since Patterson died. I don't think he'd skip out on dinner without at least texting her."

"Where could he be?" I'm trying to keep the shake out of my voice, but panic is chewing away on my insides. This is all my fault. I need to find him. Tell him how much I care. Tell him I did all this for him.

"I think we should head to that office," Martin says. "Just to make sure he's okay. Don't you?"

"Yeah. Maybe he just lost track of time," I say, even though I don't believe it. If something happened to him, I'll never forgive myself.

"Maybe…" Martin sounds skeptical.

I call up to Nic's apartment one last time.

There's no answer.

"Harriet?" Martin says in my ear.

"I'll be at Steven's in five," I say. "Be out front."

We hang up.

"I've gotta go," I tell Mindy.

"Who was that?"

"Martin. Nic's not at his parents. Not answering his phone. We're worried, so we're heading to the last place we know he was."

Mindy's mouth hardens. "Then I'm coming with you."

CHAPTER THIRTY-NINE

NIC

September 12
5:37 p.m.

A *gun.*

I paid enough attention in high school English class to remember that once a gun appears, it's only a matter of time before it goes off.

I have to get out of here.

"There's been a misunderstanding," I say, holding my hands up in front of my chest. "I'm clearly in the wrong place. If you don't mind, I'll just grab my phone and get going..."

The gun is dangling by Luke's side. "Actually, I do mind," he says.

My hands are shaking. I shove them into my jeans pockets.

I need my phone. It's so close, sitting on the edge of George's desk just a few feet away, but Luke's between me and it.

"What's that?" I say loudly, eyes on the empty hallway behind him.

"What?" He twists toward the door, and I dart forward. I reach out, fingertips brushing the case...

For a moment, I think I have it. Then it starts buzzing, catching Luke's attention. He turns, grunting when he sees me. I lose my grip, and it drops to the floor with a clatter.

Luke shoves me, and I fly back, slamming into the sharp edge of the windowsill, pain shooting down my legs. I stumble forward, one step, two—then something hard crashes into my skull, and my vision explodes white. A scream rips from me, long and loud.

"That was a very, very dumb idea," Luke says.

I shrink back against the wall, sinking down into a crouch, hand pressed against my throbbing head. Trapped. Helpless.

He pulls a phone from his pocket and presses it to his ear. "Hey," he says. "We got a problem. I just walked into my office and got a nasty surprise. What? *No*—A person. A man. He was in George's office. Looked like he was going through his computer. You gotta get down here so we can figure out what to do with him."

I gulp a breath as Luke hangs up.

"And now, we wait," he says, swiping my phone off the floor.

It disappears into his back pocket—along with any hope I have of getting out of here in one piece.

CHAPTER FORTY

HARRIET

September 12
6:04 p.m.

The four of us tumble out of the car, forming a tight circle outside the building's entrance. Martin called the cops on our way here, but there's no sign of them yet.

"Should we wait for them to arrive?" Steven asks, clutching the baseball bat that he insisted on bringing along to his chest.

I shake my head. Now that we're here, I can't wait another second. I need to know that he's okay. "We should go in."

"I agree. He might be in trouble," Mindy adds.

We all turn to Martin. "We should go in, I think," he says. "But somebody needs to wait here for the police. Steven?"

His mouth drops open. "*Me?* I'm the only one with a weapon!"

Martin looks at him incredulously. "The other day, you walked down six flights of stairs to save a spider's life. Are you trying to tell me you think you could *hit* someone with that thing?"

"I would if...*ugh*." Steven throws up his hands. "Fine. Whatever. Go. I'll stay here."

The lobby is quiet, as is our elevator ride up to the second floor.

"It's that one," I say, as we exit into the hall. "Second door to the right."

But I freeze in place. *He's probably fine*, I tell myself. His phone ran out of batteries. He lost track of time. He—

"Are you okay?" Mindy whispers.

I shake myself. *Keep it together*. "Yeah. All good. Let's go."

We stop at the door, and Martin tries the knob. "It's open," he whispers. "Did you lock it when you left?"

I think back, but the memory is a blur. When I left, I was mostly doing my best not to cry. "I don't think so?"

"Okay, that's a good sign. You guys ready?"

I take a deep breath. Mindy gives him a thumbs-up.

He pushes open the door.

CHAPTER FORTY-ONE

NIC

September 12

6:14 p.m.

Fifteen minutes ago, a big, brawny guy with a shaved head and biceps the size of a cantaloupe showed up. From what I've gathered, his name is Dominic, he's the one who broke into Harriet's house last week, and Luke is scared shitless of him. Which does not bode well for my chances of getting out of here alive.

"I told you, it's handled," Dominic says to Luke. He sounds calm, but the veins bulging from his neck tell a different story.

They're by the door, blocking my path to freedom. I can't tell if Dominic is armed, but I'm not sure it matters—Luke still has his gun, and Dominic looks like he could break me in half with his bare hands.

I should have signed up for jujitsu back in middle school when my dad suggested it. I should have gone to the gym more often. I should have pumped more iron instead of spending my time cooking and getting tattoos.

My knowledge of how to properly plate food isn't exactly helpful in this situation.

"When I leave," Dominic continues, "I'll get rid of him—properly. Nobody'll be the wiser."

My stomach sinks. I'm dead.

Then: a noise from the inner office.

"What was that?" Dominic asks Luke sharply. "Did you call somebody else? I told you I'd fucking handle it!"

Luke's face pales. "I didn't. I swear!"

It must be Harriet, coming back to find me.

They turn toward the doorway. Luke lifts the gun, his thumb cocking back the hammer.

I won't let them hurt her.

I lunge forward, throwing my elbow into the small of Luke's back. Except I hit Dominic. He stumbles forward, catching himself just before he topples to the floor.

"What the shit?" He swings around, but before he can get a grip on me, I wrap my arms around his waist, flinging my knee into his groin. "Fuck! You fucker!" He kicks out, connecting with my injured knee. I shriek as white-hot pain shoots down my leg. My grip loosens, and Dominic whips around, grabbing me by the scruff of my neck, yanking me toward him so hard I see stars.

"Nic?" It's Martin.

"Who the fuck is—" Luke disappears into the hall, taking the end of his sentence with him.

"Martin!" I scream. "He's got a gun!"

"Shut your fucking mouth," Dominic hisses before dropping me to the floor with a thud. He pulls his leg back, then kicks me in the side of my head, just above the ear, pain like I've never felt bursting through my skull.

Just before the world goes black, I hear it—a sharp crack, like a firecracker exploding in the night sky.

A gunshot.

CHAPTER FORTY-TWO

HARRIET

September 12

6:16 p.m.

A bang, sharp and hard. Then impact. My shoulder hitting the floor, pain blooming. I curl into a ball, arms wrapping around my head.

My ears are ringing—high-pitched, painful. I reach up, sure I'll find blood, but my fingers come back clean.

The smell of burning plastic hits the back of my throat, and my stomach heaves.

From across the room, a loud groaning. I drag my eyes to it.

Her.

Mindy, clutching her leg, red seeping through the gaps between her fingers.

Blood.

Mindy, bleeding. She's been shot.

Shot.

Oh my god.

"Harriet," she says weakly as her knees buckle. It feels like someone stuffed cotton balls in my ears. "Help." She collapses to the floor.

Martin crawls to her side, ripping off his hoodie and pressing it against the wound. He soothes the hair back from her forehead gently.

That's when I notice Luke standing in the entrance to the back offices, a gun in his hand. His eyes are fixed on it like he's not sure how it got there.

I tug my phone from my back pocket, moving slowly so as not to draw Luke's attention, and open the camera, hitting Record. I set it on the ground facing him, then try to pull myself upright. I falter, unsteady, and Luke swings toward me, raising then dropping the gun, like he's not sure if he's willing to use it a second time.

His mouth falls open as he takes in my face. "Harriet Baker?"

I ignore this. "I heard Nic when we came in. Where is he?"

Luke shakes his head. "What are you…what are *you* doing here?"

"Just tell me where Nic is!"

"I don't know who Nic is, but if you're talking about the guy I found in here, he's in the back with—"

"I hear a siren," Martin interrupts. His face is pale, his white hoodie soaked red with Mindy's blood. "The cops. Thank god."

"Is she okay?" I ask.

He shakes his head, and my stomach drops.

I look at Luke. His ruddy face has paled. On the way here, I still had doubts about how much he knew, but I don't anymore.

"You're fucked, you know that? We know the motel fire wasn't an accident. That you bribed them to blame faulty wiring. We know about the casino. And I would bet money on the fact that you killed Barbara Patterson." I'm trembling. *Where is Nic?* "You're a monster. I talked to you at that party, remember? Right before we found her body. You were *laughing*."

"I didn't kill Barbara," he says weakly. "That big shelving unit fell on her."

"Oh please," I say. "You killed her, just like you killed George."

His mouth twitches, the gun in his hand trembling. "You shut your fucking mouth! I had nothing to do with what happened to George!"

A man appears behind him. Bald, muscular, with gelled black hair and wild eyes. Not someone I'd want to run into in a dark alleyway. Who the fuck is he?

He nudges Luke's arm. "I heard a gunshot. You shoot that lady?"

"I...yeah," Luke says gruffly.

"Nice one. The cops are here. We gotta split."

"But what about the rest of them? About—" Luke jerks his chin toward the back offices.

"Taken care of."

A chill runs down my spine. What did they do to Nic?

"And these guys?"

The man shrugs. "Kill 'em?"

He says this so casually, like he's suggesting they go get brunch. Like killing people is a hobby of his. How does Luke know this guy? Did *George*? How would George—old, buttoned-up George—have met someone like this?

Luke hesitates, clearly not thrilled by this idea. But I'm pretty sure it doesn't matter what Luke wants. I'm pretty sure if this guy decides to kill us, we're dead.

"If you do that, you'll be looking at a triple homicide," I say, tripping over the words in my hurry to get them out. "When the cops catch you. Because they will."

The large man snorts. "Sure, doll. Sure they will."

"They're nobodies," Luke says to him. "And it'd be their word against ours. Who'd believe them? The right people will back us up—"

The man frowns. "I don't know."

The wail of a siren cuts through their conversation, loud now and closing in.

Luke's eyes dart around the room. "I swear to god, Dominic—it's fine, okay? Do you hear that? The cops are *here*. Like you said, we gotta go."

Dominic. I don't recognize the name. I wonder again who he is. How Luke knows him.

Dominic sighs. "All right, fine. Have it your way. It's your ass on the line. But"—he looks around the room—"you'll keep your fucking mouths shut about me if you know what's good for you. I was never here. You understand? All this was Luke's doing. Right, Luke?"

He claps a hand down on Luke's shoulder, hard, and Luke flinches.

"Right," Luke says. "Yeah. All me. Nobody else."

"Good boy." Dominic yanks him across the room. At the door, he turns back, pressing a finger to his lips. "Remember—not a word."

As soon as the door shuts, I run to Mindy's side. Her eyelids are fluttering, her face drained of color. She looks terrible.

But even so, relief washes over me.

"She's alive?"

Martin nods. "For the moment, but the bleeding's heavy. I'm doing what I can, but I need the EMTs up here, stat. Steven needs to tell them to hurry."

"Can I do anything?"

He shakes his head. "I got it. Go find Nic."

I nod, hurrying toward the back offices. As soon as I get through the door, I see him, slumped on the floor next to George's desk. Still.

Too still.

"Oh my god!" I rush to him, press a hand to his back.

It's moving. He's breathing.

He's alive.

A sob escapes my lips.

"I'm so sorry," I whisper. I crouch beside him, brushing the hair from his forehead. My fingers catch on something sticky. When I pull them back, they're red.

He's bleeding. I don't know what to do. He's bleeding, and I'm useless.

"I found him," I scream. "His head is bleeding! His head! He's breathing, but it's his *head*. What if—"

"Do you need me in there?" Martin calls. "If you do, I need you to come out here and hold this on Mindy's—"

A loud bang. Then a shout, "Police! Hands where we can see them!"

"Okay, okay!" Martin starts explaining who he is, what happened.

"We're in here!" I call, unsure if they can hear me through the chaos. I'm about to get up when Nic's arm jerks. "Nic!" I press my hand against his cheek. It's cool, clammy. "Nic. Are you okay?"

Nothing.

This is all my fault. I left him here, all alone.

"You have to hold on. Please. You have to. I'm so sorry. I messed up. I…I can't lose you. Please."

What if he's not okay and I never get the chance to tell him how I feel? How much I care? How incredible I think he is, how lucky I am that he's even willing to give me the time of day after all the stupid shit I've pulled.

I don't know if I can live without him.

Tears are running down my face, dropping into his hair one by one.

"*Harriet?*"

My head jerks up.

Kozel is standing in the doorway.

And he looks furious.

CHAPTER FORTY-THREE

HARRIET

September 12

6:24 p.m.

I launch myself at him. "This is *your* fault!" I spit at him. "You told me you thought the investigation was being rushed. Why didn't you fight it? Insist on investigating other suspects? Or, wait. Maybe you're in on it too. I wouldn't put it past you."

I don't care if he's a cop. I don't care if he arrests me.

He could have stopped this.

He *should* have stopped this.

He glances over his shoulder and then takes a step into the room. "Harriet. Please. Stop." His voice is low and urgent. "I've been… Since our dinner, I've thought about reaching out to you. I said too much. What I told you—I shouldn't have. But also—" He's only about a foot away now, eyes pleading. "Listen." His voice drops. "Before they come in. What I'm about to tell you—you say you heard it from me, I'll deny it. You got it?"

He waits.

"Fine," I say through clenched teeth.

"Good. Look. LIPD is... It's worse than I thought." He shakes his head. "The corruption runs deep. I'd heard rumors, sure, but seeing it with my own eyes—it's something else. Jones and I have tried pushing back against Sharkey and his crew, but we haven't had any luck from the inside, and my hands are tied for now. But listen to me: I do not think Sara Allbright is guilty."

"Detective Kozel?" Someone's heading toward us.

Kozel stiffens, talking faster now. "I know you and Nic are looking into it. Jones and I both know. Normally, I'd tell you to stop. But don't. Okay? Don't stop."

Through the open door, I see a cop.

Kozel clears his throat. "We have a man down in here," he says loudly.

We lock eyes one last time, his pleading.

I give a small nod, and he turns to join the other cops.

CHAPTER FORTY-FOUR

NIC

September 25

9:03 a.m.

I feel like I live in this damn hospital.

First, it was two nights to treat my head injury; now it's daily visits to see Mindy. I've spent more time here over the past two weeks than in the rest of my life combined.

"Nic, nice to see you today," Mindy's nurse says as I walk into her hospital room.

"Hey, Nic!" Mindy says from the bed. A massive cast encases her leg. Dark bruises linger under her eyes. But each day, she looks stronger.

Her second surgery Wednesday morning went well. According to the nurses I've talked to, she's healing up fast. Barring any surprises, she should be released tomorrow.

I settle on the edge of the bed. "Hey, Mind. How're you doing?"

She gives me a thumbs-up. "Good. I can't wait to get home tomorrow, see my cat, sleep in my own bed."

"I'm so sorry," I say for the hundredth time.

She replies as she always does: "Nic, it's not your fault. I'm just glad *you're* okay." She puts her hand over mine.

A part of me worries I might be leading Mindy on with these daily visits, but we've been friends for two decades. Plus, I feel responsible for what happened to her.

She could have died, and it would have been my fault.

Well, actually, it would have been Harriet's.

Of all the people in the world, she brought *Mindy* to that office?

Martin? He's an EMT. He knows how to handle himself in difficult situations.

But *Mindy*? She's so gentle. So innocent.

She needed a blood transfusion when she arrived at the hospital. They said it was lucky Martin was there; if it hadn't been for him, she would have died.

I'm so angry at Harriet that even the thought of her name sends my blood pressure soaring. I've barely spoken to her—not for lack of trying on her end.

I needed space to think.

Still do in fact. How can I ever trust her again? She was using me. All she cared about was that stupid fucking job, and once she got it back, she was going to disappear. Just like she did eight years ago.

"Any word yet on whether they've found anything linking Luke to George's death?" Mindy asks, as she does every day I'm here.

I shake my head. "Nothing."

The cops tackled Luke in the parking lot as he was sprinting toward his car. He was arrested on the spot.

Martin's since heard that the cops were on his trail even before Harriet and I got involved. They'd found security footage of him arguing with Barbara outside the walk-in fridge right before she died. Plus, he'd left enough DNA at the scene to clone himself. Sharkey and his corrupt cronies were left with no choice; they were going to have to charge him.

Criminal mastermind, Luke is not.

He's facing charges for murder, attempted murder, bribery of government officials. My hope is that he'll be behind bars for a long, long time.

Mindy, bless her heart, managed to email the contents of Barbara's binder to a reporter at the *Pleasantville Times* just days after she had surgery on her thigh. She asked me before she did, wondering if she should give it to Harriet instead, but I told her to go for it.

Maybe a dick move. But Harriet is familiar with those.

The ensuing article kicked off internal investigations at both the LIPD and the LIFD. County investigators were brought in. Michael Krischer, the fire inspector who signed off on the faulty wiring report, was put on leave, and his cousin, Ryan Krischer, who sent the invoice for thirty grand to George, was brought in for questioning.

As it stands, the two of them are potentially facing multiple charges, including racketeering, money laundering, and fraud.

The mayor's office is claiming total ignorance. DiPetrio threw her cousin under the bus, blaming him for everything and firing him from the zoning board.

And even with all that, Sara's still in jail. The jail on the mainland now, where fights break out daily.

"I don't get it," Mindy says. "What happened to George *must* be related to what happened to Barbara. Do you think"—she drops her voice to a whisper—"Dominic did it?"

I swallow. Martin made us all promise not to tell the cops about Dominic, and as far as I know, Luke hasn't either. We don't know who in that department is trustworthy and who might be tangled up with what Luke and Dominic had going on. If they tip him off that we talked, he'll come for us.

Mindy's a sitting duck. She can't even get out of bed. She'd be in an enormous amount of danger, and I won't allow that. Not again.

"I don't know," I say and then change the subject. Mindy doesn't deserve to have the stress of all this weighing on her right now. She needs to focus on healing.

Toward the end of our chat, a doctor walks into the room. He's older, maybe around forty, with salt-and-pepper hair and a beard. His face lights up when he sees Mindy.

"Ms. Washington. Always a pleasure," he says, smiling at her over his clipboard. Mindy turns beet red, and seconds later, they're deep in conversation.

Huh. Maybe I don't have to worry about leading her on after all.

Mindy giggles at a groan-worthy dad joke, and I rise to my feet. I don't want to interrupt their conversation, but I'm due at my parents' house soon, and it's pretty clear my time here has come to an end.

I make my excuses and head out.

I text my mom as I stride down the hallway, letting her know I'm on the way. Ever since the office incident, she's insisted on me staying in almost constant communication with her.

I round a corner and slam straight into someone.

"*Ow!*"

It's Harriet. Who else would it be?

"Oh! Hi," she says, tugging at the bottom of her T-shirt. Her cheeks are red. She clears her throat. "Are you... Did you... Were you seeing Mindy?"

I nod.

"Oh. Right. Cool." She stuffs her hands into the pockets of her shorts, eyes trained on the ground. I've never seen her like this before—nervous, stumbling over her words like she's not sure what to say. "I...uh, can we talk—"

"I gotta go," I say, cutting her off. She's texted me *I'm sorry* so many times I've lost count, but I'm still not ready to hear whatever it is she wants to say.

I wonder if she's still writing her article. The one in the *Times* focused on the island's corruption—zoning scandal, the casino, Barbara's death, Luke. But there was nothing about Sara.

Does Harriet even care? Or did she drop the story as soon as the juiciest bits went public?

Sara needs me, but I'm wondering if it's better if I continue on alone. No blue-eyed distractions. No wondering about other people's motives.

Harriet's face falls. "I really need to talk to you."

I shake my head. "I can't yet. Okay?"

She chews on the bottom lip I kissed. "Please?" she says. "Nic."

Her pull is magnetic, and I can feel my anger slipping.

I remind myself: She was going to leave me. Again. Maybe she would have said goodbye this time, but that doesn't change the fact that she never told me it was her plan all along.

I can't trust her.

"Sara's still in jail, you know," I say. "They're trying to say Luke didn't kill him."

"I know," she says. "Of course I know that. That's what I want to talk about. I want to help. Please—"

I cut her off. "I'll see you later, Harriet," I say. And I walk away.

CHAPTER FORTY-FIVE

HARRIET

September 25

9:52 a.m.

I push into the nearest bathroom, desperate for a moment alone so I can finally allow my tears to fall.

Nic has every right to be mad; I know he does, but I wish he would just listen to me for a minute. I'd tell him he was right. My priorities were all mixed up. I'd somehow missed the forest for the trees.

The article isn't what's important. Sara is.

He is.

More practically, I need to share what Kozel said. How he told me that he doesn't believe Sara's guilty. He told me to keep pushing, but I haven't been. Since the gun went off in George's office, I've been paralyzed with indecision, fear, worry. And the one person I want to talk about everything with won't give me the time of day.

On the other end of things—Frankie. My article. That *Times* piece.

After Frankie saw it, she called me, ranting into my voicemail about how I'd been scooped.

Since then, I've been ignoring her numerous emails, texts, calls—each angrier than the next. Telling me I better come up with another angle if I want to ever get my job back.

I don't care about that fucking job anymore.

I just want to get Sara out of jail.

I brace myself against the counter, studying my reflection in the mirror.

I need to stop avoiding this. I know what I need to do. I've known since the conversation Steven and I had in his apartment. It's time I finally fix this.

My phone's heavy in my hand as I dial her number.

She answers on the first ring. "Harriet, where the *hell* have you been? I've been trying to reach you for days. *You're* screening *my* calls? Are you fucking kidding me? We have to talk about that *Times* article—I should have known you couldn't handle this. I should have known I couldn't trust you. I should have known—"

I want to hang up and go hide under my bed.

I force myself to speak. "I—"

She keeps going. "You fucked up majorly, Baker. You have one shot to fix this or you can kiss your chance at working at *Humans* again goodbye. You told me initially that girl Sara's the real story. That little Podunk paper didn't mention anything about her. Maybe go talk to her again. Play up the doubt. People love stories about pretty girl killers. Look at Amanda Knox. They're *still* making shows about her!"

"The entire point is to get Sara *out* of jail!"

Frankie scoffs. "At this point, her being behind bars *helps* you. If she gets out, you're shit out of luck. The corruption angle's been done. It's over. So get the fuck to work. We can call her…*Hot Killer Chef*. Or something like that. Send me some copy ASAP. I'm waiting forever. You're lucky I'm even giving you another chance here—"

"Actually," I say, finally getting to why I called, "I'm not writing that."

A pause.

"Not writing what?"

"Anything." I'd rather be unemployed for the rest of my life than work for this bitch again. "I'm not writing *anything* for you."

A beat of silence, then an explosion. "Are you *fucking* kidding me?" she screams.

"Not kidding at all. If I do write something about all this, I want it published by someone I trust. Someone who's familiar with the word *ethics*. Not someone who fired me to protect their own ass. So sorry, not sorry, but I quit."

"Harriet." Frankie's voice is a low growl. "If you do this, you are *done*. Do I make myself clear? You will never work in this town again. We will sue you for breach of contract—"

I laugh. "Do your worst. You might remember you never had me sign anything?"

She's still screaming as I hang up.

I catch my reflection in the mirror. My cheeks are warm, my eyes glassy and wild.

I look completely unhinged.

A loud laugh escapes through my lips.

I want to text Nic and tell him everything but decide I should finally respect his wish for space.

I've matured so much in the last five minutes.

That call to Frankie revived me. I'm more determined than ever to solve this fucking thing.

But how?

Was George's murder connected to the casino? If so, maybe he and Mayor DiPetrio had a falling out and *she* killed him? Or maybe Sharkey got nervous that George was going to expose his corruption? Or Fire Chief Dutton? Or...or...

My mind is spinning with questions. I don't know what's important anymore.

What I need right now is to clear my mind.

Talk to someone who has nothing to do with any of this.

"Harriet!" my grandmother exclaims as she opens the front door to her townhome. A smile stretches across her face. "We weren't expecting you!" She hesitates. "Were we?"

I pretend like I don't hear that. "You weren't," I say.

"Are you here to say goodbye?"

"Goodbye?" It hits me—my dad and Cynthia got back late last night, which means Vicky is leaving for London soon. "Oh, right! Yes. Of course. When does she leave? I wish we could have spent more time together."

After Mindy was shot, Vicky was amazing; she brought her food in the hospital, checked in on me daily.

I'm going to miss her.

"Tomorrow," Gogo sighs, her wafer-thin hand drifting to her collarbone. "Who knows when she'll be back? I'm not getting any younger. In another ten years...who knows where I'll be?"

"Gogo! Stop." I hate it when she talks like that. With her recent memory slips—no. I can't think about it. I came here to decompress, not pile on more worries.

"Well, it's true, Harriet," she says. "When you get to my age, death is something you learn to live with. That said, I do want to spend more time with my daughter before it takes me. I wish Vicky had never left New York. She had a whole life there, but she never looked back. I do understand why, but I miss her every day." She leads me into the living room. "Have you ever seen pictures of her back then?"

"I don't think so."

"Here." She pats the couch. "Let me show you. She took that city by storm, I tell you." She walks over to the bookshelf by the window, crouching in front of it, her knees cracking loudly. "Let me see...oh yes. Here we are." She tugs an old, spiral-bound photo album out of the row of books and brings it to the couch. "Vicky stored some of her things here when she moved overseas." She flips to the first page and taps a photo. "Look at my girl," she says with pride.

It's unmistakably a much younger Vicky, with the hair to prove it. She's wearing a graduation cap and a long purple robe.

"Her graduation from NYU," Gogo says. "What a day! She was so excited. I thought she'd stay in that city forever. She loved it so. She had so many plans..."

She flips through more pictures, taking me through Vicky's mid-twenties. We're almost to the end when Gogo yawns.

"I need to make my tea." She sets the album between us and stands. "Would you like one?"

"Sure. I'll make it!" I'm not sure she should use the stove.

"Thank you, peanut, but I can handle it. You're as bad as your aunt, hovering like I'm a child. I'm perfectly capable, you know."

I swallow my argument. How much trouble can she get into when I'm sitting in the next room? "Okay. Yes, I'd love one."

She disappears into the kitchen, and I pick up the album, absent-mindedly flipping through more pages. Vicky on the tram to Roosevelt Island. Vicky in Washington Square Park. Vicky standing beneath a gold banner that reads *Happy Birthday!*, her arm slung around the shoulders of an attractive man.

An attractive man who's somehow familiar.

Have I met him before? Maybe they came to visit at some point?

Gogo's head pops through the doorway. "Milk?"

"What?" It takes me a second to register her question. "Oh, sure. But—hey. Who's this guy?"

I turn the album so she can see it.

"Hold on. My eyes are no good anymore." She walks to me and cranes her neck toward the photo. "*Oh!* Oh my. That's Vicky's fiancé."

"Fiancé?" I didn't know Vicky had been engaged. "What happened? I didn't think Vicky had ever been married. Or…is she divorced?"

"Oh dear." Gogo sinks down next to me. "It's a very sad story. We don't really talk about it. It nearly broke her. He died the weekend before they were supposed to be married. It was tragic. Vicky was inconsolable, understandably. She moved to London about two months later."

I'm stunned. All this time, I thought Vicky moved to London because she was a free spirit. I had no idea that she was running from heartbreak.

"That's *awful*," I breathe. "Did I ever meet him?"

Gogo frowns. "Not that I remember, but...let me think. You could have, I suppose. But you would have been quite young. A year, if that? I doubt you'd remember him."

The kettle starts whistling in the kitchen.

"I'll go fix our cups," Gogo says. She pats my hand and climbs to her feet.

I study the picture again. I *swear* I've seen that face before. It's something about his hair...the shape of his jaw. He looks a little like John F. Kennedy Jr., actually—

Wait.

I grab my phone off the coffee table and scroll through my photos until I find it—the picture of the obituary I found in George's desk drawer. *Adrian Pruner (1977–2001)* written beneath a black-and-white photo of a man who looks a hell of a lot like JFK Jr. The man who Matthew's mom told us died in the warehouse fire George set.

I hold the phone up next to the picture in Vicky's album, my heart thundering in my chest.

And I see that I'm right.

The man who died in that fire is the same person standing next to my aunt.

CHAPTER FORTY-SIX

HARRIET

September 25

11:02 a.m.

I set the album on the couch and scoot away from it, like putting distance between myself and it will erase what I just saw.

Vicky had a motive.

Gogo comes back in clutching two saucers, cups balanced precariously on top of them, glass rattling against glass.

I hurry over and take them from her.

"Are you feeling okay, dear?" she asks once we settle on the couch. "You look pale."

"I..." I shake my head. I have no idea what to say. I can only imagine what my face looks like.

"What is it?" she asks.

"I..." I swallow. "Um. How did Vicky meet him?"

She takes a tiny sip of tea. "Who?"

"Her fiancé. Adrian."

"Oh!" Gogo sounds surprised. "I haven't thought about that in years. I think they met through George, actually. When Vicky moved up to New York for college, your dad put Vicky and George in touch. You know how your father and George were close until...well. Until your parents got together and George became a total asshole, pardon my French. Not to speak ill of the dead, but I still don't understand *what* your mother saw in him."

George introduced Vicky and Adrian.

"Do you know..." I cough. "Um. How did George and Adrian know each other?"

"I'm not sure. You could ask your aunt, I suppose. It's been long enough that she might be open to talking about it."

"She's upstairs?" I ask.

Gogo nods.

"I'll go say hi."

Gogo smiles. "She'll love that. She really wanted to spend more time with you while she was here, but obviously the last two weeks haven't gone as we expected. And now, who knows when she'll be back? I might not even be around."

She's repeating herself again.

My thumb finds its way between my teeth, and I start gnawing at the edge of my nail, something I haven't done since I was little.

"You will be," I tell her with more confidence than I feel.

"I would love to see Vicky more." Gogo's voice wobbles. "It's hard, having her so far away..."

I leave her with her tea and take the stairs up to the second floor two by two. The door at the end of the hall is cracked, and there's movement inside.

I stop halfway to it.

What am I thinking?

My aunt's fiancé died in that warehouse fire. So what? It might not mean anything.

It might be a coincidence.

That would have been an awful long time to wait for revenge. I'm being silly.

I'm turning to head downstairs when the door opens.

"Harriet!" Vicky says, her face lighting up. "I didn't know you were here. Come in, come in!"

She disappears into the bedroom.

She's acting so normal. Smiling. I'm being ridiculous.

I slowly walk down the hall and stop in the open doorway. Her suitcase is on the floor, mostly empty, and clothes are scattered across the bed.

"I was talking with Gogo just now. She said you're leaving soon? Tomorrow was it?"

A shadow passes over Vicky's face. "Actually, Sunday. Have you noticed her memory has gotten..."

"A little shaky?"

She grimaces. "Maybe more than a little?"

"Maybe," I say.

Vicky couldn't have killed George. Right? She couldn't have. I'm losing my mind. It's been a long few days. I need to get out of here.

Vicky picks up a pair of jeans and starts folding them. "Well. Either way, I'm glad to see you. How are you? How's Mindy?"

"She's doing a lot better, thanks. I actually just came up to say goodbye. My mom's expecting me at home soon."

"Ah," Vicky says, her mouth tugging into a slight frown. "Well, maybe we could grab coffee later if you're free?"

I picture it—sitting across a table from her, trying to act normal.

"I can't. I'm sorry."

"Okay. Well. Maybe tomorrow then."

I nod, forcing myself to meet her eyes. "Maybe tomorrow."

I'm at loose ends. It's almost midnight, and I'm lying in bed wide awake. I've been scrolling on social media for two hours, trying to drown out my racing thoughts. But Adrian's face keeps sliding back into my mind, no matter how many Reels I consume.

I haven't said a word about my suspicions to anyone—not even Nic. I should. His sister is being held in that hellhole of a prison on the mainland, and I know he's terrified about what may happen to her there.

If what I think I know could help her... But every time I consider it, I picture Gogo's shaking hands.

As much as I've been trying to deny it, Gogo is sick. Not just her memory. *Her*.

If it's true...if Vicky murdered George...it might kill her.

I need to slow down. I have no real proof. Yes, Vicky was about to marry a man who died in a fire George might have set. Yes, she was at my party the night he was killed. Yes, it's all very strange, but maybe it's just a coincidence. Coincidences happen every day! This would be a massive one, but it's not impossible. Right?

What do I know for sure?

Mrs. Carter overheard George shout *This is getting pathetic. Let it go* shortly before he died.

George and Luke's relationship had been going downhill before George died. The two of them had gotten involved with very scary people like Dominic.

Several people overheard George arguing with someone in the basement.

George had an illegitimate son who went down there to talk to him and—

A thought hits me.

Matthew said he and George weren't yelling, but did he hear the fight on his way down the stairs?

I scramble upright.

A quick glance at my phone tells me it's 11:53 p.m. Late. But Vicky is leaving the country on Sunday. It can't wait.

I scroll through my recent calls until I find Matthew's mom's number.

She answers after several rings. "Hello?" she says through a yawn.

"Hi, Ana," I say. "This is Harriet Baker? We met the other day when—" *When we accused your son of murdering his father.* "Um, when we came to talk to Matthew?"

"Harriet?" she says. She doesn't sound happy, but at least she doesn't hang up. "Why are you— Are you aware it's almost midnight?"

"Yeah. I know. I'm sorry to wake you, but I really need to speak with Matthew. It's urgent. Please."

There's a long pause. "What could you possibly have to say to him that's so urgent you had to call in the middle of the night?"

I clear my throat. "Well, I'm sure you remember Nic's sister is in jail for George's murder? It's about that."

"I don't want him involved in that, Harriet."

"I'm not trying to drag him into anything. Just one question, I promise. Then we'll leave you alone. I—"

She cuts me off with a tired exhale. "Fine. Hang on."

The minutes tick by, but finally, Matthew's voice fills the line.

"Harriet?" He sounds annoyed. "Why the hell are you calling my mom's phone? You woke her up."

"Hey. Yeah, I'm really sorry about that. I know this is weird, but I just have a quick question—really quick, I swear. It'll take, like, one second."

"It's already been more than one second," he says.

"Right. Sorry."

He sighs. "What is it?"

"Well. I was wondering. The night of my party. You said you and George talked in the basement?"

He yawns. "Yeah."

"Did you hear anything on your way down there?"

Matthew's quiet for so long I start to wonder if he hung up.

"Hello?" I finally venture.

"Sorry, I was thinking," he says. "He was alone when I found him in the wine cellar, and I didn't hear anything out of the ordinary on my way down—"

My heart sinks. "Nothing at all?"

He huffs. "Let me finish. I was going to say I didn't hear anything, *but* there was this woman coming up the stairs who ran straight into me. Knocked me off-balance, and I almost fell down the rest of the flight."

I hesitate. If I ask the next question, I'm pretty sure I'm going to get an answer I don't like. Do I really want to know?

I think of Nic telling me that I'm just as selfish as I was in high school. About how he's put his family above everything else. The lengths he's gone to in order to help Sara. He deserves to know the truth, and I care about him too much to not do everything in my power to give it to him.

I dig my fingernails into the soft skin of my palm and ask it. "Do you remember what she looked like?"

"Nope."

"Not at all?"

"I mean, not really. I didn't see her face—she was moving fast. But once I regained my balance, I turned because I was going to yell at her. She was already too far away, but I saw her from the back. She had brown hair."

"How long was it?"

"Jesus. This is way more than one question, you know. I don't know! Short! Chin length, maybe?"

I can tell I'm starting to lose him, but I can't stop now. "Do you remember what she was wearing?"

"A T-shirt. Jeans. Not a ballgown like all the other freaks there."

Vicky.

I thank Matthew, apologize again for waking his household up, then sink back into my pillows.

Vicky argued with George in the basement.

Which makes it even more likely that she stabbed him out on that beach and then left him there to die.

George was a terrible person, but he was still a human being.

Was it an accident? Self-defense? Or straight-up, cold-blooded murder? Did she come back to the island to kill him? If she did, why now? Why wait so many years?

I don't understand.

Before I do anything, I need to know for sure. I need to talk to the one person who can give me answers.

Vicky.

CHAPTER FORTY-SEVEN

HARRIET

September 26

8:02 a.m.

It's bright and early when I pull into Gogo's driveway. I would have preferred to do this somewhere else, but I'm running out of time.

I find them in the kitchen making breakfast. It smells like toast and coffee in here—homey and familiar. It reminds me of childhood mornings when my parents were out of town or too busy to take care of me, and I'd end up staying at Gogo's for nights on end.

"Harriet!" Gogo says. She's reading a newspaper at the table while Vicky cooks at the stove. "I was hoping to see you today."

"Hey, Gogo." I kiss her cheek, stifling a yawn as I straighten. After my conversation with Matthew, I slept for a grand total of an hour.

I still can't believe this is happening.

I walk over to the stove. "Hey, Vicky. Are you busy?"

"Just finishing this up," Vicky says, gesturing to the pan. "Gogo's breakfast." She smiles at my grandmother.

Do I really think this woman could have *killed* someone four weeks ago?

I watch as Vicky plates the eggs. "I was wondering," I say once she's done. "Could I talk to you for a sec? Alone?"

"Me?" she says. "Sure." She puts the frying pan in the sink and the plate in front of my grandmother. "Back shortly," she says, patting Gogo's shoulder.

I follow her into the living room. She settles on the couch, but it feels too close. The doorway to the kitchen is *right there*. I need more distance between this and Gogo.

"Actually, could we talk upstairs?"

"Oh." Her brow furrows. "Sure."

"It's just...Gogo is in the kitchen," I say quietly. Maybe as a warning.

I want to throw up.

Upstairs, Vicky perches on the edge of the bed, her legs dangling off its side, feet not quite touching the floor. She looks young. Much younger than she is. She pats the empty space next to her: an invitation, like we're going to have a casual chat.

I can't sit next to her. Not right now.

Instead, I perch on the arm of a chair in the corner.

"So what's up?" Vicky asks. I can't read her expression.

I wipe my sweaty palms against my jeans. "Well, yesterday, Gogo showed me some old photos. From when you lived in New York." I pause. "And I saw something."

She raises an eyebrow. "Something?"

"A picture. You and a man. Gogo said he was your fiancé. She said he died the weekend before your wedding."

Vicky flinches. "Adrian," she says softly.

"The weird thing was…I recognized him."

"You recognized him," she repeats.

"Yes. From an obituary I found in George's desk drawer. I've been looking into all this with Nic Allbright, the brother of—"

"I know who Nic Allbright is," Vicky interrupts.

"Right. Well, if Sara's found guilty, she could spend the rest of her life in prison. I don't want an innocent person's life ruined by something they didn't do. Do you?"

Vicky's eyes have dropped to the bedspread.

"*Do* you?" I ask again, more forcefully, like my heart isn't pounding against my ribs.

"Of course not," she says finally, so soft I almost miss it.

I stand and start pacing across the carpet. "Good. I didn't think you would. This is where we stand. I figured out a few things. First: When you moved up to New York for college, my dad connected you with George. Sometime later, George introduced you to a man. Adrian. The two of you fell in love. Got engaged. Were set to be married. But instead, Adrian died. In a fire that George was rumored to have set."

Vicky's silent.

"The night of my party, George was overheard arguing with someone in the basement. For a while, I couldn't figure out who it had been. Then a caterer told me that he was on his way down there when someone ran into him heading up. Someone with brown hair. Jeans. A T-shirt. Less than an hour later, George was dead."

Vicky meets my eyes. I swear she's aged ten years in the last three minutes. "What are you trying to say, Harriet?"

"I'm saying—" The words catch in my throat. "I'm saying that even though we don't know each other well, you've always been someone I admire. And I don't believe that you could live with yourself if you let Sara spend her life behind bars for something she didn't do."

Vicky's mouth wobbles.

"I want to help you, Vicky, but you have to be honest with me. There are so many things I don't understand. Like—why kill George now? Adrian died so long ago! And at my birthday party of all places? There were tons of people around. I thought the reason you came back was to help out with Gogo—to see *me*—but it wasn't, was it? You came back to kill him."

"No!" she says sharply. I tense, but then she crumples forward, head in her hands. "I didn't—no. I never wanted to see him again! But then your father asked if I could come help out with Gogo while he was traveling, and I thought…I thought I could deal. Gogo can't handle an international flight anymore, and I was desperate to see her. I thought I could avoid him. But then I learned about the party. Okay, I thought, one time. I can handle one time. It shouldn't have been hard." Pain contorts her features. "But that night, I went down to the basement to fetch a bottle of the wine your grandmother likes. He found me down there. I tried to leave, but he wouldn't let me." She pauses. "Your stepfather was not a good guy, Harriet. He was always a pretentious prick, but once he moved to New York, he got so much worse."

"I know," I say.

"When your dad put me in touch with George, he was trying to be kind. Thought it would be nice for me to have a hometown connection in the big city. It was before your parents got together, before George's business started to take off. He was still...mostly decent. At least at first." Her mouth twists. "Once your parents started dating, I saw George less and less. But I was still on the list for the swanky events his company would throw. I went to one thinking... I guess I naively thought I could play middleman, try to broker peace between the three of them, which obviously didn't work. Instead, I ended up meeting Adrian. George always invited Adrian's bosses to those things to schmooze them. He was trying to convince them to sell their property to him. We hit it off immediately. It was like a fairy tale, Harriet. I loved that man so much."

Her mouth trembles.

"Anyway, a few months later, Adrian told me he'd started hearing rumors about George—he wasn't paying his contractors. He was cutting corners with safety codes. Still, I never thought he'd do something so awful as..." She swallows. "Adrian was the property manager at the warehouse. There'd been break-ins that summer, so the owners had asked him to be on call. When the alarm started going off, he left our apartment and drove straight there."

"I'm so sorry, Vicky," I say, but she's lost in the memory.

"I was sleeping when the cops knocked on our door. They said they tried to get him out, but the fire exploded without warning... We were supposed to get *married* in five days! He was my love. My life. And George destroyed all of it."

She's crying now.

"I couldn't understand it. How the fire had started. How he had died. I needed answers. And once I started finding them, I was appalled. Furious. No one would say anything on the record, but *everyone* knew it wasn't an accident. Everyone knew George had paid off certain people to say it was. I went crazy with rage. I couldn't stay in that city."

"But why now?" I ask again.

A flare of anger lights up her face. "Down in that basement, George tried to pretend like nothing had ever happened. I asked if he remembered Adrian, and he said he had no idea who I was talking about. I tried to stay calm, but all I could think was how unfair it all was. George, with his beautiful house, all his money—some of which he made by *killing* my *fiancé*! When I took a pair of plastic kitchen gloves from beneath the sink and then slipped that knife from the block, I didn't let myself think about what I was doing. I just wanted—I don't know. I don't *know*!" Her voice is rising. "Then the rain started, and I found George in the living room. I told him to meet me out on the beach—*alone*—or I was going to tell everyone what he'd done. I said I had proof that fire wasn't accidental—a lie, but he didn't know that. He laughed, but some part of him must have believed me, because he came."

"And that's when—" It's hard to get the words around the thickness building in my throat.

She nods. "That's when it happened. I was already there when George arrived. He started yelling at me, telling me I was pathetic—that I needed to move on. All I wanted was an apology! An acknowledgment of what he'd done. But when I said that to him, he lost it—red-faced, screaming threats. Totally out of control. That's when I put the gloves on. I was just...I don't know. I think I could tell things were about to get bad—really, really bad—and I was right. A second later, he shoved me to my knees. Said he was going to fucking kill me, and the next thing I knew, his hands were wrapped around my throat."

She brushes her fingers against her neck. "I couldn't breathe. Couldn't think. The knife was tucked into the waist of my jeans, and I wrenched it out and...and I did it. I stabbed him."

I'm trying to process everything she's saying. George, taunting her. George, wrapping his hands around her throat. Squeezing.

Vicky desperate, left with no choice.

All the terrible things George did for the sake of a dollar.

Suddenly, I remember: The night before my dad left for Europe, Vicky was wearing a turtleneck. I remember I thought it was cute.

Her tears are coming fast and hard, streaming down her cheeks. "I *killed* him, Harriet. Do you know what that does to a person? I can't eat. Can't sleep. I feel like I'm losing my mind. I'm sorry. I'm so sorry."

"He was killing *you,*" I say. "He was strangling you."

Gogo's failing health, her memory loss. It might kill her if Vicky ends up in prison.

"I wasn't thinking clearly. I wanted him off me..."

"It was self-defense."

She wipes her eyes with the hem of her shirt. "It doesn't matter. I brought that knife with me. You're right, Harriet. I don't want an innocent person to go to jail for something...something..." She inhales. "Something I did. Your ex-boyfriend is a detective on the case, correct? If you call him, I understand."

"I'm not going to call him, Vicky. Listen. I have a plan."

I take a seat next to her on the bed and start outlining the plan I came up with last night. As I talk, her head starts shaking, slowly at first, then faster and faster.

"Absolutely not," she says once I'm done. Her expression is stern. "Harriet, you're an adult, but I am your elder, and I will not allow you do something so risky. Not for me. Especially not when I'm guilty."

"Vicky—"

"No," she says with a shake of her head. "I'm going to the police. Like you said, it was self-defense. They'll understand."

"Are you serious?" I cry, rising to my feet. "*Understand* it? The police here are corrupt as hell. Did you read the story in the *Times*? About the casino? The motel fire? They're in on everything! The system is broken on this island. You tell them what you did, you're looking at life behind bars, and I won't let that happen. Gogo needs you, and so do I."

Vicky falls quiet. "All right," she says finally. She sounds exhausted. "But on one condition. If we're doing this for Gogo, then I need to be here for Gogo. I'm going to stay on the island." She tries to smile. "Plus, if there's any sign your plan isn't working, I'm telling them everything. Got it?"

"I got it," I say.

CHAPTER FORTY-EIGHT

NIC

September 26
9:28 a.m.

Loud knocking wakes me.

I grab my phone from my bedside table and let out a groan. It's not even ten o'clock. Too goddamn early for a visitor. Particularly given the night I had. I lie back down and pull my pillow over my head.

After my run-in with Harriet at the hospital, I went straight to Martin's and proceeded to get shit-faced. Not normally how I handle my problems, but it seemed like a good idea at the time.

Now, not so much.

Whoever's at the door better have a damn good reason.

More pounding.

"*What?*" I yell, which does nothing to stop them. If anything, it gets louder. "Jesus, fine."

I drag myself upright, throw on some sweats, and head into the other room.

Another bang.

"Fucking hell," I mutter. I swing the door open with a bang. "What?" I bark, seconds before my brain registers who's on my doorstep.

Harriet Baker, a brown paper bag clutched in her hand. In the other, she holds a cardboard tray with two coffees. She's beautiful. Of course she is.

I remind myself that I'm supposed to be furious with her.

"I brought bagels and coffee? From Bageltelli's?" she says, like that's supposed to make up for waking me at the ass-crack of dawn after I explicitly told her I needed space.

At least she has the decency to look nervous.

"I don't eat gluten," I say, lying through my teeth. I love gluten.

Her face falls, and I'm hit by a pang of guilt. Maybe I'm leaning into this whole pissed-off thing too hard.

I sigh. "Fine. I like it. Bageltelli's is delightful. But bagels don't explain what the hell you're doing here this early."

She glances at her phone. "It's nine thirty a.m.?"

I stare at her, unsmiling.

She holds out the bag like a peace offering. "I'm sorry for showing up like this, but we need to talk, and you're screening my calls. It has to do with the case. I think..." Her face crumples for the briefest of seconds.

I brace myself for very bad news.

"I think...no. I *know* who killed George."

It takes my brain a beat to catch up. *Not bad news.* "Are you serious?"

She sniffs. "Yes."

"Then why do you look so upset?"

Her lower lip trembles. "Can I come in so we can talk?"

"I…yeah. Fine. Come in."

She sinks down onto a ratty old armchair I stole from my parents. "Want a bagel?" She sets the bag down on the coffee table. "I need food before I can talk about this."

My traitor stomach growls. "Fine," I grumble.

"Everything, cinnamon, or plain?"

"Everything, thanks." I pluck the bagel from the bag.

She watches with wide eyes as I take an enormous bite. I get the feeling she got that one for herself. I take another big bite. She's forced her way into my apartment; I get to pick my preferred bagel.

"Great. That's fine. I'll have the…cinnamon one." She makes a face. "Coffee?" She nudges the tray toward me.

"Thanks." I grab one and take a long sip. "Okay. You're sitting. You're eating. Now tell me what you know."

She sets her bagel on the table, untouched. "After I ran into you yesterday, I went to my grandmother's house. And—" She chews on her lower lip. "I stumbled onto this."

She hands me her phone. On its screen is a photo of a man and a woman, their arms wrapped around each other.

I look up at her. "I don't get it. Who are they?"

"Do you remember the obit I sent you that I found in George's desk?"

I nod.

"Well. Gogo was showing me photos of Vicky when she was

younger, and the guy in that one—next to my aunt Vicky? He's the guy in it."

"Wait." I pause, mid-chew. I'm trying to process this, but my brain is moving at the speed of a slug. "I'm confused. Your aunt knew him? How? Why?"

She picks up her bagel and starts tearing it into tiny pieces. "Because they were engaged. His name is Adrian. He died in the warehouse fire we think George set up in New York."

I slowly put down my bagel.

"I had no idea until yesterday. They were set to marry a week later."

I repeat it to make sure I understand. "George set the fire that killed Vicky's fiancé? A week before they were supposed to get married?"

"Yes."

"Harriet," I say slowly. "Are you trying to say you think Vicky killed George?"

Harriet hesitates. "No. I'm saying I *know* she did. I talked to her."

I jump to my feet. "Then what the fuck are you doing *here*? My sister is behind *bars*, Harriet!"

She doesn't move. "Vicky says it was self-defense, and I believe her. George was strangling her."

I glare. "So?"

"So! So you know the LIPD won't give a shit that she was protecting herself. For all we know, they're *all* corrupt."

I can't believe what I'm hearing. "That may be so, but *my sister*, Harriet—my *sister* is in *jail*! What are you saying? That Sara should give up her life so your aunt can walk free? Your aunt who, need I remind you, is a killer?"

"No!" she says. "Can you sit down? That's not what I'm saying, okay? I have a solution. One that will save Sara *and* my aunt."

"What makes you so sure your aunt deserves to be saved? She killed someone, Harriet."

"Are you—Vicky isn't going to do this again. No one else is in danger!" Harriet's mouth sets in a hard line. "George was horrible. He was a predator, an arsonist, and a *murderer* too! He almost killed a *child*—Martin told me all about it. If that kid had died and Martin had found out George was responsible, don't you think he would have wanted to kill him too?"

At the mention of Martin, I sink down to the couch. "Maybe. But he wouldn't have."

"Sure, but what if George attacked him? Strangled him? What would he have done then?"

"He would have fought back, obviously, Harriet. But Vicky had a knife *with* her! Why'd she bring it unless she was planning to use it?"

Harriet winces. "Yeah, I agree that part is...not great. But remember their argument in the basement? George was *screaming* at her. That's probably why she brought it. She was scared he'd—"

I don't even know why I'm still listening to this. I cut her off. "You know what? I don't care. You could list a million reasons why your aunt should walk free, but at the end of the day, I'm not trading my sister's life away. This conversation is over. I'm going to the cops."

"Nic," she says quietly. "Please. Give me five more minutes. Just five. I'm telling you, I think I have a solution. For Sara. For Vicky. For all of it. Please."

CHAPTER FORTY-NINE

HARRIET

September 26

9:54 a.m.

I pull out a file folder from my bag and set it on the coffee table next to our forgotten bagels.

"What is that?" Nic asks warily. The fact that he's still sitting next to me gives me hope that maybe he'll be open to what I'm about to suggest.

I start talking fast. "The day we went to George's office, I managed to knock a bunch of files off his desk on my way out the door. I wasn't exactly in the mood to clean them up, so I shoved them in my bag. In one of them, I found an email exchange between Dominic and George. Martin was right. Dominic is Mafia."

Nic flips open the folder and starts reading.

Encouraged, I scoot closer to him. "As you can also see, Dominic's last name is Russo. His family owns a company called Big Load Excavating. I found a bunch of articles about the Russos. Associates of theirs arrested for assault, bribery, racketeering—you name it. And every single one of those articles mention their ties to organized crime."

"Organized—" Nic's jaw drops. "You're serious."

"Dead. I also found the address for Big Load. It's up in Elizabeth. I say we go talk to them. In person."

He sets the paper back in the folder. "In *person*? Absolutely not. Unless your goal is to end up at the bottom of the Hudson River. Is that what you want?"

"We need to find Dominic for my plan to work!"

"You've lost your fucking mind, Baker. Do you really think we can just show up there and say we need to talk to Dominic Russo? Are you sure you don't want to die? Because it sure as shit sounds you do."

"They're not going to kill us in their place of business. That would be an incredibly stupid move on their end. But they might be willing to make a deal. See the thing is, I have Dominic on video. It ties him to George, Luke, to the shooting. I'm sure he has priors. If the cops saw it, he'd be in deep shit."

Nic's eyebrows shoot up his forehead. "You have him on *video*?"

I smile. "Yeah. After Luke shot Mindy, I started filming. I figured it might come in handy."

"You are..." He trails off without finishing that sentence, and my brain spirals filling in the blank. I'm—*what*?

Annoying? Amazing? Absurd? All of the above?

"Christ," he says, shaking his head. "The fact that I'm even considering this is—I've lost my fucking mind, clearly. What *is* it about you that..."

I study him. The muscle jumping in his jaw. His clenched fists, the way he's avoiding my gaze.

I need to apologize. I should have as soon as I walked through the front door.

I clear my throat. "I need to say something. I called my editor."

Nic's head turns.

"I told her I'm not writing the article for her. What I'm doing—it's not about getting my career back." I bite my bottom lip. "Or maybe it was at first. But then I got to know you again. You think I don't remember you from back then, but I do. I do. This is about helping you, your sister, your family. Because I...because I care about you. So, so much—"

I cut short, my cheeks wet with tears, throat tight with emotion.

Nic's face softens. For a beat, he shuts his eyes. When he reopens them, he looks me in the eyes for the first time since I walked in here. I wince, reminded of those long moments after I found him on the floor of the office. Before I knew he was okay. When I thought I'd lost him for good.

"I can't believe I'm about to say this," he says. "But fine. Let's try it your way."

Nic's sitting in the passenger seat, wearing a serious expression and a dark green T-shirt that matches his eyes. The drive up to Elizabeth was quiet. I don't know about him, but I've spent most of the time sending silent pleas into the universe for it all to go smoothly. For Dominic not to shoot us on sight.

"Take a right at the next street," he says. "Are you sure you want to do this? I understand why you say you do, but we could be walking into a hell of a lot of trouble, Harriet."

I turn at the next street. We have a plan, and we have to stick to it. It'll work.

It has to.

"It'll be fine. We have a plan. Plus, Dominic seemed like a reasonable guy, didn't he?"

Nic laughs with no humor. "Not even a little. You might remember he kicked my head in? I spent two nights in the hospital?"

I wince. "Okay, fine. He's a little violent. But he let us go instead of shooting us! That has to count for something, right?"

"Uh-huh, sure," Nic says. He points to the street up ahead. "That's it! Turn there. When he let us go, I'm assuming he didn't know about your video?"

I flick on my turn signal. "I mean, no."

"Mm-hmm."

"Even so! He has no reason to hurt us! We're just asking for a simple exchange. We have something he'll want. He can do us a favor we need. Easy-peasy."

"I think most people call that blackmail."

I scowl at him. "Semantics."

"There it is!" he says. "See the sign?"

I squint through the dirty windshield. Sure enough, looming up ahead is a large, rusted metal sign that reads Big Load Excavating. The place takes up the whole block.

Now that we're here, my bluster has faded.

"Do we just walk inside?" I ask once we're parked and out of the car. I'm peering through the links of the fence surrounding the property. It's tall, topped with sharp coils of barbed wire. In the center of the lot sits a squat, one-story office building, a parking lot full of heavy machinery beside it. Two huge warehouses loom in the background. A couple guys mill around out front of one, but otherwise, the place looks quiet.

Nic shoves his hands into the pockets of his jeans. "If we want to talk to them, yes. Going in there is pretty much a necessity."

I swallow. "Okay."

I don't move.

"We can leave if you want," Nic says quietly. "We can drive back, go to the cops, tell them what Vicky did and—"

The mention of my aunt shakes me out of my stupor. "No. *No.* We're going inside."

I take a deep breath and start walking toward the entrance.

CHAPTER FIFTY

NIC

September 26

12:34 p.m.

"Hi, there. My associate and I are hoping to speak to Dominic Russo?" All things considered, I sound surprisingly normal.

The woman behind the desk looks up from her computer. She's chomping on gum and is at least two decades younger than I first thought.

"Ex*cuse* me?"

"We're looking for Dominic Russo?" I repeat. I can't believe we're doing this. Except Harriet's right, in a way. If we went to the cops and told them about Vicky, I don't foresee them being sympathetic to her claim that George had attacked her first.

The receptionist snaps her gum. "Why?"

"We have—"

Harriet elbows me out of the way. "We need to show him something."

The woman is unmoved. "You need to *show* him something?"

"Yeah. And he'll want to see this, I promise."

Her eyebrows shoot up. "*Excuse* me?"

Harriet is fucking this all up. I'm about to jump in when a voice calls from the back hallway, "Ariana? The contractors from the city here?"

"Actually, boss," Ariana says, eyeing us. "It's two randos. Says they're here for Dominic."

"Dominic?"

A man emerges from the back. His black hair is slicked off his face, and his nose is crooked, like it's been broken a few times. He's short, wide, but something about him sends a chill down my spine.

His gaze is cold and flat as it travels between me and Harriet. "What do they want with Dominic?" he asks.

Ariana shrugs. "Dunno. Whaddaya want with Dominic?" she directs to us.

"Um..." Harriet says.

I cut in. "Hi, there. I'm Nic Allbright. And you are...?"

"Ariana," the woman says.

Right.

"And your boss...?"

The man arches a single eyebrow. "Me? I'm the owner of Big Load Excavating. Tony Russo. Dominic's my kid. What'd he do now?"

"If possible, we'd love to talk in private. No offense," I say to Ariana.

She snaps another bubble with her gum and shrugs.

"We have..." I glance at Harriet.

"A proposition," Harriet finishes. Not the word I would have used, but okay. Sure.

Tony smirks. "A proposition, huh? Well, who am I to pass up a *proposition*? Come on back."

His office is large, with shiny leather seats and a wide oak desk that probably cost more than most people make in a year. I've never been to a mob boss's office before, but it's much less threatening than I expected. If I didn't know better, I'd think Tony was just another overpaid CEO, hiding a lack of empathy behind expensive furniture.

Tony takes a seat behind the desk and gestures for us to take the chairs on the other side.

"Is Dominic here?" Harriet asks.

"He's…around," Tony says, brushing this off with a wave. "But don't you worry your pretty little head about that. Anything you want to say to my kid, you can say to me. In fact, *better* you say it to me. Dominic can be a bit of a live wire."

I rub my head where Dominic kicked it. Is it my imagination, or is it still sore?

"What'd you say your names were?" Tony asks. His eyes land on me. I lick my lips. "Nic. Nic Allbright." I'm suddenly grateful to be on the other side of a desk from this man. It hides the fact that my hands are balled into tight fists in my lap.

"And you?" Tony directs this to Harriet.

"Harriet? Baker?" She says it like it's a question.

Tony leans back in his chair. "You look familiar, Harriet Baker."

"Me?" she squeaks.

He nods. "I never forget a face, and I'm sure I've seen yours. Where'd you two meet my kid anyway?"

"Um." Harriet glances at me. "Well. We had a little encounter with him the other day."

"Oh yeah? An encounter, huh? Where?"

Harriet's quiet. Little beads of sweat have popped up across her forehead. She looks close to a panic attack.

I brace myself and take over. "Look, I'll be straight with you."

"Great," Tony says. "I'd appreciate that."

I tilt my chin at Harriet. "Her stepfather is George George."

Tony picks up a pen and starts clicking it open and shut. "George George? What sort of silly name is that?"

"He was murdered about a month ago," I say.

Tony's lips tilt down.

"And?"

"And that's how we know Dominic. We met him at George's office. Well. *Met* is being generous. I was there and Luke barged in and he called Dominic and then I ended up with a head injury and Mindy ended up shot—"

Tony sighs. "You've lost me, son. Look, if you can't explain what you need from my kid, I'm going to have to ask you to leave. I'm a busy man. I don't have time for whatever this is."

"I just— He *assaulted* me."

"Well, that's your word against his, isn't it?" Tony rises from his chair. "I think it's time for you to go."

Harriet finally stirs. "No. Wait." She tugs her phone out of her bag and sets it on his desk. "I have something you need to see."

The video of Dominic is cued up on the screen.

"Watch it," she says. "Dominic's on it. I started filming moments after Luke shot someone. In fact, in this video, Dominic and Luke are discussing the shooting. It's very interesting."

Tony slowly sinks back down to his chair.

Harriet continues. "The thing is Luke and George were involved in some seriously bad shit—murder, bribery, arson—a lot of which has become public recently. Whether you were involved in it or not, this video proves that your son was. I'm betting you don't want it getting to the cops. Could bring unwanted attention to your *business*."

Tony's face darkens into a scowl. "Dominic didn't tell me he was there. That kid needs to get his head on straight. But if you turn that video over to the cops, I promise—you'll be very sorry."

My stomach lurches. We're going to end up buried somewhere on this lot if we're not careful.

"We're not. We *won't*!" she adds hurriedly. "But we just want something very simple in return."

Tony's chin tucks into his thick neck. "Let me get this straight. You're here to *blackmail* me?" He looks like he can't figure out whether to laugh or shoot us.

Harriet's cheeks redden. "I'd rather call it an exchange."

"What is it you want exactly?"

A bead of sweat runs down my back. I clear my throat. "My sister's sitting in jail. She was charged with George's murder. The cops have a ton of evidence, but it's all circumstantial. She didn't do it."

Tony's mouth pulls to one side. "What makes you so sure? I think it's possible you might be a little biased, kid."

Harriet pipes up. "We're pretty sure his sister didn't do it, because we're pretty sure we know who did. Someone I care about a lot. Someone I'd prefer didn't go to jail."

Tony crosses his arms against his burly stomach. "This is all fascinating stuff. But what the hell does this have to do with Dominic? Or me?"

"Well." Harriet clutches the arm of her chair like a life preserver, but her voice is steady. A swell of admiration rises in me. "Luke's already in jail. He killed Barbara—the town librarian—and he shot our friend Mindy. Almost killed her. He's a real piece of shit."

"No kidding," Tony murmurs.

"So we were thinking. Why not put one more murder on him? We were thinking your organization could help persuade him to confess to George's murder too."

Tony's mouth falls open. He presses a hand to his heart. "My *organization*? You mean my excavating company? What makes you think I have the ability to do anything like that?"

"Call it a hunch."

Tony snorts. "And if I don't?"

"Well, I used to work at *Humans*—"

"*Humans?*" He sounds impressed. "That tabloid, right? My wife loves that shit."

"Yeah. Well, then you know. They love scandalous stories. And they're great at digging into people's lives. If you know what I mean."

Tony whistles. "First blackmail, and now *threats*? You, young lady, have some real cojones."

Harriet grins. "Thank you. Though why would it matter if

they looked into you, right? You're just the owner of an excavating company."

Tony snorts a laugh. "Touché. You're lucky you caught me in a good mood, you know that? Some days, I wouldn't give two shits about helping Dominic out. He's my kid, but he can be a real pain in the ass. What you're asking though? It isn't that complicated. But how do I know you'll hold up your end of the bargain? That you won't just go ahead and release that video anyway?"

"Because we don't have a death wish," Harriet says.

Tony smirks. "Fair point. All right. You have a deal."

CHAPTER FIFTY-ONE

HARRIET

September 26

1:03 p.m.

We don't speak until we're back on the sidewalk.

"We did it," Nic says with wonder. "*You* did it."

He lifts me off the ground, swinging me around and setting me down on the curb. It happens so fast that I barely register his arms around me before they're gone.

I want to say something momentous, because he's right—we really just did that, *holy shit*—but then our eyes meet, and whatever I was going to say slips right out of my head.

"Harriet—"

"Nic—"

"Can I go first?" I ask after a moment.

He nods.

I take a deep breath. "I care about you. A lot. What happened in New Rochelle, in George's office—all that was real. I've realized so much these past couple weeks. I was holding on to my life in the city because...well, because I didn't have anything else, really. When I lost that job, it was like I lost myself. My identity. But after spending time with you, seeing how much you care about your family, how much you're willing to sacrifice for them...it makes me want more. You're amazing, and I am so, so sorry for everything I've done."

He steps closer and grabs my hand. "Harriet." His voice is rough and low and sends a bolt of warmth through my lower belly. "You are the most frustrating person I have ever met, but you're also funny, kind, and a total badass. I wouldn't have been able to do any of this without you. You're so driven and focused and have such a big heart. When you learned what Vicky did, you could have just kept your mouth shut and let my sister take the fall. But you came to me. I don't know if you see it, but you also care about the people around you—so much so that you were willing to risk your life making a deal with a Mafia boss to help them."

He steps forward, closing the gap between us, cupping his hand to my cheek. His fingertips caress my skin, and my breath catches.

"Harriet?"

I lick my lips. "Yes, Nic?"

"Can I kiss you?"

I smile. "Hell yes, you can."

Our lips meet hungrily. Our tongues touch, tangle, and god, it feels so good. So right.

My hand pushes through his hair, and I pull him close, wrapping my leg around his upper thigh. His fingers slip under the waist of my jeans, fingers running along my skin. He squeezes my butt, and I moan.

I don't care that we're on a public street, that it's the middle of the day, that other people could see us. I just want him—all of him—right now—

"Get a room!" someone yells.

We jump apart. Nic's chest is heaving, my body so flushed I feel like it's on fire.

Idling on the street is a big black Lincoln, its engine humming low. The back window rolls down, and Tony's head appears. He cackles with delight. "Kidding. Get after it, you crazy kids. But fair warning: The cops like to roll through this area. No idea why, of course. But you might want to take this elsewhere."

And with that, he's gone.

Nic and I burst out laughing.

"No idea why cops might hang around here," he says.

"None at all."

He hesitates. "I guess we should head home?"

Even though all I really want to do is keep kissing him, I nod. "I'll drive fast."

His mouth pulls up into a smile.

Have you ever experienced a three-hour car ride with sexual tension so thick that you could cut it with a knife?

Because I sure have.

Back at his place, it's a race to get out of the car. As soon as we do, we can't keep our hands off each other—in the front foyer, the elevator, the hallway outside his apartment door.

Once we're inside his place, we crash together again, this time with nothing to pull us apart.

I don't kiss and tell, but suffice it to say, it's amazing.

CHAPTER FIFTY-TWO

NIC

September 27

9:08 a.m.

The text arrives from Martin bright and early Sunday morning. We're still asleep, so I don't see it until I wake up a little after nine.

When I read it, I bolt upright in the bed, taking the sheets with me. Harriet groans beside me.

"What is it?" she mumbles, still half asleep.

"It's done."

Her eyes open, and she grabs the phone from my hand. "Are you serious? Already?"

She reads Martin's text out loud. "'You're not going to believe this, but late last night, Luke Dalio confessed to George's murder. Sara's off the hook. You didn't hear this from me, but barring anything unforeseen, she should be out by the end of the day.'"

"She's getting out," Harriet says.

I nod, afraid to speak because of the lump in my throat.

We did it. We actually did it.

My phone rings. The screen reads *Mom*.

"Nico," Mom cries when I answer. "Sara's getting out!" She sniffles, her voice breaking as she continues. "I can't believe it. Barry told me that the awful man who killed Barbara confessed last night. She's free. My baby is free! Things are finally turning around for us, Nico. Everyone who canceled jobs will come crawling back, and I can tell them vaffanculo!"

Vaffanculo essentially means *fuck off* in Italian. Literally, it translates to *go do it in the ass*.

"Mom! Please don't do that."

Mom lets out a loud laugh. "You really think I would do that, Nico? I would not! I will happily accept all our clients back. I'm not that stubborn, although I know you think I am. I know you think you need to protect me. I still can't believe you and your father kept the fact that you were in the *hospital* from me. That better never happen again."

Shit. "How did you find out about that?"

"Martin told me."

That rat bastard. I make a mental note to tear him a new one the next time I see him.

"He shouldn't have done that, Mom."

She scoffs. "He absolutely should have. It made me think about things. The way you put your life on hold for me all those years ago. You think I don't know that you started the catering business with me because you were worried about us? You're a good son. And now it's time we repay the favor. I'm going to find a new manager. You're fired."

"*What?*"

Firing is what happens to Sara. Not to me.

"Well," she says, backpedaling, "only if you want to be. You can keep working as long as you like, but I wanted you to know the option is there. You don't have to feel stuck here anymore. Of course, we might need extra hands sometimes. And you'll need to train the new person. And your sister can be unpredictable, so—"

It goes on like this for at least two more minutes, but by the time we're saying our goodbyes, it's clear that my mom is serious about letting me go if that's what I want.

It's terrifying, but I feel free for the first time in years.

Harriet puts her arms around me. "Are you okay?"

I reach up and wipe my cheeks. "I'm so much better than okay. I adore you, Harriet Baker."

The words are out of my mouth before I can stop them.

Shit.

There's a beat of silence, during which I die about a thousand deaths, but then she says, "I adore you too," and the world rights itself again.

EPILOGUE

HARRIET

December 24
4:23 p.m.

A tree twinkles in the corner of Nic's parents' living room, casting low light across the crocheted stocking hanging from the fireplace mantel. Under it sits a small pile of wrapped presents Nic and Sara brought for their parents to open later. The room is small, but there's real love here.

From the kitchen comes the sounds of arguing—Sara and her mom, bickering about how to best prepare the lobster for the Feast of the Seven Fishes.

"Hey." Nic comes up behind me and wraps his arms around my waist. He kisses my cheek, and my heart tugs, as it always does for him.

"Hey," I say softly. I sink into him and nuzzle my nose into his neck.

"Gogo and Vicky should be here soon. And"—he hesitates—"your mom."

I stiffen. My mother and I haven't spoken much since Sara's release; I moved out about a week after and in with Vicky and Gogo. Partly because I want to be able to spend however much time Gogo has left with her. But if I'm being honest, I also want to keep an eye on Vicky.

She's still talking about turning herself in—telling me after one too many drinks that she can't live with the knowledge that an innocent man is in jail in her place.

I keep reminding her that Luke Dalio is *decidedly* not innocent. He was going to spend the rest of his life in prison anyway for murdering poor Barbara Patterson, who was only trying to do the right thing.

But it doesn't seem to help. I'm hoping with enough time, her guilt will fade, but I guess we'll have to wait and see.

I spin so I'm nose-to-nose with Nic. "Why is *she* coming?"

"It's Christmas Eve, Harriet. She's your mom."

"In name only," I mutter.

When I told her I was moving out, she didn't understand. In fact, she totally lost it. We ended up in a huge fight, me finally saying all the things I'd never said. About my lonely childhood. About how she always made me feel like I didn't matter.

We haven't spoken since.

"You're the only family she has," Nic says. "Otherwise, she was going to spend tonight alone."

What he says reminds me of Ruth Carter, all alone in her big house at the edge of the ocean. Spying on the neighbors. Lonely and bitter.

Is that how I want my mom's life to turn out?

"I guess," I say. Nic's taught me so much about forgiveness and family, but he also doesn't understand how complicated it is with my mother. Not really.

Sara walks up to us with two glasses of white wine. "You want?" she asks with a shy smile. Since getting out of jail, she's taken over most of Nic's responsibilities at the catering company, which has allowed him to enroll in some classes online at the Auguste Escoffier School of Culinary Arts. He's currently taking a couple courses on sustainable culinary practices, and he *loves* it.

I take a glass. "Thanks."

There's a knock on the front door, and Sara's head jerks up.

"I'll get it," she says, hurrying to answer.

Steven, Martin, and Maggie are on the other side. Maggie's holding a bouquet of flowers. She smiles at Sara.

"I brought these for you," she says. "Thank you for inviting me tonight."

Sara's cheeks flush red. She seems to have developed a bit of a crush on my friend.

I suspect it's mutual.

They all come inside, talking over one another as they settle around the room. My mom, Gogo, and Vicky arrive a short while later, Gogo clutching Vicky's hand like a life raft. Her memory has been slipping even faster these past few weeks. Now, there are times she'll forget bigger things: names, places, how to get home from the supermarket.

It's breaking my heart apart piece by piece, but I am so grateful to be here with her.

And I am so glad I didn't pursue that job with *Humans*.

I'm still trying to figure out that part of my life. I don't know if I'll ever go back to journalism. If I do, it won't be at a place like that.

In the meantime, I've been working part-time at the library, and believe it or not, I sort of love it? I don't know if I'll stay there forever, but for the time being, it's perfect. Mindy and I have become great friends. I was there for her when things turned sour with the hot doctor she met during her hospital stay. I know she'll find the right person someday soon. There's no one who deserves it more.

I manage to avoid my mother until we're about to sit down for dinner.

She catches me on my way out of the bathroom. "Harriet," she says. "Hello."

I don't want to do this now. Or ever. The only thing I've ever wanted from her was to love me, and that was always too much to ask of her.

"Mother," I say, wondering if I can edge around her and escape.

She looks down at her feet. "I...I wanted to say I am sorry."

I must have misheard. "Excuse me?" I ask.

Her mouth dips into a frown, but it disappears quickly. "I'm sorry," she repeats. "I... My therapist—"

I blink. "Excuse me," I say again. "Your *what*?"

She ignores this. "My therapist and I agreed that I owe you an apology. So I am sorry. I should have been..." Her fingers tremble as she fidgets with the collar on her oxford shirt. "Better. To you. So I'm sorry."

I'm silent.

"Okay?" she asks impatiently.

"Sure?" I say, not sure how much I mean it.

She winces. "I'm not good at this. But if you're ever willing to sit down and talk about things, maybe with my therapist there too, I would be very grateful. For the opportunity."

I'm at a loss for words.

"Please, Harriet?" she whispers. She looks so small, so sad. My heart pulls.

"Okay," I say. "Yeah, we can do that."

Her face relaxes. "Thank you. I… I'll see you at the table." She hurries into the bathroom and slams the door, leaving me to stare at it with wonder.

We're almost through dinner when there's a knock on the front door.

"Are we expecting more guests?" Mrs. Allbright asks from the head of the table. "I thought we were all accounted for, but…"

Nic's on his feet. "I'll get it." He disappears into the living room.

A minute ticks by, then another.

"Where is he?" Sara asks finally.

I shrug. "I'll go see."

Steven and Martin exchange a small smile. "We'll come too," says Steven, throwing down his napkin on the table.

"Me too!" Maggie says with a level of enthusiasm I don't quite understand.

"I can handle it, you guys," I tell them.

"I'll come too," Sara says, standing with a smirk.

I blink at them. "What—" I shake my head. "Okay? Sure."

I'm halfway out of the room when the scrape of chairs against the hardwood floor stops me. A backward glance tells me that now *everyone* is up and out of their seats.

They're following me.

"What the hell is going on?" I ask Maggie. She's paused next to me, wearing a giant grin.

"Nothing," she says, and Steven elbows her. "Just go, Harriet!"

I give her a weird look. "Fine," I say and walk into the living room.

Nic's standing by the open front door. Next to him are Mindy and my dad and Cindy.

Nic smiles. "Harriet." He licks his lips. "Hey."

"Hey?" I say, wary all of a sudden. Why is Mindy here? Why is my *dad*? I don't care if it *is* Christmas, Nic should know better than to gather my parents under one roof. Especially now that Cindy is (shudder) pregnant.

"Hey," he says again, glancing around at the crowd. "I...actually, um. Would you be up for going on a little walk with me?"

"But we're in the middle of dinner?"

Maggie nudges me. "Harriet!" she hisses.

"What?"

She motions with her chin to Nic. "He has something he wants to *ask* you," she says, widening her eyes.

Something he wants to ask—*oh.*

Ohmygod.

My heartbeat kicks up. Is she saying what I think she's saying?

Is he...

"Harriet?" Nic asks.

"Um, right. Sure. Yes. Of course."

Maggie squeezes my arm, and I walk over to Nic. The room is quiet, so quiet, like everyone's holding their collective breath, like they all know what's about to happen.

"We'll be right back," Nic says.

As soon as we're through the door, I hear the room break out into loud whispers.

Nic quickly shuts it and turns to me. "I thought we could walk down to the beach?"

"Okay." My voice sounds shaky. He takes my hand, and I realize it's slick with sweat. I don't want to get my hopes up about what's happening. Maybe he just needs some fresh air. Maybe he wants to watch the sunset. Maybe he suddenly decided he wanted to feel the sand under his toes. Maybe my dad showing up was random, and he's giving me an escape from whatever the hell my parents are about to get into. That would be just like him, so sweet and thoughtful and kind.

I could be wrong about what I'm thinking, I could be, and if I am, that's okay. It really is. I know it would be fast. Hell, if Maggie or Steven told me they were engaged to their partner after only three months of dating, I'd tell them they'd lost their shit. But *everything* about us has been fast. Fast and amazing and so, so right.

Sometimes you just know. And man, do I know.

Even though I'm technically living with Vicky and Gogo right now, I spend almost every night with Nic, and waking up next to him has quickly become my favorite thing. Seeing him in those early morning hours, studying his face, listening to his soft breath. I've fallen so deeply in love with him, in a way I never really knew existed outside of rom-coms and fairy tales.

I would give anything to spend the rest of my life with him. Wake up next to him every single day. Have kids with him—

"Harriet?"

His voice cuts into my rolling thoughts. He stops. We've reached the stairs up to the path that runs parallel to the dunes. Beyond them is the ocean.

"Are you okay? You're being awful quiet."

I nod, but I am so, so not okay.

If he doesn't ask me tonight, I'm going to ask him. I'm not waiting because of some antiquated patriarchal rule. I'm a human person! I can take charge.

"Are you good to go out to the beach?"

"Sure," I manage, my voice awfully small for someone raging about feminism inside her head.

The sun dips low into the sky as we hit the sand, painting the sky with reds, oranges, and deep burgundy. Nic's hand is warm in mine.

"Do you wan—" I start to say but cut off when he stops abruptly.

And then he sinks down to one knee.

Holy shit. I was right. This is happening.

This is *happening.*

"Harriet Baker," he says. "You are the most frustrating, stubborn, opinionated woman I have ever met. But you're also deeply loyal, incredibly intelligent, and funny as hell. I love you. I love you so much that I can't imagine my life without you in it. I know it's only been a few months since everything that happened, but here I am..." He swallows. "So here I am, wondering. Harriet, will you be my wife?"

In his outstretched hand is a little blue box.

Everything about this moment is perfect: the roar of the ocean behind me, the cool wind brushing against my cheeks, the man in front of me.

Especially the man in front of me. He's seen me at my most stubborn, frustrating self and loved me for it instead of despite it. He's given me a place that really feels like *home* for the first time in my entire life.

I've never loved someone more.

"Yes." I manage to get the word through the thickness in my throat and out into the salty air. "Of course I will." I tug him back to his feet.

He rises, reaching down to brush off his pants, but as he does, I launch myself at him.

"I love you!" I say as we tumble to the ground together, landing in a pile of limbs. I straddle him, peppering his face with kisses. "*I love you I love you I love you.*"

He's laughing, his arms wrapped around me. "I love you too. Do you want your ring now?"

"No."

His face falls. "No?"

"No, I mean, yes. I do. But I want to say something first, if that's okay?"

He nods.

"Nicolas Allbright, you are by far the best person I've ever known. You make *me* want to be a better person. I was a fool back in high school not to immediately lock you down, and I'm lucky that you stayed single long enough for me to realize my mistake."

"I stayed single because I compared everyone to you." He says it quickly, like he's embarrassed by his admission. His admission that just might be the most incredible thing anyone has ever said to me.

I can't help it; I'm crying now. "See?" I wipe at my nose. "This is what I was talking about. You're amazing. Also, I will have you know that on the way here, I decided *I* was going to ask *you* to marry me if you didn't do it first."

He laughs. "Well, I'm glad we were on the same page."

"We were. We are. I can't wait to spend the rest of my life with you." I lean down and kiss him, our mouths meeting, his tongue pushing into mine. A moment ticks by and then another as our kiss deepens, my roaming hands finding his waist, ducking under the hem of his shirt to his bare chest. I press myself down against him, my fiancé, my future husband, the man of my fucking dreams—god, do I want him—

Then, to my great disappointment, Nic pulls back, clearing his throat. "Uh, Harriet, as much as I love what we're doing right now, there are children"—he gestures down the beach—"watching. Can we put this on hold until later tonight?"

"I suppose," I grumble, but I'm smiling down at him.

"Good." He kisses me one last time, and then I climb off him.

He doesn't move.

"What are you doing?"

He pulls himself up to his knees. "The first time around, I didn't get to put the ring on your finger properly...so here we go again." He opens the box. Inside is a ring, one that I recognize.

Gogo's wedding ring. She doesn't wear it anymore; it no longer fits over her aging knuckles, and honestly at this point, it's probably for the best. There's a high probability that she would lose it.

Tears build in the corners of my eyes. It's a gorgeous piece of jewelry and one that's so meaningful.

"Gogo wanted you to have it." He slips it over my trembling ring finger. "She said she couldn't think of a better place for it to end up."

"You're amazing," I whisper.

"You're not so bad yourself, Harriet Baker," he says with a smile.

He wraps his arms around me, and suddenly, I'm home.

THE END

READING GROUP GUIDE

1. Sara is a strong suspect for George's murder and is the only person being prosecuted by the police. Did you believe she was guilty, or did you think she was being falsely framed? Why or why not?

2. Harriet and Nic have never investigated a crime before, let alone tried to find a murderer. If you were in their shoes, how would you have approached the investigation? Was there anything you would have done differently?

3. How do you think Nic's loyalty to his family shapes his character and his choices throughout the story? How does this differ from Harriet and the relationship she has with her family?

4. Harriet feels strongly that Barbara Patterson had serious motives for murder. What did you think? Did Barbara seem like a worthwhile suspect, or was there someone else who you found suspicious?

5. Nic has a difficult time letting go of the past. Do you think Nic's unresolved feelings make him treat Harriet unfairly, or were his feelings justified? Have you ever held a grudge over the way someone treated you in the past?

6. Harriet's efforts to find out the truth of who killed George lead her to overwhelming truths about the world she thought she knew. What did she do with the information she learned about her small town? Did you agree with how she handled it, or would you have taken a different approach?

7. The relationship Harriet has with her mother is often tense and strained. How are they different from each other, and why do you think it is so difficult for them to get along? Have you ever had a similar relationship with someone in your own family?

8. Harriet is a complex character who undergoes a lot of growth throughout the novel. What mistakes did she make along the way, and how did she learn from them? Overall, did you like her as a character?

9. Kozel tells Harriet that the corruption in LIPD "runs deep" before encouraging her to continue fighting for Sara's innocence. Several characters struggle with corruption from those ranked above them. What would you do in their shoes? Would you take the risk and speak out?

10. Who was the real murderer, and did you expect the twist? In retrospect, what clues might you have missed?

11. Nic and Harriet have a complicated history, and while trying to solve a murder, they begin to, inevitably, fall in love. What did you think about their relationship? Do you think they made a good team?

A CONVERSATION WITH THE AUTHOR

This book is a perfect mix between a whodunit mystery and a romance. What inspired you to mix those two genres?

Thank you so much! I think often while writing whether what I'm creating is something I as a reader would pick up in a bookstore. Romance/rom-coms and mysteries are two of my favorite genres to read, and I thought, what better than to combine them on the page? They complement each other so well—one is more internal and character-driven (romance) and the other more obviously external and plot-driven (mystery). When they're mixed together, the reader gets the best of both worlds.

There are so many strong personalities and vivid characters in this story. Where do you get inspiration for your characters? Are any of them based on real people in your own life?

Ha! If they were based on real people, I'd never tell. 😂 I do admit to stealing names of real-life people at times (my husband's grandfather was actually the chief of police in a NJ shore town many years ago, and his last name was Sharkey, but he wasn't corrupt, I promise!). My inspiration for my characters really came from the story itself. Once I could hear the voices of my main characters, I started to think: What types of people might populate their world? And digging deeper: Why is Harriet the way she is? Might it have something to do with her mother? Their relationship? And from there, Harriet's mother came together in my head. Similarly, Nic's mom, sister, and the list goes on.

Throughout the book, Harriet struggles with what she wants for her future. Is this based on a time in your own life when you struggled to know the path forward?

Oh, absolutely! My mid-twenties were a hugely difficult time—I wasn't sure at all what I wanted for my life, where my place was in the world. Harriet's struggle to figure out her future and, more importantly, the type of person she wants to be in that future really mirrors a lot of what I went through at that age.

In your opinion, what elements make a story a "page-turner" for readers? What do you focus on when writing to make sure readers are on the edge of their seats?

Pacing is a huge element of why readers remain engaged in a story, but it's a delicate balance. Sway too far in either direction and you run the risk of losing the reader (and obviously, every reader has different tastes, so some people really enjoy a veryfastpacedstory and some enjoy a sloooower mooooving oooone). That said, to me the most important element of the story is the voice and characters. If the reader finds that they want to spend time with your characters, I really believe they'll stay with the story even if pacing lags (or speeds up) too much—and even if they figure out the killer in the first act!

This story has so many great twists! What does your process for writing look like? Did you have a clear vision from the beginning, or did more of the story come to you as you kept writing?

I am not much of an outliner (although I'm trying to grow that muscle right now because I know it would make my life a hell of a lot easier in the long run). For this story, I started with a picture of a woman in her mid-twenties, lost in her life, celebrating her birthday in a place she does not want to be at all. I always knew the person who dies would be her stepfather, but in a very early formation of the book, it opened at a restaurant in DC! A lot of the twists came to me as I wrote and discussed the story with friends and family. In fact, I have to credit my husband for giving me the idea for Dominic and his family!

Did you always know who would be the murderer? Or did you have a few different options?

Honestly, I can't remember if I knew who the murderer was before I started writing (probably not though—see my earlier comment about not being much of an outliner, ha), but I definitely had it figured out before I got too far into the book.

Would you want to be a detective yourself? If you could solve any unsolved mystery, which one would you choose and why?

Ha, while I've never really wanted to be a PI or cop, I will say that I'm nosy as all get-out, and that part of the work (i.e., the part where you get to dig into people's lives) intrigues me to no end. That said, I'm sure it's much less sexy than it seems on the screen/on the page, so I think I'll stick with pretend detective work for the moment. 😉

Amelia Earhart's disappearance has always fascinated me; there's something about the fact that so many very bright people have attempted to solve the mystery and failed that makes me even more curious about what really happened to her.

ACKNOWLEDGMENTS

It's funny that this is my fifth (!) book but feels a little like debuting all over again. A new category (adult!), a new publisher (Sourcebooks!), a new group of readers (you!)—so exciting, and so, so many people to thank.

To my editor, Olivia Turner, for falling in love with Nic and Harriet and all of Logan Island. Your editorial letters are incredibly insightful, and without them, this wouldn't have become the book it is: swoony, twisty, and all-around fun. Thank you for answering my questions, no matter how small, for sending encouraging GIFs, and for all the brainstorming sessions. You're an incredible editor, and I'm so grateful to be working with you on my adult debut (and on Mindy and Kozel's story next!).

To everyone at Sourcebooks for all your hard work getting *It Happened One Murder* out into the world and into the hands of readers. To Beth Sochacki and Jennifer Steinhagen in marketing, to Aubrey Clemans in PR, to Mary Wheelehan in production, and to everyone else at Sourcebooks. I cannot tell you how much I appreciate everything. You're such a wonderful team, and I am so lucky to have you supporting my writing!

I *adore* the cover of this book, so a special shout-out goes to Emma Rogers for creating such an eye-catching, perfect design for Nic and Harriet's story. It's absolutely beautiful!

To my agent, as always: Andrea Morrison, agent extraordinaire, who loved Nic and Harriet from the jump and encouraged me to keep writing. Without you, this book truly would not exist. You've been in my corner through every step of my writing career and always answer my emails, no matter how neurotic (and trust me, some of them are *very, very neurotic*). Thank you. You are the best.

To Genevieve Gagne-Hawes (again!) (always!) for her keen editorial eye and helping me shape this story into something so much better than it had been. Every time I get to work with you on a project, I'm so thrilled because you're incredible.

Thanks to Claire McLaughlin at Terrace PR for supporting the PR efforts for this book. I appreciate all the phone calls and brainstorming sessions and your willingness to think outside of the box. You've gone above and beyond for Nic and Harriet, and it's so lovely having you on my team!

And to Hayley Burdett Wilmot; Sofia Bolido and Maja Nikolic in global rights at Writers House; and Olivia Burgher and Hilary Zaitz Michael at WME: Thank you.

Thank you to all the absolutely amazing authors who I was lucky enough to have blurb this book: Tamara Berry, Allison Brennan, Gloria Chao, Amelia Diane Coombs, Alissa DeRogatis, Karen Dukess,

Carlyn Greenwald, Mia P. Manansala, KJ Micciche, Bellamy Rose, Sienna Sharpe, Alicia Thompson, Emily Wibberley and Austin Siegemund-Broka, and Ashley Winstead. I can't tell you how appreciative I am that you took the time to read *IHOM* and say such kind things about it. I'm happy to return the favor anytime!

Kathleen, thank you for all the slaps. I'd never finish a draft without them. You better write another book with me someday (mostly so I won't have to write the entire thing myself… jkkkk, mostly so we can renew our trauma bond).

Rita, I cannot tell you how happy I am that I found Writopia and YOU! I love coteaching with you, bullying you, and spiraling with you. And to all my Writopia coteachers (Jordan—we miss you!) and students, you're awesome. Never stop writing!

To my sister Tori (who once asked me to name a character after her but probably didn't expect it to turn out quite like this) and my entire family (both Lawson and Kowit sides), I love you all!

To all my friends near and far, thank you for supporting my books, coming out to my events, and being early readers. Remember what I always say: I don't care if you read it as long as you buy it!

Thank you to the em dash, which I will *never stop using*! I am your biggest fan. To the word *snorted*, which I started using while writing *The Agathas* and somehow continue to use even though you're sort of gross (no offense, but you are!): Thanks for being there whenever I need a character to express disgust, which is more often than you'd think. Thank you to the exclamation point, which I have not only overused in this paragraph but in every single email I've ever written. (!)

A HUGE thank-you to my coffee machine, without which I would never write one page, nevertheless an entire book (or books). You are my hero. You are my salvation.

To all readers near and far, thank you for being amazing and keeping literature alive in a time when it's so, SO desperately needed. To all the librarians who are working so hard to protect our freedom to read, thank you from the bottom of my heart.

And finally, to my Kowit boys, who allow me the space and time to write, who talk me down when I'm 44 percent of the way through a draft and am thinking about throwing my computer out the nearest window (defenestration! Great SAT word), and who give me the best hugs on the planet! I love you both so much.

ABOUT THE AUTHOR

Liz Lawson is the *New York Times* bestselling author of The Agathas series (cowritten with Kathleen Glasgow), *Murder Between Friends,* and *The Lucky Ones*. Her books have been featured by the *Today* show, *People* magazine, Barnes & Noble, and more and have been translated into fourteen languages. She lives in the DC metro area with her family and two very bratty cats.

Visit her on TikTok and Instagram @lzlwsn or her website lizlawsonauthor.com.